STORM AT
DUSK

L. G. Jenkins

Book Two of The Merit-Hunters series

Grace & Down
PUBLISHING

Cover design by Liz Carter
Map illustration by Sarah Jenkins
Art direction by Sarah Grace

Printed in the UK

This book you're reading is a work of fiction. Characters, places,
events, and names are the product of this author's imagination.
Any resemblance to other events, other locations, or other
persons, living or dead, is coincidental.

Dedication

For Stephen and for you, the reader.

Map of Tulo

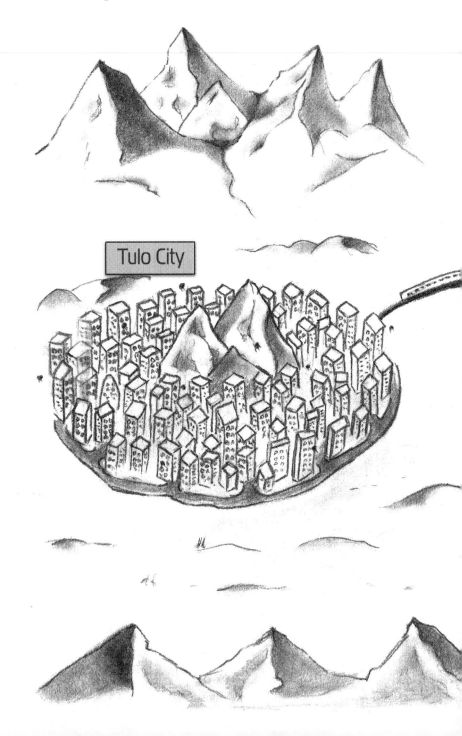

Tulo City

The Side

Old City Ruins

The Country & Forest

COMMAND NEWS ALERT

The voice of Arneld Hevas

It has now been thirty-nine and a half days since the Liberation Day attack. No amount of time that passes makes the loss of the victims any easier. We come to update you on our fight against the Rogue.

In the last week, we have seen a 40 per cent increase in the number of house arrests, detaining those suspected of Rogue activity. The majority of these arrests were conducted on the Outer-Rings and in the Side. We have also uncovered some rare, underground operations in the Inner-Rings.

To keep up with this effort, and in addition to the security measures already in place, we are introducing these new precautions:

- Watch-tampering checks are now in place for entry into all workplaces, homes, and for the use of public and private *SkipSleep* ports. These checks will continue in all sky train stations and for all shop and drone transactions.

- The Purification process for Side residents will now include a longer and more thorough application stage. This is to ensure allegiances to the City and its system are genuine, and that all applicants will become *loyal* citizens once their two years of Glorified service is complete.

- As always, it is a citizen's choice how they use their time but if no merit is recorded after forty-eight hours, our routine checks on time-wasting will now include a more extensive investigation into a citizen's activities and whereabouts over that lull period.

- We are sticking with our decision to re-open passage to the Side for Purification duties and the need for key pre-redundant workers to continue working. Robotics is still working towards key developments in areas such as sky train maintenance to limit Side residents entering the City for any reason other than Purification.

We are sorry to introduce even more restrictions on our citizens, who we treasure and congratulate for their diligence so far, but it is important we maintain a united front against the Rogue. These violent and erratic Unworthies will not destroy what we have all worked hard to build.

The merit system ensures that those, like you, who contribute to a greater Tulo are rewarded with a life they deserve. The scores on your wrists reflect how you have used your time and skills for the welfare of all of us. With this in mind, we are doubling the merit reward for any successful reports of suspicious activity, because if we all work together, we will make Tulo safe again.

Keep alert and remember that Progress is Strength.

CHAPTER
ONE

It was disappointing, infuriating and confusing all at once.

Genni Mansald couldn't move; she stared at the icons swirling around the televised sphere in the distance, bright against the twilight view of the City. Her digital notes on the large, oval table flickered in the corner of her eye and a hypothetical glue stuck her dress to her chair. Mafi swiped the air and dismissed the hovering presentation, and didn't even look at Genni with her penetrating lynx-like eyes.

Her words from moments ago spun around Genni's head.

'Angi will be taking the lead on this now.'

She watched Angi as everyone left the conference room; she had that annoying, delighted look on her face, like her merit had been quadrupled. With the way she was tapping on her wrist, Genni had no doubt her Personi feed was pending a new, boastful update.

That wasn't a bad thing; it's only what Genni would have done, but it surely shouldn't be Angi doing it. Despite her welcome appearance and her 'I know everything' façade, Angi's attention to detail was shocking, she couldn't delegate and she got visibly stressed. Maybe

Genni could outstage her and Mafi would see she was better for the role. Except, really, Genni knew she wasn't – Angi had a background in marketing and she didn't. Jun had only pulled her into the team because of her chemical knowledge of the product.

Still, Angi was younger than her. That felt wrong. How could she now be leading a team, along with the accompanying merit bonus, and Genni still only be a junior? Had the attack not happened, Jun would have praised her name to Mafi and she'd be getting the promotion or the extra merit that was well due. Had the attack not happened, everything would be different. For one thing, Jun would be alive. *How can you be so selfish? This doesn't even matter.*

She couldn't help herself, though. All she could think about was how she could do that job. She'd learned enough about the target personas, the content for each stage of the funnel and the various tactics for acquisition. She shared some of this in the meeting, adding the 'thoughts and input' Mafi had requested. It didn't even feel worth it now; she should have stayed at home and continued with her painting. Yet, she dragged herself in, quite passionately, actually, only to be sidelined.

Stop it. This is ridiculous.

She reminded herself she couldn't expect to be offered a leadership role, not even in her department. It also wasn't fair on Angi; they got on well, often spending their ten-minute lunch breaks together, chatting about work and, very occasionally, their limited lives outside of it.

She was torn, not wanting to care so much. With everything that had happened in the last year, she longed to break the grip that work and merit had on her. It had almost killed her once.

But seriously – Angi?

A strange look from Mafi pulled Genni from her chair, as if to look attentive.

It wasn't long until she arrived back at her desk, making sure to sit down gracefully while internally she was slumping into its swivel. The Beauty Dome was buzzing within its glittering, pink-frosted walls, faces and merit scores beaming from the staff board.

Maybe it was time for a new job. After all, she was a stronger person than she was twelve months ago. It was probably all holding her back, she considered, as she watched her colleague Hyi fill his glass from the water dispenser.

Maybe she should go for it; find a more accredited and merit-worthy job. That would solve a few problems in her life: her relationship with Ajay would be more stable as he was less likely to leave her for some gifted M-520; it would also elevate her in the eyes of her parents, not that she really knew why she cared. She hadn't even bothered going to see them, not fancying returning to the Glorified Quarters, even just for a drink served by an M-200 Unworthy from the Side.

Hyi turned from the dispenser, walking past her, cradling the cold glass in his right hand. Genni took a deep breath and opened her Watch mirror, examining the statistics around her face as they fluttered across the screen.

Your moisture levels are at their optimum, but there is significant swelling around your eyes. Here are some products to help with that.

Genni swiped mindlessly to scan the eye mask options and clicked on the top-rated option. The dreaded red message spanned across the product page.

Merit validation warning: M-490 and above. Only the most Worthy can have skin this smooth.

She sighed, flicking back to the list and buying one of the lower-tiered options, letting the voice of technology wash over her in a mist.

SkipSleep can also help alleviate the symptoms of fatigue.

The screen, as usual, pinpointed the location of Genni's nearest accessible port, just upstairs in the Dome. *Always use SkipSleep responsibly.* She closed it, tempted to go upstairs and have the boost, then work on her actions before morning; how else could she better Angi and show her leadership potential?

Staring lethargically through her screens, Genni calculated the exact details: she could not only get her reports in early, but also improve their quality; then research deeper into the desires of the market in this post-attack world and present an entire campaign fleshed out with product placements, marketing messages and campaign creatives. Her mind began to whirr.

What is it that people really want?

Before tapping at her desk to begin, a news alert flew into her left-hand screen, stopping her with the burden of a familiar heaviness. Was she really doing this? Planning deliberately to undermine someone she liked, just to better her own prospects? All for a stupid reason. She knew that even if she did the work, it was outside of her role description; she was a product analyst, not a marketer. Idiotic. Genni closed her tabs and didn't need to expand the news alert as the face of Arneld Hevas hovered centrally over the office floor, willing workers to lift their heads from their desks.

In the last week, we have seen a 40 per cent increase in the number of house arrests, detaining those suspected of Rogue activity. The majority of these arrests were conducted on the Outer-Rings and in the Side.

Genni scanned through the write-up of the new precautions on one of her screens. *When will this end?* Arnold Hevas had been like a glitching video, saying the same things over and over, the hopeful things only overcast by more difficulty and even more questions. Everyone, including Genni, seemed to be wondering how much Command was in control of this, and it was frightening. If they didn't know what the Rogue were doing, what hope did the rest of them have? She looked through more updates, seeing the face of Lillie Trumin from Command security who facilitated the Rogue's entry into the Quarters on Liberation Day last year.

Genni pondered over her picture, surprised at the large reward figures by her name, even though she'd caused so much drama. She was hard to look at. Harsh facial features, aged skin and greying hair that fell in a plait over her right shoulder. It was surprising that no suspicion was roused about her in the first place; she looked obviously criminal. If Genni were to paint a felonious character, the shadow under her stern eyes would be the exact shading she'd use.

A shiver fluttered down Genni's spine, giving her chills, so she turned back to her work and immediately put her earphones in, letting them crawl through her brown, mousy hair to secure themselves around her head.

Is there anything positive out there at all? Where are all those Purification success stories now?

Still distracted, Genni flicked through some newly released products she would never want or need. She was disappointed at the lack of content, though she shouldn't have been surprised. Most commercial endeavours had been completely sidelined; the same anti-Rogue advert taking up all the space. *Surely, we have to keep living?* She hadn't had a Tulo Tia in weeks with the bars still being closed. Of course, she considered, she could make them at home; the tiny drop of ethanol in each glass wouldn't be an expensive investment, but it wasn't really the drink she liked. It was the fact it was made for her, and its association with socialising, that gave it its refreshing and relaxing power. She supposed that the news update was positive in that sense. A 40 per cent increase in arrests was a good dent and the sooner they squashed this Rogue problem, the sooner she'd have a Tulo Tia.

She continued scrolling through, trying to ignore the alerts interrupting the flow: news of arrests, tutorials for reporting activity; evidence to prove that drones weren't corrupt and the improving developments of interrogation androids. There were new models of *SkipSleep Pro* in situ and those more aesthetic solar panels were hitting the mass market, but that was it. Slouching back on her chair, Genni couldn't turn herself off from it. The Rogue was everywhere, on the news, in her Watch, in the workplace, in her head. She remembered the man who she met the night of her accident, a few months before the attack. She could still hear his voice, falling on her like an ominous blanket of darkness, and his harrowing face following her into her dreams. *He was going to kill me.*

Genni breathed, feeling the tingle in her fingers and the shake starting in her legs beneath her desk. No, no, no. She needed to get out. The office started to become like a blurry watercolour painting, out of focus and lifeless. So far, she had been able to prevent these things from triggering her memories and her fear of that man and their encounters – that night, at the attack and in her nightmares.

No. She had too much to lose to let it affect her so badly.

She needed to relax.

There was her painting with the foxes, standing unfinished at home.

Jumping up and dismissing her screens, she pulled the back of her mint-green dress away from her sweating legs, and grabbed her handbag. She headed for the exit, trying not to bend her ankle to the will of her cream heels as she rushed.

'Genni, you're going home?' Angi invaded Genni's path; Genni noticed the upturned collar of her baby-pink blazer. She let the thought go, her anxiety to leave too strong.

'Yes. I'm going to turn in for the night.' What a stupid thing to say. It was only 10.46 p.m.

'Why don't you have a boost?' Genni admired the shine of Angi's neatly cut blonde hair grazing her shoulders, one side cutely tucked behind her left ear. Her wide blue eyes were captivating and almost convinced Genni to have the boost she suggested.

'Oh, I mean I'll do some work from home. I've obviously got my port there,' she lied, not having had a boost at home since her overdose, another reminder of that night. Looking at Angi again, she noticed she had no bags beneath her eyes. 'What do you use for puffy eyes?'

'Revive by Inspire.' Angi smiled. *Angi has an M-490 score?* Genni stopped herself from expressing her shock and jealousy that Angi could buy what she couldn't.

'Anyway, I've got to go.'

'Alright. Well, look out for my messages, I may need some tasks from you by tomorrow morning.' Angi's tone was authoritative and patronising, so Genni left with a feeling of resentment as she strode through the sliding doors, the air outside alleviating both her panic and her annoyance.

Ajay wasn't picking up his Watch, annoyingly; passing time on the sky train would have been much easier if she could rant about Angi and how her boss didn't appreciate her, and her dry eyes and that man who gave her the eye outside, and frankly, about her whole life being intolerable. *Would speaking to him really help, though?* She considered how miserable he'd been. Maybe he would tell her to get a grip in that sharp, brutish way he had been talking to her recently. Still, she wanted to hear his voice, even if it was the monotone version. He would pick himself back up soon and Genni couldn't blame him for being distant, what with everything around them right now. She glanced up at the carriage screen to see more depressing alerts and, looking down at her wrist, she decided to try Ajay again.

'Excuse me,' a voice croaked from behind her.

Genni flipped her body around to find an old lady, standing there in an extremely baggy, polka-dot dress. She was clutching onto a lit-up cane, trying to squeeze past, tapping it onto Genni's leg, whether intentionally or not, it wasn't clear.

'You're standing right in the carriage. Sit down, dear.'

It was intentional. Genni felt sad at the disingenuity of the 'dear' before realising that standing in the middle of the carriage was awkward, especially when empty seats were available. She slithered backwards into one and commanded her Watch to ring Ajay again.

It was odd that he wasn't picking up. The only time that had happened was when he took that wild trip to the Side. There was still something about that which made Genni feel nauseous. It didn't quite add up. Was he with another girl? Genni cursed herself, just like every time that thought came into her head. She knew it wasn't true. It couldn't be. Sometimes she hated the creative side of her brain, it always took her down imaginative routes, often unhelpful and intrusive. She swiped to check the Visual Positioning Guide.

Ajay was at home. Ace was there too.

She looked over their two faces pinned to the coordinate of Ajay's apartment and then flicked to call Ace.

As her Watch rang into her earphones, she glanced down the carriage to see if the old lady was still around. She was a few seats down, staring at Genni disapprovingly until she jerked her wrinkled face towards a young boy with a fringe covering his eyes. Still the ringing persisted. Ace wasn't answering either. *What could they possibly be doing? Oh no – they haven't started gaming again?* Ajay's merit was already falling with the missed work; surely Ace wouldn't let him. Would he?

She wouldn't cope if she had to reconsider their relationship because he was falling into a merit coma. Was that fair? She had no idea; he wouldn't tell her anything to let her know if it was fair or not. So of course, her fluttering brain would have to make up its own mind. Though there might be a reasonable justification for his solemn behaviour. She should just ask him, but was she overthinking it? Glancing at the screen, she saw the train was one stop from Ajay's. After mulling it over, Genni decided she should at least check on him.

Mum calling.

Not now, Mother. In a fumble of fingers to hang up the call to Ace, Genni accidentally accepted her mother's. She wanted to whine but instead, greeted her mother with a smile.

'Genni, sweetheart. Would you believe it – you're actually alive! Boris, she's alive!'

Genni could hear her father's distant laughter above her mother's cackle. Given the circumstances, it was pretty insensitive to be laughing about her absence from their life as if she'd died. She stared at her mother on the camera and got irritated by her hair; why did she have to scrape it back so tightly? It gave the illusion that her blonde highlighted locks were stuck down with some sort of plastic film, though Genni often thought it was reflective of her uptight demeanour. Standing in their regally decorated bedroom, Genni could see her mother's golden dressing cabinet displaying some statistics behind her plump, moisturised face. She had never been overweight, but naturally on the weightier side, which was where Genni got her hips from, completing her hourglass figure – mostly a blessing, but definitely irritating when buying trousers, as most were too baggy for her scrawny waist, yet a real squeeze over her bum. Though, of course, her mother never had that problem, revelling in the delight of the Glorified tailor-made clothing service.

'Yes. I'm sorry I haven't been around much,' she lied.

'Much? You've not been around at all.' Her mother's eyes flicked distractedly at whatever other content was active on her screen. 'Ah, that's the one. In white or grey?'

Genni found it strangely comforting that the whole City had changed yet her mother seemed exactly the same; self-involved, cocky and too busy with 'more important' matters to have time for her daughter. At least her father made the effort to walk out the Glorified Gate and have lunch with her from time to time. Though they hadn't done that for a while either, which was nice.

'Mum? Did you want something?' Genni moved her legs under her seat to save her feet from being run over by a man's self-rolling suitcase.

'Oh, yes . . .' Her mother looked down then, ruffling the collar on her silk blouse. 'We're moving house.'

'Again?'

'Well, yes, we had to. We're far too close to Command, so we're building a place further up the mountain.' Her mother's eyes ran across the camera again before she shouted, forcing Genni to remove one of her earphones. 'Boris, do we want the pool chairs in white or grey?'

'So, what is the house–'

'What?' Her mother roared, moving herself from the bedroom into the corridor where multiple pictures of Genni and her brother, Rod, hung decadently along the wall.

'Where are you?' Her mother made her way down the grand spiralled staircase, across the marble-floored entrance and out onto the front driveway. Genni got flashes of their multiple hover cars being cleaned by a young boy with red hair. He was new, so she wondered if they'd finally given 'Number Two' that reference for the completion of their Purification. So maybe he was the new 'Number Two'? It was always confusing growing up in the Quarters, when no one addressed their servants by their real names. It was never obvious whose Number One or Two people were talking about.

'White or grey?' her mother howled. The camera was now by her side, giving Genni a view of the ceiling.

'Mum, shall I call you back?'

'No, hold on.' Her mother's face was back and Genni could see her father, lounging out in the front garden space, scrolling on his Watch. She imagined he hadn't been sitting there for long and she could just spot his concentration face as he worked off his wrist. The freedom he'd earned, she supposed. 'Boris, white or grey?'

Her father responded, too mumbled for Genni to hear.

'Black? I don't think they have black.'

Pause.

'Black won't go.'

Another pause.

'What about white?'

Pause again.

'They won't get dirty. Number Three will clean them daily.'

Ah, so red-head must be Number Three. So there's still a Number Two? No citizenship for her, then?

Genni used to think it was funny, yet something inside her had shifted to sympathise. That poor woman. She'd come from the Side, served those tyrants for two years, only to be refused a reference. Doesn't she deserve it? Working that hard to be Purified from The Guiding Light should mean she was a merit-worthy citizen now. *She was also unlucky to end up with you. You really can be monsters.* Before she went momentarily insane listening to them squabble over the colour of the pool chairs, Genni silenced her mother.

She'd ring back if she had anything else to brag about. Genni could hardly fathom how she was birthed from such narcissistic characters. Though, to be fair to them, they'd done well; a Glorified house up in the small mountains in their sparkling, luxurious bubble and two children earning merit, admittedly one better than the other. She stretched her neck, forgetting them and briefly looking over at the boy sitting opposite her. The laces of his boots were untied, stains crawling up the bottom of his trousers and he slouched torpidly, but he had nice eyes.

Remembering Ajay, Genni peered at the digital display and slumped her shoulders; she had completely missed Ajay's stop.

CHAPTER
TWO

He remembered the first time he heard his voice.

With the questionable freshness of the vest against his skin, Ajay didn't react as he flopped his body through the curtain. Its texture would have surprised him if he'd considered its plastic, wax-like coating. It was dirty, though Ajay could hardly feel the sand stuck on the curtain's surface scraping the skin of his arms. Getting outside, the sun was shielded from his swollen, bruised face by the shading of the towering trees above him.

He remembered the first time he saw Ace, how he'd felt instantly inadequate against his superior strength, looks and fashion sense.

If Ajay had lifted his head, he would have considered the trees; marvelled at them, never imagining that he'd see them from this angle. From where he was, stumbling through his existence, the chunky, smooth trunks rose high into short branches, sprouting out like flower petals into glorious displays of green. Ajay didn't see it, though, as he kept his gaze down at the thin layer of sandy dirt covering the hard ground, barely recognising his own legs carrying him.

He remembered the first time Ace spoke and how happy he felt that someone other than a drone carrying coffee had interacted with him.

'Come on.' The man forced Ajay forwards, his grasp firm. Ajay obeyed, briefly seeing his accomplice's scarred face through a well of tears. If he'd looked back, he would have seen the shack he was held in; a grey tin box with a curtained door, standing alone in the trees.

If he had the strength, Ajay would have examined it further, thinking about what it was before. An old storage container, or part of a hover vehicle, upturned and repurposed? Instead, he remained ignorant of his surroundings, without the energy to whack the fly away from his ear as its wings battered briefly against his eardrums. Staggering down the dry path in the boots he'd been given, in-between the trees and foliage that lined it, Ajay did manage to recognise some Fo Doktrin with its huge orange-dusted leaves that would stain his newly gifted trousers, but he didn't care.

He just remembered the first time he and Ace shook hands and how he hoped his hands weren't too clammy.

'Seriously, we haven't got all day.' His accomplice had stopped a few metres in front.

Ajay lifted his dry eyes to notice the bottom of the man's lightweight trousers, covered with the orange powder and deeper brown stains. He shuffled forward, not noticing the small lilac flowers between the dominance of the Fo Doktrin leaves. Rustling past, he managed to look up at the trees, their magnificence foreboding and ominous until he saw birds flying beneath them. He didn't feel anything as he heard them tweeting. If he was level-headed, he would have realised such a sound hadn't graced his ears since he left the Side, where on rare occasions a bird would be heard and sometimes seen.

He remembered the first time he lied to him; he'd told Ace he was born on the Inner-Outer Ring but Ace wasn't fazed, despite coming from a Glorified family.

'A few things,' the man said, but Ajay couldn't bring himself to absorb his voice, much coarser than before. 'Our camp is set within a 300-acre perimeter. You are not permitted, unless for duty, to cross the line.'

Ajay, not really listening, became numbly aware of a dull ache in his stomach.

'We have Diverters at the border,' the man said. 'Those guys lead the drones away from the camp, and the Spotters will alert us if any get through.'

It was a painful, growing hunger, like he hadn't eaten for weeks. He widened his drooping eyes, recognising the crisp thirst in his dry throat and a dehydration headache. Part of him longed for water, the other didn't care. One voice telling him to run, the other bidding him to meet his fate.

A small lizard, unlike one Ajay had seen before, scuttled fleetingly across the path. With his head still down, Ajay thought how easy it would be to squish it under the sole of his borrowed boots.

'These are Alert Bands.' The man lifted up his Watchless wrist to show Ajay a small, red band. 'If these vibrate, a Spotter has sent the signal and we hide.'

Hide where? He would have asked the question if he thought it was important, but at that moment, nothing was.

He only thought about how, without hesitation, Ace had invited him out for drinks and introduced him to everyone, just like a friend would.

Ajay had never really considered the feeling of knowing he was going to die. Even during the attack, it wasn't like this; probably because he had the brawn to survive. It was as if with each step forwards, an overpowering anaesthetic was travelling further into his blood, desensitising everything. He didn't even flinch when a thorn spiked at his legs.

It wasn't how he thought he would go. Not part of the grand plan. He'd always imagined slipping away silently in a king-size bed, snuggled under premium silk sheets in the master bedroom of a Glorified house. He would be thinking proudly about all his achievements in progressing Tulo's technological ability and how proud he was of his children – all accomplished with well-numbered wrists. They'd be there by his bedside, along with their mother, who in recent years had had Genni's face. That's what he committed identity fraud for, why he became Ajay Ambers and left Karle Blythefen behind; that's the life he wanted.

Instead, he was walking lifeless through the desert-forest which he'd only ever seen from a distance. He was battered, bruised and preparing to meet death straight in the eyes.

He didn't let himself think any further about Genni. She'd be OK. Devastated by what he'd done, but OK eventually. It was Ace who kept coming back. Flickering like a digital photobook in his brain. That first time they met, the study parties, and the hours spent on *Revolution Combat*; the drinks between work, gossiping about girls, every game of tennis Ajay would win and every treadmill race he would lose. He always thought they'd be friends until wrinkles destroyed Ace's good looks. They'd both end up in the Retirement Village looking over the golf course, reminiscing over the days that had passed and missing earning the merit that had got them there.

But reality wiped it all out.

His unmoving body. The anguish in those wide, vacant eyes.

Ajay didn't bother mopping away the tears that began slipping down his discoloured cheeks and off his aching chin, like a wet paintbrush left on the side of its can. The man's voice continued echoing around the trees, arriving at Ajay as only a muffle of sound.

How could I have left Ace there? It felt like the right thing at the time, but now as he thought about his still body left alone in his apartment, being prodded and examined by drones and Command medics, he couldn't handle it. He owed it to Ace to stay, to look after him, to show how sorry he was for what he'd done. The merit had driven him to it, but he had chosen to throw the fatal punch. If only Ace hadn't threatened to report him, if only Ace hadn't chosen to save his merit over his best friend. That wasn't fair, it was what anyone would have done – merit is everything, and why would anyone give it up for a liar, a cheat, an Unworthy?

Ajay replayed the moment over in his head, the memory of tying Ace's arm to the *SkipSleep* port as fresh as the blood that came from his arm when its needle ricocheted through it.

Ajay's legs now fell from beneath him and he toppled to the ground, his sobs silent and contained.

The man rushed back towards him, attempting to pull him back up.

'Just kill me,' Ajay muttered. 'Just do it.'

'I'm not going to kill you.' He pulled Ajay to his feet.

'You will. Why not just do it?' Ajay looked down at the dry skin and the stains along his arms – he'd tried to scrub off Ace's blood when they'd let him wash, but it was on him forever.

CHAPTER
THREE

Was it the right thing to do?

Had posting it been too reckless? Could it be taken back?

It was another failure on the ever-growing list. If only time could be reversed, then unproductivity wouldn't be eating into her like rust degrading metal.

Genni pressed her fingers to her forehead as if to press pause on her mind. Breathing in, she rested in the strong fumes of wet paint. She'd wanted to come home and paint; it relaxed her, made her feel more whole, and seemed to allow her to reach something other than suffocation. Sitting on her stool, her apron covered in coloured splatters, she admired the work of art propped up on the easel.

Strawberry-red foxes ran between the pinks, yellows and reds of the beautiful garden. Genni hovered her fingers across the flowing waterfall, almost hearing its trickle, before gazing again at the dancing ball of light she'd placed centrally in the painting. It was a curious thing, like a great white fire crackling with destruction. When Genni saw it in a dream, she knew she wanted it; it had this attraction, this pull. Wiping her face, she hoped she would dream about the garden again, or dream about anything. It felt like a gift she'd been given. They'd replaced her nightmares about the Rogue, even though she was constantly reminded of them. It was all anyone was talking about, all anyone was blaming things on.

It was stupid to post this one on *Personi*, she decided.

Walking to the kitchen, looking at her wrist, she scrolled passed an advert on parenting merit and tapped at her post to refresh the feed; still only seventeen loves. She twisted her lips in disappointment and turned back to the painting. What was it about her recent posts that people didn't like? She missed the rush of her Watch pinging every few seconds like when she'd posted her first collection. Was it just a novelty for everyone? No longer uplifting enough to help them be more effective? Genni didn't understand what she'd done wrong, drawing the conclusion that the City didn't like her work and that it was and always would be a waste of time.

No loves, no merit, no worth; she ripped the apron from around her waist and threw it to the floor. As she tried to breathe and tell herself she was stronger than this, her Watch rang.

Pearl calling.

Sigh. She'd hoped it was Ajay. Genni leant on the table and tried to look happy.

'Hey, Gen. How are things?' Pearl's long, shining black hair flowed down her shoulders over a low-cut floral dress. Following Pearl's eye movements and expression, Genni knew she was vainly checking the prominence of her lip scar in the camera. Genni took a moment to brace herself; what was Pearl after this time?

'Yeah. Not too bad.' Genni sighed, also looking at herself on the screen. A mess; her hair looked like it had been mauled by some creature, and it and her forehead were graced with a coating of white paint. Even with a deformed lip, Pearl trumped her on the glamour every time.

'Painting?' Pearl's mouth curled into a half-patronising smile.

'Just finished.'

'Was it the foxes one?'

'Yeah.' Genni glanced down sullenly, picking at the dried paint between her fingers.

'I saw it hasn't done great.' Pearl sounded sympathetic. *You don't care enough to give it a love yourself though, do you?*

'I don't get it. People liked it before.'

'Well, you've gotta keep them engaged. Blocking the comments won't help.'

'The original feedback was hardly constructive.' Genni thought back to some pretty degrading comments on her first posts. It didn't bother her too much; she had expected it and she had become very good at blocking out negativity after growing up in a pit of it. It was down to her newly developed coping mechanism. She imagined any bad thoughts physically getting trapped inside a brown chest in her mind, one that she locked and stored away, meaning that thought wasn't allowed any space.

'If I can be honest, it's pretty, but foxes and a waterfall aren't motivational.' Pearl stroked shiny lip balm onto her lips. 'I can help you. I'll just record.' She started tapping at her Watch screen, Genni seeing the list of merit activities reflecting in Pearl's eyes.

'No, it's fine. I don't—' Genni hesitated, realising she was being selfish. Shouldn't she always let people educate her and get the merit for it? What kind of friend would she be if she didn't?

'That's OK. I've got lots on anyway,' Pearl said, boastfully. Genni was relieved yet still uncomfortable enough to move the conversation on.

'Have you heard from Ace or Ajay?'

'No, I haven't,' Pearl responded. 'He's been acting up lately. Ajay, I mean.'

'I know. I was going to pop by earlier but I got side-tracked. Ace was with him, but neither of them will answer my calls,' Genni yawned.

'Hmm, maybe they're gaming again.'

'Please don't. I've had that thought.'

Pearl's slight grunt fell into her next words. 'Anyway, Gen. Reason I rang is I saw Blake earlier and he's doing really well.' Pearl's eyes sparkled into the camera. 'He's got his new legs, and I'm gonna feature him on my channel for the Bounce Back campaign. And the Tulip Twins have gotten in touch and want to collab with me. Isn't that insane?' Pearl squealed, widening her mouth in excitement, her scar moving with it.

Wanting to put her fingers in her ears, Genni mustered up the strength to act enthusiastically.

'Wow, Pearl. That's—' Genni paused. 'Incredible.'

'I know.' Pearl flicked her hair over her right shoulder. 'Obviously, I'm trying to stay professional and keep my fangirl moments to a minimum. Overall, though, it's amazing to see the positivity coming out of the attack.'

Positive for you, Genni thought, questioning again why they were still friends, before remembering Pearl had long been a staple in her life, and how attentive she'd been during Genni's recovery. Calling at least every other day, sometimes on the Watch, sometimes in person. Still, it was incredible how Pearl often seemed completely oblivious to everything going on outside of her nearly Glorified bubble. *Of course, though, Pearl is happy when things are good for herself. Then again,* Genni rethought, *who isn't?* She had to admit, a lot of famous Glorifieds had encouraged people to keep merit-making and to move forward together; their quotes and pictures plastered all over the Social Sphere ball.

Genni pulled her hair down and ran her hands through it. 'So Blake's got his legs? How is he merit-wise?'

'Oh, fine, I think. He's got the compensation extension.' Gasping, and putting her hand over her mouth, Pearl's voice took on an even higher pitch. 'I wasn't supposed to tell you that. Please don't say anything.'

'I won't—'

'Please, Gen, don't. He was crazy about people not knowing.'

'Pearl, it's fine. I won't say anything.' Genni felt an ache in her heart for Blake.

'OK, thanks.'

Genni understood Blake's embarrassment, reminding herself of her desperation to avoid merit compensation after her *SkipSleep* overdose last year. Not only did it not go far enough, most people would rather be stripped naked in the streets than be seen being compensated. Even after the attack, while there had been a brief 'acceptance' time, opinions soon returned to normal.

When she really thought about it, the embarrassment didn't make sense. It was like with the colleague who sat three desks behind her. She had crooked teeth; that was as much Genni knew about her at the time. Though once colleagues found out Crooks received extended compensation because her husband lost his job and was borderline Unworthy, she didn't last long. As with most compensation cases, the extension for missed work ran out and Crooks was taken off the Beauty Dome's staffboard. Thinking about her, Genni felt scared for Blake – would he have the strength to work, have boosts and contribute to keep up? Genni was uneasy with it. She needed to stop painting now. There were people out there needing compensation and she was wasting her time on futile things. She let her body sag, yawning again.

'OK, hun, you clearly need a boost, so I'll let you get off.' Pearl was walking across her office, gracing Genni with the sound of her heels. 'Let me know if you want anything signed from the twins. Love ya.' Pearl blew a kiss to the screen.

Tapping at her Watch, Genni hesitated over Ajay's name.

Why is it always me calling him?

She flicked the screen off in protest before dragging her cumbersome body through to the bedroom. Closing her eyes, she slipped into the sweet danger of sleep, shutting it all out.

Her Watch vibrated and Genni opened her eyes.

Rolling over, sweaty in bed, she felt angry, and her breath was sharp, head foggy. She tried to piece together fragments of the dream she'd just had.

There was Pearl making it to M-500.

'I've made Glorified before I'm twenty-six. What have you achieved?'

Her father.

'There'll be no Unworthy in our family.'

Her mother? Maybe? And Genni was a fox, in the beautiful garden at one point, ripping down all the fruit and . . . did she attack Pearl?

Shaking her head and wiping her face, she forgot all about it as she checked her Watch.

No merit points have been added to your merit score in two hours, four minutes, and fourteen seconds. Is it time to do something of worth?

02.40 a.m.

She groaned. She'd overslept.

CHAPTER
FOUR

Ajay fell back to the ground as the man forced him up by his arms. 'Just do it. Make it stop,' he pleaded.

'Come on. Get up.' Before the man could say any more, they stumbled into a clearing, and Ajay heard a new sound. A confusing, harrowing sound.

It had been a while since he'd heard a baby crying. If he ever had, it was always in a safe place; in the arms of a sane, compassionate person. Instead, this child was exposed to the sweltering heat of the Country, with the savage and inhuman characters who had presumably bred it.

A baby doesn't belong here. Not in the Rogue.

Ajay tentatively edged himself forward, stopping still at the edge of the clearing. He saw people, too many people; some carrying pots or baskets of food, others hanging out laundry between the trees. It was as if a bustling crowd from an Inner-Ring street had been transported and distorted, rushing around with a backdrop of trees and sky, rather than skyscrapers and billboards. Ajay felt the need to shake his head furiously, almost to knock himself out of what must be some sort of hallucination.

No matter how hard he tried, it remained the same. Children ran between the trees, disturbing the paths of adults, giggling and playing catch; all of them wearing dark, dirtied clothing.

The cry came again. Ajay turned his throbbing head to see a small, helpless thing bundled up in cloth, snuggled in a man's arms who was walking away, down under the ground until he disappeared beneath what looked like a large, open trap door. They were all over the place and people moved in and out of them, comfortably and without hesitation.

As he watched the baby disappear into the pit, a ball trickled to his feet; a bright yellow ball. He bent down, his knees clicking, and picked it up, with grains of hard sand scratching his fingers.

Looking up, a small boy with beaming brown eyes gazed at him expectantly. Ajay stood, speechless, his curiosity going wild.

'Sorry. Can I have it back?' The boy spoke so softly Ajay almost didn't hear him, but he instinctively threw it back.

'Thank you.' The boy elongated his words playfully, running away to re-join his friends. Ajay watched them all, and something twinged within him. A memory of Tara, his sister, giggling into the sky, as he pushed her round on the Side's faulty merry-go-round. 'Faster, Karle, faster!' she would shout, her laugh contagious.

It felt so unnatural, enough for him to question if the boy was even real. Whenever he'd imagined the Rogue out in the Country, planning their cunning plots and murderous ordeals, children were nowhere in the picture. There were even old people here; he spotted a man about his grandma's age reading a book on a small log, leaning forward to spoon some green substance into his mouth from a bowl.

He wasn't sure his brain, usually so quick to process information, could take much more of it, especially now he was distracted from Ace and could come to terms with the identity of the man who brought him in.

He looked at him, the scar across his dimpled cheeks a distortion which teased the possibility that it could be someone else. But his bold, familiar eyes settled the matter. It was definitely Ajay's childhood best friend. It was definitely Callum.

Ajay thought back to the hour after they'd taken him, when Callum revealed himself in that little shack. When he'd first opened his eyes, Ajay had expected to see the inside of the bag that had been over his head, but there was sunlight. It was bright, splintering through the small window of the shack, revealing the three people in there with him. Maze, an ugly, shirtless man with guns criss-crossing across his chest, a woman who hardly spoke, and Callum, who Ajay hadn't recognised at first.

Maze had spent time teasing Ajay, like he had as they'd travelled, beating him for being a 'City-lover' or whatever, until Callum moved Maze out of the way – and that's when it had happened; when he'd walked into the light, bent down to meet Ajay where he was, tied to a chair, and addressed him with those familiar eyes.

Ajay felt cold, thinking of the moment, watching Callum now in the midst of all these people. His hair was still a light-brown colour, but longer and floppy, kept back from his face with a dirty, red fabric headband.

The freckles he was once embarrassed by had faded or were distorted by the scars on his right cheek.

'Hey, Jessy,' Callum hugged a small girl with freckles, who stopped assisting a woman in folding yellowed bedsheets and giggled at Callum as he fluffed her hair up playfully.

How can he be here? Ajay asked the question again, the same as he had when he'd first seen him, and his heart dropped in his chest. It had been over ten years since he'd last seen him in the shopping centre. They were just two Unworthy boys, having sneaked in from the Side. Ajay knew it was his idea, to try to experience the Worthy life, to see that canteen full of exclusive foods and dress up in clothes way beyond his merit status. Callum had wanted to leave and yet he was the one who got caught, tasered to the ground by drones, gifting him with the scars Ajay could now see. *Was that really my fault too? Did I let him down, like I did Ace?* Ajay didn't want to think of the answer, but subconsciously he did. *It's not the same. Callum could have come home.*

Ajay happened to glance at the woman folding the sheets. When their eyes met, she turned instantly aggressive and as if she were protecting her cub, grabbed the girl away from Callum and pulled her down into the hole in the ground, not shutting the door above it. Ajay didn't react, though he didn't understand. Was it because his face was bashed up? They could blame his kidnappers for that.

'Come on, let's keep walking.' Callum drew him away. As he felt Callum's fingernails dig into his skin, Ajay fell back to his concern for the baby, until he reminded himself that it looked as if it was loved. That only invited more confusion: *How can the Rogue have a community like this?*

When Ajay had realised it was them who had hauled him into a van from the Outer-Ring street, a welcome dread had fallen over him. Even though fear infected everything within him, he was happy he was going to get what he deserved. Ace wasn't supposed to die. It was only right that the debt was repaid. Yet now, it didn't look like they were going to kill him, despite the reminder of their brutality in the throbbing bruises on his face and in his ribs.

Any moment he'd wake up from the nightmare. His mind whirring, Ajay walked with Callum into another cluster of trees. They were called Baffle Trees, he knew that much. The only known tree species in the Country; numerous and, among other uses, the key resource for building commercial furniture. There wasn't much else to think about them, other than the graceful way their wide, branchless, cylindrical trunks were sun-kissed, patches of light glowing on them like contour make-up.

What is that?

Ajay's focus darted from the trees to the mountainous pile of junk metal between them, just grazing the path. He recognised some parts: a bent door from a Blitz Oven; cracked mirror screens from dressing tables and wardrobes, now black and silent; and the rusting carcasses of *SkipSleep* ports with their needles removed. The question of what they were used for faded as he stared at the ports; the first ones he'd seen since his own became a weapon. They had been like a body part to him, always accessible and useful, but they were capable of so much destruction. He thought of Genni lying lifeless in his bed after her accident, and Ace . . . lying . . . dead . . . in . . .

The pain pulsed up his chest again, taking his breathing and his balance. He tripped on a root but managed to catch himself and knock back his emotions, distracted by where he and Callum were. They had arrived at a much smaller set-up; just the one pit and a small induction hob on the ground, plugged into a miniature, battered solar panel.

A small man with huge arms, which made Ajay wince, was sitting on a fallen tree trunk, steam covering his face from a bowl.

'New recruit?' Something green was churning around his mouth. One look at Ajay slowed his eating down, as he gave him the same incriminating stare as that girl's mother. It was like they knew him, somehow, and their opinion of him wasn't good. Ajay looked down at his hands, dry and still tinted red. *It's on me forever.* They already saw him for what he was – a killer, a criminal, an outcast, an Unworthy. He didn't blame them; he supposed that's who he was. *But they're not any better.*

'You've got to be kidding me, Cal.' *Cal? He'd always been Callum.*

Callum approached the man, talking quietly, leaving Ajay to absorb the surroundings. Trees spanned every direction, and he had a sudden urge to run but there was no way of knowing which way might be his best chance of escape.

A crunching of dry leaves snapped him back to find the man walking towards him, allowing Ajay to see him more clearly. He was probably in his late thirties, with a shaved head, and his left eye curled in on itself lazily.

His broad shoulders and domineering stature gave him a thunderous presence, which Ajay didn't intend to offend.

The man grunted, peering at Ajay closely, examining his bruises. 'Fine, but if I get any trouble, I'll give him back.' He turned back to his food, stepping over the solar-powered cooker and sitting down. 'I'm done with the ration. Have you tried getting these things to work?'

'I'm fine with cold food.' Callum smiled while also eyeing the green mixture in the bowl before excusing himself and only giving Ajay a passing glance.

Part of Ajay wanted to go after him, plead with him not to leave him behind for whatever the short man had for him, as if Callum was some sort of comfort. But he stayed still, knowing that the freckled-faced boy from his childhood was gone and the man walking away from him was just another stranger. Vulnerability cut through him like a knife. *Why am I here? What do they want if they're not going to kill me?*

He focused back on the sound of the children echoing through the trees. *How can those who killed over 100 people last year be raising children? Who will those children grow up to be?* It's inhumane; just like he himself was, killing Ace, and then leaving him . . . but then again, he had a good reason to leave.

'You got your suit?' The man spluttered through his green-coated lips.

Ajay watched him, the lazy eye making it feel as if the man was looking beyond him. *Suit?* The word triggered a moment in the shack, when Callum and the woman were discussing how they didn't have a suit with the extra length for Ajay's legs, before throwing him one that 'would do'. He hadn't given it any attention, his mind only burdened with questions over Callum and pain over Ace.

He slowly shook his head. 'I left it.' He gulped, bracing himself for a harsh reaction.

'Oh, for Tulo's sake.' The man plonked his empty bowl down on the ground and rose from the log, causing Ajay to jump back. He could now see the full extent of the tight fit of the man's T-shirt against his muscly arms and chest.

'I'll go get it. You need some shut-eye before we head out.' The man sighed and was gone before Ajay could respond.

Shut-eye? As in, sleep?

It felt so inappropriate, as if the man had just asked him something deeply personal on the first time of meeting. He'd not had anyone suggesting he sleep for years. It was not something people said or even talked about, just a lust that lay under the surface, and if ever indulged in, kept very quiet. Not blurted out like that. *Get some shut-eye. How dare he.* Ajay then realised it was broad daylight. He looked up at the trees again, light splintering through their green cover, a solid reminder he wasn't in the City any more. Things were different and *SkipSleep* was as useable as its broken ports in the trees.

So, he was supposed to sleep? The last time he had done that purposely for a good length of time was in the Side, after Grandma's bedtime stories or late-night chats . . . the pain came back to his chest. *How can I save her?*

His thoughts broke as he heard a cough not far from him, beyond the other side of the log. He scanned around to find a man was sleeping there, curled up in the fetal position, sniffling in the dirt. That's when Ajay noticed them, a few more bodies sporadically dotted around him, out in the open, in different directions. Asleep.

Ajay felt his knees buckle with trepidation as another thought occurred to him. He was supposed to sleep, unprotected, in the midst of killers?

That wasn't going to happen.

CHAPTER
FIVE

Ajay remembered one particular time at the gym, when he was pounding the running belt, listening to music and watching his stats rise next to the animation of his body. Its thighs turned red just as he started to feel the burn on his own. He probably continued until the calorie count hit 500 or the merit earnt was to his satisfaction. Ace was with him, repping weights and complaining that the machine was wrong after giving him a muscle tear warning. Ajay admired the way Ace would never be second best; it was one of his most admirable qualities, never letting other people be better than him; it kept him driven.

Ajay rolled over in the dirt, trying not to think about the memory, when Ace asked Ajay how he really felt about Genni. It was just after he finished on the belt and looked out from the Sports Tower, watching drones zip in and out of each other's lines. Ace had mocked about being a reference on their marriage application, and then backtracked to be one for the straightforward termination procedure. He even tried to claim he should earn merit commission when they had high-flying kids, just because he had introduced them. Ajay remembered the conversation so vividly. He spent most of the time telling Ace to pipe down as they'd only been dating a few weeks, but he knew why it was so ingrained in his mind. Because everything Ace was ridiculing him for, about a Worthy marriage and successful kids with Genni, was what he imagined he could have. A dream he'd envisioned even when he was Karle, looking out from that thin Side window, over the City skyline. A tear trickled down his cheek as he thought of her.

I'm sorry, Genni, for what I've done to you. For the pain you'll feel when you find out. You deserve better. I know I need to let you go, because if I don't – it'll kill me.

Thinking about Ace and Genni didn't make the sun set any quicker or make the uneven ground more comfortable. It only made him more uneasy about his position in the Rogue, surrounded by murderers, of which he was one. He was still trying to convince himself that they weren't the same. What happened with Ace was an accident. A tragic, heart-shattering accident, not a calculated, unrelenting attack on civilians. It was different. It had to be.

He had to let Genni go, but would he be able to let go of Ace?

As his mind skimmed across the water of his life, bouncing off key events that propelled him forward to where he'd ended up, he considered how it was all encoded into his very being, weighing him down. He had so many desires, regrets, hopes and fears. He'd lost the hope of ever being Glorified, what he'd desired more than anything, and the fear of never getting it led to the regret of fighting with Ace. All of it was gone. Different. *Does that mean he died for nothing?*

Something invaded his ear, loud and fizzing.

Startled, Ajay sat up, flicking out his arm as the buzz battered his eardrums. He whacked the bug away, feeling its little body rebound from the back of his hand.

'Eh, don't do that.' The stubby man emerged from his pit as a silhouette, the low light hiding the details of his face.

Ajay didn't ask why not, assuming that the things might sting. He looked at the insect regaining flight and second-guessed. Or did the man care because it was pretty? It was small, delicate with sparkling wings, their edges trimmed with an orange glow. Ajay observed as it bobbed gracefully through the evening air, its spindly legs hanging softly below its body. At first, there was just the one, until Ajay looked up and it was like an emerging lightshow; the tops of the trees covered in their glitter, resembling moving stars.

Now watching him gathering his things, Ajay considered how the man didn't strike him as one for aesthetics. *The glowing things must sting.*

'Come on.' The man grunted in his direction. 'Get up.'

'I didn't actually sleep.'

'Nothing new, then,' Ajay thought he heard him grunt. He didn't like it, but he willed himself not to care.

Ajay hurled himself up from the ground, his long legs feeling feeble. He was clearly past the hunger pains. His stomach had ached incessantly all through the day while he thought about Ace but also kept alert for any sudden attacks from those around him, all of whom were rising now.

The ground seemed to open up everywhere, more pit doors flying open from underneath the leaves and dirt.

He froze, internally panicking that there may be one beneath him and he'd be catapulted across the ground. That was delusional; he'd weigh them down and trap them in, *obviously*. He wiped his tired face as even more figures emerged through the coming night. Part of him felt intimidated, the other, indifferent.

'Well, Haro.' A high, stern voice. 'What have they dragged in this time?' Ajay took a deep breath as he watched a tall woman address the short man. Haro; so that was *his* name.

'Nothing much.' Haro shrugged. 'City-lover.'

Timidly, Ajay attempted to pick up the suit from the ground, patting the dry dirt with his large hands in the dark. *Where is it? Where is it?*

'Not for long, I hope,' she tutted. 'He can hardly see.'

The woman spoke above the fluttering of wings, before the space filled with light. Ajay saw the suit, no longer folded, lying a few inches from his right hand. He looked up to see her long brown hair flowing down to her waist as she walked away from the Watch torch she'd put on the log beside him. She too was wearing a suit, the light bouncing off the black, shiny material. Staying silent, he stood up, as two or three more people appeared.

'Ah, a newbie.' A baby-faced boy with short, black hair gave Ajay a cunning smile. He must have been about sixteen. *So young.*

'Who's taking him, Haro?' A man with broad shoulders casually fetched a laser gun from inside his pit. Ajay heard the clicking of the load and saw the red flashes of its awakening as the man held it to his chest.

'I'll take him.' Haro wiped his nose ungracefully. Ajay was fixed on the gun, just like the ones *they* used in the attack. *Monsters.*

'Looks like he'll be agile enough.' The tall woman curled her lip, examining Ajay, as if under a microscope. 'Are we heading west?'

'No, east. Spotters' orders.'

Spotters. Callum had used that word, but Ajay couldn't remember why. *What are they talking about?*

The woman nodded, picked up a black, rubber sack and rolled it up.

'They better have cleared it that way, I'm . . .' Haro paused, quickly glaring at Ajay. 'Why are you just standing there? The suit doesn't wear itself.'

Ajay fumbled with his suit, awestruck, not understanding what was happening. 'Why? Where are we going?'

'We're going to work.' Haro came close, his lazy eye twitching in the night light. 'So put on your uniform.'

Ajay didn't argue, even though that didn't really answer his question, it only confused him more. He swiftly held out the suit in front of him before putting his legs into it, and the crowd dispersed around him.

It was almost painful to squeeze himself in, wriggling the tight rubber-like material around his body. Uncomfortably, he slipped the all-in-one over his torso and struggled to zip up the back, his entire body feeling like it was being constricted. Looking down, he quickly pulled on the socks to cover his olive ankles exposed beneath the hem of the short trousers. They were clearly going out further into the desert-forest, and they needed some protection, otherwise, why the guns? And why would he need to be agile, as the woman had said? Ajay couldn't imagine he was ever going to be agile in this thing. Everything felt so compressed he was surprised he could still breathe.

'Let's go, team.' Haro marched past him, the chafing of his small legs in his suit loud. 'You're with me.'

Everyone trooped forwards into the forest, illuminated by the fluttering of the sparkly bugs above. Ajay scuttled after Haro, skipping slightly through the foliage, trying to get used to the strange sensation of walking in a skin-tight prison.

Fear fell stronger over Ajay, almost enough to make him feel cold as he sweated. Scrunching up his eyes, he tried to stop focusing on the bright red lights that ran through the laser guns in front of him; cradled in the arms of the men leading the pack. As he saw them, he saw the attack; Jun's body, the screams of agony, the resulting chaos and the inevitable aftermath. He suddenly grew angry. *These* people deliberately set off bombs to hurt those he cared about. Blake – how was he doing without his legs? And Pearl – with her lip? Genni and . . . Ajay stopped.

He couldn't think about the people back home. It was too hard. Everything was too much to process. What did Haro mean by 'going to work'? His limbs began to shake as the fear and emotion poisoned his body into paralysis. *I've got to get out of here. Don't I? But how could I?*

Then it cut through him like an electric shock, making him gasp quietly.

Laughter.

Not evil or sinister but genuine, light and friendly laughter. Was he deaf to it before? Through the dark, he could make out two teenage girls flirting with that baby-faced boy and a few other women chatting as they walked arm in arm. Ajay looked at Haro, a few metres in front of him, who nearly tripped over, losing the rhythm of getting his small legs over the increasingly uneven ground. One of the shiny flies bobbed closer to Haro's face and he lifted up his index finger, letting it rest there as he walked, its glow illuminating Haro's admiring eyes. *So they don't sting and Haro likes pretty things?*

Ajay had so many questions, curiosity drilling into his brain like a wound-up screw in the back of his head. As the thing flew gracefully off Haro's finger, Ajay noticed he had a wristband where his Watch should have been, similar to one Callum had. Some information came back to Ajay. *They vibrate when the Spotters do something.* He was distracted by talking behind him.

'If you managed to do that, he would have your head, and I ain't helping you when he does.' Ajay turned to see a skinny lad with his suit-balaclava half off his face walking with two other men; he stared at Ajay, unpleasantly.

'Can we help you?' he spat out, with a slight stutter in his voice.

Ajay said nothing, just shook his head and turned back to walking.

'Wait a minute, that's the guy Tri was talking about.' Another man picked up his pace to get a better look at Ajay, who didn't say anything but walked quicker.

'Nah. He ain't that tall, is he?'

'How would you know? You've only seen a portrait of him – idiot.' The guy came closer to Ajay's face, which must have been slightly contorted by the fresh bruises around his eyes. Ajay contemplated cursing at him.

'It is definitely him.'

'This is a good spot.' One of the men with guns shouted across the group, the others lifting their torches up into the trees, scanning around as if to reassure themselves they were alone.

Ajay was aware of the sudden pace of everyone's movements as people started to throw down bags and pull out long ropes, helping one another tie them around their waists. *What are they doing?*

'Oh, man, I think you're right.' The three men were still staring.

'Who is he?' The third one started to rummage in his sack, also pulling a rope from it.

'He's that lad they patched through from the inside. Command has their best detectives on him.' The men looked back at Ajay who was slowly walking away until he heard the whisper.

'They found a dead civilian in his place.'

Ajay's heart stopped. He didn't want to hear any more. *They all know? They can't; not everyone has reacted like they recognised me.* Then Ajay thought of Haro objecting with Callum, and the woman who had pulled her child away. He was surrounded by criminals and yet they believed him to be the dangerous one? Hearing Ace belittled to just a 'dead civilian' broke him further and if it wasn't for Haro pulling him towards a tree, he would have cowered.

'With me.' Haro came to an abrupt stop at the base of the tree. 'Hold this.' He threw his rucksack into Ajay's arms and prised a rope from it, wrapping it around his waist.

Ajay, distracted, holding back tears, barely noticed as people wrapped their ropes around tree trunks and pulled themselves up speedily.

'You do much climbing or anything at that place in the City?' Haro tied a precise triple-knot, pulling it tight to his waist with quick, snappy force. Ajay assumed he meant the Sports Tower.

No, he hadn't, and he tried to remember how merit-worthy it was, as if that mattered.

'Huh, you'll learn,' Haro grunted dismissively.

He got a Watch from the bag and gave it to Ajay for light, then he pulled an empty sack from the bag and clipped it around the left-side of his rope. Ajay looked at the Watch, tentatively flicking through it; most of the main components were offline; it was basically unusable.

'You've got long legs.' Haro briefly looked at him, before pulling the balaclava over his head, completing his suit.

Ajay didn't know why it hadn't hit him before that moment. They couldn't be, could they? Ajay knew how drones worked; the propellers, the motors, the transmitters and receivers, the speed controllers, the landing gears and the infrared cameras. The latter would allow them to see targets even at night. Ajay pinched part of the suit material on his arm, thinking. If his assumptions were correct, the suits combined some sort of silica aerogel with a wavelength emitter, which absorbed the infrared, thermal radiation their bodies produced. If any drone were to fly above the trees, they'd be virtually invisible to them.

That. Is. Brilliant.

His thirst for intellect was going wild. *How could they have done that, out here?* He didn't know what to think about; Ace, the attack, the suits, the Command drones, or what everyone was doing around him. Everything was moving so fast. Haro grabbed another rope from the bag, and threw it around the trunk of the tree. Ajay looked up, examining the bare tree trunk that ran up, branchless, at least 20 metres high.

Haro wheezed, tying both ropes together on either side of him, and then planted his small feet on the side of the trunk and hoisted himself upwards.

'Come on. Fill your sack,' he called out, pointing at the neighbouring tree and then the bag.

Then he moved upwards, at speed, Ajay watching in amazement. The little man displayed incredible strength; the bulging of his biceps visible in the Watch light. Soon Haro was halfway up the tree and Ajay looked down into the bag, where he saw another set of ropes curled up like sleeping serpents.

Absolutely no way. He's got to be joking? How could someone with no experience survive climbing a tree of this size with no safety net? They could create these suits but they didn't have anything to run or fly up a tree for them to fill up their sacks with . . . *wait, fill the sacks with . . . what?*

CHAPTER
SIX

Why can't I be someone else? The question was niggling her subconscious as Genni pounded her fingers against the desk, trying to ignore the jelly feeling in her legs. She had to get through all this work quickly, and Angi was bothering her about the use of one word on an information document. *It. Doesn't. Matter. Angi.*

She still couldn't believe she'd overslept by sixty-four and a half minutes. What was she thinking, not setting an alarm, only to be woken by a merit warning?

And now she was sinking in work with only a few decimal points on her merit count for the evening and Mafi was after her and there was some other person in operations wanting to know the timelines for the product release, even though all of that was held in the shared drive, and she couldn't go to the library to focus because the time to get there with all the Watch-tampering checks was time she didn't have and now another message had flown into her inbox and her fingers hurt because of how hard she was typing . . . and then she stopped and cried into her hands.

If she was going to avoid *SkipSleep*, she had to get better at the sleeping thing. She told herself to get a grip and power on; what had passed couldn't be changed, but it didn't stop her berating herself for it. No one else at work would do that. She always knew she was below the standard, this only proved it. Breathing slowly, sniffing up the tears, she hovered over Angi's message, asking Genni why she had been unavailable for the last two hours. For one thing, it was not any of her business, but it kind of was, because Angi was leading now. What could she say, because the truth wasn't good enough? She couldn't even claim she was volunteering, with the summer camp being on hold after the attack, so she scrolled down her Watch to find the title of an educational movie. *The Power of Plants for Well-being and Productivity.* That would explain all the new plants growing in the office, Genni thought as she skimmed over the researchers' names. She sent it off to Angi, with a friendly recommendation and the merit available for the watch. She decided to trust that Angi wouldn't look at Genni's recent merit count and figure out that Genni couldn't possibly have watched it in the last two hours. *Would Angi really have time for that?*

She briefly glanced at Angi's score and seethed when she saw it. M-499. She'd be at M-500 – Glorified – by the end of the year, along with Pearl, and probably everyone else she knew. They'd all get there before her. *Pathetic. Will this ever stop?* All of it took her back to her dream, and how if she were to paint it, it would be a whole series of convoluted pictures. She imagined a watercolour of Pearl in a ballroom dress being pounced on by a fox. It was all so stupid. Scratching her head and feeling the dryness of her hair, she left her work and wandered to the fridge to grab a bottle of iced tea. *Shouldn't I have ordered a drone to the window instead? That would have saved time.* But the walk was refreshing and the iced tea felt cool and crisp as it slithered down her throat. Sometimes drinks by drone could warm as they travelled, so this was better, and she *had* remembered to order a cleaning drone so the place looked tidy. At least one thing was.

As she went for another sip, a sudden loud banging startled her and she threw iced tea down herself.

For Tulo's sake. Who is that? She stared at the door as the knocking continued, before a voice followed.

'Are you there?' Her brother's familiar tones immediately made Genni's blood boil. She couldn't be bothered with him now, but he did sound urgent, so she swiped open the door. As soon as she did, he didn't even look at her. He barged past, his strong body knocking her sideways. She wiped the liquid from her face and shouted at him for his rude entry.

Initially, he scanned around the small living room and forced his way through Genni's entire flat. Still standing by the door and listening to him throwing stuff about, Genni didn't know what to think. The confusion intensified when three or four drones flew through the door, forcing her to duck.

He was back in the living room, looking out the window while the drones continued to search around her place.

'What are you doing?' Genni stared at his back as he looked out into the City.

He twisted his domineering body towards her and cut her with those sharp eyes.

'Where is he?' Rod demanded, irritation in his tone. 'Where's Ajay?'

His body looked tense, his fists clenched and shoulders back tight.

'What do you mean? Probably where he always is. Work? Home? Why?' Genni was unnerved.

Rod squared up to Genni firmly, so close she could see the tidiness of his shave. 'Seriously, Gen. If you know where he is, you have to tell me.'

Genni stepped back, flinching with confusion.

'OK, Rod. Calm down. What's going on?'

He gave her space, but his urgency remained. 'When did you last see him?'

'I don't know.' Frustrated and struggling to think clearly, Genni hesitated. 'Maybe a few days ago.'

Rod stared at Genni, viper-like, before kicking the side of the table and storming back towards the window, hands on his hips, the moonlight shining on his white shirt.

'Rod,' Genni spoke hesitantly, moving towards him, slightly vulnerable in her sleeping T-shirt and knickers but more concerned about him ordering the drones to scan the apartment again. 'What's going on?'

Watching the movement of Rod's chest in his anger, her anxiety heightened. What had Ajay done? Or was this a joke by Rod and her parents to get her to work harder? That made zero sense. Completely irrational. So, what was it?

Her brother turned to her, and for a moment the gravity in his eyes softened and it instantly made her uncomfortable. This was serious. Whatever *this* was.

'You better sit down, Gen.' Rod reached out and put his hand compassionately on Genni's arm. Her heart started to pound. That was very unlike him. She was freaking out internally, not knowing what was coming. It couldn't be anything too bad, she hoped, maybe just something accidental and she'd see Ajay soon. So she sat down on the sofa, making sure to look at Rod expectantly.

Rod pulled round a kitchen chair, scraping it along the wooden floor and heightening Genni's impatience. *Just tell me.*

Rod sat down in front of her, clasped his large hands together and sighed. 'Earlier today, we found Ace in Ajay's apartment.'

Genni knew that they were together, she saw it on her Watch. Why did that matter?

'Gen, I'm sorry, but we found him dead.'

What was that word? It sounded like *dead* but she must have misheard him.

'Sorry?'

'Dead, Gen.'

Did he mean passed out from drinking too much? Ace hadn't done that very often, but on Liberation Day a couple of years ago, *dead* would have been a very appropriate word to describe him. No, Rod probably meant sleeping. So tired that he'd indulged in sleep? Ace didn't do that, though. Anyway, why would Rod care about Ace's time-wasting, and why would Ace be in Ajay's apartment, without Ajay? Rod couldn't actually mean that Ace was dead, dead. That would be ridiculous.

'We found his prints all over the body, his Watch left behind and the fire escape chute open.' Rod's words cut back through the moment. She'd missed a lot of what he'd said.

'Whose prints?' Genni's throat was drying.

'Ajay's.' Rod was blunt, the softening of his eyes diminishing.

'All the evidence is there.' Rod nodded. 'And there's more . . .'

'No.' Genni protested. 'This is a joke. I saw Ace on the VPG and he was fine. Look, I'll show you.' With a determined energy, Genni swiped at her Watch and projected her screen to show Rod the little pins of Ace and Ajay, happy and merry, in his apartment.

Flick, flick, tap and there it was. Genni refreshed the screen. Over and over. She stared in disbelief.

'You were saying?' Rod was patronising. Was he serious? He was using this moment, this heart-wrenching moment, to play the 'I was right' move? She felt the urge to lash out, scratch at him with her nails until blood seeped into his white shirt. But a trivial sibling dispute was insignificant as she looked at Ace's pin, floating in Command, covered in a red mist with a medical symbol beside it. Was that there before? It couldn't have been or she'd have noticed it, wouldn't she?

'They did their best to save him, but he had lost too much blood.'

'I don't—' Genni couldn't grasp her breath, gawking at Ace's red pin.

'Gen.' Rod leant forward and touched her knee, but she felt numb. 'There's something else.'

She didn't want to hear what it was, as she instantly assumed it was about Ajay. It wouldn't be like him to just leave Ace there. It must have been an accident; Ace tripped and Ajay went to get help. But that made no sense because the medical service would have been alerted. So why would Ajay leave? There had to be something else going on. He must be in trouble.

'I've got to find him.' She stood up, flicked off her Watch and shuffled tentatively into her bedroom, Rod following behind her.

'Gen . . .' He stood as Genni pulled some trousers on and didn't even bother changing her top. She moved towards the door, the zip of her trousers still undone.

'Gen!' Rod insisted, his heavy footsteps reaching her as she felt the strong grasp of his hand around her arm.

'I'll find him, Rod. He's probably in trouble,' she rambled, 'with whoever really did this. I'll find him and—'

'No,' Rod said as she swiped the door to open it. 'He's not who you think he is.'

There it was again – the softening of his green, menacing eyes. Genni felt a kick in her stomach, no longer because she thought Ajay was in trouble, but because she knew Rod wasn't lying.

'What do you mean?' Genni slowed down, catching her breath.

'You might want to si—'

'I don't need to sit down, Rod. Just tell me.'

Rod sighed.

'OK. He's not Ajay Ambers. He's called Karle Blythefen and he was born on the Side.'

As Genni listened to the words and processed them, she realised that perhaps Rod was right. She should have sat down. Her legs buckled beneath her and she fell heavily, with Rod and the walls around momentarily turning to mist.

'OK, sit down.' Rod led her stumbling body to a seat.

Genni felt his strong grip on her arms as he steadied her, listening to his heavy grunting. For a split second as things had blurred, she'd hoped it had all been another dream.

Rod had just said that Ajay wasn't Ajay. That he was from the Side. Yep, that was just as unbelievable as Genni metamorphosing into a fox and biting Pearl's face off. And the whole thing about Ace being dead, and Ajay being the murderer?

Except, it wasn't a dream. If it wasn't a dream, then it must all be a joke, because she had to hold on to something that meant this wasn't the truth.

Genni watched Rod as he paced in front of her. Rod had never really liked Ajay. He'd always looked at him like an Unworthy on the street, like he was worth nothing. Genni reminded herself that the part about Ace must be true. The Watch showed it. A pain ricocheted across her chest, but she knew she didn't have the capacity to grieve now. She needed to understand why Rod would want to set Ajay up, or accuse him of this. Was it because he, and her parents, thought it was Ajay's fault she wasn't Glorified yet? If he was out of the picture, then she might make it? Though that also made no sense; Ajay worked at Prosper, Tulo's biggest bank, and he was higher merit-wise than her. In fact, she'd always assumed her father thought highly of him, despite only really meeting him a few times. So, what was this?

'Why are you here, Rod?' Genni felt the exhaustion in her eyes again.

Rod started. 'To find Karle Blythefen.'

Genni wanted to laugh. *Karle Blythefen.* It sounded made-up and Ajay definitely didn't look like a *Karle.* He was too cool, confident and . . . that just wasn't his name. Genni refused to believe any of it.

'You're lying.' She shook her head and looked down at her legs, quickly zipping up her trousers.

'I'm not lying, Gen.' Rod crouched and started swiping at his Watch. What was he going to show her? Some edited videotape of Ajay in the Side, or a fake identification card of 'Karle' with Ajay's face on it?

And then, there it was on Rod's screen. Ajay's face, somewhat less mature, with shorter hair and smoother cheeks, next to the name *Karle Blythefen*. It occurred to Genni that this was the first picture she'd ever seen of Ajay taken before she met him. That didn't prove anything, though. He was private about his childhood because of what happened to his parents in that hover vehicle accident. It couldn't have been easy merit-making after having that weight of loss and grief hanging over him as a teenager. Talk about trauma.

So it made sense for him never to show her anything, or introduce her to the grandma who'd raised him. *And come on,* she thought, as she gazed over the identification card further, *Blueberry Bliss Lane?* That has to be false. Sounds like some cheap, knock-off Tulo Tia cocktail. She wasn't buying it. What still didn't make sense though, was why Rod would be doing it?

'What do you want?' Genni attempted to dismiss his screen herself.

'You can't seriously think I'm making this up?' Rod's green eyes were wide. 'It's all here. We matched Ajay's prints back to the real him.'

'You've made that up. Did you get one of your girlfriends in graphic design to draw it up for you?'

'This is straight from Command. His Watch has been examined – he tampered with it to change his name and score.'

'And how would you have access to that classified information?' Genni said, agitated.

'I work for them.'

'Right, so who in security have you seduced?'

'No, Gen. I work in security. I'm a Compliance Detective for the CSB,' Rod said. 'You really think I'd settle for some entertainment job?'

Genni initially thought that Rod had completely lost it. Then a dark sadness drifted through her. She knew Rod was telling the truth. That last part, at least. There had always been part of her that never understood why someone like him, bold, cocky and vain, would get merit from organising events. Even as kids, he'd wanted to play the head Command Officer, or the drone that led the pack. He was right, he'd never have settled for a job that wasn't of maximum impact, and he'd always be in places Genni never expected him to be. Further Downtown or in the Outer-Rings. She'd never really questioned why, but this made sense. He fitted the bill for the Command Security Bureau perfectly – protective, powerful but aloof enough so the public never quite understood how they operated.

And if that made sense, and Rod was telling the truth about it, and about Ace being . . . then, it seemed reasonable to believe he wasn't lying about Ajay.

Genni sat back in her chair, feeling sweat under her arms and her breathing getting shorter. She stared forward, not knowing what to say, or even what to think. All she could hear was the drones humming, the two of them floating in the kitchen, awaiting further instructions.

Ajay can't be . . . he just . . . when did he . . . how did he . . . how was I so . . .

'Genni?' Rod said. 'Look, do you know . . . Gen!'

Genni jumped at Rod's volume and held him in her gaze, trying to fix her mind on what he was saying.

'Do you know where he could have gone?'

'No.' Genni cleared her throat. Apparently she didn't know anything about him.

'OK. You stay here.' Rod stood. 'And tell me as soon as you hear from him. Got it?'

Genni nodded, slouching further and further into paralysis. Did he not realise how hard this was to hear? Clearly not, she thought, as he bounded from the room, drones with him, and left her in a bewildered state.

CHAPTER
SEVEN

It tasted like rubber. Ajay expected it to be sweet, maybe slightly soft, not chewy and bitter. He pressed it to his nose, the aroma also disappointing him. Deciding that it couldn't be ripe enough, he put it with the other pieces of fruit and stared lifelessly at them, sitting in his sleeping spot.

It had only taken him a moment after Haro had started to climb to realise they were collecting fruit from the Baffle Trees. It was unlike any fruit he'd had before; each piece the size of a tennis ball and red in colour with a hard, tough skin, though not hard enough that Ajay couldn't cut into it with his hands. He was glad he'd never eaten it before, he thought, picking sticky pieces out of his teeth. It was disgusting.

So exhausted, he wiped his eyes lazily, hoping maybe he would sleep. Feeling uneasy about the notion, Haro's gruff voice ground against him.

'Don't leave them. We're on a ration.' Haro squeezed out of his suit, making a wet, squelching sound as he prised the material from his skin.

'They're not ripe yet.' Ajay briefly glanced at Haro's small, half-naked body. With the speed at which the guy clambered up those trees, it wasn't surprising his chest was ripped and muscular.

'They're ripe.' Haro didn't look up. 'Eat them.'

Ajay looked back at the fruit. *They can't be ripe. There's nothing to them, in taste, smell or satisfaction.*

'What do you call them?' he asked Haro, who stood on the edge of his pit.

'Rank.' Haro wiped his sweaty hands on his thighs. 'Let us know if you find anything better.' Haro smirked, lowered his pit door and disappeared beneath the ground.

Ajay moved on and thought about what he'd learnt on the walk back from overhearing climbers' conversations; the glowing flies were Wingsparks, the lilac flowers were Duskdrops and there was something else called a Toxlizard. Intrigued by nature and happily allowing it to be a distraction from the weight of grief on his chest, Ajay wondered about the fruit's real name. 'Baffle Fruit' would be the logical answer.

Ajay screwed his face up as he took another bite of his unsatisfactory meal; it was like chewing into the meat of a hover vehicle bumper. *There must be more than this to eat.* Rolling the fruit over in his hands, he began his calculations. Presumably the boiled down Fo Doktrin, the green mush, didn't give them enough protein, so they need something more substantial. Why not go out and find some wild Ginel, or eat the birds, or even one of those lizard things? Thinking about what he'd read about the behaviour of wild animals, he concluded that perhaps there were very few of those left. If the Rogue had been here long enough and established themselves as the top of the food chain, any surviving animals had probably evolved to stay away. Ajay looked up, eyes blanched slightly by the sun, and listened to a small bird sing.

What about the birds? There were enough of them; small, fist-sized things whizzing from branch to branch. Ajay considered what they would taste like, before realising there wouldn't be much meat on them anyway. With the way they blitzed about, the effort that would go into catching one would not be worth the gain. Yet still, he'd seen bigger ones, with striking blue beaks and brown, intricately woven feathers. He'd seen their large wing span, gliding above the trees, spiralling the air and diving to catch their smaller counterparts in their talons. Why not eat them?

Biting into the fruit again, he realised how long it had been since he'd thought about food without the added merit consideration. Usually he'd be stressing about how much merit might be deducted or if he had enough merit for a certain product. Here, none of that mattered. He didn't know how to feel about it. Uneasy, he heard whispers growing behind him.

'Did you see him trying to climb that first one?' It was a youthful voice, followed by flutters of laughter.

'Where did Cal say he found him?'

'He knew him once, apparently. Thought he could help us.'

'They just don't get the tough ones any more, do they?'

'You didn't hear about him?' The youthful voice again. 'He's on the run. A murderer.'

'Really?' The responding voice sounded vaguely surprised. 'Well, you wouldn't have thought so. Quivering like a fox pup, when he was barely up the tree.'

Ajay continued to chew and swallow painfully, trying to avoid heaving.

It always came back. No, it never left. The weight of what he'd done physically pulled him down to the dirt; he turned onto his back, letting the slow tears trickle away from his eyeline into his hair.

Thought he could help us. So Callum kidnapped him to assist them in whatever they were planning next? It was almost laughable. There was no way he was going to get involved.

He's on the run. That wasn't fair. He never intended to be. It probably gave the wrong impression when he left Ace and ran towards the Side, to try to get to Grandma before Command did, because they'd go for her first.

He thought back to what the boy said on the climb: 'Command's best detectives.' *Insider knowledge.* So they still had people on the inside? How? And even more disturbing: Command was pumping big resources into finding *him*, presumably because they believed him a threat, tied up with these people.

That wasn't the truth. He'd turn himself in, if he knew it would ensure Grandma's safety. And even though he had nothing good to eat, in a camp barely surviving, he hated that he was almost freely existing in a life without Ace. Worse yet, it was a life he had created; his own stupid, desperate creation.

Sobbing silently, every part of him hurt for hours until he tumbled into sleep.

A clattering of metal forced Ajay's limbs to twitch and eyes to open.

His vision brightening, the tall woman was stirring a pot over the flat induction hob on the ground. Tasting the sweat running down his face, Ajay was aware of how sodden his clothes were. Lying by the heat of the hob, under a desert sun, was surely not the best way to avoid dehydration. He jumped up and moved to the other side of the log behind him, clattering into the solar panel in the process.

Steadying himself, he realised it wasn't day any more. Evening had set in and people were milling about, getting ready to climb again.

'Eh, watch it.' The woman looked as if she would hit him with her spoon. 'If you break that, we're screwed.'

Ajay assumed she meant because of the power ration that Haro had mentioned. They seemed to be conserving electricity for the higher priority items such as charging the laser guns or keeping the refrigerators and water dispensers going in their pits. All of it still drummed towards Ajay's main question – how did they get all these resources? From the ones on the inside, maybe, but Ajay was more intrigued about the logistics.

He reached for his suit.

Looking at the woman, cradling over the pot, he tried to see if she was taller than him. She'd tied her almost body-length hair up and already had her suit on. Her cheekbones were well-defined, and Ajay noticed how the skin was slightly strained around her eyes. He guessed she was in her late thirties, but her body looked as if she could be twenty-two. Slender and well-toned, he watched her take the pot from the stove and sift out boiled Fo Doktrin leaves into a bowl before mashing them down with a spoon. A homemade *SkipSleep* boost.

'Do you mind if . . .' Ajay spoke instinctively, his growling stomach talking.

'You can have the scraps.' Her blue eyes struck into him.

He took the bowl from her, still watching as she ate. He mirrored her and almost gagged, triggering a memory of a green smoothie in the City. *You get used to it after a while.*

'Yeah, awful, right? Don't even have any sugar to improve the situation.' She sat poised with her spoon hovering below her mouth, sounding both amused and irritated. Ajay stayed quiet. 'Maybe they'll actually give us something decent on the next drop-off.' She blew into her spoon, the steam rising over her face and disappearing as she ate.

'Drop-off?' Ajay coughed, the sharpness burning his throat.

'Did Cal not explain?'

As Ajay shook his head, she grunted and put her bowl on the ground.

'Seriously, it's like I have to do everything around here. When was I given the role of the mother?' Sighing and scraping her hand over her head, she looked at Ajay calmly. 'Every now and then we get cargo from the City. Mostly water barrels and food and a few scrap materials for the Architects to work with.'

'From the people on the inside?' Ajay swallowed again, struggling, while thinking about the mountain of materials in the next line of trees.

'Right. We call them Moths. Though there's not a lot of them left, so the infiltration of the resource planes is harder.'

She took a solemn swig from a silver, metal water bottle and then reached it out to Ajay.

'Here.'

Ajay hesitated. His eyes widened at the bottle.

'What? You think I'm going to poison you?' she smirked, clearly trying to stop herself from laughing. 'You just ate my cooking, didn't you? Look, if we were going to hurt you, I definitely wouldn't be involved. Take it.' She pushed it closer, letting him grasp onto the metal bottle, its touch cool.

'Thanks.' Ajay sipped, feeling relieved as the water washed out the remaining taste of leaf.

'There's a dispenser in Haro's pit. Sorry, there's no ice.' She took the bottle back from him, staring. Ajay touched the healing bruises on his face, which still throbbed on and off. He then looked at his hand, also bruised, remembering how it hit Ace's face.

Looking down at the bottle, she rolled it in her hands. 'I'm Charlene.'

Instantly, he associated her name with his grandma's; Karlane. Reminders of her everywhere, just like with Ace; the pain, guilt, longing and regret never leaving.

Ajay nodded to her in recognition but he assumed she already knew his name, the news about him from the inside having made its way through the camp.

She suddenly sprang up and sat next to him. 'I was thinking, seeing as you're new, you could help me with trying to convince the Architects to sort out better suits. I mean, they're disgusting aren't they? I noticed yesterday how you're having to wear socks because yours are too short. Me too.' She stuck her leg up to reveal her exposed ankle. Ajay watched her, not a clue what was going on.

'They surely could come up with something a bit more comfortable and workable. Surely the drones can't see camouflage joggers either? Oh, man, I used to love my joggers. Just lounging back after a hard day's work. Don't get any of that round here, I'm either sleeping on the hard ground or darting up the trees, which I don't mind; we've all got to do our bit. But I'd really prefer an outfit that didn't give me a permanent wedgie.' Charlene sighed and shook her head. 'We've really been slumming it since . . .' She paused, sadness in her eyes, quieting her voice. 'Everything.'

There was so much to process in her fast-paced monologue. The suits, joggers, what? Second, what was 'everything'? The attack? *Have things changed as dramatically here as in the City?*

The bizarre moment was broken by an angered shout behind them.

'Give it back!' The baby-faced boy then cursed, his body tense and cheeks red with rage.

'Come and get it,' another lad said, holding a piece of fruit, which was presumably stolen, by the way his pursuer looked ready to kill him. Ajay watched as the playground scuff unravelled and others intervened to pull the lads away from each other.

'It's always like this in mating season,' Charlene said, unaffected and turning her head back to Ajay. Mating season? *What in Tulo does that mean?*

'I thought they were friends.' Ajay recalled seeing them laughing together on the previous night's walk to the climbing spot.

'Hmm,' she grunted before turning to Ajay excitably. 'We could be friends, though, I don't mind. I need a new one after Seph let me down. She sleeps down that way. We don't talk now.' Charlene looked distastefully into a space to the right of them, then peered down, playing with a hair tie between her long, slender fingers. She smiled, almost sympathetically. 'I'll help you to climb. You need to know what you're doing. For the sake of all of us.'

Ajay nodded, not wanting to refuse and feeling overwhelmed by her.

'You remember what Cal told you about the perimeter?' She paused. Ajay thought; he remembered what he couldn't before. They couldn't cross the perimeter of the camp without permission. There were the Diverters who led Command drones away from the camp, and then the Spotters who alerted them if any did get through. The memory of Callum holding up his wrist donning that small, red band flitted in his mind but his face must have been blank.

'Oh, you're kidding me. He didn't bother telling you? I'm going to whip that headband out of his floppy hair and—'

'No, no. He told me. I remember.' Ajay almost enjoyed her light-hearted passion.

'Oh, good.' Charlene sighed and stood. Ajay appreciated her height, just taller than him. *Wow, that is unfortunate for a woman.* He silenced the thought, wondering if it was time to stop thinking about people in such a way; it never did him any favours.

'Get your suit on. Also, please don't let anyone see you've wasted them.' She swaggered away and pointed down at his uneaten pieces of fruit.

Wasted? What does she mean? The woman made no sense; he was going to eat them before they left. Picking one up, he tore into it. The once-green flesh had turned to a mouldy brown. Already? They lasted less than a day? *Seriously,* Ajay thought, *how are these people surviving?*

Armed with new and recalled information, the thought of escaping came back. He'd thought about it during the climb. If he could get out, then maybe he could make it back to the Side and still ensure his grandma's safety. His family would always be connected to his crime, and with the house arrests he'd witnessed, he didn't imagine Command would treat them well.

That wouldn't be the only reason to escape; he'd also be free from the vermin he was living among. While not all of them seemed to display the characteristics of the Rogue he thought he knew, being with them wasn't the best scenario. Escaping surely couldn't be that difficult. All he'd have to do was pass the Spotters in the trees, sneak past all the Diverters at the perimeter, hide from Command's drones, and trek out into the Country, figure out how to get to the Side, hunt for food on the journey and not get burnt by the persistent sun.

Ajay put a palm to his face, knowing he'd have to find another way. He heard a faint rumble from underground. Now knowing what that noise meant, he threw the rotten fruit into a nearby bush as Haro opened his pit door.

CHAPTER
EIGHT

'Don't worry, you're doing well,' Charlene whispered from the other tree. 'Just push up again on your heels.'

Ajay felt his legs buckling together and the sweat congregating around his butt cheeks. It was beginning to itch, which wasn't helpful. While the drop beneath him was heavy on his mind, he was thankful that Charlene's voice was a distraction, despite her having to be quiet. He looked at her through his goggles, her eyes bright and pulsing in the night light.

'Come on, we do have to get back down tonight, you know.'

'I can't . . .' Ajay's arms were clasped around his rope, its fibres burning his skin.

'You've got all the way up here. Just one more push and you can get to that branch.'

He looked at Charlene's somewhat comfortable position on one of her tree's branches, picking fruit and throwing it over her head into the sack on her back.

'I . . .' Ajay couldn't bring himself to do it. He knew all he had to do was push against the tree, hoist himself up, and flip his left leg over the branch. It was easy, but the drop beneath him was making things complicated.

Part of him wondered if he could get to the very top, what he'd be able to see. The Side? The lights of the City? He was disorientated in terms of location, not really knowing how deep or far the desert-forest ran and where they were buried within it. His thoughts turned to the largest Baffle Tree, the one towering above the rest. If he saw that, it might give him some idea of where he was. Looking up, he dismissed any chance of seeing the view; he'd have to go higher up this tree than necessary, and he couldn't even make it to the fruit.

Breathless, he fixated on Charlene. 'I can't.'

'OK. Let's try this.' Charlene's legs were swinging beneath the branch she was sitting on. 'What do you want more than anything?'

'What?'

'Like a thing. What do you want more than anything?' Charlene pulled the cord at the top of her sack to close it. 'For me, it would be a five-course meal, three courses of which would be dessert.'

'That's what you want more than anything?'

'Well, no, what I want more than anything is my life back, but to imagine that is more difficult. So tell me, what is it?'

He couldn't bring himself to tell her it was to reverse time; where Ace was still alive, and the accident never happened, and he wasn't the one to cause it.

'I don't know.'

'Oh, come on.' Charlene had her arms crossed. 'There must be something.'

'Fine.' Ajay paused. 'A Glorified mansion.'

'Seriously?' He couldn't see her expression but he imagined from her tone, it wasn't one of delight.

'Fine, when you push up and reach for the branch, imagine the mansion and don't stop until you get it.'

'OK.' Ajay nodded. He could do this.

'OK, now go on.'

Ajay pushed up on his legs, pulling his body out wide until all he needed to do was move his leg over to the branch. He looked to his left, it was right there . . . and at first, he did try to imagine the mansion; with Genni, his job, the score on his wrist. Yet that wasn't what he really wanted. Not any more.

OK. Imagine something else, then.

He could have imagined Ace, but he knew in his heart he'd suffer with that weight forever because it couldn't be changed. The branch instead transformed into a vision of his grandma, safe, untouched, not harmed by his bad decisions. He took a deep breath and shifted his body to the right position, throwing his leg over and stabilising himself on the branch.

'Woo, yeah.' Charlene's celebrations were comical though Ajay had forgotten how to laugh. He breathed out, the tree's leaves tickling his neck through his suit. He wanted to smile at his legs dangling above the drop, but reality still had him chained. He never should have left Ace. All he wanted was to know his grandma was safe, but it was futile. The moment Callum and the other Recruiters took him from the Side terminal had stolen any hope of helping her. Hadn't it?

Thinking about it now, the whole thing was stupid. Running across the City, covered in Ace's blood and terrorising commuters with the sight. It was a miracle the Tulo Police Department drones hadn't got to him first, he reflected. Was it a miracle? Wouldn't being arrested be better than being kidnapped by terrorists?

All of it was so ridiculous. He should have stayed with Ace, but the terrified Karle inside him had taken over, thinking about everything Grandma had done for him. As he sat on the tree, memories rattled through his mind again like a *Personi* feed: the birthdays, the trips to the playground; their chats on the hill, the bedtime stories; their late-night gossip. He couldn't just leave her to Command, but what could he do all the way from the forest? There must be a way for him to do something, but he would have to be more strategic this time, and strategy, until recently, had always been his strong suit.

With his feet firmly back on the ground, and a sack only half-full around his waist, Ajay felt as if his whole body could collapse. He blinked back at the branch, a mix of emotions falling over him like a blanket. Warm because he'd achieved something; cold because no part of him should be happy about it. Not when his family was at risk and Ace haunted his every cell and muscle.

'You smashed it.' Charlene patted Ajay on the back as she slithered the ropes off her waist.

'I only got half a sack,' Ajay spoke lazily, briefly feeling lost that he wasn't receiving exercise merit, before something on the ground caught his eye.

'Eh, that's not bad on the first climb.'

He briefly glanced up. Charlene was untying her long hair, letting it flow in waves over her shoulders. He knew she was watching him as he stared downwards again. 'I'm saying the first climb because I'm not sure the first one counts if you didn't even make it up the tree . . .' Charlene paused, like she was waiting for a response. 'Wow, you're really upset about it?' She came closer. 'What are you looking at?'

Ajay watched the small forest mouse burrow its way between the leaves until it stopped, stood on its back legs and reached for a leaf, nibbling adorably across its blade; he wished he could hear the tiny, intricate workings of its teeth and just be taken into its little, straightforward world.

'GET IT.' Charlene pushed him aside, throwing her long body onto the foliage, the leaves bowing down to her weight. Rustling around on her knees, she spread her hands over the dirt, patting around with speed in a frantic manner like someone who had lost something precious. Then she stopped, sighed and flicked her head back at Ajay, her blue eyes growing brighter with the rising sun. 'You idiot. If you see anything you could eat, grab it! Don't stand there gawping like it's a nature show.'

Ajay wasn't sure what to do. In the moment when he saw the mouse, he didn't immediately think of food, which was, he agreed with Charlene, idiotic. Yet he hadn't wanted to touch it. As he thought about the succulent taste of meat between his teeth, he knew he wouldn't make the mistake again.

Charlene glared at him further, as if she was waiting for an apology. Ajay might be grateful to her for helping him, but there was no apology passing his lips. He wasn't planning on staying any longer than he needed to, so perhaps he should be wary of being friendly with her. After all, it wasn't like he agreed with her and her friends' values; attacking the City the way they did.

'Never mind. Come on.' Charlene stood, and pulled her sack onto her back, leading Ajay back towards camp.

A man then marched towards them.

'What did you find, Charl?' The broad-shouldered man with a bristly beard spoke flirtatiously, ogling Charlene with his grey eyes.

Charlene stroked her long fingers through her hair and sighed. 'Nothing. A mouse got away from us.'

'Gutted.' He rubbed the edge of his badly shaven chin, joining Charlene, with Ajay staggering slightly behind them. He glared at Ajay over his shoulder, making him feel like a piece of meat. 'Who's the lanky lad?'

'Oh, my apologies. Bad manners.' Charlene grabbed Ajay, who stumbled forward, losing the feeling in his legs as the lactic acid hadn't worn off from the climb. 'This is Ajay.' Charlene leant forward slightly and cupped her hand to her mouth as if to whisper. 'He's the wanted one.'

Ajay had never really cared what these people thought of him but that one, for some reason, hurt.

'Ah, right. Yeah, I've heard about you from my girl.' The man grinned, not looking the least bit bothered about what he'd 'heard'.

'I actually wondered if you could get a message to her. I was thinking about the rationing for the next drop. If there's enough water barrels for washing this time, I think we should really get some better shampoo. I know the cheap stuff is easier to get, but it doesn't give you a proper clean, you know? I don't know if you've noticed, Ajay,' Charlene cocked her head at Ajay as the three of them moved back through the trees, 'but we all stink and if we could just get our hands on some good products, life might be more tolerable.'

Ajay had noticed, but he had nothing left within him to care. *Why bother when you have no merit to live for?*

'I think there's more pressing concerns than shampoo, Charl.' The man laughed in an appeasing way, but there was enough irritation behind his tone for Ajay to spot.

'Mex, good climb tonight?' A small, skinny girl with blonde hair and a muddy, pink headband appeared from the right. Ajay noticed Charlene's face immediately turn sour.

'Not the best. The Toxes must be breeding like wildfire.'

'We best get a move on, actually, Ajay. The sun is rising so they'll be coming out.' Charlene pulled Ajay forwards, dismissing the others and striding through the forest with vigour and determination. Ajay followed her, allowing himself to be pulled along with her fierce grip pinching his skin through his sweaty suit.

'Man, I hate her.' Anger pulsed through her usually bright eyes. 'That girl, there. Stay away from her. She's a right camel.'

'What did she do?' Ajay's curiosity of childish politics took over for a moment.

'I'm not talking about it, but trust me, she's bad news.'

Weren't they all bad news? Charlene seemed to calm down, as if the distance from the foe was strong enough medicine to heal the wound that had been suddenly torn open. As they walked further in silence, Ajay started to wonder about these Toxes they were referring to. They were lizards, he knew that, having overheard that the other night, but what threat did they pose?

'Hey, Charlene.' Ajay spoke hesitantly.

'Hmm?' Charlene turned to him, looking welcoming.

'What's the deal with the Toxes?'

'Toxlizards. You really weren't listening when Callum brought you in, were you?'

Actually, Ajay was pretty sure Callum hadn't mentioned anything about any lizards. He bit his lip.

'They live out here, mostly in nests underground made of twigs and stuff.' Charlene's knowledge seemed simplistic. 'But the important thing to know is that they come out during the day and gather the fruit for their young. It's breeding season at the minute, but they don't tend to come near the camp.'

'So why can't you climb during the day, though?' Ajay deliberately didn't say 'we' but he was intrigued as to why they subjected themselves to such uncomfortable sleeping conditions.

'Well, for one thing, any drones that Command sends would see us easier.'

Ajay felt dumb. So dumb. That was obvious.

'But mainly, you want to avoid Toxes. They're not particularly vicious, I don't think. Only when they feel threatened or have their babies with them. I mean, I've never seen one, but if you did happen to get bit, there's no coming back from it.' Charlene paused. Ajay considered how stupid it was, then, for Charlene to jump like a lunatic into those leaves to find the mouse. What if a lizard was lurking? Charlene readjusted her sack on her back and grunted. Ajay wondered if he should offer to carry it. No, he shouldn't be making friends. He was leaving – somehow – and anyway, he suspected she wouldn't care for charity.

Breathless, she continued talking. 'That's why you should always check your fruit before eating it, yeah? And keep your gloves on.'

'What do you mean?' Ajay was so curious, keen for new information.

'Their saliva is poisonous, but dries a dark colour so we know if anything's been contaminated. Though they rarely touch fruit they don't eat.' Charlene grunted again as they neared the camp. Ajay spotted Haro, walking strongly, the sack on his back bigger than him.

'Callum really didn't tell you any of this?' Her eyes carried a look of concern, as if it was completely out of the ordinary for Callum not to relay the information. Maybe he had. Ajay struggled to remember most of what he'd said when he'd walked, beaten and numb, out of that shack, but he thought he would remember something about fatal, toxic lizards.

'You look worried.' Charlene smirked slightly. 'Don't tell me the boy who conned Command when he was eighteen is afraid of lizards as well as heights?'

Ajay's mind froze for a moment. The Moths really did have information on him. He needed to know more. Knowledge was like a drug to him, it always had been. He had so many questions about this place and the people here, and how – he stopped his rambling mind. What was the thing he wanted to know more than anything?

He thought back to the tree and Charlene's question:

'What do you want more than anything?'

Ajay didn't need to know more about where he was but how to *get out*. To know his family was safe and not to become part of anything else where people would get hurt. The lines on his record in that department were already full enough.

Charlene cut through his thinking as they caught up with Haro on the edge of camp.

'Anyway, hopefully, we'll find a better spot tonight.' Charlene sighed, tying her hair back up, almost going off-balance as the fruit on her back weighed her down.

'No climb tonight.' Haro breathed heavily, shuffling his rucksack and walking as if a wall was being pushed against him. 'Just got word from the rest of the committee, there's a storm coming.'

So there was a committee, and Haro was part of it? Ajay remained attentive.

'Oh, actually giving some instructions, are they?' Charlene seemed to clench her jaw. 'What's the plan? We're going to starve soon.'

The plan? Another attack? Those words made Ajay cold, down to his deepest vein. He had to get out.

CHAPTER
NINE

Genni played it over in her mind. She'd felt so nervous, probably trying to act aloof by stroking her hair or something. The way he spoke, the way he looked, everything about him was what she liked; soft-eyed, not overly bulky and his messy, black hair gave him that charming, rugged allure.

She asked him about Prosper, trying to avoid just falling into his eyes. He probably tucked that hair behind his ears, the way he always did. She was like a foolish teenager, everything about him catching her off-guard, even the way he leant on the bar, edging ever closer to her and sending her feelings rampant.

Until she relaxed into it and got to know this new, beautiful person.

There were no warning signs that night they met. His story was completely ordinary, other than the unexpected death of his parents. Genni thought it over again as she sat lifeless on the sofa. That night they'd effectively ignored everyone else in their group and she remembered feeling so thankful that Ace's mother and her own were friends. Without their relationship, Ace never would have introduced her to Ajay. It was like they'd known each other for years; how they talked, laughed, even danced, earning a bit of merit in the process.

Yet sitting there, numb, staring forward into nothing, Genni knew she didn't know anything about him at all. Her flat was silent but she could still hear the hard grating of Rod's voice.

Ace is dead. Ajay killed him. He's from the Side.

Ajay was a flawless liar. There wasn't anything on the first night that suggested he wasn't raised in the City. Nothing. She quizzed him on everything from his grandma's best dishes to his favourite childhood memory. Did he even have a grandma? The way he used to praise her and all the marvellous stories she'd tell him. Everything about his childhood made Genni feel as if she had lost out in hers. Was any of that even real?

Genni felt her head starting to burn. Her throat dry, she willed herself to her feet, still thinking about it – he was a normal guy. A normal but beautiful guy. There was no way this was real. *It's an alternate reality,* she thought as she reached for the cupboard door and set down a glass. Staring at it for a moment, she wondered about all the times he'd been late to meet her. Or when he hadn't picked up his Watch. Was he there? Out on the Side with this family on Blueberry Bliss Lane? Genni closed her eyes and she could see the identification badge spinning around on Rod's Watch screen again.

Karle Blythefen.

Genni shook her head, looking down at the empty glass, the rim playing tennis with her falling tears.

Pulling herself together, she placed the glass under the water dispenser and watched as the initiation light turned on and the water fell. She got lost in memory again.

'What did you say your grandma did, Ajay?' Her dad had definitely asked him that when they'd all had dinner, most likely stuffing his face with a forkful of potato as one of the Side servants filled his soda glass.

'She's a health adviser,' Ajay had said, and Genni was confused, sure he'd told her she was a physiotherapist. She hadn't said anything, believing he'd just misspoken.

The cold cut deep into Genni's skin as the water fell over her fingers under the dispenser. Pulling her hand away and shaking the water off, she downed the glass to help her thirst. So, the 'health adviser' thing was a slip-up from a well-thought-out backstory? Was it? Genni didn't know. She didn't know anything. Did he really like to watch the storms with her when they came? Were camel burgers really his favourite? Was he really a fan of the Tulip Twins, like she was? Did he even love her? Or was she merely part of his plan to become Worthy? It was all so confusing.

Looking down at the goosebumps on her bare arms, she felt cold even though she was sweating. No wonder he wasn't answering her calls, and was acting so off after the attack. He must have been terrified, his time running out. Things started to add up as she leant against the breakfast bar for support. That's why he insisted on walking everywhere and why he wouldn't eat out for dinner, or why he'd been missing work and not having boosts. He would have been caught instantly with the new security checks. Could it really make sense? Was it really true? *Of course it was,* Genni thought, as she reminded herself of the surest sign of all.

When she and Ace caught him.

That time when he said he'd gone to the Side to 'help with the wildfire effort'. She was so unbelievably naïve.

Both she and Ace were. It was right there in front of them. A compulsive liar sitting on a sofa, water glass in hand, laughing at them both. It was all her fault, the signs were there, she'd just let him manipulate her. He'd blinded her with his charm and false commitment so well that even when Rod had told her the truth, she thought he was playing games with her. She was weak. Pathetic and weak.

Looking down at her legs, water splashes on her trousers, she watched them crumble to the wooden slats of her kitchen floor. The breakdown started as she held her stomach and hunched over. Everything was painful; she couldn't bring herself to think about what people would think of her. How her friends, parents, colleagues would react. It would be everywhere; nowhere to hide. There was no doubt in her mind that Command would make this big news. A manhunt for her man. A murderer.

Ace. She hadn't even begun to think about the reality of that. A life without Ace. Another thought came: if she'd always lived a life without Ace, she never would have met Ajay. Or Karle. Or whoever he was. That disgusting sociopath who had most likely ruined her life. She could feel anger moving inside her like flames.

All the times he made her feel Unworthy. When she had her *SkipSleep* accident and he considered leaving her; when he'd tell her she was wearing too much make-up, or a dress she was wearing wasn't as nice as another one; when he'd indirectly make her feel bad for eating something she shouldn't. Genni felt her breathing quicken and blood rush to her face. All those times he'd willed her on by pointing out his number was higher than hers. And yet, he was the real Unworthy all along.

'I HATE YOU!' Genni shouted into the apartment so loud her throat cracked.

She cursed as she rose in rage, wanting nothing but to destroy anything she could. He'd helped her pick this flat when she hit M-420 and everything about it felt dirty. She swept the empty dishes off the breakfast table, letting them smash across the floor. Stepping on a shard, but not stopping from the pain, she bounded into the living room, snot and tears streaming from her face.

She turned to her latest canvas and lifted it from the easel, before hesitating and dropping it to the floor, unscathed.

Running to the bedroom, she screamed through her teeth and picked up every digital photo of his face and threw them to the ground, feeling satisfied by breaking their screens. Screaming again, she relieved her dressing table of her make-up, hairsprays and other products, all of it crashing to the floor. The vases and their flowers were thrown towards the walls and the clothes hanging in the wardrobes were ripped from their hangers. Genni felt like she couldn't even feel herself, as if she was possessed by someone different. As she stood in front of her mirror, she heard the beep of technology as it started to explain her trousers were becoming off-trend.

'SHUT UP!' Genni picked up a hairspray can and launched it at the mirror, causing a spider's web of cracks. The screen moved in glitches and shut down, leaving Genni staring at herself, breathless and ugly.

Sitting on the bed surrounded by the massacre of her anger, only her paintings intact, Genni stroked the paintbrush charm on her bracelet.

It was one of Ajay's more thoughtful gifts.

After everything she went through last year, it was like a statement that he accepted her meritless painting habit. Genni felt soft inside as she looked at the charm, blurred by the tears in her eyes. Wiping the snot from her nose with her T-shirt and trying to control her erratic sobs, she thought about the times when she knew she'd loved him. There were almost too many to count. But did she just love a fictional character? Someone that didn't even exist? Whoever he was, he wasn't *her* Ajay. That was just something he created to fit some sort of mould. Though there was one thing Genni couldn't shake. That feeling that she did know the real him, revealed only in rare moments.

They were sitting in reclining deckchairs by the roof pool, a bolt of lightning cracking in the Country, flashing wildly beyond the shimmer of the artificial lights.

Ajay probably celebrated how awesome it was and she would have agreed. Watching the storms was often the only quality time they had. Life would have been normal; grabbing dinner out, stopping for boosts, working through the night after exercising and socialising. So she always cherished those moments, sitting calmly with him, watching the simplistic beauty and power of nature.

It was the time she'd asked him if he ever wondered what was out there, beyond the City, and they talked, and they laughed, and it was the first time he'd told her he loved her.

Genni sobbed.

Looking at the shattered glass on the floor, she saw how it resembled her heart. A fragile glass heart that had been blasted apart inside her, the pain of its shards cutting through every nerve in her body. She crumbled into a ball on her bed, crying into the apartment, thinking over his response when they had joked about living in the Country.

I think it would be nice, just to have you.

She couldn't bring herself to believe it was all lies. The love she had for him was real, even if it was never real for him. He had manipulated her to the point of her emotional obliteration and still, she loved him. It was sickening, but she couldn't let it go.

CHAPTER
TEN

Rod inhaled, holding the device steady in his mouth, feeling its vapour slither down into his lungs.

The meeting around him became a blur, and as he puffed again, he studied the photo of Ajay swirling around in the middle of the table. Ajay's smug, calculating eyes stared at him; his black hair groping his ears, neatly and professionally. His perfectly straight smile was carried by his pathetic, vile mouth. He was the only person who had ever truly fooled Rod; every other idiot in life had been unable to manipulate him into anything. Not even his own father had managed to force his hand. Yet this guy, from the Side, emotionally abused his dear, younger sister, also managing to hack into the system and consistently put Rod off the scent. Something had always felt wrong about him. At first, he'd blamed his uncertainty on an innate desire to protect Genni – that any man wasn't going to be good enough for her. Yet as time went on, and Ajay got seemingly weirder and Genni further discredited the family name, he'd disregarded that reasoning.

He took another drag of his *SkipSleep Pro*, starting to feel its effects as his mind fog cleared.

A recurring thought; why hadn't he seen it? His experience on the job meant he *should* have seen it. Especially after the psycho's pathetic attempt to cover up that printed photo of a Side friend or relative. Rod questioned it at the time when he and Ajay went for that drink. Ajay was anxious and erratic, the photo flying out from his pocket with the little girl on it, in sweet braids and holey tights, clearly not from Worthy neighbourhoods.

Yet he had decided to believe Ajay when he claimed she was his niece which, he defended himself, she could have been, despite something familiar in her eyes. *Where had he seen her before?*

He also should have trusted the alarm bells the time he caught him sweating, mucky and dishevelled outside the Quarters, like he was waiting for someone. If only he had acted on his gut feeling, then they wouldn't be wasting time trying to find him. Though he had to hand it to Ajay, he never expected him to be bold enough to do what he had. Ace's face came to mind.

The guy was clever. Brutal and clever.

'Are you with us, Mansald?'

Rod pulled his gaze away from Ajay's picture slowly, turning to Jona at the head of the table.

'What was that?' Rod sat up and casually slipped his *SkipSleep Pro* back into the pocket of his jacket.

'An update on the interviews, please?' Jona's eyes were irritatingly insistent.

'Right.' Rod coughed and addressed the others around the CSB board table. Officers Trye, Unn and Lang all typed notes on the desk while Rella seemed to avoid looking Rod in the eye, until he spoke and she gave him a subtle, flirtatious smile.

Looking back at Ajay's face, Rod proceeded to give his update.

'Both interviews with the friends, Pearl Pedro and Blake Sentra, were inconclusive. Neither gave us any leads on Ambers' whereabouts.'

Rod recalled the interview with Blake in his small, claustrophobic apartment, standing on his new plastic legs and continually throwing up in the kitchen sink. Clearly hearing one friend was dead and the other a murderer caused a weak stomach for some.

'It was the same with Mila and Jaxson,' Jonas chipped in.

'I think it's safe to assume that Ambers' immediate inner-circle knew nothing.' Rod stroked the edge of his clean chin.

'Including the victim?' Rudney Cedna, the lead on the Country search, leant forward on the table, the sun catching the dark shadows under his eyes through the wall-to-ceiling windows.

'I'm pretty sure Ace was oblivious. There's nothing to suggest otherwise.' Rod sipped from his glass. 'In fact, with the evidence of struggle at the crime scene, I'd guess he'd found out before he died, and we can't find a motive in Watch records or in the nature of their relationship to suggest any other reason for Ambers' actions.'

There was a moment of quiet and Rod appreciated the thoughtful nod Rudney gave in response.

'Good, thank you for that.' Jona swiped and removed Ajay's face from the middle of the desk, replacing it with two other faces. 'We'll pick this case up later. For now, let's move on to–'

'Hang on,' Rod spluttered slightly in his surprise. 'That's it?'

'We can discuss the details of the Ambers case afterwards, Rod.' Jona leant back in his chair. 'We just needed an overview. There are other items on the agenda.'

'What about the family? Surely they're a priority.'

'We've taken the measures we can for now.' Jona seemed to hesitate, flicking his eyes awkwardly at the others. 'Later, Rod, please.'

Grinding his teeth, Rod complied. Why couldn't he bring them in? And why was examining the evidence from their house taking so long? They'd never needed physical evidence for *their type* before. Rod didn't like it but he held his tongue.

'Rella, an update on the interrogations, please.'

'Sure.' Telusa Rella sat up straighter, softly scraping the sides of her light, tied-back hair. Rod listened, her sweet voice a drug to him, a distraction he couldn't quite keep at bay. 'The use of androids in the interrogations has returned good results this week. In addition to the convict, Lillie Trumin, we have now identified these two Rogue insiders.'

Rod listened as he watched the two unfamiliar faces swirl in front of them; two men, both average-looking, one with light hair tied in a ponytail with a scar above his right eyebrow, and the other with a rounder face and no hair at all.

'Mat Horri, thirty-three, worked in Transport. He was caught recalibrating Command cars' routes, clearing them on the system, which allowed safe passage out of the city. Mainly to the airfield.' Telusa stood and gestured with her hands, making Rod wonder if she was nervous. 'This means we are pushing harder on officials who operate in the Resources Transport Department. If there's anyone helping them use the resource planes, we'll find them soon.' She leant over Jona to tap on the desk, her long, gemmed necklace falling forwards as she did so. 'And Ben Jakobsin was found to have been assisting Trumin in the identification frauds leading to the attack.'

'Two people?' Rudney spoke, hands across his head, eyes sharp on Telusa.

'I'm sorry?' Telusa raised her eyebrows at him.

'You've made it sound impressive but you've only found two people.' Rudney pointed a chubby finger at the man's scarred face.

'That is a significant improvement, in that we hadn't caught *anyone* last week.' Telusa was annoyed, Rod could tell; her voice was getting lower, sounding similar to when she ranted about the lazy, incompetent juniors on her team.

'A significant improvement? Are you kidding?' Rudney snapped.

'That doesn't include people who don't work at Command.' Officer Trye chipped in, darting her eyes anxiously from Telusa to Rudney.

'That's my point. This is not . . . not good.' Rudney swallowed. 'We're two months down the line and we're nowhere near where we need to be.'

'How do you know that?' Jona stared at Rudney. Rod kept quiet, listening to the unravelling time-wasting discussion. 'We have no idea how many people they have on the inside.'

'It's got to be more than two. With what they pulled off.' Rudney loosened his tie under his plump chin and breathed more heavily. 'You're telling me that we can develop freaking robots to fix bones and we don't know how many people are right under our noses.' The table shook as he bashed it with his fist. Rod wasn't surprised Rudney was so animated, seeing as Lillie was on his team. *Your attempt to hide your embarrassment is pathetic.*

'With respect, Rudney,' Telusa spoke confidently, not the least bit fazed, 'we're all in an unprecedented situation, having to develop our techniques on the job, not really knowing what will work and what won't. It's going to take time. I'd appreciate a little bit of patience on your part.' She paused. 'I don't think that's too much to ask, given the circumstances.'

Rod raised his eyebrows and looked down at his feet, trying to conceal his smirk. *Go get them, girl.*

While he appreciated her bravado, she did need to step up. Rudney, frustratingly to Rod, was absolutely right – finding only two was poor. He reckoned he'd have found at least ten by now if they were there to be found. *You haven't found Ambers yet. That's different.* He battled through his thoughts. Ambers was on the run, not working among them. It was a harder case but still, it stung not to have found him.

Rod started to fidget, picking the edges of his leather seat. He wanted the Rogue to be found but not as much as he wanted to leave this insolent lot to themselves, as his job wasn't going to get done sitting here.

'Can you submit a report to me, then, Telusa?' Rudney calmed himself. 'I'd like to see what the androids are trying.'

Telusa nodded with an agitated twitch in her lip.

'OK,' Jona sighed, tapping his desk. 'Let's try to keep our heads, shall we? Rudney, what about the search in the Country?'

'Joann, you wanna take this?' Rudney looked at Officer Unn across the table, who was pressing her pupils to readjust her blue-pigmented contact lenses.

She sat up straight, tapping the desk and clearing her throat. A satellite map of the desert-forest appeared, its vast surface-area covering the breadth of the table. 'There have been several sightings by drones over the last few weeks.' She pressed the desk again, glancing at the map where pinpoints flashed up in different locations. 'The drone recordings show individuals running until we lose connection as they take them out.' Stroking the top of her short, spiky hair, she presented some video footage over the map showing a man dressed in dark clothing, sprinting between trees until he turned and fired lasers at the drone, and the scene turned black.

'All of these incidents, at first, seemed to follow a pattern.' Rudney drew on the table, lines appearing in red between the coordinates on the presentation. Rod followed, seeing how the first five seemed to form a rough arc or circle. 'Until . . .' He tapped, and pins appeared in more random locations across the acres of forest.

There was a slight pause in the room until Jona spoke.

'Do you think they're trying to divert from where they're based?'

'Potentially.' Rudney grunted, shuffling in his seat. 'So, the next step is to try to identify the right cluster around their actual location.'

'So, you're telling me,' Rod leant forward, creating his own entertainment, 'that we can programme freaking robots to fix bones and you haven't found them yet?'

Telusa sniggered, as the others looked shocked.

Jona sighed. 'Rod, please.'

'Why don't we just take out each of these zones?' Rod asked, pointing at them and still holding a smirk on his face. That would be his way of doing things, then they could get back to their real jobs.

'And how do you propose we do that?' Joann was stern.

'Oh, come on.' Rod laughed impatiently. 'Jokes aside, we have all this resource. Let's just get rid of them.'

Rudney started. 'And what trained army do we have?'

'Enough to take them on, surely,' Telusa cut in.

'Not nearly enough. Command guards are not trained for that sort of combat.' Rudney rubbed his eyes. 'And we don't have enough weaponised drones.'

'Plus, we don't know their numbers or how many weapons they have,' Joann interrupted. 'There are many unknowns.'

'Well, don't use men. Weaponise more drones or even the resource planes.' Rod gestured, dropping a bomb with his right hand. 'Get them from above.'

'That would destroy a lot of the forest.' Officer Trella spoke up, for once.

'Welcome to the meeting!' Rod snarled at him, watching him cave into himself.

'Rod, I can't ask you again,' Jona commanded. *Then don't,* Rod thought, slumping back in his chair, disgruntled, his mind turning back to Ajay. He could have gotten closer to finding him in the time he'd been dealing with this incompetence.

'There's another consideration now, too.' Jona glanced around the table, all of them looking at him. 'A conspirator from a house arrest yesterday revealed they have children, which not only implies bigger numbers, but also complicates any sort of thoughtless attack.'

'That didn't stop them from attacking us,' Telusa growled.

'There weren't any children killed on Liberation Day,' Joann responded.

'And that excuses them, does it?' Rod barked.

'No, of course not.' Joann swallowed. 'But we shouldn't take on their mentality, killing whoever and whatever.'

'How do we know the conspirator wasn't lying?' Telusa asked. 'To protect themselves.'

'The state the guy was in after the arrest . . .' Rudney paused and grunted, a stern yet joyful look in his eyes. 'He wasn't lying.'

'Right, let's bring it back in.' Jona glanced at his Watch before dismissing the forest map, it fading into nothing so all that was shining in the room was sunlight. 'With this information, the Hevases are keen not to put the children's lives at risk, as they could contribute to society in the future. The matter of sporadically attacking is therefore already settled.' Jona stood, tucking the back of his shirt into his trousers. 'We'll come together again tomorrow when we'll also be getting an update on the new Watch model. For now, back to our cases.'

Rod didn't hesitate. *Finally.*

He jumped from his seat, letting it roll away behind him, and followed Jona from the meeting room.

You're mine, Ambers.

CHAPTER
ELEVEN

Sitting on a log, Ajay thought about The Guiding Light properly for the first time since Ace died. He hated it, that hadn't changed. It was the reason he was where he was. If it had never existed, his family wouldn't have followed an ideology against Command's, and he could have been just like a City kid. There would have been no reason for him to become a criminal. He could have earned more than M-200 the usual way and Ace would be alive right now. But he remembered how as a small kid, he liked it. It made him feel sick now, but he did. Its cheery voice would bounce off the walls and he would admire its body of small, microscopic lights; veins of sparkles projecting from its hardware.

He even had a favourite story.

'*There was a chief on the railway line who had twenty-eight workers under his command.*' Or was it twenty-nine? Ajay wondered as he watched Charlene packing things into a bag a few blocks of trees away.

'*One day, they completed the day's work early as there was a dangerous sandstorm coming.*'

That was it, and when he counted the workers, there were only twenty-seven or twenty-eight of them. One was missing and the chief went out, not stopping until he found him.

'*Stop, rest, and know I'm fighting for you.*'

Ajay remembered how cleverly The Guide would match the tension of its voice to the rhythm of the story. His brain ran away with the algorithms responsible for that function, before returning to a memory.

One time when he was older and listening to that story, Ajay was distracting Callum, who was sitting with his mother across the table. They started pulling faces at each other until his grandma suggested they could go and play. Happily, they darted through the Side streets, running past homes, seeing other children gathered around The Guiding Light and then others in the playground. Ajay had grown jealous of the very few kids whose parents didn't listen to it. They never had to sit quietly, listening to the same mind-numbing stories, now etched into his memory like an overplayed educational movie. Thinking about it made him clench his fists uncomfortably, but he knew it was a waste of energy, so he focused on Callum.

He probably challenged him to a race up the hill.

'First one up the hill gets the merit.'

He would have zoomed past the mail office, bakery and ration stations; weaving across into the desert sands, spotting the City to the south. He would have beaten Callum, every time.

Ajay rarely thought about him. Ever. It was only when his life fell apart in the City that Callum crossed his mind. Yet there were good memories there, and his family was good to Callum; all the dinners and the helpful gestures, especially when his dad left.

He rolled some fruit over his hands, examining it diligently for any signs of dark lizard spots. There was a niggly feeling in the back of his mind he wanted to dismiss; that he'd done to Callum exactly what he'd done to Ace.

To Genni.

To so many people.

Sidelining them for his own selfish desire, no matter how it affected them. He swallowed, trying to ignore the omnipresent lump in his throat.

'We're both in Haro's pit for the storm. Here.' Charlene gave him a knife to help ease the destruction of his nails when prying open the fruit's hard shell. By asking her more questions over the last hour, he'd learnt they were called Kakafruit. It was something to do with their history; one of the first babies born in the forest had called it that and the name stuck.

'I was thinking I'm going to move to sleep by you. It's got more tree cover and I thought you might like the company.' She smiled graciously without giving Ajay the option to refuse. As she returned to the entrance of Haro's pit, she helped him connect a solar panel to a bashed-up air-conditioning vent.

They were so resilient. A trait built up after generations of angry Unworthies surviving, growing strength in numbers and in ingenuity. That had impressed Ajay. The thought made him squirm inside. While he was fascinated by their use of technology and their unbelievable ability to survive, he couldn't get attached to them. Not after what they'd done. Yet part of him couldn't help but be curious – and, of course, there was Charlene.

Watching her standing by Haro's pit, smiling and laughing with him as they worked together, Ajay couldn't figure her out. She didn't seem murderous; she seemed angry, sure, but not a killer. Nor did Haro. While he was grumpy and closed off, he cursed Ajay for hitting a Wingspark. How could he ever physically hurt another person? Ajay thought about the children as he bit into the rubber fruit; they were raising children – sweet, innocent children. There was a battle brewing inside him, questioning if these people were in some way – good?

He'd tried to bring up the attack with Charlene, without much success.

'Can I ask . . .' He'd kept his voice down as they'd arrived back at camp, Charlene quickly pulling off her suit. 'Were you involved in the attack last year?'

Charlene had hesitated, her eyes static, as she'd pulled her suit from her waist. After a moment, she stood straight and seemed to exhale as if anxious.

'No, I wasn't, not in the way you think.' She'd spoken softly, glancing around at others. 'But keep your voice down, we don't talk about it much.'

'You don't talk about it?' Ajay tried not to sound irritated. 'After what you did to people?'

'It wasn't all of us,' she'd spat with a stern look. 'Things have changed around here, OK? But I don't like talking about it, so can we just drop it?'

'OK.' He smiled briefly and set about taking off his own suit as Charlene nodded and walked away. Watching her, he hadn't been particularly satisfied; in fact, he was even more intrigued than before. *What has changed around here?*

As these thoughts ran across his mind, he knew he needed to clear it. It didn't really matter what they did or didn't do, *he* needed to refocus on his plan to escape.

'I'm just going for a walk,' he called over to Charlene, who flapped her hand at him in response. Why did he even feel the need to tell her?

He stopped, closed his eyes, and leant against a tree trunk, reminding himself of everything these people had done. They didn't deserve any of his gratitude or appreciation.

Ace's eyes wide. The coffee table smashing. His cry; his long, painful cry.

The songs of the birds turned to Ace's screaming. Every silent moment turned back to him and Ajay cursed himself. He could use all the birds and lizards and fruit and questions he wanted to distract himself from what he'd done. The facts remained the same: Command was after him and so they should be; leaving his Watch in his apartment may have slowed them down, but not by much. They'd have gone to Genni first, expecting that to be his obvious hiding place.

How is she dealing with this? Ajay looked up at the trees again, remembering her face and the way her freckles came out beautifully in the white sunlight. She hated them, he loved them. He thought about how good it would feel to kiss her again.

She probably hated him, and she should. He wasn't worried about her and Command, she was protected by her father's merit power, not that she'd even done anything wrong. She was so much stronger than she realised. She could forget him and be successful. Not able to think about her too much, Ajay moved on.

His grandma and the others had no protection; they were vulnerable and he needed to do everything he could to help them get out, flee, go into the Country and save themselves. He didn't even know if that was a feasible plan.

Grandma always knew this would happen. He shook his head and slapped his hands to his face, reminding himself of everything she'd given him and Tara. Even a small part of Ajay wanted to save his father, despite all he held against him.

Could he still solve the problem? Protect his grandma and his family from those who might suspect their hand in his crime? *Think straight.* He pulled himself up taller against the tree trunk.

I've been in the Rogue for just under a week. Have I? I'm not sure. They might not have found anything substantial enough to warrant an arrest yet, but his family surely would have been questioned. Ajay had no idea how the CSB operated, but he needed to do something. He would go insane if he didn't.

What do I need to do?

Escape from these messed-up people and, maybe, get to the Side. Then I'd know if they're safe, or I could get back to Command and try to plead their innocence. Well, I can't do that without being directed out of here, and survive a trek across the desert, which would be nothing short of miraculous.

How did they get me here in the first place?

Perhaps they can transport me back.

There's no way they'll do that. I know too much about them. I'm still a City-lover, a threat.

What else is there? They have communication devices to speak to the Moths on the inside. Could I get my hands on one of them? And do what?

OK, take another step back. Who goes to the City? The Recruiters.

Callum.

Ajay lifted his head and set off to find Callum immediately. Almost stumbling through the vegetation, he wondered if he would ever get used to the uneven ground. Hopefully he wouldn't be staying long enough to find out. Night was setting in and Ajay could see the storm clouds gathering above the trees. A strong, sweet smell invaded and warned of the coming rain. Genni might be watching the storm tonight, without him. *Stop it.*

He reshifted his focus back to Grandma getting arrested.

Bumbling forwards, Ajay knew Callum didn't owe him anything, but he owed his parents, for being so kind to him and his mother all those years ago. That might be enough.

Arriving at the main camp, Ajay tried to stay discreet as he walked in among the families, all getting ready for bedtime. He watched as children disappeared into the pits, wondering if they were read stories, and what sort of stories they would be. Would they be wholesome, or plagued with anti-Command propaganda? Being taught how to hold a gun? As he continued to walk, he saw a man carrying his sleeping daughter in his arms, who wore cute, pink pyjamas covered in little fox heads. Ajay smiled to himself as he saw how proud the father looked, holding on to his child like she was the most precious thing in the world. Without his permission, he turned soft inside.

'Get him out of here.' A squalling voice disrupted the moment and Ajay turned to see a woman standing at the edge of her pit, pointing at Ajay with rage in her eyes.

Man, they really hated him. Did they seriously think he was a threat to their children? He may be a so-called 'City-lover' but he was also on the run from Command. Didn't that technically make him an enemy to the City and therefore one of them? Not that he wanted to be.

'You shouldn't be here.' Callum pulled him aside into the next line of trees, holding a bag over his shoulder.

'Sorry. I needed to talk to you.'

'What is it?' Callum didn't keep eye contact with Ajay but gazed past him. It was like the way Haro would look at him with his lazy eye, except, of course, Callum didn't have one.

'My family.' Ajay tried to move his head to be in Callum's eyeline. 'Grandma and my parents. Command might suspect their involvement with me.'

Callum said nothing, continuing to look everywhere but at Ajay.

'And I'm scared of what they might do to them. There's evidence at their house. The computer I used. I need to get back to them. To the Side or Command. To try to—'

'You're not leaving.' Callum's bluntness took Ajay by surprise. Stunned, he thought of the baby-faced, polite boy he used to know. It was always Ajay who had the upper hand in their friendship; he chose the games to play and the places to go. He always won the race up the hill.

'Look, I know I messed up before. But they're . . .' Ajay tried to talk.

'It's not about what happened.' The taser scar across Callum's cheek was bright red and brown even as the light became dim. The wind started to pick up. Ajay didn't believe him. 'I had to get out.' He breathed calmly, remembering the chase with the drones they had in the shopping centre. 'And I know I dragged you into it. You never wanted to go in the first place.'

Callum gave no response but finally looked at Ajay, gratitude dashing across his pupils until they turned cold again.

'Why didn't you come home? After Command let you go?' Ajay asked, stepping a foot closer, but Callum took two more back.

'After they beat me, you mean,' Callum said curtly. 'And yeah, you're the reason I'm here.' He pulled the red band from his sweaty head and ran his fingers through his floppy hair.

'Command beat you?' Ajay was momentarily shocked before getting distracted by Callum's tone. 'Wait, you mean to say you don't want to be here?'

'That's not what I said,' Callum sighed. 'The storm's coming. I've got to go.' Callum tried to push past Ajay, readjusting his bag on his back.

Ajay wasn't having it and moved to stand in his way. 'Look, if you can't get me out—'

'It's not that I can't get you out, it's that I won't. The new committee will need your help soon, so you may as well let that one go.'

As Callum tried to get by again, Ajay smelt their mutual stench and contemplated Callum's words. Under no circumstances was he offering them this 'help'. Though Callum referring to the committee as 'new' was interesting. Shaking his curiosity away and determined, he skipped back in front of Callum.

'Look, you know my family. They were kind to you.' Ajay grabbed Callum's arm, and Callum glared down at his grip. 'When you next go out to recruit, can you check up on them or do something to protect them? I'll owe you.'

Callum grunted, forcibly flicking Ajay's hand off his arm. 'You already owe me. I'm not doing you any more favours. Now, get out of my way.'

Their eyes fixed on one another for a lifeless moment and Ajay could hear his heavy breathing, seeing that his friend was no longer there. That was about right. He knew he wouldn't help Callum if things were the other way around.

But this was about Grandma and his own conscience. He couldn't live with himself if what he'd done to Ace caused her death too.

'Please!' Ajay stopped tears from forming but Callum continued walking.

Feeling the first drop of rain on his nose, Ajay was even more bewildered when he saw the device popping out of Callum's rucksack. He'd recognise The Guiding Light anywhere. Seeing it triggered instant frustration. Why did Callum have one? Too many questions he probably didn't deserve the answers to.

He looked up at the angered sky, knowing he needed to get back, but he already felt as if he was in a dark, impenetrable pit.

CHAPTER

TWELVE

The outside world felt like a carnival. Everything was a kaleidoscope of blurred colours, swirling around her. The beeps, bleeps, horns, electronic flickers and buzzes of the City were a cascade of sound, feeling so much louder than ever before.

Genni, eyes glazed over and body flopping, was tempted to return to her cave of destroyed possessions. To escape from a chaotic, unruly world of activity that jarred so powerfully with her ever-growing emptiness. Her breathing started to turn into something erratic and, clutching onto her handbag, she didn't even know what she was doing. She felt drunk on heartbreak, unable to walk without barging into others. Their staring, threatening eyes passed her by until she tripped over her own feet and fell to her knees, snapping her surroundings back into clarity.

'You OK?' a woman said, bending down to help Genni up, her long chestnut hair falling over her arms.

'Yes. Thank you,' Genni sighed. 'Was obviously going too quickly.' She brushed herself down, suddenly feeling vulnerable about her outfit; the trousers she'd thrown on were heavily creased and a few watermarks remained, splattered in places.

'Well. Take care of yourself.' The woman smiled sweetly without removing her sunglasses.

'Thanks.' Genni felt comforted by the woman's graciousness; a surprise in her current dark sense of reality, reminding her that Ajay's betrayal and the other rejections she'd suffered weren't all there was. There were more people, nicer people; it just felt like a quest to find them. Part of her wanted to scrabble after the woman to thank her again for her small act of kindness, not having remembered another time when a stranger had helped her so willingly. All she'd done was something tiny, but to Genni it was a stark, emotional moment.

Until the sorrow returned and she felt vacant again as the woman disappeared into the crowds.

Taking a deep breath and controlling her thoughts, she lifted her Watch to check herself and put concealer beneath her dried-out eyes, before then boarding the sky train, and condemning herself for even thinking about going to the Side.

She was heading there, she reminded herself as the train tilted on its route, because there must be another piece to this messed-up puzzle. Loving Ajay had always been so easy that some of it had to be true. She couldn't merely sit around her apartment, or pick herself up and get back to work when the search for answers felt so heavy. Nor could she let Rod hold her hostage, telling her to stay here or there. It only occurred to Genni then that if Rod really was in security, which did bizarrely seem to check out, had she disobeyed a direct order from

Command? A small feeling of regret creeped in. What was she doing?

In a panicked motion, Genni stood up, anxious to get off. The train silently swooped to a stop but she didn't move. It was like something had fixed her feet to the ground, willing her to stay on board. *For Tulo's sake.* She cursed herself for her indecision and slumped back down into her seat.

It was probably too late anyway. She could come up with some convoluted excuse and play the daddy card. It paid for him to be one of the biggest businessmen in the City, even though that get-out clause was nauseating. Besides, she thought as she stared numbly at the moving adverts above the head of a small child chewing gum, those from the Side weren't all bad. Those going through Purification who served her family were pleasant, sometimes even pleasant enough for Genni to like them. What was her name, her favourite? *Lanie.*

The first time Genni met her was after the bald one with hairy arms was let go. It was amazing how quickly the useless ones got dumped; her friends' Purification candidates always lasted longer. It was probably because her parents were the worst to work for – over-demanding, pedantic and basically unpleasant to be around. Maybe it was better for them to fail Purification and end up back in the Side, Genni considered. Her mum had lied and said that Hairy Arms had finished the process, when Genni knew, even at ten years old, that the constitution required him to work for a Glorified family for two years, and it had not been that long.

But that was the day Lanie started and Genni remembered the exact moment they met. She was sitting on her bed, flicking through the education curriculum on her tablet and struggling with a maths problem. Lanie walked in holding a questionably folded pile of sheets and her large hips carried her around the room as she pulled off Genni's bedsheets. She'd asked Genni to help her, and Genni remembered thinking it was rude, and she didn't need educating on that skill. Once she was eighteen and in the City, she wouldn't sleep enough to warrant changing them regularly, and for what she did need, a cleaning drone could do it. And anyway, they were there to do the work, to earn their citizenship, not to have ten-year olds helping them out. Yet at the time, after a few moments of small talk, Genni had felt drawn to Lanie's warmth and gentle demeanour, so she held down one side of the sheet while Lanie pulled the other over the mattress.

She ended up asking Genni what she was reading. Genni lied and said she was good at maths. She felt nervous her parents would walk in at any moment and batter her for chatting with the help. Lanie told Genni she liked to read something called a novel that took longer than ten minutes to finish, which made Genni's head spin. Ten minutes' reading something that wouldn't help you contribute? *That's why they never achieve anything on the Side,* Genni thought, as she watched drones drop off outside as the sky train accelerated.

Even back then, Genni had a plan for her life. One that was straightforward; study hard every day before she turned eighteen, get a job at Command, climb the ranks, dismiss any dead weight she met along the way, and make it back to the Glorified Quarters before she was twenty-five. She never admitted to anyone she'd just copied it from Rod's digital timeline on his bedroom wall. Now, fourteen years later and watching the City zoom by, she was as close to the Quarters as Ajay was to being Worthy. Holding back more tears, she let her failures wash over her.

Downtown, Outer-Outer Ring.

The voice of technology disrupted her thoughts and she looked out at the last sky train platform. The memory of Lanie faded, the doors to the now-empty carriage slid gracefully open, and Genni looked out into Downtown, unsure whether to disembark.

CHAPTER
THIRTEEN

Genni hadn't been this far out since the night of her accident – memories flickered.

The side effects of the overdose, the feeling of nausea so strong she couldn't contain it; the struggle to know what was real, and arriving here, Downtown, to find her usual administrator gone, and that man from the Rogue in his place. She could remember the way he looked at her, a terrifying stare that spoke clearly even into her intoxicated state. He was going to kill her, and if she hadn't had help getting away, he would have done. Just like the Rogue took the others, using their identities to get into the Quarters that day. Genni remembered the headline: *The Victims of Rogue Impersonation: some bodies found, others still remain lost.* Genni knew why; it could have been her.

Everything in her mind told her to stay on the sky train because wherever the Rogue were, whether still Downtown, in the Side or out in the Country, stepping off here meant stepping closer to them. It also meant edging nearer to the Ajay she believed she knew. Potentially. If he existed.

I need to know, don't I?

Her body pushed her off the train, feeling the gentle breeze as the train glided back towards the City behind her. Genni felt frozen in place, staring numbly forwards, recognising the bridge that led to Downtown. The therapist, who no one knew about, had told her not to come back without careful preparation, not without working up to it, because the environment would trigger those same feelings of trauma she felt that night. It seemed he was right; she was trying to ignore the tremor in her legs and the tight wheezing of her chest. Especially as she could see the road where the hover vehicle hit her after she ran; closing her eyes, she could see its lights slamming into her body, sending her skyward. *Stop it, control the thought.*

As she turned her feet robotically away from the bridge and walked slowly down another main street, a new feeling passed over her.

I could get a fix.

The more she walked, the more it felt right to turn around. Sauntering more slowly through the crowd than she was accustomed to, she tried to distract herself with her surroundings. A crisp packet skidded across the pavement as she marched through it, an unfamiliar sight. Having always been so conscious of anyone seeing her in Downtown, she'd never even considered the litter or how bland and box-like the buildings were. They looked almost like what they had on the Side, or what she had seen online. Everything was depressingly grey; houses with only one or two windows; Unworthies laying out on doorsteps and a nasty smell Genni couldn't identify.

Trying to close her nose, Genni wrapped her arms around herself, not looking at anyone who passed her. Even as a group of children ran past, giggling and shouting, it was like an all-consuming thunderous wind. That was when she realised how much she was shaking; she was terrified. *What am I doing to myself?*

She saw the entrance to the rusting rail platform and had never felt more vulnerable in her life. Going to the Side was a suicide mission. Not only were the people there ideologically dangerous, but the merit deduction for the trip would be sacrificing a week's work. What she'd achieved in the last week flashed through her mind; leading that meeting, educating Mila on more efficient eating methods; finally filing that report that had been hanging on the bottom of her list for months, and a few intense sessions of exercise at the Sports Tower. The painting of the foxes and the garden came up, but she dismissed it quickly. All of what she'd done in the last week would be eradicated by trying to find an answer about someone who had been playing her for the last three years as part of some twisted story of his own. *Really, Genni? Turn around. There's something better back there.*

She stopped, trying to turn off her mind. She couldn't think about the enhanced *SkipSleep*; she couldn't go back to it, not after everything she'd done to recover. Scanning over the billboard above made things worse. *Suspicious about your neighbour? Report it on your Watch.* The grey background meant the advert merged into the buildings' walls yet the bold, white callout gave the words nowhere to hide. The rotating secondary banner was disorientating as Genni tried to read its spinning contents.

562 arrests have been made this month on the back of anonymous civilian tips.

As Genni thought about it, a group of Command guards and TPD drones moved past her in unison, as if approaching some sort of battlefield, just as she also spotted a home cordoned off with flickering 'crime scene' barriers. She wasn't the only one in a war. The whole City was messed up. There was nothing positive or fun or free.

That's when she remembered how it would feel.

That high.

The overcooked drugs would pulse through her veins, and she floated through life on a cloud, and she felt amazing. Energy, clear and clean, allowing her to thrive.

In the time she'd spent thinking about it, the Side had become a distant memory. She stopped at the bridge, eyeing the opening to the market stalls of Downtown on the other side of the river. It was stupid. She couldn't do this to herself, but what else would stop the pain? She had no other answer. No, there must be a way. *You can handle this, Genni. Be strong. Go home, grieve, move on, don't give up.*

Just as a small ounce of strength grew within, she unsilenced her Watch and briefly scanned her message log. Pings came in one after another like a catapult of rocks falling on her, stopping her from breathing.

22 missed video calls – Blake, Jaxson, Mila, Pearl, Mum, Dad

62 unread messages

Some work-related but most of them flagged as urgent.

Blake: *Gen, where are you? Rod has been here. I can't believe what's happening. I need you.*

Jaxson: *Gen, ring one of us. I've just been to your place. We're worried.*

Mila: *Gen, I just can't believe it. Ring me.*

Pearl: *I'm lost for words, Gen. I might have extra breaks today. It's too painful. So hard to believe Ajay would do this, but if it's true, you can obviously do better and he'll get what he deserves. Call me, babe.*

Dad: *We need to get a hold of this. Genni, I've talked to my contacts to make sure you are not associated with this scandal. Come on, girl. Ring us.*

Mum: *Genni, dear, I always thought he was no good. Come home for a little while, maybe?*

Blake: *Gen?*

Jaxson: *Gen?*

Mila: *Gen?*

Pearl: *Gen?*

Dad: *Genni?*

Mum: *Genni, darling?*

No, no, no.

She couldn't handle it. She wasn't strong enough. She needed it.

Nothing else on her mind, she turned off her location and silenced her Watch again before marching over the bridge back towards her darker past.

It looked different from before. Quieter. Less people. The stalls had been cleared out, cardboard boxes upturned and straying across the ground. Glass from the lanterns littered Genni's path and the fairy lights had been torn out, the remains of them hanging down like still snakes.

There was no one here. Genni felt her heart sprint in its beat, her breathing tight and throat closing as she started to panic. Tears fell down her cheeks as she rushed towards the familiar door where her administrator used to be, hoping he might have come back.

'Please, please,' she cried, falling through the metal door, seeing nothing but an empty room. No vials, no *SkipSleep*, nothing. Falling to her knees, she held her hands tight to her mouth to muffle her screams. It was the one thing she had hope for, the only escape she knew. A thought came as she broke down. Was there a way she could tamper with her port at home, to get more than the four-hour allowance? It still wouldn't be the same. Whatever they put in the enhanced stuff was what she needed. What she wanted.

Everything was gone.

Ajay.

Ace.

Everything.

'Excuse me, are you OK?' A light voice came from behind her.

Genni jumped to her feet, startled and embarrassed, to find a man with short black hair staring at her with concerned eyes.

'Yeah . . .' Genni wiped her eyes, trying to compose herself. 'I was just . . . erm . . .' She breathed and fell silent, not looking at him. 'I'm going . . . going.' She left the room and he didn't get in her way, moving aside.

'Are you sure?' he asked. Genni looked back, not really taking him in, but noticing a small mole on his neck.

'Yeah. Sorry. I didn't mean to bother anyone.' Genni felt cold again, stroking her arms.

'No, no you didn't. I was only walking past.' He tightened the straps on his green rucksack so it shifted further up his back, grimacing as he did so.

'Well, I'm fine now.' She paused, smiling as she felt her heart rate normalise and her Watch vibrate to tell her so. 'Thank you.'

'I didn't do anything.' He smiled back.

Genni just shrugged her shoulders. 'OK, well, bye.'

'Bye. Sure you're OK?' he asked once again, his brown eyes holding her.

Genni nodded before walking away, thankful that he had somehow intervened. He didn't know it but him being there, instead of the drugs, and caring for her gave her a slightly new perspective. Genni had no doubt that if the drugs were there, they'd be in her body now.

She'd lied of course; she wasn't OK, but she did feel slightly better. Better enough to try and heal, and forget all about ever going back there.

CHAPTER
FOURTEEN

The ground above them rumbled, under a roaring sky that beckoned sizzling lightning bolts.

Ajay, silent, pulled his balaclava over his head and observed the people around him through flickering candlelight. Charlene, sitting next to him, was chatting away, her squawking voice accompanying the noise of the thunder outside. Ajay needed to stretch his legs out but there wasn't room with the eight of them huddled together in Haro's pit. He sat with his legs close to his chest and his bum going numb.

He grimaced as he tried to get comfortable, causing Charlene to notice him.

'It should pass soon.' She looked up at the roof, before turning back to the two women beside them.

'Don't wish that, Char. We need it to lash it down tonight.' Haro sat on the other side of Ajay, staring forwards.

Charlene sighed and leant back against the carved-out wall of the pit. Haro dismissively glanced at Ajay and then looked down at the ground, deep in thought. Ajay stared back at the roof, thinking of the water barrels getting filled. Though much of the water supply came through the drop-offs, they were getting slimmer, so he appreciated Haro's sentiment.

This squish wouldn't be so bad if he didn't have to wear his suit. Ajay highly doubted that Command would send drones out in a storm unless they'd been upgraded for protection against the frying of a motherboard if lightning hit it. Yet, they wouldn't particularly care about a few broken drones if it meant catching the Rogue. So Ajay concluded, as he could feel the sweat running down his spine, wearing the suits was a safe call. For them.

It was the first time it occurred to Ajay that he could, theoretically, run past the perimeter to give away their location. It now seemed the obvious thing to do. Then he could get away from them, Command would eliminate the threat and Tulo could return to normal. He may even be able to plead for his and his family's pardon after his heroic actions. His thoughts tracked back. He still wasn't sure if he wanted to be pardoned; he didn't deserve any mercy or forgiveness after what he'd done to Ace. And . . .

What if the Rogue caught him escaping first?

He recalled his recent experience of their brutality when they took him. He was dreaming about something so bright. So white. Burning like fire and somersaulting gracefully through the air. Like a wafting piece of silk. It was a lion. A flower. Then a tree. Until it was only the whisper of his name. That's when Ajay opened his eyes to darkness. At first, he thought everything was a dream – Ace and the attack – until memories returned. He had just been at the Side terminal. As he breathed, hot air had shot back at him and his vision cleared, allowing him to make out small specks of light being let in through whatever was over his head. He noticed his wrists and ankles were tied; then he heard muffled voices and heavy footsteps not far from his head.

He had wanted to panic, thrash about like a fish out of water, scream and groan for help, until he recognised he was in a vehicle, moving, being taken somewhere. Ajay remembered now that he thought it was Command and he was surprised it had taken them so long. It was only when he thought about the speed of the vehicle and the lack of turns in its movements, that he realised they must have been going beyond the City lines. He'd tried then to move discreetly, grinding his teeth as the ties dug further into the skin of his wrists. That's when that Maze guy, identifiable through his distinctively gruff voice, had seen he was awake. Ajay could smell the rubber of boots and tasted his own snot. It was only then that he realised he was crying; more tears than he thought possible.

Ajay tried to stop thinking about it. He didn't want to remember the way Maze patronised him or the several hard kicks he drilled into his stomach, making him curl up like a fetus. He couldn't focus on how many times Maze punched him around the face, still covered with a bag. He also wanted to avoid thinking about his own cowardice. At the time, he wanted them to kill him, just to make his guilt and shame go away but now he didn't want *them* to have the satisfaction, nor did he deserve to just escape the consequences of his actions.

Was he a coward for not trying to run now?

Was he procrastinating under a weight of fear, longing to avoid another beating? His face wasn't so sore any more, but that didn't mean he was strong enough to take it again. Even if he wasn't brave, Ajay decided there was intelligence mixed up in there too. He shouldn't do anything reckless or stupid. Escaping would need to be more strategically planned than sprinting out into the dark, perpetual forest.

Looking around Haro's pit, Ajay's thoughts turned to its strange resemblance to a bare and basic little house. They'd dug further outwards to make room for shelving where Haro stored chipped bowls and plates, and a small hook hung on its trap-door roof to let the candlelit lantern illuminate the space. It did its job, allowing Ajay to see most people's faces.

There was the baby-faced boy, who fought with that other lad about the piece of fruit. He was laughing hysterically with another, weightier boy, his weight exaggerated by the tight rubber of his suit. There were then two petite twin sisters; Ajay guessed, around mid-forties, their black hair identically tied up in small ponytails. The one on the left, eating fruit, seemed to always be in pain. The other sat bolt upright and held a bored stare as she listened to Charlene. There was someone else too. Ajay couldn't tell if it was a man or a woman sitting behind Haro. They had their back to the group, head down in-between their knees, swaying. Ajay pulled his eyes away when Charlene's voice got louder, fighting against the thunderous volume above.

'I've been trying to beat my time. I can't get anywhere as fast as you two.' Charlene looked at the twin who was staring down into her open Kakafruit. She didn't respond.

'Us shorties are probably a bit lighter.' The other twin smiled. 'It would be better if we had long arms like you.'

'All we need to do is genetically engineer a person with my arms and your body stature and we'd have our greatest climber.' Charlene twittered a laugh before launching into further dialogue.

Ajay zoned out of the conversation again, thinking of his grandma, sad and frustrated that Callum refused to help them. It was hard to stomach. Especially after how good they'd been to him, taking him in as their own. It was after Callum's dad left for Purification, which apparently wasn't a surprise to Ajay's parents. He overheard them once in the kitchen, talking about how he didn't follow The Guiding Light and left without as much as a goodbye. Callum's mum was devastated to the point of becoming ill, so Callum came to live with them for a bit.

Ajay had felt annoyed at first when Callum took up residence on his bedroom floor. As he grew older and he thought about how Callum's mother had picked herself up, he did wonder about the difference that Callum-free month had made, and all the years of kindness from his family that followed. Particularly when Callum himself disappeared.

Yet, years later, Callum didn't even have the courtesy to merely find out information about his family's welfare. It was hardly too much to ask, was it? If, as Ajay had assumed, they somehow still used the Side to access the City, it would take Callum no time at all to sneak his eye through a window. Were they there or not?

He didn't know if he had the right to be angry with Callum. Part of it felt justified, the other not, as he was the man who selfishly ignored Callum's pleas to go home in the shopping centre. If only he'd listened, Callum wouldn't have ended up buried under a mountain of drones and literally scarred for life. Not to mention what

Ajay had done to his other best friend. Ajay stopped himself from thinking about it; denial seemed to be the best method to stop himself whimpering like a child in front of people he shouldn't like.

And he didn't like them.

Mostly.

He wondered if this was *it* for him; living out his hollow existence, with bad people, his heart always heavy. Thunder tore above him as Ace's face tore through his mind.

Looking again for distraction, he glanced at the wall beside him. There were a couple of photos of Haro with a pretty woman holding a baby, standing in front of a convenience shop. Not unlike the ones Ajay used to see on the Outer-Ring.

'This is you,' Ajay said to Haro, who was staring at his feet, holding a water bottle between his legs.

'Used to be.' Haro raised his head, sneezing and blowing out the candle. Everything went dark as more thunder rattled above.

'Oh dammit.' Haro's voice was loud in the darkness after the talkative twin squealed, insisting the lads at the back stopped making ghost noises. Listening to Haro striking another match, Ajay pondered over the photo again through the new flicker of candlelight.

'I'll be glad once the storm passes. These things suck.' Ajay noticed Charlene's nod of agreement. She'd told him how they harnessed the storm's energy to generate extra electricity, and how she got 'unnecessarily slammed' for using the charging banks for her earphones in the middle of a power ration.

'I enjoy listening to music as I try to sleep. What am I supposed to do?' she'd said as they'd made some Fo Doktrin soup earlier that day.

Ajay hadn't lost his curiosity over Haro's photo.

'Did you own this shop?' He spoke almost instinctively, having become used to Charlene's willingness to answer his questions.

'Yeah.' Haro turned to Ajay, his lazy eye less obvious in the dim light. 'That's my wife and my little boy. Though he's not so little any more.'

'Where are they?' Ajay didn't even consider it a forward question, until everyone else in the pit went quiet.

'Ajay, let's talk about something else,' Charlene jumped in.

There was a brief moment of awkwardness as Haro held Charlene's sympathetic eyes. Ajay realised he'd hit a nerve. It was a stupid question. Looking again at Haro's wife, her hair not unlike Genni's, he cursed himself. It could hardly be a happy story, as his family weren't there with him.

'No, that's alright, Charlene.' Haro spoke gruffly. 'It's time he knew some stuff.' Haro coughed with his hand over his mouth. 'If he's your friend, as you say, don't you think we need to set him straight?'

CHAPTER
FIFTEEN

Thinking on Haro's words, Ajay felt excited by the prospect of new information, but he glanced at Charlene through the dappled candlelight in the corner of the pit. She had told Haro they were friends? That was a strong assumption. He'd never actually agreed to that, she had just decided. A small part of him felt warm, which then made the rest of him feel twisted. And what did he need setting straight about, exactly? He already knew what they were.

'He's fine. He knows what we're doing here. No need to labour the point.' Charlene's attempt at bluntness didn't pay off, a slight flutter of anxiety in her voice. Ajay's instinct was to say he had very little desire to be there, but he stayed quiet, wanting the conversation to play out to his advantage.

'Does he? Do you not realise he's probably planning to escape?' Haro's head flickered to Ajay, who felt a sudden dryness roll like a ball down his throat. Serious backfire. He looked briefly to the pit roof, contemplating making a run for it. Seven people against one weren't good odds.

Charlene didn't look at Ajay, nor did she respond, indicating that she knew it was true.

'You lose anyone on Liberation Day?' Haro addressed Ajay, his question sending even the whispers of the teenage boys quiet and a timely crack of lightning zapped above.

'My friend lost his legs.' Ajay answered the question, trying not to sound angry, his voice still coming out cold as he gritted his teeth. 'And I got shot.'

'Ouch.' Haro looked at him with sudden sympathy, then back down at the water bottle between his legs. Charlene hissed beside him and Ajay swore he saw her hand move compassionately towards him until she hesitated. Ajay didn't bother mentioning the trauma they'd put Genni through. And everyone else. Nor did he want to reface the experience of her co-worker, Jun, being killed right in front of him mid-conversation, his dead body flattening him to the ground.

Haro sipped lightly from his bottle. 'I've seen the way you look at us. As if you're above us, more righteous. Then, I know you're no fool.' Ajay didn't move his eyes from Haro's, the candlelight bouncing off his shaven head. 'If you knew what Command has done – is doing – you'd change your mind about us. We're not the enemy, kid.'

Haro's reference to him as 'kid' sent shivers up Ajay's long spine. Lillie used to call him that. The woman who'd helped him hack into the City, who turned out to be one of *them* all along. Her menacing eyes and long braided hair flew back to him, anger simmering in the pit of his stomach.

'Liberation Day didn't happen the way most of us thought it would.' Haro placed his bottle down and rubbed his hands together as grains of dirt fell from above. 'It was only ever meant to be Command.'

Ajay was flooded with confusion. Was Haro saying the attack wasn't planned? It was so meticulous; hacking into the Watches, the shootings, the second round with the bombs.

'Unfortunately, a few of our more . . . *unstable* people worked with some Moths to carry it out. Including Pete, our old leader.'

Charlene moved uncomfortably at the sound of the name. She breathed slowly before she spoke. 'It was devastating. Not only did people die but now we're in more danger, the food is running out and Command, well . . .' She swore.

Ajay's brain was going mad. Some things falling into place, others still unanswered. 'So you just wanted Command? That doesn't make any sense. Even before the attack, you took lives to get into the Quarters.'

'Again, that wasn't us.'

'What, so none of you were meant to bring guns?'

'They were only meant for certain heads.' Haro sighed. 'Strategic violence creates opportunity, while sporadic violence just causes chaos.'

'And that's OK, is it?'

'How do you think they won the revolution you all celebrate?'

'So, what? This is a new revolution?''

'Exactly.' One of the teenagers chipped in, with a triumphant air in his voice.

Haro raised a stocky hand at him as if to tell him not to get too excited.

'We need to bring down the system that has stolen everything from us.' Haro stared deep into Ajay, almost like he was trying to manipulate him to his will. 'Stolen everything from *you.*'

'It stole nothing from me,' Ajay said, confident, knowing the system was flawed but ultimately, it gave him life.

'Are you sure?' Haro raised an eyebrow.

Ajay didn't respond but remained thoughtful as he peered back at the picture of Haro and his family. 'The shop went out of business when new drones came in, right?'

'Yeah.' Haro nodded and stroked his chin. 'Command gave me nothing. Not even the minimum merit compensation. My score was just short of eligibility.'

'And your wife?' Ajay was reminded of Sam, who he'd helped last year. It didn't feel like too long ago since he had that ex-Glorified in his bed who hissed as Ajay had stitched up the nasty cut in his leg.

'She managed to get a progressive job in robotics. But I only managed one in retail . . .' Haro sighed again. 'You get the rest.'

Ajay went quiet, glancing again at the photo of Haro's wife. They looked happy. Until his low merit would have taken her away, probably for her to find another man and for his child to call someone else father. That was the way it worked. It was the rhythm of life. If last year Genni hadn't made it through, Ajay would have lost her but there was no way he'd have blamed Command for that. It would have been a result of Genni's incompetence and her decisions. Just like Sam; he'd made the decision to lie to his wife all those years ago, no one else did. And Ajay himself, *he* hacked his way in instead of waiting for Purification and *he* ended up killing Ace.

To join a resistance because of your own inabilities seemed a pretty weak argument. Without thinking, Ajay allowed this thought to manifest as a small but obvious eye roll.

Haro laughed, irritated. 'You think it's my fault?' Silence filled the pit as Ajay didn't respond. 'Right?' The candle struggled to stay alight as Haro's breath disturbed its burn.

'Well,' Ajay paused. 'It seems . . .'

'What? Irrational?' Haro leaned even closer to Ajay, his lazy eye clearer and the smell of his breath potent.

'You think Nissi and Martha here are unjustified to stop a regime which, when they lost their parents in the River Bar Disasters, offered no explanation or merit support?'

Ajay glanced at the twin sisters. Is that why one of them seemed so messed up? He looked at her, curled up in a ball, arms around her knees. Haro's voice was loud again.

'You think Jaco's father is wrong to hate Command after losing his job to care for his sick mother?' Ajay could give them that one. That did seem a little unfair. Just a little, though, right?

'You think that Charlene is unjustified to be angr–'

'Don't! You have no right.' Charlene pointed aggressively at Haro who held his hands up in surrender, as much as he could in the squeeze. Charlene calmed and Haro looked back at Ajay.

'Come on, you must see it.'

Ajay said nothing. What was there to say? His brain rattled through it all: the house raids, the arrests; the way they had the security dome ready for the Quarters, in case of any threat. *Surely necessary because that's the way society works, not everyone agrees, not everyone complies and those measures should be put in place?* The system had its flaws, he could give them that, but overthrowing it in a way that took people's lives still seemed radical.

'What about them? Your people who planned the attack on civilians?' Ajay leant forward, still pressing for more.

'They're not *our* people,' Charlene snapped before Haro answered.

'A lot of them are dead. Killed by Command. Others on the run. Don't really know, don't really care either,' Haro sighed, resting his head on the wall.

'Who's in charge now? And why am I really here?'

Haro cackled. 'That's a good question. Us on the committee are technically in charge, but no one wants to take full responsibility, not after what happened. Saying that, Ki has tried to take a lead. He's our best Architect. A bright guy, but he's complicated and not a leader, nor does he have the expertise we need.'

Haro looked at Ajay again, smiling through the candle's flicker in a way that made him curl inside. *He,* Ajay, had the expertise they needed. For what? The pit was then plunged into a new level of darkness, but not by the absence of light. A sinister laugh came from the corner of the pit and it felt louder than the thunder. It was sharp, bringing goosebumps to the surface of Ajay's sweating skin. Everyone looked to the space behind Haro, to the unidentified person who had started to shake, rocking with their knees to their chest and speaking with a croak.

'My Rolfa was alive. Until she was dead.' The voice confirmed to Ajay it was a man – and an aged one.

'Who's Rolfa?' Ajay whispered to Haro, intrigued and uneasy.

'Probably his imaginary lover.' Haro sat back casually. 'Just ignore him, he's not right in the head.'

Ajay glanced around the pit to see the others' reactions as the old man continued to talk in rhyme.

'Rolfa was alive. Until she was dead. They all came in and took her head.'

The uneven rhythm and strain of his voice was spooky. Scanning around as more lightning flashed through the small cracks in the disguised roof, Ajay could see no one else cared. Haro focused on the candle while Charlene examined her fingernails; the teenagers had returned to their childish sniggering and the twin sisters looked to be settling down to sleep.

'Rolfa was all fine with taking her time,' the man continued. Ajay decided to take Haro's advice and ignore him.

'The Light dances from its case, telling us to seek the place.'

'What did he say?' Ajay sat bolt upright and attentive, recognising something familiar. 'What did you say?' Ajay spoke loudly. There was a pause as Ajay tried to see the face behind Haro. It was covered by long wisps of bedraggled, greasy grey hair and he could just see the excess skin of his neck moving as he spoke.

'Rolfa . . . Rolfa . . . Rolfa.' His sentence was getting stuck.

'Did you live on the Side?' Ajay asked.

'Of course he did,' Haro interjected. 'Where else would a madman come from? No offence.'

Ajay ignored Haro, the voice of the man too harrowing not to notice.

'Rolfa was alive. Until she was dead. They all came in and took her head.'

'Who's they?'

'Rolfa was alive. Until she was dead. They all came in and took her head.'

'Who took Rolfa's head?'

'Seriously, mate. I wouldn't bother.' One of the boys laughed. Ajay didn't remember them ever being 'mates'.

The old man went almost silent, mumbling words so quietly Ajay could only just make them out.

'This was never the plan, from the original clan.'

Deciding not to take it too seriously, he sat back with the man's words running over his mind.

They all came in and took her head.

So, yes, Command has been violent. With the house raids and . . . Callum. Ajay remembered how his face was pressed into the ground, contorted by the tasers of the drones. Whatever they did to him was enough for Callum to retreat to the Rogue, rather than back home.

Were they right about Command? Justified in hating them? Wanting them dead and the system overthrown?

No.

No.

No.

Ajay couldn't let them mould him. More than ever before, he wanted to get out.

CHAPTER
SIXTEEN

Genni slowly became numb to the constant ricocheting pain festering inside.

Two days had drifted by since her near relapse and she listened to the howling storm tapping on the windows of the Beauty Dome. She was still thankful for the lack of the enhanced *SkipSleep*, and a caring stranger in its place, but she had managed to repress everything. Staying Watch silent to her friends and family was probably the most successful tactic in her strategy. She couldn't face them yet. Everything had to stay buried deep down, hidden, until she could feel normal again.

It was getting harder not to face it. Every time she left the office, she checked the VPG to ensure no one was waiting for her at home. The few times Blake or Pearl were, she had managed to wait them out by going to the library. No one had attempted to catch her at the office yet, but it was only a matter of time. Genni held on to that control of not wanting to talk, because she wouldn't have it forever. Because she knew, wrapped up in all the excruciating Ajay stuff, there was Ace. It was only fair to him to remember their friendship and grieve.

She wasn't ready, though. Along with the pain of his loss came the heartbreak of Ajay's betrayal. To ignore it felt better, and working was the best way to do it.

A message pinged and she paused typing at her desk, her attention drawn away from her current report. Mafi wanted to see her in her office. Genni gulped; did she know about Ajay? Did she know who and what Genni had been associated with? Would that put her job in jeopardy? Genni felt her breathing falter. She couldn't lose work. That would mean no merit, no boyfriend, no prospects and, more importantly to her in that moment, no distraction.

Half-hoping that the message would disappear and that it was only her imagination, she hesitated before walking across the Beauty Dome, her eyes flicking anxiously across the other desks and screens. Her colleagues were oblivious to what was going on in her head. What would they think of her if they all found out? *Because they will, won't they?*

There'd been no news from Rod on the hunt for Ajay, which she could only assume meant he would soon be publicly wanted. His face could be plastered all over the place, where there would be no escape. She stopped a tear escaping from her right eye and straightened herself up, walking with more confidence. No one else could empower her, but her. She could fight her case – she had nothing to do with Ajay's dirty criminality – that was the truth.

As she took the gliding elevator up to the Dome's first floor, she closed her eyes and let the classical music fall over her like a sheet of comfort. As the doors slid open and she eyed the door to Mafi's office at the opposite end of the walkway, she spoke to herself clearly and tried to believe every word she said.

Everything is going to be OK.

Sliding gracefully into the chair Mafi had offered her, Genni forced a loose, casual smile. Mafi returned it subtly, her dark eyebrows rising. Genni didn't look anywhere but at Mafi's face, trying to interpret what this could be about. The view through the pink-tinted, triangular window panes was all a blur. Mafi didn't look angry, or concerned, or fearful. To Genni's confusion, she looked – pleased? She had never seen her look this relaxed, even when they hit last year's ambitious targets.

'Are you feeling better?' Mafi asked bluntly, more as a formality than a genuine question of empathy.

'Sorry?' Genni blanked out.

'Yesterday?' Mafi glanced at a screen over her desk, dismissing it as she spoke.

'Oh, yes, sorry.' Genni recalled she worked from home yesterday, claiming to be sick. 'Much better, thank you. Just a passing thing, I think.'

Mafi nodded. 'Nothing we need to be concerned about?'

'Not at all. Why would there be?' Genni smiled, nervously.

'With your history and the attack, it's good to keep an eye.' Mafi leant forward in her chair. Genni couldn't wait for her overdose and breakdown to be forgotten. Would they ever be?

'Anyway, to business.' Mafi coughed to clear her throat and Genni held her breath for whatever was coming.

'We have been incredibly impressed these last few months, Genni.' Mafi tapped at her desk after patting down her tightly tied hair, and Genni's employee log appeared above them. 'Your performance metrics are improving, your hourly log has been exquisite and you've almost met all your objectives. After . . .' Mafi paused and looked at Genni, who felt her eyes widen. 'Well, I'll be honest, I never expected it would be you I'm having this conversation with.'

Genni didn't say anything, still unsure of how to feel. Mafi swiped the screen away and leant further forward on her desk, the cuffs of her white blouse creeping out from under her suit jacket.

'We're planning a restructure and we're considering you for a new role.'

Genni opened her mouth to express her disbelief, but Mafi held her hand up to stop her.

'It's conditional, you need to continue at this pace.' Mafi lowered her hand. 'It would be heading up testing for the Skin Division. As you know, we need to move with the times.' Mafi sat back again and crossed one leg over the other. 'One small niche being the scar-concealing products, of course.'

Genni nodded, remembering the pitch meeting for the new post-attack range she attended last week. In a state of shock, she didn't notice the silence and how that was her cue to speak.

'Genni?' Mafi raised one of her thin, well-groomed eyebrows.

'Yes . . .' Genni paused. She thought she would come out of here without a job, not the chance for a better one. 'I'm honoured. I . . .' She swallowed hard. 'Thank you.'

'Well, there's nothing to be thankful for.' Mafi stood, the sound of her heels tapping across the hard floor as she approached the door. Genni left her chair, weak at the knees with relief. 'You haven't got the job yet. If you do, there'll be no one to thank but yourself.'

'When can I find out more?' Genni was flustered, trying to straighten her twisted skirt.

'I'll schedule another meeting next week, as I have a 10.30,' Mafi said, both of them peering at their Watches to see it was 10.28.

Mafi held out her hand for Genni to shake.

Genni, still surprised, immediately took it; a firm and hard grasp. The concern that Mafi might notice her clammy hands quickly faded as the door slid closed. Her momentary high almost materialised as a giddy dance on the walkway hovering above the office floor. It was amazing. She'd worked so hard and now she might actually get close to Glorified. Then she could stick it to her father and everyone else who thought she wasn't good enough. This was her chance. She couldn't let it slip.

Letting it sink in as the elevator glided down, she briefly thought of Ajay and the sadness crept back in. It took her excitability down a notch but didn't completely extinguish it. Mafi had shaken her hand. *Mafi*. The formidable, nothing-impresses-me Mafi. She wished she could have someone to boast to. Maybe Angi, or Dan, or she could ring Pearl? More sadness came back. A reminder that she wasn't talking to Pearl because she couldn't face the pain. Walking back to her desk, still with some joy in her stride, she would continue with her report.

Mafi said it. The job wasn't hers yet, and if she got it, it would be because of her. She swiped her activation pad to get back to it and thanked her Watch for its encouragement.

Have a happy merit-making day, Genni.

A few hours later, on returning from a toilet break, Genni noticed the vibe in the office had changed, like a wave of darkness engulfing every worker in its breaking. Faces faded from concentration into restlessness and alarm.

As she approached her desk, the murmuring started and uncomfortable looks were thrown in her direction. Did they know about her conversation with Mafi earlier? Their faces wouldn't be painted like that if so. Would they? It had to be something more discrediting. People stared at Genni and then stared at one another anxiously as the movements of news updates flickered on people's screens.

The murmurs fell silent as Genni walked deeper between the desks, until Angi's footsteps filled the space.

'Genni, shall we go outside?' Angi grabbed Genni's arm protectively and pulled her forward.

'What's going on?' Genni whispered.

'Hey, put it on the big screen,' a man shouted from way across the office floor, and everyone's eyes flicked to the presentation screen hovering next to the staff photo board.

Ajay's face appeared. A picture of him she'd seen many times. Smiling, his black hair tucked behind his ears, his perfectly straight white teeth. It was the Ajay she thought she knew. Yet it hung beneath a 'wanted' callout for murder. There was more information she didn't bother to read.

Gasping and breath escaping her, Genni pulled her arm away from Angi.

'Let me help you,' Angi pleaded, standing still. Genni walked backwards at first, catching a last glimpse of the disapproving yet compassionate faces. Why had she brought Ajay to work events? Or even introduced him to anyone? He was too big a part of her life to just let go. Circumstance made it impossible.

Turning and running, she didn't want to wait for anything else. She staggered from the Beauty Dome out into the muggy, desert air, tears streaming down her face. Feeling sick, she fell over by the fountain in the plaza, the wisps of its water streams cooling her down. She anticipated another inundation of calls from the others. Her Watch would stay muted, she couldn't cope with it; not with all these emotions mixing up inside her like a tornado. Never had she felt so angry, so hopeless, so broken, so full of hurt and hatred that her insides felt cold. Yet there was a small glimpse of hope in the form of this new job. She could go back in there, head held high, and smash it.

It was hers for the taking, but all she wanted to do was fall to her knees and cradle them, rock back and forth like an automatic baby cot. Ajay was never going to leave her. She couldn't help it. Even if he was a bad man, a killer, he was still part of her and she had to understand what happened. It would take time to heal, but Genni wasn't sure what she was even healing from. Was she only collateral damage to him? An insignificant secondary character? Genni knew the answer to that question probably wasn't in the Side, but his family were; a part of him she never knew.

Genni groaned inside; she had too much to lose. She had tried to ignore any thought of going there. Yet as she looked around, she only saw Tulo mirroring herself; angry, hopeless and broken with house raids, violence and trauma spinning on the billboards. There was no escape. Breathing erratically, she tried to think straight, and wiped her eyes. She was both thankful and offended that Angi hadn't followed her out. She didn't think about what they were saying inside. Instead, Genni thought for a moment about the girl she used to be: the one who sat on her bed, swiping through her study tablet, unsure if she could achieve the life she was supposed to, but ambitious enough to try. As she looked towards the sky train station, she was briefly comforted that even after all of this, she still had that determination left – to find some sort of answer.

CHAPTER
SEVENTEEN

A few nights had passed since Ajay and the others sheltered in the pit, but a storm still fought hard inside him. What Haro and Charlene told him had only confused him more. It was like he was on a slow, self-deprecating loop: don't sleep, force down some leaves; think about Ace, hate himself. Then think about Grandma and hate himself. Try to master an escape plan and hate himself when he fails. He would think about the attack, how it wasn't the original plan, that some people here might be good. Then he'd wonder if he should stay. Next he would hate himself for even considering it, before attempting to climb and then hating himself some more. Until he came right back full circle.

He'd wanted to find the madman from the pit again, to ask him more questions about his rhymes that could mean something, but he decided that wouldn't help at all. Not if he couldn't get out. Plus, he hadn't seen him since the morning after the storm. He'd watched him stumble away across the forest, still mumbling his tales above the rustlings of the battered trees. Now looking at that same spot with tired eyes, Ajay felt another spark of determination. He moved to enjoy the electric fan where Charlene was sitting with the twins and started to calculate a strategy again, desperate not to get pulled into whatever plan the committee had.

If the Recruiters go out to the City, they must be moving at night. Otherwise the drones would see them through the forest? The Spotters, the guys who issue alerts if any drones get through, and the Diverters, who send the drones off track, couldn't be working beyond the perimeter. So the Recruiters surely wear suits to avoid drone detection.

Then what?

They couldn't just have a vehicle and move freely across the desert. Unless there's some sort of Old City infrastructure underground? There's decades' worth of architecture above the surface, ruined or reused; who knows what lies beneath that the public doesn't know about, but surely Command knows. Think, think.

Ajay leant over Charlene, without a word, grabbing a bowl of soup she'd prepared.

'A thank you would be nice,' she snapped, before returning to a conversation with the others. Ajay grunted, barely hearing her.

What else comes to the forest? Or who else?

The Resource Workers used to collect raw materials until the planes replaced them. What if they were using the planes? Somehow hacking into them to divert the course to where they wanted. You're stupid. Command would be all over that. So, what? They just sneak on and off without any security breach at all? It wouldn't be out of character with Command's previous naivety but they're so ruthless now, surely they wouldn't miss that.

Of course.

Ajay hesitated in picking up his spoon.

The Moths.

He remembered Charlene saying they infiltrated the planes for the drop-offs, so could they also be clever enough to use them for sneaking people in and out? It must have been how they transported him too, after being kidnapped and knocked out cold by Maze's boot.

'You're wasting it. Eat it before it goes cold.' Charlene's eyes were fired up, staring at Ajay's untouched bowl of soup.

Wanting to roll his eyes, Ajay tolerated her orders and slurped at the plant juice. People had become even more precious over food since the storm, which had ruined a lot of the nearby plant life. The lizards were also mating like mad. More lizards, more contaminated fruit, more plant juice. With the darkness he was feeling, Ajay fancied going on one of the hunting shifts. He wouldn't mind venting his frustration by obliterating the lizards' tiny bodies. He certainly couldn't take much more of *this*. His family was in danger, and he was sitting around, picking fruit from trees, listening to Charlene bang on about some insignificant tripe, all the while feeling himself growing closer to her and others.

His mind turned to their motives to take Command down. *So they do that, destroy the merit system and then what?*

Ajay couldn't finish his thought.

He saw someone new between the trees.

He dropped his soup.

The bowl and spoon clunked on the ground.

Ajay ignored Charlene's screams of annoyance.

He bounded forward, losing control of himself.

'Hey!' he roared, his legs quickening in fury.

His prey turned her head and her face made Ajay sick.

The sunken lip, dry, piercing eyes and that greasy braid hanging over her right shoulder.

Lillie, staggering, looked like she had aged years, but Ajay didn't care.

He just wanted to hurt her.

Her laugh was horrible.

It taunted Ajay straight through to his vexed lungs. Breathing heavily, he stopped beside her, fists clenched and eyes determined. He should knock that sinister laugh straight back into her throat. Something made him stop. He didn't know if it was Charlene screaming after him, or Lillie's laugh throwing him off, or perhaps her dishevelled and drunken appearance telling him she'd already suffered for what she'd done to him. Looking at her, the greyness of her face, the limpness of her arms and the emptiness of the bottle in her right hand, Ajay thought back to when they'd first met. He was scared in that small room with the pink curtain, where they shook hands and she agreed to create his new identity. She was like a fantastical creature to him, beautiful and unexplainable. Yet somehow she'd transformed into this back-slumped old hag. Ajay wondered if it was his future. Turning to drink while on the run, nothing to live for but the bottle.

'Fancy bumping into you, kid.' Lillie's voice seemed more strained, less gritty.

'You . . .' Ajay couldn't find the words.

'You look bad.' Lillie leant against the trunk of a tree.

'Ajay, how do you know her?' Charlene touched Ajay's arm, squeezing her fingers into his suit.

Ajay couldn't speak, eyeballing Lillie, who drained drops of ethanol from the bottle and threw it into the dirt, smashing it around her feet.

'Oi!' Charlene objected. 'The children play through here.'

'Alright, Long Legs, I'll go fetch the maid,' Lillie smiled as she slurred, her menacing eyes directed at Charlene, who curled her arm around Ajay's, almost like a need for protection.

Stepping back, Charlene tugged at him, but he wasn't leaving. He stood his ground. The evening was setting in as Wingsparks emerged, their buzzing and shining a blur to him. His eyes were only set on Lillie.

He couldn't think of anything else but the way she'd left him in that underground bar not long after the attack, when he was so desperate he couldn't hide it. She could have helped him. Lillie clearly knew about the new Watch model that was coming or something else about Command's plans. If she had told him, rather than leaving him stressed and panicked, not knowing how he would escape, then maybe he could have coped better. Maybe he would have been more methodological in his planning, and he would have been calmer when Ace came round and maybe . . . Ajay couldn't even think of it.

If he let himself believe it, he would kill her.

'So what's been happening, kid?' Lillie was too casual.

'Why didn't you tell me?' Ajay didn't move his eyes from her.

'Tell you what?' Lillie smiled and slurred. 'Oh, about me being a Roguey-poguey?'

'No.' Though Ajay realised that information would have been nice. 'About the new Watch model, about Command's next plan.'

'Kid, you are clever,' she garbled. 'How did you find these things out?' Lillie stepped forward and almost lost her balance. She laughed into the lilac evening sky, the laugh etching into Ajay's brain, taunting him.

'Ajay, how do you know her?' Charlene repeated, sounding curious before retreating. 'Let's just get back. We're setting out soon.'

Ajay felt Charlene's arm tug on his own again. Maybe he should go back; this pitiful excuse for a person wasn't even worth his time. But he couldn't help it, he couldn't move. Dark emotions swarmed his brain, having been building up for the last few days. His legs felt loose on his waist, as if they could drop off. Standing there, he was concerned he might cry with the hatred he felt. There was no way he could go back when she was wandering through the trees at her leisure. Had she made herself useless even to the Rogue? So in her intoxicated state, she seemed harmless?

Eventually, he decided hurting her wouldn't help anything. He was trying to get out. Beating up some middle-aged madwoman wasn't going to facilitate his plan, even if it was possible.

Taking a deep breath, Ajay felt his feet turn and he looked at Charlene willingly, ready to go back.

'So who are you, then, Long Legs?'

Both Ajay and Charlene stopped and looked back, to see her staggering towards them again.

'His friend.' Charlene sounded defiant, despite what she said being a lie. He still hadn't agreed to that.

'Oh, his friend!' Lillie laughed again. 'Well, be careful.'

Ajay froze, piercing his eyes into her, willing her to stop talking.

'We all know what happens to *his* friends.' Lillie stared at him with a crooked smile, running a finger across her throat and projecting a slicing sound through her teeth. It was as if the moment happened in slow motion. Ajay's thoughts instantly went to Ace and the circumstances of his death.

If she'd helped him, maybe Ace never would have died.

Uncontrollable rage stole Ajay's every movement, sense and thought. It all felt like a dream, blurry and indistinguishable, where he was a raging fire setting out to engulf Lillie until there was nothing of her left. The first punch was straight around her jaw, throwing her small, slim body down quickly. She fumbled around till she was on her back, still laughing, willing Ajay on. Clambering on top of her, Ajay ignored the buzzing of Wingsparks in his ears and Charlene's screams for help. He wanted that smile off Lillie's face, but as he went for the second punch, he stopped.

Heaving his breath, he caught a glimpse of confusion in her eyes. The same confusion he felt. Why wasn't he punching again? Another disgusting smile grew across her face as stronger men pulled him back and he struggled to break free; they dragged him away between the trees, his suit getting covered in Fo Doktrin stains, and all he could hear was her laugh echoing through the emerging darkness of night.

CHAPTER
EIGHTEEN

Arriving at the Side, Genni didn't know what to think about first. She couldn't decide if the pain of the merit trickling away from her wrist was more pressing than the state of the desert between here and the City. Why would Command leave it all out there? Glass, old market stalls, rubble, remains of buildings, all of it crumbling away in the sand. There was talk of the Old City ruins, but not really. It was a forgotten era. She'd never heard anyone question what came before the Revolution, because why would they? Still, she'd have assumed that Command would be diligent enough to get rid of the debris which, she noted, was destroying an otherwise breathtaking landscape. At least the lost merit and the foolish adventure she'd undertaken had given her one thing: a view of the desert from ground level. The distant peaks of the mountains reminded her of the tough wisps of meringue nests, and the forest looked ominous and deep. It was all beautiful. Unlike where she stood.

As the train crawled away from the platform, she hugged herself. It was hot but she shivered. Was she sure about this? It would be easy enough to wait for the unnervingly empty train to return, and go home.

But that would be a real waste of merit then; she'd committed as soon as she'd swiped on and ignored the merit deduction warning.

Her brain was starting to feel mashed; a piece of dough being kneaded around her head. She'd barely taken a moment to breathe since running from the office, only stopping off at home to change. The whole journey through the Outer-Rings, she had tried to talk herself out of it. She'd even turned around twice, telling herself she didn't need to know who Ajay was and she was stronger without him. There was no way she was giving up her achievements, the new job, for him. The second time she turned around she'd noticed a woman about her age sitting by the riverside. Her eyes carried deep, blue bruises and her bare, skinny arms cradled her knees. Catching her eye, Genni didn't see any plea for help, merely the loneliness she felt herself, the helpless agony of being alone. Still walking and not strong enough to approach the Unworthy girl, Genni begged herself to feel peace by walking away from the Side, telling herself it was the right thing to do . . . but a hard weight in her stomach forced her to stop and turn back. That's when she held her breath and did it: jumped on the train and took the deduction, the pain of it almost too much to bear.

Now she was here, she took things slowly, putting one sandalled foot in front of the other. She hesitated along a long stretch of poorly constructed pavement, sand scratching her glittery painted toes. Genni took in what she could see; desert to the left and the same to the right but with a faint outline of the forest through the heatwave. Fo Doktrin was sporadically dotted in the sands, the greens and oranges of nature, colours richer than her eyes had seen before. A strange feeling of warmth spread through her as she looked out to the vast expanse, away from the familiar comings and goings of life. Stopping for a moment, she looked towards the forest and could see the tallest Baffle Tree spreading its branches across the sizzling sky, through which she could see dots flying. She wondered if they were drones or birds.

While she'd love to walk into the desert and never come back, she remembered her reason for being here. To find the truth. It was only temporary beauty, anyway; the real joy was back in the City and in merit. She had so much more to give, but this nightmare hanging over her was interfering. Maybe that was why she came, for some sort of closure, or understanding, or empowerment, or proof?

Nope, no peaceful scene of nature can calm the storm in my mind.

Closer to the buildings, it looked a little like she'd seen on the news; the sand hill was domineering and the buildings were undesirable, not even good enough to house a fox. Some further up looked more like skyscrapers, with old water towers rivalling their height, making her wonder how far and wide the Side really went.

Not everything was the same as she was led to believe by the media, though. Some of it looked similar to the City; people everywhere, some jogging, others being carried in lower-model hover vehicles. There were drones too, but Genni noticed how none of them held any deliveries. As they flew, children ran parallel, hand in hand, across a street decorated with bright buntings and littered with tables where people stood offering small pieces of food. There was no tantalising smell from any coffee stops as Genni was used to, and people stood by the stalls, chatting, not rushing away. It reminded her of the old stalls Downtown, except people weren't being shifty. There, Worthy people would hide themselves behind sunglasses and exchange exclusive, high-merit products for chocolate, ethanol and cigarettes. Things they'd usually lose merit for, they were able to enjoy with their reputation unstained. Genni had always ignored it, but now, looking at the untoxic workings of this market, the contrast was clear. She wondered if she looked like a lost child, her head twitching in every direction when she heard a plethora of different sounds: the opening of paper bags for groceries, the shouts and greetings, the bashing of shoes together outside doors and the gleeful squeals of playtime. Genni stared for a minute, first at a man farming food from an allotment, then at a playground at the end of the street and instantly, she felt sad. She watched the movements of a little girl, making her way across a row of bars in the air, her precious fingers gripping to the purple-chipped metal, her legs swinging precariously and her face full of determination. She made it across two bars, then three, then all six, leading her to jump and shout with excitement. Genni watched as a man, probably in his late twenties, swooped her up into his fatherly arms and congratulated her on her insignificant achievement. This wasn't the Side she'd seen on the news at all.

'You alright there?' Genni jumped at a croaky voice coming from her left, owned by a skinny middle-aged woman with greying hair and wearing a practical blue jumpsuit.

'Sorry?' Genni responded, spaced out.

'Are you OK?'

Genni held her breath, assuming she was a street seller. She waited for the product screens to appear and for the woman to force something on her, as they always did in the City. What was it going to be? Menstrual-blockers, book files, mood-enhancers? Instead, though, the woman raised her unkempt eyebrows, and held Genni with a concerned gaze.

'I'm . . .' Genni paused, clearing her brain fog, noticing the woman was standing behind a table displaying cakes and bread. Genni looked past most of it but appreciated the smell.

'Are you wanting something?' The woman spoke tentatively.

'Yes, I think so,' Genni lied. No other words seemed to come. 'Maybe that.' She pointed at a brown cake, assuming it was chocolate-based. What was she doing? She felt so out of place, enough to make her lose her senses. She couldn't afford any more deductions today, but by the time she realised, the woman had packed the cake into a bag.

'Here. Two credits.' She flipped the bag over itself and handed it to Genni.

She took it, glumly raising her arm to the woman's handheld scanner and winced at the transaction ping. How much would it take? Genni glanced at her Watch. Her merit score had remained the same.

Genni stared, confused, not understanding how it was possible. It had been laboured into her since birth that too much sugar drained your energy and productivity and so merit deductions were necessary. How could they be sparing her now?

'You're not from round here, are you?' The woman laughed. She was friendlier than any stranger she'd met before, like she had too much excess energy. Her skin was also glowing, in a smooth, consistent way.

'Why didn't it take anything?' Genni continued to observe her beautiful complexion, despite her caterpillar eyebrows.

The woman shrugged her shoulders. 'What's the point of taking something people don't have?'

'But I do.' Genni showed her wrist.

'Good for you.' The woman picked up some tongs and started straightening the cake display. 'We make these ourselves; they're not registered on the system. So, you can have all the brownies you like.'

No, thank you. So you don't have access to any merit-exclusive products? You must do, though, for your skin to look like that.

The woman looked up again. 'Why are you here?'

'I'm . . .' Genni hesitated as a man stopped at the table, jogging on the spot, his breath heavy.

'Hi, Cara. Sorry to interrupt. Is my usual ready?'

'Sorry.' The woman addressed Genni. 'Here, Den.' She handed him a plastic bag, its bottom pulled tight by its contents. He was sweating and Genni noticed his wrist was Watchless. How was he tracking his exercise without it? *He isn't. Why wouldn't he?*

Before she could think about it, he'd run away, the sun reflecting off a bald patch on his head.

'Sorry about that.' The woman placed her hands on her hips. 'You were about to say something?'

Genni drew her eyes away from the jogging man. 'Do you know Blueberry Bliss Lane?'

It doesn't sound like a real street. Is there any chance this could still all be lies?

'Sure. The first right after the playground.' The woman pointed and Genni noticed some blue oil smudged on her hand. Had she been working on a hover vehicle? Making cakes, selling them, and fixing cars? *I thought they didn't do anything useful?*

Genni felt her head spin; there were too many questions coming, but she had to remain focused on why she came.

'Thank you.' She didn't look at the woman as she marched away towards the indicated street.

She became distracted again all too quickly. She spotted a few billboards and felt grateful for something vaguely familiar. Yet she was disappointed to see no offers or deals, no new products or *Personi* posts, only adverts for Purification. *How did people live like this?* It was so simplistic and dull. They had no aspirations, knowing full well that they could attain something better, if they just applied for it. Her thoughts turned back to the man jogging, not even bothering to wear his Watch. *How can they not care about merit? What would that feel like?*

Genni saw a few more groups of people standing around, chatting. She examined them closer, some were wearing Watches, but were they recording? *Were they talking about anything to help them become their most effective selves?* Somehow she doubted it. Next to them walked a pregnant woman and Genni stopped still, not remembering the last time she'd seen one. Her huge belly ballooned under a blue, stained dress and she walked as if every part of her was breaking. Genni had been taught that choosing to be pregnant was careless; growing successful children in the lab was more sensible. She remembered her mother's dismay when a family friend chose to give birth naturally.

'Nine months of exhaustion and minimised activity. The girl's a lunatic.'

Genni watched as the woman hobbled around a corner, holding her back with one hand. Genni's mouth felt dry as she walked deeper into the street, lined with overflowing, fly-infested bins. Another absence became clear. She scanned every wall, shop display and house window. There wasn't one screen or poster with the words 'Progress is Strength'. Not one.

It was like a different world. A meritless, terrifying world.

Genni wondered again if she should turn back. She didn't belong here. No one should. It was against Tulo's purpose for people to exist like this. The constitution rang around her head: *Each individual is fairly rewarded, according to the time they dedicate to moving society forward. Merit is a statement of status: one earnt, not simply given.* Why don't they want that status?

It dawned on her then that she didn't know the number of the house. As her eyes darted between the different-coloured doors, she was confused again. Each side of the street was like one long building, but with several doors dotted along it. *Were there really that many houses crammed in here?* They'd be tiny. It was inhumane. Then again, it wouldn't have been too bad for Ajay and his grandma. Just the two of them would have coped, but it must have been difficult with those little windows.

Then, when she saw the sign by a chipped, green door, her trivial thoughts faded.

The Blythefens.

She recognised the name instantly. *This is it.*

She would meet the grandma he'd always raved about and maybe she would get some answers. Genni forced herself up the small steps and looked for the door screen. There wasn't one. There wasn't even an activation pad. She looked down to see a brass handle midway down the door. Did it even slide? It must have been old. It was unlike any door she'd ever seen. Tentatively, she knocked on it, looking around and not wanting to attract attention.

As she waited, she self-consciously shimmied her hands through her hair to increase its volume. The door swung open and Genni was welcomed by a petite woman with greying hair, wearing a pale dress with a frayed hem. Genni was surprised how young she looked to be someone's grandmother.

'Hello.' Genni spoke confidently despite the fear inside. 'You must be Ajay's . . .' Genni paused and painfully corrected herself. 'Sorry . . . Karle's grandmother.'

The woman's brown eyes sparkled with a sort of strange surprise. 'You know Karle?'

Genni nodded, not wanting to say any more while standing vulnerably on the doorstep.

'Come in. Come in. His grandma is upstairs.'

Genni instinctively stepped forward before pulling herself back again.

'Wait, so who are you?' Genni asked.

'I'm Karle's mother,' she said warmly, still holding the door open.

'You're his . . .' Genni couldn't speak, all moisture in her mouth disappearing.

No, no, no. You're supposed to be dead. You died with your husband in an accident. A faulty hover vehicle prototype.

Genni instantly realised how obvious a lie that was. Feeling frozen, she stared angrily at the concerned, but very much alive, mother. She couldn't breathe. Needing to get out and not scream in the face of a stranger, Genni turned in fright, almost slipping down the small steps that led up to the door. She started to run, everything inside her shattering all over again. Not seeing, with tears blocking her vision, she tripped on an uprooted pavement slab. She hit the ground, but didn't feel anything until soft hands on her shoulders helped her up to her feet.

Genni looked again into the woman's kind brown eyes and then up at a tall man whose eyes she knew. Ajay, but thirty years on. She supposed it was right for the dad to be alive too.

They were speaking to her but it only came as muffled noises at first.

'We'll get you cleaned up,' she heard him say as she came round. He looked as worried as his wife.

'I'll get some iced tea sorted. How about that?' the woman said, compassionately stroking Genni's arm. Her touch felt warm.

Genni couldn't speak and wanted to say no, but as she touched her lip to see blood on her finger, she knew she had to go with them. After all, this is what she had come for – the truth.

Genni stared lifelessly at the glass of iced tea, mindlessly baffled by its lack of ice cubes. It looked lonely without them bobbing on its surface. *They must have a good fridge if they don't need ice.* Though she noticed the lack of condensation on the glass, sat static on the dirty, white table with chipped legs. Having not said a word since Ajay's parents caught up with her outside, she decided she could avoid talking if she drank. Cupping the glass hesitantly, she sipped, hoping it would settle her stomach, sick with dread. The iced tea was warm. Managing to avoid heaving, she wiped the side of her mouth discreetly and watched Ajay's mother divide a pot of soup into individual containers. What was she doing?

Genni hadn't answered any of her questions, so she thought it wouldn't be right to ask her one. At first, Ajay's mother had sat next to her, on another of the uncomfortable wooden chairs, and asked her who she was, how she knew 'Karle', if she knew where he was, and told her how worried they'd been.

In the end, his mother had sighed and stood, leaving Genni to mourn at the table. The soup smelt good. Genni wasn't able to determine what had gone into it, but she guessed some fresh vegetables from the garden, as she spotted muddied offcuts by the sink. There was so much to their kitchen. Pans and strainers hung from hooks on the walls, and the open drawers and cupboards were full of cooking utensils. It was totally cluttered. It didn't even look like they had a delivery hatch. How did drones deliver their meals without coming into the house? The dishwasher was archaic. Genni had watched Ajay's father load it and give it some sort of tablet before inputting commands. Why wasn't it automatic? *Everything must take them an age.* It made even more sense to her why Ajay never had cleaning or cooking drones. Maybe it was a security thing, but maybe it was also familiar for him. If this was where he came from.

I should just go.

I've already had one merit warning on my Watch.

It was too unproductive to sit there, staring at their kitchen, if she didn't have the courage to even speak. As her legs readied themselves to walk her out, her exit was blocked by Ajay's father, wearing a long jumpsuit, splattered with the same oil stains she'd seen on the cake lady's hand outside.

'I'm going.' He gave Genni a small smile before looking directly at Ajay's mother.

'Already?' She paused in her work.

'Yeah, increased checks.' He pressed his glasses up his nose. 'They're all over the streets again.'

'Trix mentioned that to the group. I didn't think that would affect you, though.' She sighed softly. 'Could you take a few of these down to her? Then you can collect the donations on the way back.' She gathered some of the plastic containers, full of steaming soup, into a paper bag.

'I'll see.' Ajay's father paused. 'It might have to be the morning.'

'They've been working you too hard recently.' Ajay's mother wiped the worktop with quick precision. 'Is that rust issue sorted yet?'

'No. Not sure they'll give us the resources to fix it. Not with what's going on.' He took the paper bag from her before kissing her cheek lightly.

'We've got to keep hoping,' she said, pressing a hand into his chest. Her husband grunted in response and placed a black cap on his head, looking at Genni with those familiar eyes behind slanted glasses. Genni smiled slightly, not knowing what else would be appropriate. She was also distracted. What job could he possibly be doing?

As he walked away, his heavy footsteps vibrated through the house and Ajay's mother continued to spoon soup into the remaining containers.

'Your mother's coming down the stairs.' His deep voice travelled back up the hallway before the front door announced his exit.

'My mother's what?' She dropped the ladle into the pot so quickly Genni was sure it had been engulfed by the soup. Ignoring that, Genni watched Ajay's mother sprint out into the hallway, her apron dishevelled around her waist.

'Mum! What are you doing? You shouldn't be coming down. Let me help you back—'

There was a pause as Genni heard a faint whisper of response. She leant over on her chair in an attempt to see the stairs. Only then did it occur to her – the grandma. She was real.

Genni sat back, unbelieving. She had forgotten all about her in the shock of his parents being alive. Instinctively, she jumped to her feet.

'No, Mum. You can't—'

Ajay's mother sounded frustrated. 'Well—'

Another whisper.

'OK. OK. Well, let me at least help you, for Tulo's sake.' Genni listened to Ajay's mother's agitated tone and the creaking on the stairs. She felt as if she needed to make herself look more presentable. This was the woman Ajay had raved about; she'd told him bedtime stories and taught him about Tulo history, or what she knew of it. She was sweet, loving and, according to Ajay, inexorably headstrong. Ready to say what she thought, often challenging, but always compassionate. Admittedly, though, Genni's source was no longer reliable. Ajay could have lied about her too. The lady who was soon to appear in the mouldy kitchen could be a tyrant: rude, unreasonable and angered. She could blame Genni for everything. What if she hated her? What if these people could actually hurt her? Her parents once told her Side people were as capable as a malfunctioned drone. But surely she could out-fight them if they tried anything? She looked around: keys hanging on a hook, towels sitting on the side, kitchen cupboards falling off their hinges. Any of these things could be used as a weapon. Before she could bring herself to grab one, a croaky, dry voice pulled her away from her irrational thinking.

'You must be the girlfriend.' The woman stood in the kitchen doorway, her wrinkled hand clinging on to her flustered and soup-spattered daughter.

Genni felt a hard rock of saliva struggle down her throat. Ajay's grandma smiled, wide enough for Genni to know she had little teeth, but the intentionally soft look in her drooped eyes helped Genni to relax.

It was a strange feeling knowing that perhaps Ajay had been honest about something.

CHAPTER
NINETEEN

'Did you offer Genni some soup?' The old lady said to her daughter, both of them hobbling closer. The old woman was deteriorating; her hair was thin, her eyes looked tired and her saggy skin was almost yellow. Collecting herself, Genni realised she knew her name.

'Ajay told you about me?' Genni was surprised how clearly her words came out; her mouth was dry with distress and the warm iced tea wasn't helping.

'Oh yes . . . alright, alright, stop your fussing. I can go from here.' She struggled to release herself from the grasp of Ajay's mother as they reached the table. 'You get some soup read—'

'No, Mum. You need help sitting.' Ajay's mother sighed, pulling out the chair beside Genni's with her free hand. Genni sat down and considered how that impatient tone didn't suit his mother's sweet appearance. After what felt like forever, his grandma was settled in her seat, and Genni felt anxious. She felt the sharp pinch of her nails, burrowing into her own wrist. It was as if the lady was Glorified, or someone she should impress, at least, until she reminded herself of their stations; Genni was M-432 and climbing. Yet she couldn't find it within herself to demand information, just because she needed closure.

'So, love. I assume you're here looking for Ajay,' his grandma said, before coughing and spluttering over the table. Whatever substance came from her body did not look healthy and Genni avoided the need to grimace. She hadn't actually considered the possibility that Ajay might have returned home; she'd assumed he knew it would be a stupid thing to do.

'No. I just wondered if . . .' Genni paused as his grandma's coughing got louder and more severe. 'Do you need a tissue?' Genni instinctively lifted her wrist to order a box from a drone.

'Here.' Ajay's mother ran over, attempting to wipe her mother's face before a wrinkled hand batted her away. Ajay's mother was frustrated, Genni could tell by the way she gently closed her eyes and breathed deeply, her small chest rising and falling heavily. It reminded her of the way she often felt with her father.

'Sorry. I'm not in the fittest shape.' His grandma laughed forcefully as his mother softly stared at Genni.

'You didn't say you were his girlfriend?' His mother's smile was welcoming and compassionate.

'Sorry. It's all been a bit overwhelming.' Genni sipped at the iced tea, making sure to appear satisfied by it.

'Well, of course it has.' His mother looked sympathetic. 'It must have been an awful lot to deal with. With how Karle acted and what he did, which I assume you didn't—'

'Yes, very hard for you.' His grandma cut across but his mother didn't look fazed by the interjection this time. 'I always told him it was a bad idea.'

'Mother, this is hardly the time to play the blame game, is it?'

'Blame game?' His grandma coughed. 'Who else is there to blame? He's made some awful mistakes and left this poor girl in this mess.' She had a point. It was Ajay's fault. 'You look exhausted,' she said, leaning closer to Genni who could smell dry sweat and musty breath. 'Maybe you could stay the night here. Get some sleep. If you do that?'

Genni didn't respond, feeling blindsided at such a question. *You don't just ask someone if they sleep. That's personal.* And there was no way she could stay.

'So, you haven't heard from Ajay, then?'

'No, Karle hasn't been home since before the attack,' his mother said, returning to the soup. It was painful to Genni for her to keep using that name. 'Would you like some soup?'

It was gracious of her to ask, but Genni refused, not feeling like it. How could she trust their cooking, anyway? She realised his grandma was gazing at her, smiling with admiration.

'You are pretty,' she nodded, slowly. 'He always said that about you.'

'He did?' Genni felt warm, which then made her feel sick.

'Oh, yes. He told me you could live together one day and how brilliant you are.' His grandma started to struggle, hissing in discomfort as she tried to settle into the hard, wooden chair.

'Would you like this?' Genni held up the less than plumped cushion that was behind her own back, tempted to order a better one.

'Please, love.' His grandma thanked Genni as she carefully placed the cushion on her seat to support her, and Genni noticed the dark patches of sweat along his grandma's long brown dress.

'Did he talk about anything else? To do with me?' Genni felt as if her anger towards him was subsiding. *Maybe I was more than a piece in a game.*

'Ha. How long have you got?' His grandma laughed again, attempting to smile before spluttering into the tissue his mother had left behind. Genni smiled back.

'If I'm honest . . .' Genni paused. What was she doing? These were complete strangers. She shouldn't burden them with her problems; that would waste their time. She had no right to do that to them. It suddenly occurred to her how strange it felt to talk to a stranger without one of them setting their Watch to record. There was no one earning merit from this conversation, and she was unsure if she liked it or not.

'Go on, love,' his grandma pushed her, and Genni realised *they* had all the time in the world.

'I feel like I don't know who he is.'

'No.' His grandma paused as the only sound in the room was the clattering of more soup going into containers. 'I suppose you don't.'

'And you definitely haven't heard from him?'

'No. We were paid a visit by Command, their drones ripping up the place.' His grandma's eyes turned sad. Genni thought that explained all the rips in the hallway wallpaper and chips in the ceiling paint.

Genni nodded in response before glancing down at the dry, peeling skin of her hands.

'I'm so angry.' Genni held back the welling in her eyes and noticed how Ajay's mother was looking at her, soup ladle suspended in the air.

'Me too.' His grandma didn't smile this time, but moved her hand across the table in Genni's direction. 'He's done you a real disservice. As I said, we always told him not—'

'Mother, please.' Ajay's mother was back, placing a bowl of soup in front of her own mother and giving her a spoon. 'Let's not speak badly of him. Not when we don't even know—' She paused and seemed to swallow nothing.

'Oh, stop it, love. He's not dead.' His grandma spoke casually, swirling the soup around the bowl limply. 'Is there any yoghurt?'

'No, the ration was short.' His mother spoke fast, wiping her hands on her apron and tutting as his grandma huffed. 'There's not much coming now, Mum. And, to your earlier point, Ajay's life is very much in danger, if they find him.' Her words seemed like hot fire on her tongue. It hit Genni too.

The reality of Ace's death and her grieving for him had been sidelined by Ajay's betrayal. Was that selfish? Genni wasn't sure. Yet she hadn't even considered what would happen when they found Ajay. Could it mean he was dead too?

'Have you tried to find him?' Genni asked, knowing how much she cared despite burning with hatred for him.

His mother shook her head sadly. 'There's far too much ground to cover and we don't have anything that could track or communicate with—'

'What will be, will be.' His grandma slurped at the cloudy water in her glass. 'I know we're all scared but remember we need to trust.'

Ajay's mother sighed and moved her lips silently as if uttering some sort of verse. Genni had wondered when it would come up. The Guiding Light. All she knew about it was what she learnt in history at the Education Centre:

> *The Guiding Light is a holographic device created after the Revolution. These devices appeared in their many thousands and contain an ideology that existed before the Revolution took place. It promotes the ideals of laziness, over-resting and self-indulgence. It does not put the interest of all of Tulo first.*

Her experience of it checked out so far. Every one of their Side servants had been underskilled and underdeveloped. Especially Lanie. It was not a good day when her parents caught them together, reading the opening chapters of a novel. Yet the two women she was with now chose not to be Purified because of this Guide thing. Why? Genni didn't know about Ajay's grandma, but his mother was clearly skilled in hospitality. The efficiency she had shown as she managed to prepare that soup, divide it into numerous containers, sort out her ill mother – and now, she had started chopping potatoes – all in the time Genni had been sitting there ... it was pretty impressive. It was also definitely not lazy.

'Would you like to see his room?' Ajay's grandma pushed the soup away from her, the bowl virtually empty and scraping abrasively across the wooden table.

'Mother, that's hardly necessary. There's nothing up there. I'm sure Genni won't want to.' His mother set her knife beside the warped chopping board.

'No, I'd like to.' Genni stood up graciously, smoothing down her trouser legs that had risen up her shins.

'Splendid.' His grandma coughed through her next words. 'Would you help me up?'

Genni quickly and carefully placed her hands under her armpit, feeling the moist sweat around her fingers. Telling herself to ignore it, she noticed how it felt nice to do it. She was used to helping people; contributing to their reports at work, educating them on something, advising Mila on whether a pixie cut was more 'her' or not. She was a helpful person. Yet this felt a little different, as if it meant more. The thought passed as his grandma hoisted herself up, clinging to Genni's forearm with life-dependent force.

'It might take me a while,' his grandma breathed deeply. 'But you've got time, right?'

Genni instinctively looked at her Watch. She really didn't.

No merit points have been added to your merit score in five hours and twenty-four minutes. Is it time to do something of worth?

She thought of the new job. Her mind flickered through everything she was meant to achieve this week, and everything she achieved last week that was wiped out merit-wise when she boarded the Side train. It was 'Unworthy behaviour'. Something in Genni's gut twisted – a need and urgency to drop this lady and run. Get back to life.

Then, on looking into his grandma's eyes, so sincerely joyful despite her position, it pulled Genni back.

She had to see more of this place.

CHAPTER
TWENTY

'Don't mess with me, Jona.' Rod pressed his hands down on Jona's desk, staring deeply into his narrow, blue eyes. 'Why wasn't I told?'

'The Hevases say you're too close to this,' Jona sighed and let his body fall backwards into his chair. 'It is your sister's boyfriend. You're practically family.'

'So they care about policy now?' Rod turned away and took a long breath, calming himself and leaning on the glass wall of Jona's office that looked over the Command Security Bureau below; hundreds of rows with floating screens, heads down, and drones flying, carrying coffees and other products to their customers.

'We need to keep in line with them here, Rod.' Jona called up a screen and started tapping incessantly on his desk. Rod recognised the graphs of lie detector results as Jona validated the android's decisions.

'So, what? We're going to allow him to hide under some Rogue cover-up?' Rod turned back to Jona, who looked strained beneath a digital slideshow of his children floating on the wall behind him.

'We're not.' Jona held Rod's stare.

'Oh, really? So we're letting go of the whole "he's from the Side" thing, are we? Because the last time I checked, that was a crime punishable by public exposure and death.'

'We *have* exposed him. Making him part of the Rogue is arguably a harsher fate.'

Rod didn't understand what could be harsher than death. He briefly thought about the lies in the press release:

Evidence shows that Ambers was working closely with Lillie Trumin. While Trumin operated undercover within Command's premises, Ambers assisted Trumin in programmatic Watch manipulation using stolen equipment, which was found in his Inner-Ring apartment.

'And his little Side family are just left to carry on?' Rod asked, the question seething through his lips.

'The house has been searched and the evidence is being analys—'

'That's not good enough.' Rod slammed his hands down on the desk, making Jona jump slightly. Rod wanted him scared. Even though he led the board, he was not technically his superior and he needed to listen. Changing Ajay's story was anti-constitutional. *So there's rules for the rest of us but the Hevases can make exceptions for their own interests, is that it?*

'We cannot let his family get away with it.' Rod threw his arms above his head, pacing across the room, drowning in the harsh ceiling light.

'And we won't. Not if they're involved—'

'So what if we don't have any evidence?' Rod glared. 'That hasn't stopped us before.'

'That's true.' Jona nodded slowly, his lip twitching in agitation. 'But for now, we will follow their request. We cannot afford any more of your antics.'

Rod grunted, feeling the irritation lodging itself in his stomach like a lump of greasy camel meat.

'You can't tell me what to do.' Rod felt the saliva between his teeth as he spoke, pointing at Jona with a strong, threatening hand.

'If you want to keep your job, I can.' Jona sprang up, his chair rolling backwards and hitting the wall. 'We may both be detectives, but I'm the lead on this case. So, you're going to shut up, read through my notes, check through the surveillance of Ambers again and not make my life any harder.' A drone came into the room, flying through the toxic air and placing a coffee down on Jona's desk. He went to pay but Rod lifted his own wrist quickly to swipe along the side of the drone, his blood boiling. The ring of the transaction cut the silence sharply.

'For the inconvenience I've caused . . . *sir.*' Rod nodded at Jona distastefully before leaving the room, slamming the door controls with deliberate, wall-vibrating force.

Walking to the surveillance room, Rod tried to bury his frustration. He wasn't used to such cautious action. Usually, if Guiding Light believers were involved in any case, it was a charge and arrest strategy. Not this tiptoeing around and fabricating lies in the suspect's story. The whole nature of Ajay's Side-born criminality had been coated in a nice Rogue cover. It was all anyone seemed to care about these days. It was as if his job was becoming redundant. The thought unsettled him, like the scraping of a fork down his body. Striding across the main thoroughfare, Rod didn't even glance at the commoners of Command Security, sat at mirroring desks, taking mirroring citizen calls.

He took the elevator to the second floor before passing the first block of interrogation rooms. There, he spotted Telusa alone, observing an interview through one-way glass. Without hesitating, he swiped his Watch against the door's exterior to join her.

'You fired them all?' He looked around the empty room, expecting to see junior detectives, but there was only a red apple standing on the ledge of the glass.

'I wish,' she smiled, arms crossed across her chest, standing in a way that exaggerated her slender legs above thin high heels. 'One might quit after this morning, though.'

Rod leant against the glass, quickly looking at the android questioning a small, scrawny man with blond hair and crooked teeth. 'Huh, maybe I should let you loose on Jona.'

'Wouldn't be the first time,' she muttered.

'Sometimes I think I'd be better working somewhere else. Might get more respect.'

'Depends whether respect is more important than status.'

'Don't bore me with philosophy.' Rod turned around to watch the interrogation more closely, listening to the audio patching through.

'Have you ever stolen anything?' The android addressed the man in the chair, hooked up to a few screens.

'No . . . no,' the man mumbled, fiddling nervously with the cuffs of his long-sleeved shirt. 'Not that I recall.'

'This guy surely isn't one of them.' Rod watched as the man spluttered in submission to the android's questions. Yawning, Rod pulled out his *SkipSleep Pro* and puffed, offering it to Telusa.

She didn't thank him, but put her small lips around the device and continued to hold it between her fingers. They watched in a mutually acceptable silence as the subject's statistics and reliability metrics hovered beside him. Rod squinted, trying to read some of the numbers. He could understand most of them but all that really mattered was the verdict at the end.

'How many have gone through since the meeting?' Rod moved slightly closer to her, admiringly, his body almost knocking the apple off the ledge.

'Only one.' Telusa took another puff. 'Though she was almost cleared. She's probably lying about something else.'

'Hmm.' Rod nodded, considering the progress. It seemed basic but it was the way he would do it; a machine learning algorithm calculated reliability metrics based on physiological cues of the suspect. Heart rate, sweat on the palms, 'shiftiness' of the eyes. Using androids instead of human interrogators was the right call. *At least they're getting something right. Most humans are lazy, unobservant, too emotional, likely to let any old Unworthy through.* Androids could even tap into the suspect's Watch recordings to understand their natural behaviour and compare that with their actions in the interview. Any unnatural body language would be another warning sign. Enough of those would send them through to the next stage. One much more brutal and unrelenting. *As it should be.*

'What were your metrics?' Rod asked.

'What?' Telusa raised an eyebrow, still hogging the *SkipSleep*. 'What a rude thing to ask a lady, Roderick.'

'Only curious.' Rod smirked slightly. 'Any chance you could get me off the list?'

'That's very suspicious.' She tossed her head playfully towards him.

'I've got better things to do,' Rod grunted, thinking about his interrogation interview next week. He understood that no Command Worker was an exception, but surely he could be?

'Like standing here flirting with me instead of carrying out Jona's orders?' She took another small puff. She laughed again after seeing Rod's face turning sour at the mention of Jona's name.

'It would be a lot simpler if the Hevases got over their love for children,' Rod mocked.

'My job would be easier, that's for sure.' Telusa didn't stop watching the interview, eyes stern before she managed a smile. 'And it wouldn't be a great loss.'

Rod put out his hand to take back the device. Telusa peered down at it and let the moment linger, before Rod relented and retreated his hand. Staring back at the interview, the android was asking about the man's whereabouts during the attack.

'We certainly wouldn't have to bother with all this.' Telusa puffed and blew the vapour into Rod's face teasingly.

'Give it back.' Rod lurched forwards to grab the device as Telusa pulled her arm backwards.

'Now, now, Roderick. You've already had your strop for today.' Telusa raised both eyebrows this time. Rod liked the way she toyed with him.

'Dinner later?' he asked, hopefully.

'I dunno,' Telusa shrugged. 'Not sure I have time. I've got to restrategise the plane limits before ten.' Unfortunately, that was more important than dinner. Most things were.

'What do you reckon, then?' He finally snatched the device from Telusa, their fingers sliding together, before they both looked back through the glass. 'Is Mr Fidget going to pass?'

'Nah.' Telusa shook her head, sounding hopeful as her light hair escaped her shoulders and shimmied down her back. 'He's shifty.'

Rod, inhaling *SkipSleep*, coughed with amusement. 'You're joking? He looks like he couldn't lie to his mum.'

More questions and time passed as they debated his looks and demeanour, arguing their cases over his reliability until the android finished the process and enabled the algorithm. They both turned to the screen, watching the metrics rise and fluctuate until the reliability indicator turned green and the android confirmed: 'Interviewee not deemed suspicious.'

'Well,' Rod paused, taking a moment to observe Telusa's annoyed, beaten face. 'I guess that's why we let the computers do the work.'

'Oh, shut up,' she said, pushing him lightly.

'Yes, ma'am.' He stood up straight, before glancing again at the apple on the side. 'You gonna eat this?'

'Nah.' Telusa didn't look up from her Watch as the android told the man to leave. 'It's bruised.'

Rod confidently threw the apple up and caught it again, before landing a small peck on Telusa's cheek. She gave him a reluctant yet humorous look as he left. Striding from the room, he considered how his annoyance with Jona had momentarily faded. Yet he knew as he sat down in the surveillance room, it would only take a moment to resurface.

Rod bit into the apple and crunched through its flesh, tearing it apart before it struggled down his throat. It was difficult to swallow, his irritation so consuming that it was taking over his normal bodily functions. He stared blankly at the dozen surveillance screens in front of him, suspending depictions of Ajay's last known movements; the idiot running, covered in the blood of his friend. It was all a blur to Rod, he wasn't really looking at the screens, suspecting there was nothing more to find.

'Personally I think they should chip us. We're all becoming machines anyway, right?'

Rod vaguely looked at the operator beside him; a skinny, small lad with serious acne scars around his nose and chin. He didn't know his name, never bothered to ask, but Rod admired the kid's ambition. He was probably early to mid-twenties and had worked hard to be connected to high-calibre people like himself, though he couldn't comment on the quality of his work. If it was anything like his constant rambling, it wasn't good. Rod ignored him, biting another frustrated chunk out of his apple.

'It would be much quicker and probably cheaper.' The lad leant back casually on the chair, eyes scanning the screens. 'Don't you think?'

Rod didn't answer as he hit a bruised part of the apple, fluffy and unwelcome in his mouth.

'Although not sure android tech is that trustworthy yet. Especially with the way the medical ones dealt with the attack. Then again, we haven't heard anything about the interrogation results yet. How are they going?'

Rod stayed silent, trying not to register him.

'But as for the ones in the Country, it was like my mum was saying the other day, just blow the lot of them up. We know they're out there, just set the damn planes off, load the lasers and smoke 'em.'

Rod grunted, amused by the boy's ignorance, as the presence of children in the Rogue wasn't common knowledge. He decided to play along to pass the time. 'And your mum's an expert in recreating raw resources, is she?'

'That's exactly what my dad said. Ha.' The lad laughed, his voice taking on a new, excitable tone. Rod continued to half-watch Ajay, listening vaguely. 'It led to a bit of a domestic. You know, if we can genetically engineer the fruits and stuff, why can't we do the same with wood and whatever they put in *SkipSleep* and that? And before you say it, my dad snapped back with the whole "it's not natural" thing. I've always been a mummy's boy so I agreed when she—'

'Shut up.' Rod sat up, staring at the bottom right-hand screen. He lobbed his half-eaten apple into the trash chute that pinged green at its entry. 'Did you see that?'

'Oh, erm . . .' The lad followed Rod's finger to the correct screen where Ajay had emerged from an alley and stopped in the street, having almost collided with a woman in sunglasses. 'What?'

'Who checked this before?'

'I . . . I did. A few times. And Jona had a look at it.'

'Has it not occurred to you that he used the shortcuts?' Rod watched, irritated that it hadn't been noticed, as Ajay continued to nip in and out of back alleys, moving with premeditated direction.

'Well, we lost him just before the Outer-Rings. There was no further drone footage.'

'Yeah, I know that.' Rod recalled the shouting match Jona had had with another operator when the footage of the Outer-Rings didn't show any sign of Ajay. 'But where is he going?'

'The Side, we're assuming.'

'Yeah, of course that's where he's going, but how does he *know* the shortcuts?' It was painful to work with such incompetence. *And the mighty Jona hadn't even noticed it. I should be leading this case.*

'Erm . . . well . . . I suppose he might have done it before.'

'Exactly. Only someone with a detailed knowledge of that particular journey would know the most efficient route.' Rod refrained from swearing at him, though the desired effect still occurred; the lad looked degraded. *He has to learn.* 'Show me footage of the Side terminal for the last, I don't know, four weeks.'

The lad quickly rolled back the cuffs of his shirt, pulling his chair forward eagerly. Rod drummed his foot on the floor and looked at his wrist. They were running out of time. Ajay was potentially getting further and further away. Though there were only so many places he could be without transportation or equipment.

They flicked their eyes over four weeks' worth of footage of the same drab, rundown platform to see nothing but Side residents bobbing in and out of the City to litter-pick, for Purification duties or whatever it is they did. Rod sighed. No sign of Ambers. The lad looked to Rod for the next instruction, helpless on his own. *He won't make it here.*

'OK, four weeks before that.' Rod pulled his hand over his face, agitated that his theory hadn't checked out straight away. On and on the footage went as the lad's finger continually tapped 'next', the only change being the billboards as they went back before the attack; the bleak messaging returning to its previous product placements. Until.

'There. That's him.' Rod stood up from his chair, stroking the air and expanding the screen. Ajay was standing on the platform in a detestable light-grey jacket and wearing a black cap with a frayed rim. He looked so small. An insignificant body standing beneath the watching eyes of a camera lens. Rod smiled, feeling somewhat triumphant.

'Why was he going back there? Surely once he got out, he kept away.'

'Shut it. Save that, and do it again. The weeks before that.'

The lad followed Rod's instructions, pinning the footage up to the left-hand side and returning to the archive, flicking through again, but this time faster, with greater understanding of what they were looking for.

'There he is.' The lad stopped, both of them glancing at Ajay in a black T-shirt and the same, torn black cap.

'Good. Save it,' Rod said, following the footage as it also got pinned. 'Again.' Rod was transfixed, ready to see Ajay again, powerless under his gaze. 'There.' Ajay was back in the disgusting jacket. They continued this pattern twice more until the lad spoke, surprising Rod with his observation.

'They're all on a Saturday.' He breathed heavily, ordering the pinned videos out in front of them. 'Four weeks apart.' Rod straightened himself up, a smile stretching across his face as the lad spoke again. 'So he was—'

'Visiting his pathetic family every fourth Saturday.'

Well, well, well. Rod smirked cunningly at the screens, thrilled that he'd found a way to arrest them. This would play perfectly into his hands. With evidence suggesting they'd maintained a relationship with their little criminal, they couldn't escape. Whether they'd facilitated him or not, it was the perfect cover-up to eradicate a whole Side family at once.

He leant forward, addressing his accomplice.

'Check the footage in the Side for those dates. Let's make sure he goes home.'

CHAPTER
TWENTY-ONE

'Are you completely insane?' Charlene walked Ajay through the trees, the sunlight dappling on the ground. Ajay said nothing, holding his arms and soothing the places where the men's restraints had compressed his skin.

'You're lucky they didn't throw you out.' Charlene pulled her heavy hair over one shoulder. 'Your brain must be very important to them. I wouldn't have been surprised if they'd thrown you out in the desert and left you to . . .'

'Die?' Ajay said curtly.

Charlene looked back at Ajay, her eyes stunning in the daylight. 'They've never done it before, but then again, no one has morphed into a complete madman and attacked one of their own. That woman is not the nicest, I'll give you that, but she was alright before all the drink and whatever.'

'She is not one of my own.' Ajay gritted his teeth, still feeling enraged, glancing through the trees, searching for Lillie.

Charlene stopped, the pausing of her footsteps obvious and stark. She pressed a hand to Ajay's chest.

'She is one of your own.' Her eyes pleaded. 'She's not much use now but was let back in as a courtesy. You're part of us, so is she – you're on the same side.'

Is that an order? He didn't react, but stayed silent and stomped back through the trees, letting Charlene harp on.

'I overheard some of the lads talking about her while I was waiting for you. They were saying that because she was the main instigator in getting the identifications faked, she'd earnt the right to be let into camp when she fled the City. Not that I agree. She helped with the . . .' Charlene paused. 'You do know I don't agree with what happened, right?'

Ajay glanced at the truth in her eyes, one he'd always known, that she had no part in the attack. He nodded feebly and she smiled with relief before turning and marching back towards Haro's pit.

'Anyway, they were saying she's completely lost a wire because the Moth who ratted her out in interrogation was her . . . romantic interest,' Charlene said delicately as she walked, the sky turning lilac. 'I assume. They were a bit more graphic about it. Pretty disturbing. I was about ready to go and tell them to shut it. I mean, the children would be up soon and there they were, talking about the intricate, and very . . . *intimate* details of . . . Ajay?'

Ajay had stopped, fallen to his knees, letting Charlene's noise disappear. He heard the chafing of her suit as she came back to him. He was glad that Lillie had been betrayed. She deserved it. She'd taken everything from him and continued to taunt him, joking and laughing about Ace. He had lost track of time, but he guessed it had been about a week without him. So much had happened since then that it felt longer, but everything still felt as lost. Lifelessly staring down at the drying dirt, the trees standing stagnant in the humidity, Ajay felt numb. Hitting her felt good, because he'd wanted to, like he wanted to get back at these people, who hurt and killed others. He thought back to the ridicule he'd faced after they'd dragged him away from her. Maze was there and with all the rage inside of him, Ajay longed to hit him too as he boasted to others about how *he'd* taken Ajay from the streets, and Ajay had 'whimpered like a child', hands tied and a bag over his head.

They're all like Lillie – vile, horrible vermin.

'Ajay?' Charlene bent down to his level. 'Come on, let's get you up.' It was only as she wiped Ajay's cheeks with the cuff of her suit did he realise he was crying. He resisted and flopped down again, bringing his head to his knees.

'I can't . . .' he sniffed, trying to stop the tears. *This is embarrassing. Pull it together.* 'I can't stay here. You're bad people, Charlene.'

Charlene straightened up, her long physique towering over Ajay, blocking out the sun. 'You just said you believed me.'

'You want Command dead. You want to hurt people, like the rest of them.'

Charlene sighed and to Ajay's surprise, sat down beside him and leant against a nearby tree.

'You don't think I realise we're among some disgusting people? Don't you think Haro knows that too?' Charlene picked up a curled-up leaf and started pulling it apart. 'At least it's kind of like a home. People don't name you Worthy or Unworthy. We're all united, in one way or another.' She sounded sad. Ajay wondered if she always had, behind her meaningless chatter about suits, hair, food and comfort.

'Command needs to pay for what they've done to us. Look around you – we're starving, dirty, outcasts. Taking every day as it comes. Until eventually they catch us, or don't, and we run out of food or morale. You really think they don't deserve to be exposed and punished?'

Ajay said nothing.

'What about what happened to you and your friend? *They* want you to believe it was your fault.'

'It was my fault.' Ajay stared at Charlene with defiance, quickly tucking his sweaty hair behind his ears. *How can she think it was anyone's fault but my own?* It was him who cheated the system, him who panicked, him who tied Ace into that *SkipSleep* port, him who threw the final, fatal punch. Holding back the tears, he picked a few withered flowers beside him and started to twist them together as a distraction.

Charlene paused and didn't speak for a few minutes. It was some sort of miracle; he'd even heard her speaking in her sleep.

'Promise you won't tell anyone this.' She finally spoke softly.

Ajay nodded, still trying to weave stems together, but his stumpy fingers kept causing them to snap.

'I was famous, once.'

Intriguing.

'Properly?'

'Yeah. Properly,' Charlene smiled. 'My face was everywhere. Probably not in your neck of the desert, though.'

'What for?'

'I was Command's promo kid – do they still have those?'

'Yeah.' Ajay thought about the same faces on the billboards and in the videos, different Command products joining them.

'I started when *SkipSleep* was relatively new, about . . .'

Charlene paused in thought. 'Probably ten . . . twelve years ago. It was a time when motivational speeches were a big thing, before *Personi* took over.' Charlene started picking apart more of the leaf. Ajay wondered if he'd seen Charlene on anything as he'd mined through his father's Watch, or on the few trips he had taken to the City as a teenager. He watched her as she sighed and looked up towards the sky, emphasising the small spots on her chin. She seemed to be thinking, hard, before she moved her head back against the trunk and told Ajay her story.

'For some time, I was what they termed their "superstar". "You're my sensation," my mother used to say whenever I went for auditions as a kid. I was being prepared for it, growing up in the Quarters. They have people lined up since their teenage years to be their pretty representatives. When I was sixteen, I got my first job as a poster girl for Education Centre Out-of-hours Clubs. They put me in some uncomfortable clothes, not tight but not relaxing. It was horrendous. "You're a prime student," I remember the costume director saying, to help me get into character. It was a training technique. Telling us we looked great in our clothes, so we'd believe that we really were prime students, or excellent workers, or whatever part they wanted us to play.' Charlene laughed. 'It all sounds so ridiculous when I look back.

But at the time, I was like a prized possession. When I was eighteen, I had millions of *Personi* followers, attended big-scale events, and spoke the words they wanted me to speak every other week. When I got my Watch, my merit score started at M-450. It only took me two years to get back to the Quarters.'

'That's . . .' Ajay had never heard of such a quick succession, even with his own techniques. 'Insane.'

'It was.' Charlene nodded. 'It was my life. I was expected to jump that high. So, the years continued and I spent my time doing what they told me. As you can imagine, I started to get a bit sick of it.

'I was becoming like an android. No more than a drone delivering iced coffees and kale smoothies to consumers, all to plug more economic value back into society. The worst campaign I ever did was called a "healthy heart". The stuff they had me drink may have been healthy, good for brain strength and life expectations, but my heart was still lost. I despised everything they gave me. Do you know how hard it is to look "pretty" while sipping down straws full of what tasted like blended-up vomit? I thought I might get fired that day. Ha. If only.' Charlene scrunched up the leaf in her hand, the cracking sound of its dried skin filling the moment.

'Don't get me wrong, the merit and lifestyle was everything I'd ever dreamed of. My house up in the mountains was beautiful. It had a staircase that spiralled up three floors. What I loved most was when I was alone and I could relax. Then one day, as I was lying by the pool, I noticed a finger smudge on my sunglasses. And it made me smile. Because I thought, how beautiful for something to be so imperfect and it's OK.' Ajay was slightly confused but let Charlene continue. 'It was like an epiphany moment. My instinct was to clean the smudge, but then I thought, *What if I don't want to clean the smudge? Do you see?'*

Ajay blinked at her, kind of understanding.

'It felt liberating to *choose* not to look perfect all the time. Because, let's be honest, I definitely wasn't perfect underneath all that tight, painful clothing and skin-degrading make-up. They say it had moisturising qualities but it just dried everything out. There are lumps and scars all over this body.'

Ajay found that hard to believe. As he listened, his mind briefly turned back to his escape plan. Picking up a stick beside him, he started drawing a map in the dirt, his legs covering Charlene's view. He drew a line to represent his guess at the resource plane's flight path.

'The best part was, as I lay there, I realised, I am a lazy person. Or not lazy, but I'm not a workaholic. I liked to relax. I remember talking to my mother about it. She was a bit appalled. "You can't say things like that, Charlene," she said. "You might have the merit now, but you can't always just relax. Command won't allow it." I didn't laugh right in her face, though I wanted to. I knew there were people less privileged than myself who felt like they had to run themselves into the ground for merit, but that smudge got me thinking about it: *Why can't we have breaks?* If we all came to a consensus, culturally, things would be better. I thought so anyway. My father used to think I was a loony.

'I dwelt on my thoughts for about six months, still feeling like everyone, not just the Glorified, deserved some holiday time, when you don't do anything for merit, and for that to be acceptable. Like Liberation Day, but for a week or even two. The first thing I did was post a picture of me in the pool in my favourite swimsuit. It was gorgeous; bright yellow, with small red flowers dotted across it. I wrote a caption about how great it was to relax and unwind. Next thing I knew, my manager was banging my door down. "Do you realise what you've done?" She was furious. My fox, Popsicle, was sniffing around her feet.' Charlene smiled subtly, a loss in her eyes.

'Apparently, I'd stained my reputation and people at Command were furious. What got me, though, was the post got a lot of loves before it was taken down. There was an appetite for it. And I enjoyed the feeling of riling people up the wrong way. It gave me a power I never realised I had, and it added a bit of spice to my flavourless existence.' Ajay could feel her looking at him as she continued. 'Don't get me wrong. I loved all the glamour and being highly favoured and everything. But it was boring. I got a bit stir crazy. The real truth was, I did believe we needed to take time out sometimes. It occurred to me, when I was about twenty-four, having fallen back into the same old, runaround life, that there could be somewhere else to go.'

Ajay looked away from his badly drawn map and flicked his curious eyes back at her.

'Think about it. There's all that space out there. Why can't there be somewhere else to go when we want to get away for a bit? Where merit doesn't matter and life can be calmer,' Charlene sighed. 'Why not build a place to relax rather than just more of the same?'

Ajay nodded, finding the idea somewhat attractive. The concept of a holiday had never really come up; not even

Genni had suggested taking the liberty and she enjoyed relaxing more than most. He remembered the annual statistics: only 1.2 per cent of citizens above M-200 clocked over two meritless days in the last year. It was something to celebrate, alongside all the other strides taken in advancing Tulo to the next level, including expansion projects. Every year they met milestones; their society wouldn't be where it was without it – that desire to build was written in their generational make-up. *How could she suggest such a thing?*

'So, anyway. After the drama of the post calmed down and people seemed to forget, I thought I may as well give it another go. You might think I'm stupid but I was getting so claustrophobic with people telling me what I should and shouldn't do. In the end, I snapped and went for it. My posts showed me in my joggers, chilling out, eating cake, slacking off at the library, taking my Watch off.' Charlene got elated and seemed to be enjoying the memory, until the charm in her eyes turned sad. 'And I even mentioned the idea of building that place to relax. That's when things turned sideways.'

Ajay expected that. It was hardly a twist in the tale. Looking down at his map, he'd managed to draw the Side, and the Country where the desert slowly became the forest. *This is pointless.* He erased the map with the stick, its splinters sharp on his skin.

'I realised I might have been treading the line too thinly, but I thought, I wouldn't mind having a new job, doing something different. So them being angry didn't matter to me and as I said, I kind of enjoyed it.' Charlene sighed. 'Then, it was on a Saturday afternoon. I was watching *The Glorified House* and my Watch alerted me to someone at the door. I rolled off the sofa and felt slightly conscious of my hair being unwashed and in a bun, but I noticed from the window that a drone had been through the gate. I wasn't expecting any deliveries. I swiped to open the door to find a box there. Just a white box.' Charlene paused. 'It was a cake, covered in white icing, with red letters piped onto it.'

Ajay stared at Charlene, eyebrows raised, intrigued.

'It said "Eat cake, Unworthy".' Charlene's voice cracked. 'Then, it got a lot worse. Messages through to my Watch, death threats to the door, comments about my height and body. Anything people could do to hurt me, they did. I never understood why. People claimed I didn't deserve to be where I was. I suppose they took my thoughts about relaxing as a stab at them. I don't know. I was just trying to help people. Well, I thought I was anyway. At the time my brain was always fuzzy. So maybe I wasn't very sensitive,' Charlene continued. 'But what really angered me, and what I will never forgive them for, was the way my managers reacted. They had access to people in Command. What I was going through, all the hate and the threats, was completely anti-constitutional.'

'They didn't track them down and deduct merit?' Ajay asked.

'You'd think. As a general rule, they do. Somehow everything to me "slipped" through?' Charlene crooked her head. 'I think Command allowed it to happen. No, I *know* Command allowed it to happen. Because of what I was saying. They don't want anyone to leave or have breaks because of their perfectly formed constitution. They need all the contributions. "Progress is Strength".'

Charlene stuck out her tongue and made a vomiting sound. She paused and stretched her long legs along the ground.

'Anyway, the messages were painful and I didn't cope very well. I don't really want to talk about the details. When I stopped coming to work, they fired me. At first, I didn't care much. I was getting older and I could already see who would replace me. That red-headed shorty with the big bum. The thing was, this whole fiasco hadn't gone under the radar, Command had allowed the hatred of me to go public. And it was contagious. Even when people may have agreed with me, or were impartial, they still hated me. So who was going to hire me? Of course, I slowly lost everything. The house, my achievements, and my parents disowned me. "We can't have an Unworthy daughter." That's what my mother said the last time I saw her. It killed me.'

'Wow, I'm sorry.' Ajay tried not to sympathise, but it was confusingly instinctive, having grown to care about her.

'Nothing to be sorry about. I never wanted to lose the Glorified life, but once it was stolen from me I was given a new purpose.' Charlene then picked a Duskdrop flower from its stem and held it out in the palm of her hand. She spoke with defiance. 'To destroy them.' Closing her hand, Ajay watched her rip the flower between her fingers, its lilac petals falling gracefully to the ground.

She looked at him and smiled, her thoughts clearly switching gear.

'You can't go. There's no way out. Besides, Cal told you we need your help. I don't know what for, but we do.' Charlene dusted her hands off and stood. Ajay, while sympathetic, could see that Charlene's hatred had led to an irrational pursuit for revenge. *Like everyone here. Though she might be angry and desperate and broken, there's no excuse for such hatred to lead to violence.*

Ajay's thoughts paused.

Just like how much I hated Lillie before I hit her. Or how much I hated The Guiding Light and my father before I left. Or, maybe, how much I hated Ace at the moment he said he would report me. I'm the same as them? But that doesn't mean I belong with them, does it? No, it can't.

'Promise you won't try to go.' Charlene towered over him, the moon appearing above her as the sun set. She stretched out a hand to help him up and he took it, lying through his teeth, confirming the promise.

CHAPTER
TWENTY-TWO

Two days later.

'Do you think they'll bring back toothpaste this time?' one of them asked Charlene as they walked out to the next climbing spot.

Ajay dragged his feet, hoping they would find a lizard-free spot soon. It felt like they had walked further than ever. His mouth was dry and his stomach growled, complaining about the new level of fruit rationing, not that his mind cared so much. He was too distracted by his building, unrelenting obsession on his escape plan. He didn't care what he promised Charlene. *How can I get on that plane?*

'Maybe.' Charlene coughed, her throat sounding sore. 'Doubt they'll bring the shampoo I requested.'

'You should think about cutting your hair.' One of the men pulled his spade along behind him, its scraping following them through the night.

'Not a chance.' Charlene stopped momentarily as she dropped her empty sack and attempted to roll it up more tightly. 'Maybe some chocolate, that was amazing, that one time. It was the good stuff too, not that no-merit deduction, low-sugar rubbish.'

'Hmm, I would prefer some cigarettes,' the man murmured.

'You'd be lucky,' someone else said.

'What are you hoping for from the drop-off, Side boy?' The man asked as they waited for Charlene. Ajay had never spoken to the guy, one of the Architects. He glanced at his shovel while thinking he was one of those 'too pretty for his own good' kind of guys, his strong arms probably built through digging new pits in replacement camps, should they ever need to move.

'He also needs to brush his teeth,' Charlene commented as they all continued walking.

'Ha. Well, he won't be first in line after he punched up the drunk the other day.' The guy laughed, but in Ajay's mind, he was silent as Ajay laid one around his cocky cheeks.

'Hope it's not as frustrating as last time. People were so pushy.' Charlene readjusted her bag on her back. She joined Ajay and watched the men with guns in front, moving their torches up into the trees, hunting for lizards.

'Yeah, well, people are ravenous.' The Architect lugged his shovel up and placed it over his right shoulder.

'Did you hear about that lad catching that Ginel?' another guy piped up, sounding tired, pulling his sack along the ground.

'A Ginel?' Charlene sounded both excited and irritated.

'Yeah, he was out lizard-hunting and it wandered into his path.'

'Shut up!' the shovel guy responded in disbelief. 'You trade for some?'

'Nah. It was all gone by the time I heard about it.'

They all moaned over the disappointment. Mulling over how hungry he actually was, Ajay hoped a Ginel would wander into *his* path so he could have a proper meal; get a taste of all that meat from its ballooning boar-like body. He reminisced about just tapping on his wrist and a drone bowing to his stomach's orders. As if by magic. That life was gone now, for *this. Would there ever be a way to get it back?*

'Anyway, we're off this way. Have a happy merit-making day,' the Architect smirked as he walked away, carrying his spade over his shoulder confidently.

Charlene grunted at his sarcasm as they walked in silence and Ajay continued to watch the gunmen searching the trees with their touches as Wingsparks bounced through the night sky. He then looked up further. The stars were coming; one significantly brighter and more orange than the others, glowing like a dull furnace above. *That must be Curtan.* Ajay watched it, not a star but a planet, letting himself escape into nature. *And it's one of those nights where it crosses the light of the sun at the right time.* He couldn't remember the last time he'd seen it; he never stopped for long enough to really look up and appreciate the magnificence of it all. Not like this. It was only those times when he and Genni watched the storms that his life wasn't billboards, skyscrapers and merit counts. Out here, in the wild, it was beginning to feel like an escape, even though he still felt trapped.

There was something about the moment, as the dazzling dots caught him and the Ginel came back to mind that Ajay thought more about what Charlene had said. *There could be somewhere else to go.* He knew there was nothing else out there but water, mountains and sand. Yet it was an interesting notion to go out and see more of nature, more of the place in which they lived. It had never been done before. Not really. Right from when he was a child, they spoke about the vast expanse that surrounded them, how it had been explored but never occupied, as the City was the best place to be. Of course, there were the expansion projects that Command occasionally reported on, mainly to inform them that they'd been delayed yet again. Though Ajay, now that he'd lost everything else, wondered if he wouldn't mind seeing more of it.

He caught himself in the ridiculous thought. He'd never survive out there anyway, not well enough to enjoy it. *I'm going demented, stuck here with these people.* Still they walked, hoping to find a spot where it looked all clear.

'That was a complete disaster.' Charlene lumped her half-empty sack down in frustration as the sunrise was turning the sky its signature lilac.

'Not long till mating season is over.' Haro put down his own light sack. 'And there's a drop-off today. So heads up, princess.' He wandered over to his pit.

'Don't call me that!' Charlene spat at him, sitting on the log, pulling fruit from her sack.

Haro slipped off his suit in his pit's entrance, briefly looking at Ajay, who sat down and opened his own sack. Silently, he took his ration and gave the rest to Charlene, who would take it to be distributed.

'Ajay.'

All three of them followed the voice towards the opening that led to the main camp. It was Callum; his taser scars across his right cheek clear in the emerging sunlight. Sniffing and pulling his red headband further across his floppy hair, he came closer.

'I need you to come with me.' His eyes were fixed on Ajay. 'We need to talk to you.'

'Finally.' Charlene stood with some self-ordained authority. 'The committee has realised time is short, have they?' She addressed Ajay. 'You can tell me the master plan, seeing as they're keeping it all to themselves.' Charlene returned to the fruit with a slightly concerned twitch in her lips.

Ajay didn't hesitate but stood and joined Callum. *This is my chance to find out more.*

'Haro, you coming?' Callum called back.

'I'll be there soon. Start without me,' Haro mumbled, still pulling himself out of his suit.

With everything Ajay had needed to process, he recognised he'd been nonchalant about what 'help' they needed from him. The rumours, the whispers, the passing comments about why he was taken had fallen over him like a dry mist, almost evaporating into something insignificant. His desire to leave, his grieving and regret had been too overpowering. Now it seemed the time had come, he swallowed his breath, following Callum in trepidation. What would they force him to do?

'So, what do you want?' Ajay caught up with Callum as they approached the main camp, narrowly missing the stares of the others. Were they all still suspicious of him, as the 'wanted' man? Or was this because of Lillie?

Or because they knew he was going to the committee? *Ignore it, it doesn't matter.* He held on tighter to the piece of fruit in his hands.

Callum stayed quiet and led him back through the trees, out into another clearing, a part of camp Ajay hadn't been to before. There, a group had gathered, sitting on the ground, talking, and eating rotting pieces of fruit from last night's pick.

'This is the committee.' Callum spoke calmly. Ajay looked wordlessly at them. Maze, the man who beat him, was there. *Brilliant.* Ajay didn't look at him, but instead at the woman. She had a short pixie haircut, lynx-like eyes and a very forced smile.

'So, we've heard a lot about you from Callum.' The deep voice belonged to a scrawny man with a curiously refined face, wearing a tattered Command jumpsuit. Ajay's eyes instantly gravitated to where the Command symbol would normally sit above the man's right breast; he wasn't surprised to see it wasn't there, a hole with seared edges in its place.

This must be Ki. The man Haro had told him about that night in the pit; the only man willing to lead, since his predecessor had been dealt with during the attack. This Ki looked ill, malnourished even. The width of his legs was almost the same as his arms and his skin was pasty enough for a dressing table to give him a warning.

'Sit down. Here, have this. It's much better.' As Ajay sat, Ki threw over a tin, the contact of Ajay's catch making a clunking sound and causing him to drop his fruit. He looked down. *Peaches in their own juices.*

No way.

'Thanks.' Ajay was confused.

'Keep it quiet. We shouldn't really hoard things from drop-offs.' Ki smiled through a husky cough. 'Alright, I'll bring you up to speed.'

Callum sat beside Ajay but kept his distance, appearing displeased with the situation. *Yeah, well, I'm not your biggest fan either.*

'I'm Ki. I head up the Architects and do a lot of the tech stuff.' He looked softly around the circle before coughing again, placing a hand to his bony chest. 'I think you know most of us.'

'I'm Marta.' The woman with the pixie cut said curtly, a gun laying by her feet.

Ajay nodded but stayed quiet, staring at the tin of peaches, the bright yellow picture taking his attention. *How should I act here? As if I don't care? As if I do? I don't want them to hurt me or force me into anything. Would I do it if they did? Maybe there's some information I could use here so I can escape before having to answer that question.*

'So, Ajay.' Ki pressed his hands together. 'You've been with us long enough to know things are a bit unstable around here.'

'Unstable?' Marta snapped. 'We're falling apart, Ki.'

'Alright, Marta.' Ki remained casual but Ajay noticed he was picking the edge of his nails anxiously. 'I know Haro told you what *really* happened on Liberation Day.'

'That killing civilians wasn't your plan? Yeah, he told me that.' Ajay spoke bluntly.

'Well, it won't happen again.' Ki scratched his head, the sunlight bouncing off his balder patches.

'It won't?'

'None of the sickos made it back.' Marta spoke again, standing and rocking on the tips of her toes, arms crossed against her green vest. Ajay remembered the way Haro spoke about the breakout group who planned the civilian attack, rather than only infiltrating Command. He'd held the same tone as Marta; angered and disgusted.

'But . . . you still have a plan to get at Command,' Ajay commented, albeit hesitantly. 'How do you know that in the heat of whatever it is you're planning to do, innocent people won't get hurt?'

'You think you're so noble, eh?' Marta's words cut. 'We all know what you did to your friend.'

Ajay fell quiet, not taking her point lightly, clutching the tin of peaches. *What would Ace do here?*

'Let's have some hush.' Ki pressed a hand to his chest again, as if he was finding it hard to breathe. 'We don't want to harm civilians – they're victims like the rest of us, they just don't see it yet. You've seen enough of us to know we're not bad people.'

Ajay shrugged his shoulders faintly, not sure how to answer. He wanted to wait this out, see what information he could gather.

'The Moths who are managing to withstand Command's interrogations can help us move forward, but the technical side of things has to be done from here.'

Not changing his expression as he held Ki's eyes, deadpan and serious, Ajay continued to listen.

'From what we've heard from our trusted sources,' Ki glanced at Callum, who was staring into his lap, playing with his red headband. 'You could be very useful to us, Ajay.' Ki stood and stretched out his back. 'You see, our

Watch manipulation abilities have hit a dead end. Our previous asset is being . . .' Ki paused. 'Non-compliant.'

'The guy's an idiot,' Maze interrupted, hot-tempered again, looking at Ajay with hunting eyes.

'Regardless. We need someone with your understanding.' Ki turned back to Ajay after glaring at Maze. 'And given what you've been through . . .' He opened his arms as if sympathetic. 'I might be able to build up broken parts and stolen things, helping us stay warm and invisible, but I am not someone who can do what you can do.'

Ajay was slightly taken aback; he couldn't believe Ki's honesty. It was almost refreshing to hear someone proclaim their weaknesses so comfortably. Ignoring that thought, another replaced it. What if he *could* agree to it and somehow destroy whatever plan they had, allowing Command to find them? Yet that wouldn't work – would it? He didn't know. Did he even want to do that?

'What are you asking me to do?' Ajay glanced around the circle, wondering why Haro hadn't appeared for the meeting yet, thinking his presence would be comforting.

'Hack Watches,' Maze grunted. 'That's all you're good for, isn't it?'

'Shut it, Maze.' Callum pulled his headband back onto his head, leaving Ajay in disbelief that he'd defended him. 'That doesn't get us anywhere.'

'Callum's right. Our squabbles have caused enough problems.' Ki sat down again, crossing his legs.

'What if I say no?' Ajay stuttered as silence filled the circle, and he noticed an unsettling smile growing across Maze's face.

'You can't say no,' Marta held a sinister desperation in her tone.

'Sounds like the other guy did,' Ajay threw back. A quietness fell again, the noise of the nearby camp cutting through the trees.

'He wouldn't have if he'd stuck around,' Marta breathed out laboriously.

'It's perfectly natural for you to hate us,' Ki cut in, stretching his long skinny legs out across the dirt. 'We want you to help us *willingly*.'

'But that doesn't mean you won't force me to?'

'You *are* clever,' Maze scoffed, pieces of fruit stuck in the triangles between his ugly teeth.

'Stop it!' Ki grew agitated, bending his fingers into fists. 'Look, Ajay.' His eyes widened, as if he'd been injected with a strong drug. 'We are not the bad guys here.' He gestured with his arms, widely. 'You know first-hand what it's like to be labelled Unworthy, through no fault of your own. You were born into it.'

'You hated it so much you forced your way out of it.' Callum leant forward. *So that's what you think? You think you can convince me?*

'The system isn't the problem. It was all me.' Ajay was trying to be brave but his heart was pounding, he was almost expecting his non-existent Watch to tell him so. The heat of the sun was suffocating. He wasn't interested in their revenge regime, all he wanted was to get out, of course to help his family, but also just to be free from them. Or try to be. He felt as if they were getting their talons into him, digging deeper and deeper. *Don't let them mould you.*

'How can you say that?' Marta barked, looking like she was going to ring his neck. 'You don't know what people have been through.'

'At least hear us out some more. We can show you the equipment and let you know our plan. Step by step.' Ki had stood again, getting closer, inviting Ajay to stand too.

There was a moment of connection; a confusing moment where behind the bloodshot eyes, Ajay could see some sincerity. He didn't want to see it, he didn't want to feel it. It was a similar way with Charlene and Haro. His growing attachment to them was becoming a festering problem. How could he develop feelings for the group who kidnapped him and were now trying to force him to be one of them? Yet he wasn't in a position to say no. There was nothing he could gain by it, but listening might give him something he could use. *Wouldn't it?*

He subtly nodded his head, watching as Maze and Marta stood waiting behind Ki.

'Thank you.' Ki sighed in relief. 'Anything you might need, if you do decide to help us, Callum can find it when he next goes out. When is it, Callum?' Ki sounded suddenly urgent.

'Friday.' Callum, standing up, brushed dust off himself.

'Six days? No, it has to be sooner.' Ki was loud, snapping like a kid snatching another's toy. 'We . . . are running out of time.'

'That's when a Moth is next on.' Callum didn't seem fazed. 'It's Friday.'

Ajay felt simultaneously elated and disappointed. Excited, because he knew when Callum would next be getting a plane. *That's my chance, but six more days here?* He could grow more attached and, worse still, they could succeed in convincing him. *They could never. Could they?*

Ki pressed his twig-like fingers into his forehead, breathing deeply before smiling and coughing again. *He does that a lot.*

'OK.' He paused. 'We'll have to manage. Ajay, this way . . .' He willed Ajay to follow him, scratching his chest through the Command-absent hole. Ajay didn't think there was any harm in seeing what they had and how he could use it. He still held the tin of peaches in his sweating hand, wishing his climbing suit had pockets.

As he moved to follow Ki, they were all disturbed by a rustling through the trees and Haro emerged, eyes ablaze. *Took you long enough.*

'The drop-off is here.' He sounded panicked, his left bicep bulging as he balanced against a tree trunk. 'There's not enough. People are losing their minds.'

'Karle, come on, love, food will be on the table.'

That's what Grandma usually said when he was stalling after school. She was probably wearing a loose, knee-length dress and her tatty, worn-out sandals. Ajay was most likely playing with the Drainies. That's what he called them. The imaginary creatures that lived in the dysfunctional storm drains along the Side high street; he gave them wide eyes, sharp teeth and fluffy blue fur.

Grandma would have pulled him away with her free arm, the other carrying Tara. *Where is she? Dad said she went a while ago. Went where?* The thought came and went as Ajay arrived at the drop-off with Haro and the others.

Grandma had never sounded rushed walking him home; he didn't know if that was deliberate or not, but she'd always had time for him and his many questions. He'd enjoyed school, no way near as much as he would a City Education Centre, better resourced and managed, but he wasn't a City kid. Instead, every day he'd throw questions at her, probably ones his inadequate teachers had failed to answer. One day it was about the Revolution and he wanted her to show him 'the holes in the walls'.

She took him down a street and found a plain wall on the side of a small shop. Ajay examined hole after hole, sporadically dancing in some sort of pattern across the wall. Ajay remembered saying he thought it looked like a Felkar, a wild animal that hadn't been seen for years. He had felt scared as they talked about the holes and how they came from guns and how he wouldn't know how to use a gun if someone shot at him. That's when Grandma said he wouldn't have to, but he continued thinking a lot about the Revolution and its violence. Before that, he'd only assumed it was all hair-pulling and name-calling. Much like the playground squabble he was watching right now.

Ajay stood and watched as suits were torn, punches flew and people ran away with products they'd pinched from upturned crates. Ki sent Maze to break people up while he took the rest of the committee elsewhere, leaving Ajay behind to watch chaos ensue.

CHAPTER
TWENTY-THREE

What's going on? Where are the distributors? Children were crying as others screamed for the fighters to stop. A man scuttled past Ajay, clinging to a loaf of bread.

'Hey.' Ajay addressed him. 'What's going on?'

'They brought nothing.' He justified himself, pulling the bread closer to his chest before quickly running away.

Ajay followed his white T-shirt through the trees before turning back to the fight. Watching it, Ajay wasn't sure how he should feel. Should he help? Or could he laugh? Because it was kind of funny, watching these lunatics destroy each other over a few tins of fermented peas and apples that don't travel well. That's when he spotted Charlene's head towering over all the others, her face grimacing with her struggle. He groaned. *Should I get involved now?* He hovered at the edge of the scuffling circle.

'Charlene!' he said over the scramble. 'What are you doing?'

Charlene flicked her head, her hair covering the man behind her, who escaped with something Ajay couldn't see.

'What does it look like I'm doing? Trying to get my share!'

What share? That logic had clearly long gone, the distributors were nowhere to be seen and there wasn't enough to go around. The tussle he was watching was not what his grandma, school, the City and the whole of society had taught him about 'sharing'.

'Get off that!' a gruff voice demanded.

Ajay turned to see Maze pummeling another man to the ground, spitting at him while holding a crate of tinned beans. So much for Ki sending Maze to break up the fight. Trying to make sense of it, Ajay scraped his black hair back, feeling the grease between his fingers. He turned as he heard a ripping sound, created by the destruction of a man's T-shirt as a woman clawed at him.

She screamed through the trees as he got away. 'You owe me.' Ajay doubted the man could hear her, having already disappeared.

Collecting herself and wiping her nose, she saw Ajay. 'What are you looking at?'

Ajay shook his head and walked away, still fringing the action. He spotted a small girl being pulled into a pit as two women were squabbling over a packet of crisps. It was the brand Ace liked. The thought sat heavily on his chest, but the disorder around him didn't let it take hold.

Isn't anyone going to stop this? Maybe he should get in there. He *was* starving; he felt the hollow space in his stomach. If he was going to escape, he'd need the energy. Spotting a small man coming away with a few ready meals, Ajay envisioned himself tackling him to the ground. It would be easy. Simple. One quick swipe and those meals would be his. Then his body would be prepared for what he was about to do. They'd made the decision that Callum was heading out on Friday. That would be his window. If he was stealthy enough, he could follow them through the forest and jump onto the plane without them realising. As he kept his eye on the chaos, he knew he was missing his opportunity. Yet staring down at the tin of peaches in his hand, given to him by Ki, a strange sensation within him felt content: not having the desire for more, even though his stomach told him he needed it. The man was gone with the ready meals and so was everything else, the brawl starting to disperse and the toxicity hanging in the air.

Astonished at the behaviour, Ajay wandered back towards his sleeping spot, his thoughts turning back to Ki. Ajay was, of course, intrigued by this 'equipment' in the pit and the opportunity to hear their plan. If he left, was he running away from his chance to stop them? There was also something about Ki. Despite his unpleasant appearance and constant coughing, he was a genius; Ajay had now seen the generators that collected energy from the lightning and converted it into electricity. Ki had built that from broken parts. And their communication devices, the suits and the Alert Bands. It was incredible. Yet, they needed *him* to hack into something? It felt odd to Ajay that Ki couldn't figure it out. Maybe they didn't have time for any second chances, no opportunity to develop new expertise, or perhaps it was a particularly sophisticated plan – so surely this meant Ajay had the upper hand? *Can I use that? I could force them to get me to Grandma if I help them?*

He let the concept linger as he found Charlene and Haro sitting on the log, playing with their culinary prizes.

Charlene's hair was frizzy and untamed, like she'd been dragged through the trees.

'What was all that about?' Ajay breathed and stumbled back towards them.

'There wasn't enough food.' Charlene yanked at her hair, wearing a subtle smirk. 'Laz lost complete control.' Ajay tried to remember who Laz was; his intuition told him she was a distributor and probably someone he had met. He'd tried hard not to care or remember.

'Command must be finding more Moths than we thought.' Haro prized open a tin of peaches, reminding Ajay that he could eat his. 'It's getting more urgent.' He looked at Ajay intentionally as peaches slipped between his lips.

'Did you come away with anything?' Charlene caught Ajay in thought.

'Yeah . . .' Ajay shook his peaches at her.

'Is that it? I could spare you a few tins, if you like. You can owe me some next time.'

'If there is a next time.' Haro slurped juice from the tin and Charlene glanced at him dismissively.

'Sure.' Ajay took a couple of tins from Charlene, distracted. If he negotiated for Grandma's protection and assisted in their plan, would that mean he'd joined them? Is that what he wanted? He looked at Charlene and then down at the tins: pineapple rings and rice pudding. Why weren't they all like her? If he didn't help, wasn't he letting her down?

This is why I need to get out of here. I can't get attached. It all feels unbearably wrong.

'Oh, also . . .' Charlene grabbed something from behind her. 'I managed to nab one of these for you. It's a manual, unfortunately.' She shrugged her shoulders and offered him a toothbrush.

At least my breath will smell better for my escape, because I've got to go, haven't I?

CHAPTER
TWENTY-FOUR

Genni struggled with Ajay's grandma up the stairs, allowing her to take the steps first.

In the back of Genni's mind was the incessant need to leave. It had all gone too far. Her irrational emotional attachment to Ajay had screwed her up to the point of sacrificing merit, and now she was having a tour of his house? The hatred, the anger, the love and desire for him were all weaving themselves into a cardigan of confusion she couldn't help but wear. Even when she'd been high on that knock-off *SkipSleep*, close to death, her emotions hadn't been so frayed. She couldn't decide which desire was stronger; the one to run away, or the strange pull of knowing more about Ajay's childhood.

After the wrestle up the stairs, both Genni and Ajay's grandma breathed heavily, hobbling towards the door straight ahead. His grandma gently pushed it open, her swollen fingers grazing the peeling letter 'K' on its front. Genni read the name that still felt alien to her, quickly turning her head as if it wasn't there. The bedroom was a box; grey, sweaty walls, mostly plain apart from two ripped, falling posters, one for the Watch game *DroneDefenders*, the other so faded its image was distorted. Other than that, the room housed a wardrobe with a broken door, a mirror shrouded in enough dust that its function was redundant; a low bed with a dirty mattress and, in the far corner, a crooked desk. It was also dusty, except for some cleaner outlines like something had been taken from it recently.

The two of them stood in the cesspit for a few minutes and Genni had nothing to say. She cursed herself. What was she expecting to find? A magical place revealing the *true* Ajay that gave her the closure she wanted? Letters stuffed in a drawer somewhere that revealed his undying love for her and how he never wanted to hurt her? That was the moment Genni came to some sort of acceptance.

This wasn't Ajay's room; it was Karle's.

Looking back at the door, tears trickling from her eyes like drops of paint, she saw the name in bright red stickers, surrounded by smaller stickers of drones and hover vehicles. Ajay Ambers wasn't a real person. It was like what Lanie had taught her about novels all those years ago. Ajay was always a story that Karle Blythefen wrote for himself, and unfortunately for Genni, she was a protagonist, entangled in the toxicity of the plot.

His grandma's voice cut through and Genni wiped her eyes discreetly.

'Keli was right, there isn't much to look at.' His grandma sighed, pulling on Genni's arm, lowering herself to the bed. The springs bounced and squeaked as the mattress took her weight. 'He'd spend hours in here, tapping away in the corner, gazing over that skyline.' She sighed again, tilting her head towards the window.

'Were you angry when he left?' Genni didn't move.

'I could have been, but that wouldn't have helped anything. He had already made his decision.' His grandma coughed, her chest squeaking. 'His father, on the other hand . . .' She shook her head and laughed subtly. 'It took him a bit longer.'

Genni thought briefly of Ajay's father; tall with handsome eyes behind those broken glasses. He spoke in the same way Ajay did, with a sort of charming gravitas that drew people to him. Genni heard it even in the few words he'd spoken earlier, before he left.

'Does he work somewhere?' Genni asked, feeling more comfortable and lightly touching the bottom of the Watch game poster, flattening down its edge to the wall. The graphic drawing was intricately detailed, though she would have made the drones a darker shade of grey to make them more ominous.

'He does maintenance on the railway, mainly. And some community work.' Ajay's grandma seemed to be watching Genni intently, her eyes soft. 'What does your father do?'

'He's a businessman. Boris Mansald?'

'Not sure I know the name.'

Genni smiled. She couldn't believe how overwhelmingly great it felt to meet someone who didn't know who her father was. It was like a key to her prison; no need to meet some sort of expectation, maintaining a reputation created for her before she was even born. The liberation felt uncomfortable but nice. Really nice. Her thoughts turned back to Ajay's father and his mother; her hard work in the kitchen could still be heard through the clattering of pots travelling up the stairs. *They are hard workers. That doesn't make any sense.*

'I think I want to go back downstairs, now,' Genni stuttered, knowing her discomfort wasn't a secret as his grandma looked at her understandingly, her haggard skin brighter as the setting sun illuminated the room through the window. Genni didn't want to go downstairs; she wanted to get out but couldn't upset a woman who was clearly very kindhearted and trying to connect with her in some way. The place suddenly felt oppressive, like she was being pulled into some trap hole. It wasn't the real Side, not the one she believed it to be. The selfish one where they did no good for wider society, where they didn't believe that progress was strength. Yet why were they working so hard? They must be striving towards progress of some kind.

Helping his grandma back down the stairs seemed harder than going up. Genni felt exhausted; she looked at her Watch with her spare hand, multitasking while keeping her balance, both she and Ajay's grandma clomping onto each step. She'd go. *Get back home, have a boost, as realistically, there's no time for sleep.* There was the promotion to think about. She couldn't be seen slacking or she'd lose everything she'd worked for. The last six hours had been a write-off because of Ajay and his games, and Genni decided she would have to grieve silently. Not talking about it, not labouring anyone else with her problems, and she would work harder to get over him. There was no point in ruining her own life because he didn't play by the rules. In thinking about this, she grew angrier with herself. It was so stupid coming out here for some sort of answer when she could be strong enough to deal with it alone.

Her eyes moved towards the wall, and it took over her thoughts as she spotted something hanging on it, slanted in a frame. A beautiful, fantastical painting. Genni wasn't sure what it was; a mesh of bright, moving colours. It was so abstract, dark blue became light blue, interweaved with whites and yellows. Was it supposed to be a flower? A vivid representation of life in all its messiness and chaos, yet from it something beautiful could be born?

Genni couldn't help it.

'What is that?' She was eager for the answer.

'That?' His grandma asked, breathing hard, struggling to lift her head at the bottom of the stairs. 'Oh, that's a painting Karle . . . sorry,' she paused, '*Ajay* and Tara did together as kids. It's supposed to be The Guide.'

Genni slumped her shoulders, her disappointment not going unnoticed.

'Sorry, love.' His grandma laughed, presumably understanding that Genni had stupidly misrecgonised the children's painting for something more creditworthy. 'Do you paint?'

'Yes,' Genni nodded. 'I do it to relax.' *You fool. What are you saying? You already know the majority of people condemn you for it.*

'Wonderful.' His Grandma looked delighted. 'I'm surprised you have the time. Accomplished girl like you.'

'I don't, really. I mean . . .' Genni couldn't shake the instinctive embarrassment. 'I try to get merit from it.' *Who am I trying to impress? I'm above her.*

Genni fell silent, trying to avoid his grandma's eyes. At first, Genni thought the way she was looking at her was creepy, until she saw some compassion there, as if his grandma was looking into her very being, trying to figure her out in a way that could help.

'OK, Mum. You really need to get some rest now.' Ajay's mother bounded in from the kitchen, her apron covered in flour.

'Yes, OK. A little lie down wouldn't hurt.' His grandma looked back to the stairs, as if they were a mountain. Genni felt guilty for bringing her back down, not even considering that she might have wanted to stay up there. It was time to go. It was a natural departure point. Besides, two full days of no merit would mean Command could check up on her, and with the new precautions, question her about where she'd been, and that would not be good. She could easily say her goodbyes and get back to her life. She looked at her Watch and turned her notifications back on with an unmediated urge.

No merit points have been added to your merit score in six hours, two minutes and twenty-two seconds. Is it time to do something of worth?

Thirteen missed video calls – Mafi, Angie, Dad, Blake

Twenty-six unread messages.

She looked at the first message.

Pearl: *Gen, I can't believe what's come out now. I'm so sorry, hun, he will pay for what he's done to all of us.*

Genni assumed she was referring to the announcement about Ajay's facilitation of the attack and his involvement with the Rogue. She hadn't pondered on it much, what with the distraction of coming here, and it was only another string in his rope of lies. She remembered Ajay's reaction to the attack; the fear and shock in his eyes as he held her just before the bombs went off, and the sudden way he caved into himself in the aftermath.

Why would he react like that if he was part of it? Is Command lying? Why would they do that?

I don't want to think about it. Or face any of it. It's following me forever, isn't it?

She couldn't just silently grieve. In that moment, she realised it wasn't as simple as just ignoring it. It would be impossible to go on with life without facing her reality. Her family, her friends *and society* wouldn't let her. She'd have to mourn for Ace, grieve the life she expected to have with Ajay, and embrace the embarrassment he'd caused her. Was she ready for that? Could she cope? The job she *could* have was hanging in the balance, but to have that, she needed time and space to heal. The City didn't allow her that. *Maybe this place can. Just one night and then back tomorrow, first thing in the morning. That's plenty of time to avoid a merit check.*

'Can I stay here tonight?' Genni was panicked, her voice uneven with her breathing, her heart longing to rip the Watch from her wrist and store it somewhere dark and undealt with. Both women turned back to look at her with the same concerned eyes.

'Just . . .' Genni paused, not knowing how to word it. 'If you wouldn't mind.'

CHAPTER
TWENTY-FIVE

There were times when Rod wondered if his job was good for his health. Taking a deep puff from his *SkipSleep Pro*, cradling his fingers around the device's cylindrical tube casing, he tried to stop his anger controlling him. It had served him badly in the past. Yet other people's incompetence was not *his* problem.

As he let the vapour fall over him and he listened to the smooth, mechanical clicking of the elevator, he struggled to understand how he was going to talk to the Hevas family without raising his voice. This whole thing was tedious. Rod knew how things should be done. Let him get the suckers, bring them back, have them killed, and in this case, let the public know who they were. Simple. So why all this treading lightly?

His mind stood strong in that opinion, yet with his body tense, watching the digital numbers flicker higher on the elevator screen, he condemned himself for feeling nervous. They might be at the top, but they're only keeping the seats warm for people like him. *Don't show any weakness, clever people can smell it.* His father's words rang around the tight space of the elevator shaft. Rod closed his eyes, slipped his *SkipSleep Pro* into his pocket and started picking at his nail cuticles. *I can't let them smell it.*

The doors slid open to the Dome at the top of Command, sunlight hitting Rod as he stepped out into the large room with its familiar panoramic view. The artificial sky of the Quarters swept across the majestic buildings and small mountains; residents' homes and the blue spots of their swimming pools were sporadically dotted within the peaks and troughs. Rod strode through, his hands calmly in his pockets, his gaze on Jamal Hevas, who stood at the far end of the room holding a glass of bubbling liquid in his right hand. It had been years since Rod had seen him, and as he approached, he noticed the ageing of his skin underneath his thoughtful eyes; it also felt dry as Rod shook his hand.

'A drink?' Jamal's voice was strained and resistant.

'No.' Rod paused, not wanting to spend any longer here than necessary. Not with work to be done. Though begrudgingly, he remembered his manners. 'Thank you.'

Rod stood silently with Jamal, both of them staring out towards the Gate, seeing the rest of the City through the translucent security roof. The televised ball of the Social Sphere and black dots in the sky were distorted, like a dirty brush had smudged over them with its bristles.

Jamal sighed lethargically. 'How's your father? It's been a while since I last connected with him.'

He sipped his drink slowly, grunting as he swallowed. Rod didn't take Jamal as one of those people who needed to fill silence. With his mind and influence in the development of Tulo's robotics, Jamal should be someone intimidating. The kind of man people idolised. Yet all

Rod saw was timidity. Maybe it was a learned behaviour because he was always in the shadow of his wife.

'He's well. They recently moved.' Rod pointed to the west while growing agitated. He'd come for a reason. *Where is she?*

'Further up in the mountains?' Jamal asked.

Rod confirmed with a slow nod of the head. He watched as Jamal looked awkwardly into his glass, swirling it in a clockwise motion.

'I wonder how his business will fare, given the circumstances. Hospitality has taken a hit.' Jamal's eyes held a sadness. 'It's hard to remember life before all this.'

Rod agreed as they both watched a drone swoop past the window and fly directly over the Glorified walls, the roof opening up in a glittering hole, allowing it to pass through to the glazed City. Rod's irritation intensified, feeling the top of his mouth starting to itch.

'Arneld is having a house built too.' Jamal gestured towards the east side of the Quarters. 'Should be done in a few weeks. Four floors.'

'My parents' is five.' Rod sighed quietly. There wasn't the smallest bone in his body that cared about Arneld Hevas' ventures into crafting a Worthy-looking life for himself. There was too much bad press in his history to rectify that, no matter what number was on his wrist. The family had done their best to cover it all up, especially by encouraging him to be the face of 'making Tulo safe again'. Rod wondered if Jamal's relationship with his son was as taut as Genni's with their father. Surely it would be. He was arguably a bigger screw-up than her, what with all the drinking, overeating and sleeping he used to do.

239

To Rod's relief, the air was filled with the swift, repetitive tapping of *her* heels. It was a quickening rainfall pattering against glass, getting closer, like an oncoming storm, until it was on top of them. Rod breathed and spun around anxiously to welcome her. He'd heard a lot about this woman from his father.

'She's one to watch, that Esabel,' he would say. There was only one occasion, as a boy, when Rod had seen her up close. From the balcony of their grand staircase, gazing down at the Glorified in their finery while he was supposed to be in bed. She was much younger then, less aged in the eyes, and had more of a curve to her body. The woman strangely strutting towards him, her scrawny limbs drowning in a grey trouser suit, had a concerned expression painted across her synthetically even face.

Reaching them, she placed a hand on her husband's arm, politely but firmly pushing him to the side. Her eyes moved to Rod's, wide and intense, examining him, surely close enough to smell the sweat on his face. It wasn't a look he'd want to see on a dark night. *What have I done to deserve that?* He considered stepping backwards to protect his vulnerability before her eyes relaxed, shimmering with their artificial blueness.

'A hat. Ha.' She clapped her hands together. 'Yes, that's it. A hat.'

'A what?' Rod's throat was dry with his insecurity.

'Ever since I walked into this room, I thought to myself: what is that man missing?' Esabel Hevas sighed, beaming out the window, her black hair tied tightly back against her small head. 'It's a hat. You need a hat.'

She turned back to look at Rod. He was distracted by Jamal placing his glass down on a table, the chink of the contact stark and startling. Rod looked at the glass, placed down without a coaster.

'Well?' Esabel's insistent tone flicked his head back to hers.

'Erm . . .' Rod swallowed, gathering himself back up to his standard. 'I don't spend much time out, so—'

'Forget the hat.' Esabel twirled her neck around until it clicked, highlighting the protrusion of her collarbones. She sighed, shaking her head, giving Rod an eye that wasn't reassuring. 'I hear you've been an excellent contributor in the last few years, Rod. Protecting the constitution diligently. I commend you for it.' She didn't stop to give Rod a chance to thank her for her compliments. 'We've been informed of some inappropriate behaviour on your part and I've had a little look here at your previous behaviour on the job.' Esabel was swiping through case files on her Watch, pictures of Side residents reflecting off her eyes. 'I can see that your bending of the rules may have added to your success in the past.'

Too right. I get the job done.

'Yet in this case, we cannot accept it. It needs to be dealt with carefully. What that clever boy managed to do *on his own* can never be known by the general public. While you have found this evidence that Ambers had consistent contact with his family, it is not enough for you to go in there. Not this time. It would bring unwanted attention towards Ambers' true lineage and how he really ended up in the City. As you seem to have an unstable, emotional affiliation towards this particular case, which I can only assume is due to the familial connection of your sister, we have come to the decision that you are off this case with immediate effect.'

Rod was speechless, expletives running around his head. His forehead felt tight, as if the skin was going to crack.

Esabel sighed too joyfully, swinging her meatless arms at her sides. 'Well, good to get that done. You haven't got a drink. Shall we have one?'

'Excuse me?' Rod stared hard. *You foul woman.*

The blue in her eyes suddenly turned icy cold.

'Don't make this hard for yourself,' Esabel said, causing Rod's anger to simmer further.

'We can't have anything else fuelling the public's unrest, Rod. You understand?' Jamal came and stood closer to his wife, his bald head towering above her tiny frame.

'This has nothing to do with Genni. It's been my job for years.' Rod ground his teeth, hands clenched.

'Oh, for Tulo's sake, Roderick. We're not firing you.' Esabel shook her head playfully. 'Once all this nonsense with the Rogue is over, you can go back to what you're good at. We just need to prioritise.'

'What, like not just blowing up the bas—'

'Come on, now. We're not here to play games with each other.' Esabel gave him a disappointed, motherly look and tutted. 'I'm being honest with you. There's other cases you've been assigned to, making sure the City is safe *inside* its walls.' She smiled irrefutably.

Before Rod could respond, his head fogging over like a mirror in a shower room, Esabel's heels were tapping again, strutting their way out of the Dome with a conclusive energy.

'Tell your father I'll give him a call sometime.' Jamal retrieved his glass and lifted it at Rod. It didn't take him long to join his wife and disappear from the room. Rod was left simultaneously numb and livid, surrounded by a view he loved, but all he wanted to do was tear through the glass.

CHAPTER
TWENTY-SIX

It was impossible to sleep with so little noise outside. There was no rushing feet or meritful chatter; no beeps, no pings, nothing. Genni stared, wired, at the ceiling, distracted by the silence. Whenever she slept, she always fell into the comfort of a City still awake. Here, there was nothing but a wasteful night passing by. Just stillness. So still that Genni was afraid to close her eyes and leave herself vulnerable.

Sitting up, she breathed through the night's humidity and touched the bedside lamp that pathetically flickered out into Ajay's childhood bedroom. *What was I thinking, asking to stay here, in the Side?*

What was that?

She flinched at the window, hearing someone scuttle past the house. *Why does something so normal feel so strange?* Wanting a distraction, Genni stood and wandered over to the desk at the back of the room and drew her name in its dust. She stared at it, her name scribed upon an Unworthy table. *It doesn't belong there.* Instinctively she swished her hands across it, the dust particles sticking to her fingers; she rushed to rub them off. That was when she noticed the desk drawer, slightly open, tempting her to pull at the bobble handle, which fell off in her hand. *Such junk.* Placing the handle on the desk, she hoisted the drawer out and had a look inside. There wasn't much there: a few sheets of paper with scrawls of equations across them, a worn ball of string, a pair of scissors, a few expired packets of Tulo Caramels, each with a note saying 'Tara, keep off!', and at the back, a small tablet device Genni didn't recognise. Ignoring the rest of the drawer, she flipped it over in her hands. It was flat, the screen a bit bigger than her Watch face, with a hole at one end. *What is this?*

Genni tapped at it, intrigued and curious, and controls for a music player appeared alongside graphics and song titles. A voice came from it, quiet and slightly stuttered.

'Please select a track.'

Oh, I know what this is. It's one of those older music devices, player, thing-ummy-bobs. I've seen them in Educational Movies about Watch feature development. It must be old.

She tossed it over in her hands again and returned to sitting on the bed, flicking through the songs and artists. There was nothing she recognised. No Tulip Twins, no Flying High, no Peti Yuni, and they were some of the most popular artists ever. Inquisitively, she continued looking at the different titles, feeling like she was accessing some forbidden material or unheard archive, fearful to press play. Until she got over herself and selected a track. It was called 'Never-ending Sand'.

Two surprises came. The first, the lack of any statistics, nothing about the percentage of people who found it inspiring; and the second, the way it started. It was really slow-paced, a melancholy tune on a piano that didn't feel like it would encourage anyone to concentrate and be their most effective self. It was nice to listen to; rhythmic, relaxing but not motivating so Genni knew it would have a low percentage of promoters back home. *Never a merit-making listen.* Once she listened to the lyrics, she was even more astounded.

> *When everything surrounds me,*
> *The status and numbers fail me,*
> *Life is a dry and barren land,*
> *But you're the rainfall,*
> *In the never-ending sand.*

It was almost *depressing* but honest. It made her reflect; who is the rainfall in the sand? Was this person thanking someone, or hoping for someone? The feelings they described resonated with Genni unlike any piece of music she'd heard. It would definitely not motivate her to do better work, but did cause her to take a breath and spend time thinking about it. Ajay once listened to this? Maybe he didn't, but it was obviously produced for an audience, one that was willing to listen to something meritless. Genni couldn't figure out if that was liberating or terrifying. It was the same question she held over the entire place. Were these people trapped or free?

The song played on, and Genni started to lose its words as her shoulders slumped and pulled her body down, and she drifted off into sleep.

It was a dark place. Dark walls, dark furniture, boarded-up windows with a tiny speck of light glinting through. Then there was him. His body got bigger, skyscraping over her until she felt like she was falling.

'I hate you!' Genni screamed, striking her hand across his perfect smile. Her nails were shards of glass but his skin didn't cut and then someone else took his place.

'I hate you too!' The words turned into daggers flying from her mouth straight towards his face. His response fired golden arrows back at her, his calligraphic initials on their tips. They hit, it hurt. Hatred consumed everything. Genni roared at him, then her, at them, at her, then him. Only to feel her own skin cutting, the people still changing and arriving, until the light in the window grew. It got bigger and brighter, blinding Genni and extinguishing her now flaming mouth.

She woke up crying; trying to catch a breath she left in the dream. Panting, she put her hands to her face. *Is this my life now? This poison seeping through everything, whether I'm awake or asleep?*

Sitting up, she stared down at the music player on the floor and felt bitter. *I don't deserve this. It's others who have let me down.* She knew she wasn't blameless, but as she felt the rough texture of the old, inadequate mattress on her fingertips, she still found it hard to believe where she was, physically and mentally. *How am I in the Side right now? Out of choice? Why can't these feelings go away? How can they? Will they ever?*

Letting the bed bounce on its springs, she wiped the tears off her rough, unmoisturised face. Lethargically, she tried to stretch and followed a breathing technique she remembered from her meditation class subscription. *Ten sharp breaths out of the nose, followed by three repetitions of deeper breathing.*

It worked to make her feel calmer, but her mind was still racing. *There's nothing I can do to change this. I'm stuck here. Constantly running, always circling, I'll never get over it. What will happen to my score? What will happen to my job? My friends? Will I still be Worthy?*

To avoid screaming, Genni threw her trousers on and crept downstairs in search for any distraction. It was hard to find. The house was dark. Genni had never known a building to be so engulfed by night: no illuminations from outside, no billboards, drone lights, hover vehicle lights, sparkling windows, or street solar lights. Nothing. The only thing Genni could see as she reached the landing window was another advertisement for Purification. 'I love being my most effective self', read the headline, next to a lad wearing a blue suit, holding up his Watch proudly with a high merit score on its screen.

'Apply for Purification.'

I still don't understand why you wouldn't.

Over dinner, the topic seemed to come up.

'You know the tall teacher, her name escapes me . . .' Ajay's father was holding his glass at the other side of the table.

'Viktoria.' Ajay's mother blew at the steaming vegetables on her fork before sending them into her mouth.

'Yes, Viktoria. She's another one going.'

'Oh, really? OK.' His mother nodded her head as Genni moved the potatoes around her plate, grateful for the food, however bland. 'Shame to lose her.'

His father grunted. 'I think she might work with Reha and the others.'

'Really?' His mother swallowed her food. 'I thought her family weren't followers.'

'They aren't, but she is. Reha has her number, anyway.' Just then, his father seemed to catch himself, as if he'd forgotten Genni was there and the subject of conversation wasn't appropriate. He looked at her and smiled, drinking awkwardly.

'I'll go and check on your mum. See if she's ready for some dinner.'

His mother looked at her wrist. 'Good idea, before she sleeps.'

Other than those words, the vegetable roast had mostly been enjoyed in silence. Not an awkward silence, but an accepting, relaxing one. Genni didn't think much about what they'd said, still too distracted by everything else, but it was intriguing that the teacher didn't come from a Guide-following family. She had assumed all Side residents carried the ideology, that's what the City suggested anyway. Genni realised now how that would be too simple; after all, they were all people, just as complicated as each other. *But, if they don't follow it, why don't they just leave? Maybe they don't want to. But why?*

Arriving downstairs, barely able to see her hands in front of her face, Genni briefly glanced up the stairs, conscious of making any noise. She walked towards the kitchen, thinking about a glass of water. Though it would be warm from the tap, it might help the headache she felt brewing. Grimacing as the floorboards creaked beneath her bare feet, she tiptoed down the hall and stopped at the open door to the front room, a bright glow coming from within. Not being able to help her curiosity, Genni faintly pushed on the door, letting it fall open silently. There was no one in there, only a medium-sized room, the walls covered with shelves holding fallen ornaments and dry flowers. Genni followed the glow from a desk in the middle of the room, dressed in large pieces of paper, strewn about carelessly. She wondered if she needed to worry about her bare feet. If the rest of the room was anything to go by, she doubted the floor had been properly cleaned. Ignoring her judgements, she stepped lightly to find the glow was a digital photo frame.

Genni couldn't help it. She had to judge them here. It was like a shameful *Personi* feed of time-wasters. There were pictures of babies, groups of friends, laughing, hugging, out on the street, playing team sports; Ajay's father giving a struggling piggyback to another man his age; Ajay's parents dancing in the kitchen; one of his grandma tying his sister's hair into small, black pigtails. Then one of . . . Genni paused hesitantly at the thought of the name . . . there was one of *Karle* and another boy, standing together on top of a sand hill, arms thrown up triumphantly in the air, both of them wearing magnetic smiles. The pictures rolled on and Genni couldn't stop watching it, everything about it both mesmerising and barbaric. All these people, all that time wasted, achieving nothing. Yet they looked different, almost as if they were happy. Their expressions looked like they wanted to be there, for no other reason than just each other. It wasn't for 'loves' or merit, as they weren't for the public eye but private and contained. *They're crazy.*

The pictures started to repeat themselves, Genni noticing again the one of his grandma holding a baby. Her hair was much browner and her skin more elastic, but she was staring into the camera with those same caring eyes. Ajay hadn't lied when he'd told her she was forthright. Genni had been slightly offended when she'd told her to smile a bit more, earlier that afternoon. How could she smile? She was hardly in a situation to be smiling. It was insensitive and rude. Yet Ajay always said that the woman just said what she felt. As Genni thought this, she noticed his grandma's clothes as the picture faded away into another. She was wearing what looked like nurse's scrubs, and it took her thoughts to Mila. *I've hardly seen her. I'll need to find out how it's going at the hospitals now the androids are gone. I'll do it when I get back, which has to be soon.*

Sighing, Genni noticed something to the right of the frame. An oblong box, with a sign on its surface. In the darkness, she could only make out some small lines engraved into the metal and, almost instinctively, she stroked along its edge.

She shrieked and jumped backwards, falling into the wall behind, almost knocking an ornate camel to the ground. After making sure it was stable on the shelf, she looked back at the figure of light that had sprung from the box, lighting up the whole room. It was like a faceless body, just swirling around.

'Excuse me.' A voice came from behind it, causing Genni to jump and shriek again, petrified by the sudden escalation of events.

Ajay's father stood at the other side of the desk, the light illuminating his face. 'What are you doing here?'

'I'm so . . .' Genni ran towards the door, moving past him and looking back, flustered. *Remember his grandma said he had anger problems. Be careful.*

'Sorry. I couldn't sleep and I was just . . .' Genni didn't have any words. There was no excuse for her behaviour. *What was I thinking?*

'That's OK.' His father seemed to be calm, though as he swiped the wall to turn the main light on, the way he was frowning told Genni he was suppressing some emotion. There was silence. She spun on her bare feet to leave, feeling embarrassed and vulnerable.

'Wait.' His father's eyes were insistent in the electrical light. 'Did he ever talk about me? Karle?' His father breathed deeply, and reluctantly corrected himself. 'Ajay?'

Oh, of course. All the time. He always said you were a fantastic father. Genni wanted to say that. It was the type of thing she would have said to a colleague who had submitted a bad report, or to Pearl, who needed reassurance on a recent campaign that actually made her look ten years older. But she couldn't bring herself to do it, most of all because she realised his father had probably already guessed the truth.

'No.' Genni swallowed. 'He . . . he said you were dead.'

'I see.' His father nodded, eyes down, moving forward to push the door and close Genni out graciously.

She walked away but not before pausing curiously at the new voice that came from the room. It only then occurred to her. *Was that The Guiding Light?*

CHAPTER
TWENTY-SEVEN

After experiencing the madness of the drop-off, Ajay was summoned again by Ki. He'd been staring into a patch of dirt, spitting toothpaste out onto the ground, swirling it around with sips of water from a bottle. It had been years since he'd used a handheld, manual toothbrush. *Such a time-waste.*

'Hey, Ajay. Ki said you should come and see the stuff now.' The woman from the committee whose name he'd forgotten stared at him, gun close to her chest.

Washing the toothbrush out, Ajay slipped it into his pocket and followed her back through the trees, catching a glimpse of Charlene settling in for sleep. They walked in silence until they arrived at an open pit, Callum and Ki talking at its entrance.

'She didn't pass?' Ki asked, angered.

'No, but she's the only one this week.' Callum didn't mirror Ki's initial irritation. *How was he always so nonchalant?*

'OK, we can cope with that.' Ki wiped his hand over his head before looking at Ajay. 'Ah, Ajay. Good.' He strode forward, slightly flustered, and grabbed Ajay's arm, pulling him underground into the pit.

Ajay didn't know what he was expecting. He admitted part of him wondered if he was going to be immersed in an underground, technological wonderland with winding passages, people at desks, flashing green and red lights, screens along every sand-dusted crevasse in the wall. Like it was a fully resourced, slick undercover operation. Instead, he saw very little. Four or five dusty screen ports sat lifeless on a wonky digital table, shoved against the right-hand wall of the pit, accompanied by numerous old flailing wires and a plastic box carrying a mountain of dirty, dead Watches. Of course it made sense this was all there was.

Ajay stepped forward and swiped a screen port, wiping the dust from his fingers afterwards. It sprung into life, the top of it bending over the roof of the pit. In many ways, the Liberation Day attack was a meticulously planned affair; the logistics, the Watch hacking, building up their numbers over generations. Yet, for the actual technical side of it, all they would have needed was in front of him. It was exactly what he'd used, alongside the help of Lillie on the inside.

Ki stood behind Ajay, the width of the pit not big enough for them to stand side by side.

'So, the plan,' he said as Ajay gathered up one of the dangling wires, with one eye on Ki.

'We need to create a distraction to get in and infiltrate Command.' Ki paused, his struggling breaths loud. 'Liberation Day was meant to serve as that distraction. Command always had their guard down. Yet we didn't anticipate what was *actually* happening.' Ajay saw sadness in Ki's small, hazel eyes and his voice carried a heaviness that jarred with his usually light tone.

'We're not giving up.' Ki glanced down at the box of Watches. 'So, we assume you can hack in somehow, even with the new measures in place.'

There was a cough from the entrance of the pit as Callum joined them, sitting with his legs hanging over the jump and nibbling on a Duskdrop flower. Ajay grimaced; were they even edible?

'So, you get a big group back into the City.' Ajay bent down to the box of Watches and rolled a few of them around in his hand. 'And then what?'

'We do something to pull Command's resources away. Another distraction.' Ki leant back on the wall of the pit, one of the wires getting squashed. 'And then we go in, take control and start again. Without the system and without *them*.'

'Them?' Ajay noticed how Ki's tone implied something more personal rather than collective.

'The Hevases.' Ki was blunt, his mouth straight. At first, it didn't seem like he was going to say any more as he coughed. 'And anyone else in Command who made Tulo the way it is.'

'And what about the rest of society?' Ajay asked.

'People will come round once we get in the public eye and tell our stories.' Ki stood up straighter, stretching his gaunt body. 'Your story, Ajay.'

Something about the way Ki spoke, with sincerity and compassion, pulled Ajay again. Were they right? *No.* He told himself not to get emotionally entwined. Yet playing along kept his options open. He still needed a way out of here.

'So what's the plan with the Watches? How do you propose, as you say, a distraction?' Ajay could hear the loud giggle of a child outside, making the sinister conversation feel even more unnatural.

'This is the tricky part.' Ki appeared uncomfortable. 'We have an idea and we still have materials to make explosives.' He didn't look at Ajay as he spoke, nor did Callum shift. A moment of silence festered in the pit like mould.

'You're going to do the same thing?' Ajay couldn't quite believe it. They were planning to do exactly what those who betrayed them did? He felt a sudden fear; they'd be going back again to hurt people he knew. He tried to breathe calmly to avoid an emotional trigger, dismissing the memories of the first attack. Maybe he could be the one to stop them. If he stayed. 'Why . . .' Ajay hesitated, trying to make more sense of it. 'Why do you think that doing the same thing will change anything?'

'Not quite the same thing.' Callum jumped down into the pit, his arms out as if to reassure Ajay. 'We plan to do it strategically.'

'So no civilians get hurt,' Ki cut in.

'How can you guarantee that?' Ajay blurted out.

Their lack of response indicated they couldn't. He looked around at the screens again, knowing he had to get away from the Rogue, but he couldn't leave without trying to convince them of a better way.

'Just blowing stuff up isn't going to change anything. Say you get into Command and take over. Abolish the system, what do you do with the public then? You'll end up starting a civil war.'

'Well, we're running out of time.' Ki glanced back at Callum, as if asking for support. Callum didn't say anything, only looking at Ajay considerately.

'If it's the system that's the problem, you have to show people why,' Ajay continued.

'Command is the problem,' Ki snapped as he stuttered into a coughing fit.

'But doing the same thing will only give the same result.' Ajay raised his voice over the coughing, hoping his words were working.

Please, please, don't hurt anyone else.

He stared at Ki, following his receding hairline down to his harsh stare. There was something about him that started to unnerve Ajay. Something sinister buried deep, some chain binding him to his course of revenge. And what was with all the coughing? Why was he so unwell?

'We can iron out the details, I'm sure,' Ki finally said, gasping for air and whimpering from the fit. 'Are you going to help us or not?'

Ajay needed to think this through. He couldn't leave knowing they might hurt others, but he also couldn't stay. Not having the time to process it properly, he tried to carry the conversation further. If he made sure Callum *had* to leave on a resource plane, he still had the option to escape with him.

'What about the new model they're developing? I can't imagine they will waste time in putting it through.'

'I thought you knew about that. We have intel on it.' Ki spoke with no air of concern. 'It's still in development, not public knowledge yet. But we can get information on the features and mecha—'

'It's no use to me unless I have the hardware.' Ajay didn't really have an idea whether it was or not, but it would be convincing enough to suggest his potential commitment.

'So you want one of the prototypes? I'm not sure they have a finalised version yet. Callum?' Ki looked to Callum, who was still watching Ajay.

'Yeah.' He took a moment to come round. 'Last comms said they do, though that was a while ago.'

Ki looked back at Ajay, optimistically.

'A prototype would be a start.' Ajay flicked on all the screen ports and observed the main frame, tapping at the desk.

'I understand. OK. Cal, do you think they could get one for you?'

'It's possible, given they've got time.' Callum's voice was a monotone as he pressed his headband further back through his greasy hair.

Ajay agreed but another question loomed. 'Aren't you concerned this is going to take too long? Command will be here soon. As you said, there isn't a lot of time.'

Ki seemed to consider this. 'I'm more concerned about the lack of food than Command. The Diverters seem to be working well to stall them for now.' Ki's smile fell flat. 'If the lizards carry on mating like they are, Command won't have an enemy left. It wouldn't surprise me if they already know that.'

Ajay nodded slowly. It was a tight situation and he felt thankful he'd soon have nothing to do with it. Or could he? His mind was whirring; he could negotiate a deal or even use their plan against them, maybe to strike a deal with Command, to protect Grandma, or even himself.

'You think we'll last long enough?' Ajay asked, still playing along. This was like living his old life when deceit was his primary practice. He didn't know how to feel about it. Something felt dirty.

'We should be able to manage.' Ki pushed himself off the wall as Callum moved out the way.

'Oh—' Ajay said, instinctively, his empty stomach talking. 'Why don't we eat the birds? The larger ones?'

Ki coaxed his head to the entrance, perhaps listening for the birdsong.

'The Bluebeaks?' he smiled. 'They eat the lizards, the toxins run in their blood. They used to be handy for population control but slowly, the drones are—'

'Scaring them away.' Ajay finished Ki's sentence before following him out of the pit, giving one last solemn look at it; the head of operations for the attack that ruined his life.

That night, Ajay knew he needed to make a decision.

The options had been looping in his head like the sky train around the City's rings.

Option one: help the Rogue and negotiate a deal with them for his release.

It's a feasible idea; hack into the new Watch models, to somehow create chaos and infiltrate Command. Could that be done in a peaceful way, which meant no death or injury? Probably not. For one thing, Command would not hesitate to shoot *them* down, so Ajay would still have a part to play in some sort of murder. Hadn't he done that enough already? No. Yes. Of course he had. Yet it wasn't all his fault. Was it? Maybe it wasn't. Callum said it, if he wasn't born on the Side and Command didn't punish him for something he couldn't control, he never would have hacked into the City in the first place. So, technically, *technically*, the Rogue were kind of right.

Command is to blame. Although . . . Ajay rolled over, looking up at the daylight sky. It was definitely *his* doing what happened to Ace. Yes, he'd established that. *Stop circling.* OK, so helping the Rogue was not an option. Surely? Or maybe it was.

Ajay groaned and spun back onto his other side, the consistent chirping of the birds focusing his thinking.

'Would you pack it in?' Charlene whispered next to him. 'You're worse than a child!'

Ajay flipped over again, his back to her, disgruntled at her mothering. He almost told her to put her noise-cancelling headphones in, before remembering they were on a power ration again. Things were getting dire. Malnourishment, little sleep and no electricity; it was starting to take its toll. No wonder the drop-off yesterday was so bad. It wasn't his fault he couldn't sleep. He considered putting his eye mask on, but his mind would still remain alive. If he were to help the Rogue, what did that make him? Slowly, he was rejecting the idea while still clinging on to how much simpler it would be.

Option two: escape. Follow Callum – his suspicions about the use of resource planes confirmed.

Perhaps option two was the better way. The planes couldn't land anywhere in the forest, as it was too dense, so they must stop on the border and the walk there couldn't be far. So, he'd only have to follow Callum and it would be at night so he could easily be discreet enough. What about the Spotters at the perimeter? On their lookout for drones, they might raise an eyebrow at another body sneaking through the trees. Then again, he could walk close enough to Callum to make it appear as if they're together.

Ajay closed his eyes and shook his head, amused at his rambling mind. *You fool.* That would never work. He'd have to be very close, but not close enough to be breathing down Callum's neck, and far enough away to give himself space to hide if Callum turned around. Who, if they were together, would walk like that? He'd either get caught by the Spotters or by Callum himself. So following him, basically, was a real risk. Yet it wasn't impossible. Then, he'd get onto the plane behind him and answer questions later? There might be something left of his old friend that would understand his reasoning. It would be too late once the plane had departed anyway.

So, then, what? *I'll go to the Side.*

What? Just hop off the plane, hail a hover vehicle, swing around the Outer-Ring, pop along on the Side train, muse at the breathtaking views, and knock on the door for a cup of tea? *You're an idiot, Ajay.* He couldn't walk around liberally, he was a criminal. His face was plastered all over the place, from what he'd been told by people here. It was funny, he thought, how once it was his dream to have his face famous, perhaps for being the quickest person under thirty to make Glorified, or becoming the greatest software engineer ever for revolutionising something in his industry. Never did he think his face would be famous for murder. Ajay swallowed away the hardship, returning to the dilemma and considering option three.

Option three: to help the Rogue, but under false pretences. He could somehow get a message to Command and trade his pardon, which would also pardon his family.

He could definitely act as if he were facilitating their plan but instead hand them over. There must be a way to communicate with someone on the other side; all he'd have to do was send some sort of distress call, along with the location. No, not the location. He didn't have the exact coordinates, but he could tell them about the diverting strategy. Command was probably still trying to figure it out, what with the Diverters leading drones every which way. Yes, he could let them know that, and sign off his name. Then, when the Rogue had been captured, he could appeal for his good service to Tulo society. His grandma would be safe, Tulo restored to its previous state, and he would . . . what? He would go back to before, to his life, working and never sleeping, having boosts and drinking kale, occasionally seeing Genni and the others, but all of it without Ace? Rolling over again, the crunch of old leaves under his back, he let the tears trickle to the ground. He could never go back to how it was, not after what he'd done and what he knew. Yet, all his achievements, his merit score – was this a chance to get them all back? Yes. No. That would never work. Plus, what about Charlene and Haro and how they'd been treated, how the system had let them down?

Could he really turn them in? Charlene's light, fluttery breaths distracted him. Surely, there was too much brokenness for his life to go back to normal. And he needed to be honest with himself – if he really wanted to give the Rogue up, all he'd have to do was run across the perimeter and lead the drones back to camp. That would be a no-nonsense, Ace approach. Ajay sniffed through small tears, missing his friend before realising he'd made no progress.

He clenched his fists, frustrated. It was impossible. Maybe there was an option four: stay and do nothing.

Continue climbing trees and let fate decide. But then, wouldn't they try to force him, through violence, if he stayed and he didn't help? Right, so, go with option one, then, just do what they want. *You're right back where you started. Make a decision!*

Option one. *I'll help them.* No. He couldn't ignore that grieving within him; it didn't feel right.

For some reason, he was reminded of the time he had Sam in his apartment. Perhaps it was how he felt or the moral quandary that brought him to mind. He'd considered killing the Unworthy he'd found on the street, his leg cut up. He even considered how to dispose of his body. Ajay grimaced at the memory. In the end, though, he'd opted to look after him, like he would look after himself. Why did he do that? How did he make that decision?

Batting a fly away from his ear, he remembered.

It was Grandma. It always was.

They'd listened to another Guiding Light story, but it wasn't that *thing* Ajay listened to. He was recalling what Grandma had said afterwards. The story was about some twin brothers who had always fought, even from inside the womb. As they grew, they strived to better one another; to be richer and greater in every aspect. One worked for the government while another stayed behind to look after their father's camel farm. When their father died, the farmer decided not to tell the other brother in order to steal all their inheritance for himself. Years passed until he started to find life difficult. His camels stopped breeding, he had no credit left and business dried up. As one of his daughters fell ill from malnutrition, he knew he had to go to his brother for help. Ajay couldn't place all the details, but the other brother did help him willingly, even though hatred had pulled them apart.

Ajay could remember exactly where he was sitting on the kitchen table. The memory was so vivid it felt like it was happening now.

'What did you think of that one, Karle?' Grandma asked.

'I've heard it before.'

'I know. Do you like it?'

'I dunno. Why did the brother even bother helping?' Ajay could see Grandma's bright smile as she paused washing up at the sink.

'Because he decided to love.'

That's what Ajay had remembered that night he'd shown Sam compassion and what he couldn't stop thinking about now.

He'd made his decision. He knew what his grandma would want him to do. If they wanted him to assist in hurting people, he had to get away, but he also couldn't turn them in. It wasn't that he loved Charlene and the other, rare, tolerable few. It was just some odd, caring feeling, one that would perhaps disappear with time and distance. If he got back to the City, he could help Command then. Maybe? He saw their flaws too. They all seemed to have them, himself more than most.

CHAPTER
TWENTY-EIGHT

Rod felt on fire, a wrath so intense that the skin of his fingers was getting tender as he fury-typed on his desk, blindly flicking through the unsolved cases he'd been assigned. He hadn't seen Jona yet but when he did, he wondered how he could restrain himself from laying a hot, sharp punch around his irritating little jaw. That's what he told himself. In reality, his encounter with Esabel Hevas had left him feeling sick to the stomach. Did his parents already know? Did people on the desks around him know? Could they see his failure?

No. It's not a failure.

It was merely a directorial decision because he was 'too close' to the case. Not because of his apparent 'inappropriate behaviour' or inadequacy for the position. Rod picked at the skin around his nails and snorted. *They're fools if they think me doing my job is inappropriate.*

It had never occurred to him he'd be doing anything else. Since the day he'd got the job, he hadn't looked back. Posing as an entertainment executive felt a little underwhelming. People not knowing his true significance stung at times, but it didn't really matter.

The number on his wrist made sure people knew well enough what sort of a man they were dealing with.

Rod grimaced as he glanced at a woman's picture on an open case file; her ears were almost the size of her whole face. Swiping through, he turned back to his irritated thoughts. He remembered how the Side Eradication Project started out as merely a small venture before Command launched it into a full-blown initiative. It was fun, slowly but surely picking off the dead meat when they were no good to them. Investigating Side residents, especially The Guiding Light junkies, offering them top jobs if they chose Purification. Rod's favourites were the really tough ones. It was exhilarating; the late-night chases, arrests and eventually, well, it said it in the name – Eradication. Unfortunately, that last part was done by others back at Command. Rod's lip rose as he thought about one fat man, and how he'd chased him down an alley until it all got a little bit much. The idiot had a heart attack and collapsed. Done and dusted. All under the radar, for the sake of public opinion.

Yet this whole thing with the Rogue was sidelining his job. They were a bigger threat? Bigger than a poisonous ideology that promoted less contribution? Rod didn't buy it.

The Rogue might be little irritants but they could be dealt with in a day. Plain and simple. Side people were like a virus, subtly moving within the fabric of society, stifling its health and progress. Rod had magnetised handcuffs to many over the years who could have made perfectly good programmers, accountants, businesspeople. They wouldn't comply, so they had to be punished; no messing about, just dealt with efficiently and swiftly.

Although apparently those standards were slipping fast, he realised, noticing a pattern within the Rogue cases.

Open: 2 weeks. Open: 2.5 weeks. Closed: Inconclusive. Open: 4 weeks.

All these open cases. *Not my problem.* Rod slouched in his chair before sighing lethargically, because they *were* now his problem.

Scrolling back to the start, he read over the name briefly. Lillie Trumin. Well, that was a no-go for a quick win. She'd escaped the City weeks ago. That much was obvious and if they had to 'make the City safe inside its walls', then Lillie wasn't a priority – as much as Rod would love to be the one to find her. She looked like fun; menacing eyes, greying streaks through her plait, probably hot in her younger days.

Rod moved on. Tragi Turner. A young man with bleached hair and a huge nose. An unfortunate genetic malfunction. *He should get that put right,* but Rod quickly noticed he was Outer-Ring. No merit or credit equals no nose fix. He continued reading through the notes. *Anonymous Watch report of loitering around Downtown areas, as if waiting for someone, repeatedly looking at his Watch* . . . blah, blah, blah. So, nothing. That looked boring, and he wanted something juicy, like bursting through the door to Ajay's family, pulling his father along by his ear and doing his actual job. He had to stop thinking about it. *Next case.*

It didn't look too bad. *Seen in the Outer-Ring carrying a disabled drone with a dented side. Drone found in system and no programme tampering evident.* Another entry the same day gave details of him pulling a suitcase into his apartment before closing the curtains suspiciously. Lethargically, Rod sat up and started to type into the activity log. *Compliance Officer Mansald to lead a house raid at . . .*

A message came through. Rod's eyes snapped to his second screen as he saw its subject: Blythefen House Analysis.

The evidence from the Ambers case. He had to look. Neglecting the open case, he stroked the air to make the second screen bigger and opened the correspondence. He scanned past his own name, surprised this had come to him. He scrolled through the list of evidence taken from the house, to start reading the penultimate paragraph.

> *The only real item of interest was the computer set taken from the suspect's childhood bedroom. Log traces of software tools used to access and manipulate certain Watches have been found. Namely that of the suspect's father and another Side citizen, Theo Badds (deceased).*

Rod paused briefly in recognition of the Badds name. *Irrelevant.* He continued.

> *Based on this evidence, it is reasonable to believe that the suspect's parents, in particular the father, had a hand in providing the suspect with the equipment needed to carry out his offence. In this way, they are deemed accessories to identity theft and therefore we suggest an arrest should be made.*

Reading over the words, Rod felt elated. He could finally let them know their place. His mind swirled in a motion of images, imagining how the arrest would go. Would he target the grandma first? Or stick with pulling the father along by the ear?

Reality came back. He wouldn't be the one to burst through that non-automatic door. It would be Jona. Dull, imbecilic Jona. But . . . *hang on. They addressed me.*

Rod rattled at the desk again. According to the system, he was still assigned to the case. Had the Hevases approved the arrest? Surely they had to now. Rod enlarged the arrest request and read the words thrice over. *Arrest approved.*

Sitting back in his chair, he mulled over the facts. *The arrest has been approved. The request has been sent to me. I'm, according to the system, still assigned to the case under Jona's lead. Technically I still have the authority to do the job.*

Narrowing his green eyes, he considered how Esabel would react to direct disobedience. Not that he hadn't done it before and he had always done well, as she said herself, to 'protect the constitution'. If he did his job and did it right, they'd crown him, not demote him. Though there was another obstacle. Jona. If he had also received this request – and on a quick click, Rod could see that he had – he would need to get a team out there before him. Rod smiled at the thought. Not a problem.

He knew Jona. He wasn't slow as such, not by any City standards, but he did have his ridiculous pre-arrest ritual. Before heading out, he'd puff up his quiff, check his pore and glow percentage in his mirror, and clean his teeth. It was like an obsessive thing, Rod supposed.

Yet it gave Rod a chance – Jona hadn't even sent a team request yet and it could be any minute. If he beat Jona to it, they wouldn't bother wasting resources following him. Rod laid every other thought aside, unable to shake the notion that he needed to do it.

Without wasting any more time, Rod inputted his command, not bothering to read any arrest instructions.

Immediate action required. Team needed. Despatch in three minutes. Officer Mansald to lead.

He knew it was unlikely to work, but with everything that had gotten past this crumbling institution recently, there was a chance. And anyway, he was one of the best, so it was time to let him do his thing. After a few minutes of praising himself, standing in the elevator swooping down to the basement, a little doubt trickled in. Was he being too reckless? As the door slid open, and his team of Command guards and drones turned to him, the doubt disappeared.

Clicking his fingers and pointing authoritatively to a hover van, he felt power in his stride.

'Isn't Officer Jan the lead on this?' A guard with a visor over his face and gun to his chest cut into Rod's path.

'Yes, but he's sent me.' Rod held a strong stare as the guard looked unsure. 'You can go and ask him if you like. Waste all of our time. Or you could let us all get on with it?'

There wasn't even a pause before the guard complied, following Rod and the others into the hover van. As they swooped out from under Command, into the back of the Quarters, Rod smiled excitedly as he played out the arrest again in his mind. His wrist vibrated.

Jona: *You idiot, Mansald. Bring them back quietly but when you do, we need to talk.*

Talk we will, Rod thought. *When he crowns me for a job well done.*

CHAPTER
TWENTY-NINE

Genni could feel herself shaking and couldn't believe she'd managed to get back up the stairs so quietly. She was struggling to control her thoughts; what was she thinking, going into the front room like that? She never would have dreamed of doing that to her own father, let alone someone else's. Was she so self-entitled that she thought she had the right to rummage through someone else's property? Even if they were Unworthy. Pacing in circles around Ajay's bedroom, she didn't know what to do. She was being swallowed by something heavy and dark. She should go, having completely overstayed her welcome. That was certain.

'Genni?' Ajay's grandma's voice was strained and she fell through the bedroom door, catching her balance at the last minute. Genni moved to hold her up, saying nothing, still reeling inside. She could smell his grandma strongly; a musty reek which was somehow comforting.

'Everything alright?' His grandma looked into her eyes.

'Sorry, I'm sorry.' Genni tried to hold herself together. 'I shouldn't have woken you. I'll get you back to bed.'

'Don't worry, my mind is too alive to sleep sometimes.' His grandma let out a small laugh that ground on Genni.

What if Ajay's father heard them talking and came upstairs? She was scared of him; she couldn't put her finger on why. Genni helped to lower Ajay's grandma to the bed before closing the bedroom door and sitting anxiously beside her.

'You look like you need a bedtime story.' His grandma patted her on the hand.

'What?' Genni couldn't deal with this, standing up again with urgency.

'Ajay used to love them, you know.'

'No, that's OK. I don't like stories.'

'Everyone has enjoyed my stories.'

'Not now,' Genni grunted. 'I've got to go.'

'Yes, you do, don't you.' His grandma nodded her head, hissing as she tried to cough. 'But you can't leave in the middle of the night.'

What did she mean? The middle of the night was no different to midday. Plus, she wanted to go, Ajay's father's angered eyes running around her mind like the newsreel in the Social Sphere. Bright, intrusive, impossible to ignore.

'I'll be fine.' Genni scanned the room, feeling like she should be packing up her possessions to make the exit, but of course, she hadn't brought very much with her. She never expected to be staying and sleeping in the same shirt and trousers she'd arrived in.

'Well, can I give you something before you go?' His grandma tried to rise. 'It's in my room.'

'OK, but quickly.' Genni helped her up.

'I can only go as quick as my old legs.' His grandma hobbled to her feet, tutting at Genni for her impatience. *You don't have the right to tut at me. Stop it, Genni.*

With her legs fidgeting and her armpits starting to sweat, they arrived at his grandma's room. Genni froze for a minute. The walls were badly painted and dust clung to a lot of the shelving, but everything else was – well – lovely. She had a cute, patterned sheet on her bed, in vivid pinks and blues, with static photographs hanging on pieces of string by small, wooden pegs. There was Ajay, Tara, his parents, other smiling faces, some the same as in the room downstairs. Beside her bed was a small lamp and even more photos of her family, taking pride of place, presumably being the last thing she saw at night.

'I like to see memories.' His grandma smiled at Genni from her aged eyes.

'They're wonderful,' Genni agreed. 'Were you a midwife?' Genni stared at the image of her in a nurse's uniform, with a baby in her arms.

'Yes,' she nodded. 'It was a very fulfilling job. Though not without its frustrations.'

'Did you work here on the Side?' Genni moved slowly across the bedroom, his grandma still clinging to her arm.

'Mostly, but in the City for a time, when there weren't enough resources.' His grandma sat on her bed. 'But things have come a long way since then, of course.' She struggled with opening the drawer of her bedside table, the glowing lamp and picture frame bouncing across its surface. 'Oh, silly thing.'

'Here.' Genni moved a small wicker stool out of the way and opened the stiff wooden drawer, surprised the handle remained intact this time.

'Thank you, love.' His grandma coughed before reaching into the deep drawer, discarding other things in it; Genni noticed a few notebooks, medicine bottles and pens as they rattled against each other.

'Here we go. I thought you might like this.' His grandma held it up; it was similar but slightly smaller to the one Genni had activated downstairs. *Why would she ever think I would want that?*

'What for?' Genni asked, hesitantly taking it from her out of politeness. She kept her fingers underneath, not wanting to activate its hologram, her thoughts still on the way it had startled her downstairs.

'In case you need it.'

'You know I can't take this.' *This is forbidden.* She looked at his grandma with insistent eyes, sad to disappoint her but also glad not to be keeping it. His grandma opened her dry mouth to speak, but before the words came or Genni could give the device back, a door opened across the hallway. Its loud shriek and the subsequent rushed footsteps seemed to shake the whole house.

'Genni?' Ajay's mother sounded terrified. 'Genni, where are you?'

'She's in here, love.' His grandma strained and looked at her daughter disapprovingly as she bounded into the room. 'What's all the fuss about?'

Ajay's mother appeared flustered, fear pulsating in her brown eyes.

'They're here, Mum. Just pulled up outside.'

'Oh, get Genni out of here.' His grandma instantly mirrored her daughter's urgency, with more energy than Genni would have believed existed in her frail body.

Ajay's mother grabbed Genni and pulled her down the stairs. Genni's Watch vibrated as her heartbeat flew up. She was in trouble. Command couldn't catch her here.

She had to trust these people she didn't really know. There was no other choice.

They found themselves in the kitchen, steams strong with the smell of cooking. Genni noticed some carrots splayed over the chopping board in non-uniform shapes.

'OK.' Ajay's mother swooped a Watch up from the worktop, typing furiously. 'These are the details of our friend Reha.' She flicked her fingers on her screen, as Genni held her wrist up, letting the information transfer into her Watch. 'She's in the City. She helped us protect Ajay; she will . . .' There were noises near the front door. Ajay's mother snapped her head back.

'What . . . I don't . . .' Genni found it difficult to cope with the speed of their exchange.

The crash of the front door bursting open caused them both to duck. Genni groaned as the sudden movement played with the nerves in her back. Straightening up, Ajay's mother held her with demanding eyes.

'Go. The back door.' Her eyes jerked behind them. 'Go.'

Genni didn't hesitate but flew towards the door, hitting her hand over the pad beside it, letting it slide open. She jumped out into the garden, losing her footing, and stepping on some young cabbages. Feeling a fleeting pang of surprise as she glanced at the fruit growing in the greenhouse, Genni regretted not being able to have a closer look.

'Anyone home?'

Her feet stopped moving. That voice was something she couldn't ignore. That irritating, loathsome voice, sharpened with an unfamiliar edge.

Rod.

CHAPTER
THIRTY

For Ajay, the day couldn't come quickly enough.

The last five days had been painful; he'd been trying to distance himself more from the people around him. Every time Charlene sparked a conversation, he'd tried to disengage, longing to sever any emotional attachment. When Haro offered to tie his climbing ropes around the trees, which Ajay still hadn't mastered, his heart wanted to feel. The longer he was here, the more he would want to be their friend, and that was dangerous. Almost as dangerous as his sympathies for Ki, especially after what he'd heard about his past.

'He told me it wasn't always like that.' Marta hoisted her gun over her shoulder as they walked back from a committee meeting two days ago.

'What?' Ajay had squinted at the jagged edges of her pixie haircut as the low sun splintered through the trees.

'Ki.' She paused. 'His coughing.'

'Oh, right.'

'He overdosed a lot on *SkipSleep*. Ya know, before.' Marta looked considerate, clearing her throat. Ajay had instantly thought of Genni and imagined her in Ki's position; he couldn't bring himself to finish the thought. Could that have been her?

'He needs to rest more than most of us, so go easy on him, OK?'

At the time, Ajay had dismissed her compassion and only caught on to the tone in which she spoke. 'Go easy on him, OK?' Almost like a suggestion to an authority, as if he, Ajay, would be their leader. The meetings had been a lot of him talking, but only in his efforts to convince them not to utilise the remaining explosives from the attack, even if it was just for Command. He wanted to help them find a way to *show* the public that the system needed changing. Ajay was beginning to see that from their perspective, but never enough to agree to violence of any kind. But, he was starting to wonder – if he stayed longer, could he be convinced? Escaping meant there wouldn't be that risk.

Now that the day had arrived, Ajay felt indescribably sick. It was as if for the last five days, his body had been storing his anxiety deep down until the moment when it was most inconvenient. He would need to avoid the climb tonight. He didn't know exactly what time Callum would be heading out, and that was a problem, but he had to hope he would catch him. Briefly, on the third day, he had considered trying to find the plane without following Callum. A quick look around the never-ending, meandering mass of trees told him to forget that idea.

Back at his sleeping spot, he told himself that this was his greatest show yet. Though the part he was playing felt so unnatural, as pretending to be ill would rarely have occurred to him in his old life. Returning from his mimicked toilet trip, he thought about it. His colleagues used to hobble into the office, spluttering out their insides, yet still managing to keep their head down and work. If someone was off, everyone would always suspect the worst, because they'd have to be almost dead to let themselves lose out on the merit. Yet he wasn't in that world any more. There was no score on his wrist, no one he wanted to impress, and faking illness was an easy way to get out of the climb without raising suspicion.

Lying down again, he rested his palms on his cheeks. The small induction hob he'd tampered with in the bushes had done its job to raise his body temperature. Looking up at the evening sky, and breathing through circled lips, he didn't know how long that temperature would hold. *Come on, come on. Wake up!* He looked at Charlene, still sound asleep.

The sweat trickled down his arms and his back was a pool. He hoped his face was red enough and if so, willed for it to hold for as long as possible. Thinking about his grandma, he tried to channel the fragility he'd seen in her. Her voice was deep, croaky, and drawn out. That should be easy enough. There was also the coughing, as if there were something toxic in her lungs. *How could I make that realistic?* A Watch torch came on in Ajay's head, remembering every time the dust of Fo Doktrin leaves had tickled his throat after accidentally inhaling its dust.

Charlene turned over, murmuring and stirring, her back to Ajay. Sliding along the ground quietly, he reached into the nearby foliage and twisted the stems of a couple of leaves until they snapped in two. Being careful to avoid the dust staining his hands, he slithered back to his spot and popped the leaves under his shoulder for when the time came. So, the voice, the burning head, and the coughing. Would that be enough? Should be, along with some fake shivering to add to the fever. He was struggling with his desire to deceive; he didn't like it any more. Not like he used to. Testing his temperature again with the back of his hand, he knew this could work. He was as hot as an unfanned processor.

Charlene eventually rose from her slumber, stroking her fingers through her hair.

'Oh, for Tulo's sake.' She sounded angry. Ajay jumped and scrunched his eyes shut, after seeing her observe something stuck in her hand. 'When am I going to get a chuffing pit?'

'When you earn it.' Haro's voice came into play, alongside the sound of his pit opening.

'Another bird did one in my hair.' Charlene sounded disgusted and Ajay imagined her face behind his closed eyes; irritable, eyebrows lowered, and lips curled inwards. 'Look at this!'

Haro's laugh carried weight in the evening light as Ajay could hear others rising and suits being pulled on.

'Ajay, get up.' Charlene was calmer.

Showtime. Ajay prised open his eyes, forcing himself to imagine they were stuck together. He could see Charlene's back was turned so he twisted his body, pulled out the Fo Doktrin leaf and inhaled. The dust flew up and tingled his nasal senses, forcing him to cough violently. As a headache started to rise, he wondered if he'd thought this part of the plan all the way through. He wasn't intending to actually make himself ill. Quickly, before Charlene approached him, he took another discreet sniff, spluttering out saliva as his lungs temporarily burned.

'Ajay? You OK?'

'I had . . .' Ajay paused for effect before remembering to draw out his words, '. . . the worst sleep.'

'What's new?' Charlene smiled as she bent down, before her soft eyes turned serious. 'Wow. You look flushed.' She placed her hand on his forehead before standing. 'And you're burning up.'

Ajay coughed again, forcing her to scuttle away and guard herself with her hands. 'OK, do not come near me. I do not want that.'

Number one convinced. Now for the real challenge – Haro.

'We're heading out. Charlene, Ajay . . .' Haro barked as Ajay heard one of the lads charging up their gun.

'Ajay's got some bug or something.' Charlene walked away. 'I ain't climbing with him tonight.'

'Then he climbs alone.' Haro zipped up his suit. 'Ajay, get up!'

Ajay imagined there was a man above him, pushing down his full weight on his back. It worked well to make him rise slowly and with resistance. As he did so, he sniffed at the leaf again and coughed more violently.

'What's wrong with you?' Ajay could hear Haro's heavy footsteps. As he reached him, Ajay was on all-fours, having swept the Fo Doktrin leaves to the side. He saw Haro's boots next to him and groaned as he forced him to his feet, his grip in his armpit strong.

'Come on, we can't afford for you to be weak.' Haro bent his bushy eyebrows at him, his lazy eye examining his sickness. 'We've got children to feed.'

'I can't . . .' Ajay paused. 'Haro, I . . .'

'Enough of it.' Haro turned away. 'Go a bit slower. Some fruit is better than nothing. Now get your suit on.'

'I'm red hot . . .' Ajay stopped.

He shouldn't try to convince him, that would raise suspicion. So, he reached for his suit lethargically, reminding himself he needed to hurry up; Callum would be setting off soon. Slowly lifting his leg, he imagined the suit was made of lead, making it feel heavy as he pulled it on. Haro sighed, his small, stocky legs jiggling in agitation.

'Oh, come on.' Haro marched back to Ajay and slapped his hands away from the suit. With no lament, Haro pulled Ajay's suit roughly onto him over his clothes. Ajay hissed as its fast zip pulled his skin through his vest.

'Stop being a coward and get over it.' Haro smashed Ajay's balaclava into his chest, his Alert Band catching Ajay's torso with a clunk.

Ajay moved cumbersomely after him. *This isn't working, it needs something more.*

As they walked further, trailing behind the group, Ajay knew what to do. Looking around, he ensured no one was watching him before taking a deep breath, fixating on Haro's back. *Stop being a coward and get over it.* Ajay shoved two fingers down his throat and gagged. It didn't work but luckily, Haro didn't notice. *Try again.* He got it. The vomit that came out of him wasn't anything substantial; bits of mushed-up fruit and leaves but mainly water. Ajay considered how malnourished he must be. Another good reason for getting out, even without a clear plan on the other side.

'You're kidding me!' he heard Haro mumble, coming back to him. 'That's disgusting.' Haro retched at the smell. Despite not having much inside of him, it did stink, almost like eggy camel's milk. Ajay stopped looking at the brown watery liquid, otherwise he might throw up more.

'Get yourself back to camp,' Haro said. 'Sort it out for tomorrow.'

Ajay didn't hesitate, turning back and maintaining his lumbering pace until he was out of sight of Haro. Then, he ran.

The taste of vomit still fresh between his teeth, Ajay darted through the trees, hopping over roots and fallen branches, letting the leaves swipe at his ankles. *Please, please, Callum, don't leave yet.* Getting closer to camp, he slowed down, not wanting to disturb anyone still sleeping. As he did so, he felt the effect of lactic acid in his legs, wobbly and painful, like his calves were being pressed between two dumbbell weights. Pushing through it, Ajay retraced his plan.

Number one, find Callum. That shouldn't be too hard if he hadn't already left. Number two, follow him discreetly through the forest, being ready to stealthily jump behind a tree, from him or any drones they may encounter across the perimeter. Number three, walk close to the tree lines to reduce the chance of any Spotters seeing him. It was a risk, that part. He had no control over it. Yet he hoped that because he was wearing his suit and he wasn't going to stroll into the open, he might get away with it.

No one had ever tried it before. Charlene had made that very clear, describing the dangers of being out in the desert in detail: 'You'd be alone, no food, your skin exposed. You would wither away. Not to mention the risk of being torn to pieces.' Her description hadn't done anything to persuade him against his plan, because if it worked, he wouldn't become a predator's meal. That brought him to number four; after making it through the forest, he presumed the Recruiters would wait for the plane to arrive early morning. Once it did, he would sneak behind them and jump on as the door closed.

Finally, once he arrived at the airfield in the City, he would need to make his way to the Side. That part was a challenge and not yet confirmed. He would either walk, which he calculated would take between two to three hours, but he could easily be seen. Or he could reveal himself to Callum and try to convince him to take him. After all, he'd have already escaped. The third option was going into the Outer-Rings and finding Grandma's friend; the strange, sharp woman who'd helped him before. He thought about the last time he saw her, in that underwater bar, the reflection of water trickling over her birthmarked face as he left her there, surrounded by shelves of Guiding Lights. He never did get her name. Maybe she would be gracious, despite the way he'd been so rude to her by demanding answers like he deserved them. Having thought it over, he'd wondered if she could be the answer to protecting his family from Command entirely. After all, she'd done so much already: protecting him as a child, carrying Genni back to his apartment after her accident; offering to get him out of the City. *Why didn't he listen? Maybe she would protect him again?*

Ajay tried to convince himself it was all going to work. His fear, however, knew the opposite. There were so many risks, so many assumptions. Whether it was ending up lost in the desert or being caught by the Rogue, his mind thrummed with the same five words, over and over. *I am a dead man.*

It was the first time Ajay had seen the camp in the dead of night. Instantly feeling vulnerable in the quiet, Ajay stepped lightly behind the trees edging the deceptively untouched space. Yet beneath it, children were sleeping, wrapping their arms around handmade cuddly toys. He'd never get used to that, and hopefully he wouldn't have to. Finding a tree behind Callum's pit, he pressed his back against it to wait, crunching the bottles in his pre-packed bag. His body immediately tensed up as he heard whispers in the dark. *Who's that?* They were getting louder. Ajay couldn't make out which direction they were coming from and whether they'd soon appear right in front of him, ruining his plan before it had even begun.

There was another moment of quiet. A small breeze danced through the trees. Ajay felt hot drips of sweat sliver down and drop from his nose. He held his breath in the silence.

'You got that bag?' The voice ripped through Ajay like an unwelcome alarm. Startled, he almost slipped from behind the tree, but forced himself to freeze, and strained to hear Callum's response over his pounding heart and the opening of Callum's pit.

Coming down from his fright, Ajay celebrated that he'd made it in time. Though the way he'd jumped was worrying. He'd need to be a lot cooler to pull this off.

'So where are we heading?' Callum's voice again.

There was a pause and a thinking noise from his partner. Ajay assumed he was checking his Watch or whatever device they used to track people; the ones whose situations looked dire enough to persuade them to join. That was another thing Charlene had explained over a bowl of green mush one evening. *Nice of them to give some people a choice, rather than being taken against their will.*

'One just east Side. The other, Outer-Ring, by Cain's place. Is that close to where you're getting the Watch?'

Callum didn't respond verbally that Ajay could hear, but he did hear their movements. This was it. *Breathe. Chill out. Be stealthy.* Be stealthy? Ajay hated his own pep talks; they were about as useful as a napkin fan on a hot day. *Just get on with it.*

Callum and his companion, whose face Ajay couldn't see, started out through the west side of the forest, a direction Ajay had never taken. Shoving his own balaclava over his head, he circled around the trees, holding back slightly until he was only 50 metres behind. He wasn't close enough to hear their conversation. Observing more closely, it didn't look like they were talking at all. Perhaps they were enjoying the quiet of nature – there was something tranquil about it. Ajay didn't want to look up, he needed to concentrate on his walk, but he knew there were hundreds of beautifully shining Wingsparks above them, creating a dazzling picture with their wings.

Ajay wondered how close they were to the perimeter and whether any Spotters were up in the trees they passed, inspiring him to edge nearer to the base of the trunks.

Callum's companion pulled a water bottle from their bag. As he swigged, Ajay felt a contagious need to drink, but he didn't want to bring any attention to himself by opening his own bag. As they got further out, the foliage grew wilder, grazing his ankles. It was unnerving. Wasn't there a risk of accidentally threatening a Toxlizard? Was that possible? Did they just freely roam? Should he be looking out for them or did they not nest in this area? A voice in his head told him to go back. That would be the safest thing to do, and then maybe he could return to his plan to bargain with the Rogue. That would also mean he wouldn't let Charlene down. *Stop it. You don't belong here.*

Freedom, and getting to Grandma, needed to be his priority, so he continued towards the unknown.

CHAPTER
THIRTY-ONE

Ajay had no way of checking the time, but as he'd lost all feeling in his feet, he guessed they'd been walking for at least an hour. His shoulders were flopping, his arms dragging by his side. Everything looked the same. Tree after tree, bush after bush. He was almost bored. It felt like a bit of a let-down. Escapes were meant to be exciting, like the ones he and Ace had undergone during their all-night binges of *DesertDive*. Those escapes from desert madmen were pacey and exhilarating. Nothing like this *endless* stroll in an ethereal setting.

His tired mind stopped spiralling as Callum and his friend halted. They seemed unnerved. Startled? Worried? Ajay heard them snap at one another before they both dashed behind a tree. *What are they doing?* In his exhaustion, Ajay's instinct wasn't to do the same. Until logic kicked in. He threw himself at the nearest trunk, wrapping his body behind its foreboding presence.

Ajay heard it before he saw it. The sound he'd recognise anywhere. The beeps and bleeps all too familiar. It almost felt as if a coffee or a bagel would be landing on his desk any second. He closed his eyes. Seeing himself back in the office, back in the streets, drones like wallpaper bouncing through the skies. Opening his eyes, the skyscrapers replaced by trees, he twisted onto his front, pressing his chest into the trunk. He could see it a few tree lines away. Bobbing almost gracefully through the night, its small red lights merging with the Wingsparks' twinkle. There was a certain beauty about it; something comfortingly familiar in such an alien setting. He'd missed them.

Ajay felt a rush of movement. It wasn't a walk but a constant, hard pattering on the ground. Someone was running.

They ran, or rather hurtled, past him like a speeding hover vehicle. A Diverter. Ajay watched them sprint for the drone. *Dangerous. Do they not realise?* He had assumed they'd do this more strategically, rather than pelting straight for the enemy. Ajay stopped his breath. Watching the man, or woman, it was hard to tell, head into battle. They ran faster, holding a gun. The drone turned, its beeping more erratic as it released its red scanner, rolling out of it like a digital carpet. Ajay flattened himself against the trunk again, ensuring every part of his skin was covered by the suit. Looking back again, the Diverter still ran. Never even stopping. Sweeping straight and smoothly through the scanning field like a knife spreading butter. The drone turned, accelerated, and set off in hot pursuit, both of them disappearing into the night.

Another moment of quiet came, both in the forest and Ajay's mind. *Now, that was more like DesertDive.*

'Man, I can't breathe.' Ace would always say after the drama subsided and he'd done a fair amount of thrashing and screaming. Trying to process the memories and the last few seconds, Ajay wondered how far the Diverter would get before being tasered or they decided to shoot the drone down. Far enough away to avoid it crossing the perimeter into the camp, he assumed. *So this is the perimeter.* It was much further out than he thought. Clever. If any drones did get through, there'd be enough time for people to react from the Alert Band signal and dive into the pits, suited and booted. The thought then occurred to him: had Command not realised there were loads of randomers running about? Wouldn't the strategy become obvious to them? Not straight away, Ajay considered. 'Much of this has increased since the attack,' he remembered Haro telling him on the way to one climb. 'It's why we've got fewer climbers.'

Ajay slipped out from behind the tree a minute after he'd heard Callum move. He collected himself again, walking lightly behind them. Looking sneaky would only alert any Spotters who, seeing as this was the perimeter, were people likely to be hanging out above his head.

This is bad. Dead man, dead man. Ajay struggled with the idea of watching eyes he couldn't even see. *Ignore. Just walk.*

It was as if it would never end. He could see why Charlene could never do the Recruiters' job. Having to walk for more than two hours, without muttering as much as a word, would be literal torture for her. Callum was the perfect fit. Even as a child, he was the shy type. Ajay did regret what he'd done to him, and he understood why Callum didn't want to talk to him about anything but the plan. The image of Callum's face as Ki welcomed him into the inner circle was etched in the forefront of Ajay's mind. It was like he didn't want Ajay to help but knew they needed him, or someone like him. Callum had never said it, but Ajay was sure he was resentful, he could see it sizzling in his eyes and through the taser burns that burdened his face.

Before he thought further on it, he saw how the trees were thinning, no longer tightly packed, but distanced apart. They were trickling away, the ones remaining like the remnants of water on the side of a jug. The drips. Drip, drip, drip. Ajay estimated about twenty steps between each tree, then it was thirty. Then, forty. He was becoming way too exposed; if the two of them turned, there wouldn't be time for him to reach the next tree. His heart rate rocketed.

He watched as the two of them disappeared towards the horizon, where the trees were even more sporadic, and the bushes were becoming dried and withered. They were heading for the desert? Where would they hide? While cradling a tree, he observed Callum and his partner turning off just before the trees all but disappeared. Squinting, he had no idea where they could be going. Hiding until morning and the plane came? Ajay knew he needed to be closer. He'd get to one of the nearer trees and wait there. He spotted the tree he was aiming for, thinking it looked less bumpy than the others.

Stepping out, he drew breath. He felt a rock drop in his stomach. The grip on his shoulder was tight. A yelp escaped him, as his balaclava was ripped from his head.

'. . . west of the perimeter. Yeah . . . Ambers. Cry baby . . . I'll bring him back.' Maze spoke into a Watch, his gruff voice dirty; he smiled with an ominous joy. 'Now they'll finally kill ya.'

Ajay let the words sink in. He'd been caught. His risk hadn't paid off.

It was crazy of him to ever think it was going to work and he never even considered that someone else might be joining Callum. If he'd been thinking straight, he might have assumed Maze would be accompanying him. Like he knew he often did. He'd just been so desperate to get out, he'd missed it. How could he have missed it? The feeling of failure was raw. *I'm sorry, Grandma. I'm sorry.*

Could he say he was sorry to himself?

Would they kill him? Ajay doubted it. If they still wanted him for their plan, he supposed torture would be their next tactic. Especially because they would never trust him now. Yet, if he was branded a traitor, would some of them execute him in the night? Or perhaps the committee would hate him so much they'd be happy for an execution to go ahead? Charlene wouldn't let it happen, he decided. Or Haro. He was their friend, right?

As Maze grunted and grabbed the back of Ajay's suit, pushing him back through the rough, Ajay mulled over his stupidity some more. The whole plan had come with a cloud in his brain, obstructing his logical thinking and only allowing him to see the small chance that he could get out. *You're pathetic. How could you ever think this would work?* Ajay's insides ground as Maze began to whistle, knocking Ajay off-balance with repetitious, uncompassionate shoves. *You're a failure. Worthless. Disappointing. You may as well be killed. Everyone would be better off.*

Ajay had been trying to repress these beliefs. He wanted to live because he was surely still worth something. But

Ace's dead body told a different story. His grandma's inevitable vulnerability sang a different tune. And Genni. *Everything hurts. Genni was the love of my life.* He'd never told her how much she meant to him; he wasn't even sure he'd admitted it to himself. Yet where was she? Back in the City they loved, either having forgotten all about him in anger at his betrayal, or slumped into the darkness of a pit, just like him. Maze's hard pushes on his back didn't faze him because everything was turning numb. Would he ever feel again?

He remained in a desolate space for the entirety of the walk back, but Maze mumbling into his Watch snapped Ajay back to reality. Maze took his suit by the neckline and forced Ajay to stop.

'Now.' He whispered into his wrist.

Before Ajay knew what was happening, a wet splatter felt moist on his skull. Maze exploded into laughter, keeping his voice low and immediately pushing Ajay forward again. They were at the perimeter and Ajay could only assume that the thick, damp liquid hitting his face had conveniently escaped the mouth of a Spotter in the tree above them. Stumbling forwards again, he didn't think about it. Or he tried not to. It was difficult when the spit was crawling down his left cheek. He struggled to resist the feeling of rejection. *Why do you care? It's not like you want to be their friend.*

Ajay hadn't noticed them approaching, but two other lads took him under his armpits and began to pull him past the perimeter, back towards camp. Did they really think he would try to run now?

'Wait,' Maze said, looking around. 'Why don't we dry his tears first?'

I'm not crying. Ajay wanted to say, but he didn't have it in him. As Ajay watched Maze clench his big, hairy fists, he held his breath and took it.

There was a time at school when Ajay was wrongly accused of putting sand in the pockets of the teacher's jacket. Mr Huno ripped into him as if he'd shot his wife. Never a very nice man, Grandma had said years after when he'd died. Even though he was long gone, Ajay still remembered the humiliation and the shame. All the other children watching him drowning in his own self-pity and diminishing worth. It was like that now. Only he'd committed the crime and the watching eyes were desensitised, blurred and distant due to the throbbing of his face. He knew Charlene was there, her frame higher than all the others.

'What are you doing?' Her voice was strained, directed towards the brutes around him. Ajay couldn't make out much, but they must have dragged him through camp, for all to see. His legs were flaccid as he hung onto the arms of his captors and the taste of iron dripped into his mouth. Maze was all muscle and no brain, but man, the guy could punch.

'He was escaping.' Maze proclaimed proudly.

Charlene said nothing in response. Ajay tried to look at her, but he struggled to crane his neck. They dropped him to the ground, his knees hitting the dirt first and Ajay could see Charlene then, standing beside Haro, both peering at him like he belonged where he was.

'Oh, my.' Ki stepped towards Ajay, the rim of his shoes by Ajay's head. 'That's disappointing.'

'We should lock him up.' A woman's voice cut through.

'Lock him up?' Ki questioned, calmly.

'He was clearly going back to Command. To rat us out.'

Ki bent down to look at Ajay's bruises and wiped the blood away from his chin. 'You've made quite a mess of him, Maze.'

Of course, they'd think he was going to tell. He knew they had people on the inside, and he knew how they were managing to hide and that they were planning another attack on Command. He had plenty of information. Ajay felt as if he'd lost himself. Why didn't he consider what they would think?

'We shouldn't lock him up. We should kick him out.' Another voice rattled through his ears.

'Better yet, just kill him,' Maze piped up.

Uncomfortable whispers and murmurs came from the onlookers.

'He's on Command's side. Clear and simple. He deserves to die.'

'Don't use that word, Maze.' That was a voice Ajay recognised but he couldn't place the face.

'What? Command? They still exist. Why shouldn't we use their name? You know, I think it's time we start stripping out the cowards.' Maze invited gasps.

'How dare you!' The same voice returned, followed by an explosive wall of sound. The angered words flew across the forest, a verbal brawl that caused Ajay to cover his sensitive ears with his hands. Lifting his torso up, he watched as people pointed and gestured in fury across the circle, of which he was the central attraction.

'Everyone shut up!' Ki cried out, spitting through a sudden rage, shaking in a spasm. There was silence and Ki sighed, dropping his shoulders.

'Look, everyone, you're waking the children.' People scanned around to see the heads of disgruntled parents popping out from the opening of the pits, and Ki spoke again. 'Now, let's discuss this calmly. Shall we?' He bent back down to Ajay. 'What were you doing?'

'I need to get to my grandma,' Ajay said through his dry throat. That wasn't the whole truth, and he did consider how weak it made him look.

'Give me a break.' Maze addressed the audience. 'He played this on the plane when we grabbed him. Crying and whimpering like a baby.' He laughed, others sniggering with him. *'I'm sorry, Grandma. I'm sorry, Ace. Please forgive me.'*

It was like when he'd seen Lillie. A rage so uncontrollable and almost impossible in his current state. Miraculous strength came to his legs as Ajay launched himself at Maze, like a Toxlizard protecting its young, wanting to poison every inch of Maze's existence. Of course, he didn't get far. The sound of his back hitting the ground was sharp and his wrists stung as the others restrained him. Maze's cackle invaded Ajay's brain, infecting it with hatred.

'Come on, Ajay. You're not helping yourself,' Ki said. 'Now, what was this about your grandma?'

Ajay stopped himself from looking at Maze, trying to calm down. He had a chance to explain himself.

'My family on the Side. They're in danger. I need to know if they're OK.'

Arneld Hevas' words started to ring around Ajay's head. *Anyone suspected of having helped or facilitated unauthorised access into the City will be arrested and tried.*

'And what were you going to do? Fight off the drones with your bare hands?' Haro was there, and his deep voice was almost a comfort.

Silence came. Until Ajay remembered.

'I told Charlene . . . about them,' he said, recalling how he told her about his grandma on one of their walks back from climbing. He and everyone else looked at Charlene, who appeared startled by the sudden attention. Her gorgeous eyes were sad, arms crossed across her chest. At first, Ajay thought she wasn't going to say anything, leaving him to the verdict of the unrelenting and unloving jury.

'Yeah, he said something.'

That was it? That was all she was going to say? Ajay didn't know whether to be thankful she said anything at all, or furious she hadn't jumped to his defence. Though it was probably about right – he shouldn't expect her to be happy about this. As he pondered over it, another silence passed, longer than the last.

'This is rubbish. Let's just get rid.'

Ajay got the sense that everyone was as fed up with Maze's voice as he was. Another verbal massacre was starting but Haro stepped in.

'Stop, remember the kids.' Haro came and stood next to Ajay, who was still on the ground. Looking at his small stubby legs next to him, Ajay's helpless side longed to wrap his arms around those calves and never let go.

'There's no point in killing him. We're running out of food, fast, and he's becoming one of our best climbers.' Haro sniffed hard. 'I'll keep an eye on him.'

Despite his relief as the crowd dispersed, Ajay couldn't help but sense the resistance behind Haro's words, confirmed by the look in his eyes as he helped Ajay to his feet.

'We'll survive without a little fruit.' Maze didn't take his unyielding eyes off Ajay, his fists across his chest, marked with Ajay's blood.

'Maze, let's not make a habit of this.' Ki rested a skinny hand on Maze's muscled arm and looked at him intensely. Maze backed off, thrusting Ki's hand off him and spitting at Ajay's feet.

Ajay looked for her, but Charlene had already gone. Only a few remained.

'You've really disappointed us, Ajay.' Ki fixed Ajay in a penetrating stare. 'We definitely can't trust you now, can we?'

He sighed and walked away, his toxic cough causing birds to flutter from the trees into the morning air. Thinking about Charlene, Ajay knew he was walking into something new again; a life where not even Unworthies would be his friends.

CHAPTER
THIRTY-TWO

The next day, Ajay was desperate to see Charlene. His entire body felt like it had been through a grinder, the brutality of his beating painted across his face. It had been hard to clean off the blood without a mirror and Charlene to help him. He hadn't slept either. He was basking in self-pity. He still felt the numbness which always simmered in the background, the never-ending haze of his Unworthiness, only ever growing stronger.

'Can I borrow your Watch, please?' Her voice was higher than ever. *Charlene.* He looked up from his spot to see her long hair sweeping down her khaki jacket.

'Charlene . . .' Ajay didn't move fast but managed to hop himself onto one foot, using the log beside him for balance.

Charlene only responded to Haro, who handed her the Watch. 'Thanks.'

She didn't even look at Ajay.

'Charlene, wait.' Ajay called after her, desperate for some interaction.

'What?' Charlene turned in an irritated motion. 'Want to make another promise you can't keep?'

Ajay cursed himself. He'd forgotten all about his 'promise' to Charlene to not leave. She couldn't have actually believed him? She must have been a lot more trusting than he ever was.

'You're just a selfish idiot,' Charlene said, her eyes penetrating.

Ajay remembered; *Charlene always bears a grudge.* It still didn't stop her words feeling like a spear through his flesh.

He flopped back down, almost angry, watching her and Haro leave for the climb. *How can she say that? With the position I was in?*

After a few hours of venting his frustrations further, he decided his feeble legs could try a few paces. Pulling himself up, using the log to balance, he managed to hobble through the trees. After barely 100 metres, he was debating turning back when something stopped him.

A faint hum, a little whisper of a recognisable voice. Following the smooth rhythm of it through the trees, he saw it. The dancing figure of light, sprouting from the leaves on the ground. *Is this a dream? Why is it here? Why is it everywhere?* Pictures ran through Ajay's mind; childhood memories, in the underground bar with the birthmark woman; one creeping from Callum's bag, and that madman in the pit. His repeating mantra circled Ajay's thoughts as he stepped further towards it. *Rolfa was alive. Until she was dead. They all came in and took her head. The Light dances from its case, telling us to seek the place.*

Ajay followed its light, before stopping, not wanting to get any closer. He wasn't interested in hearing more of it, nor did he feel particularly comfortable with its listener.

It was a man, probably in his mid-fifties, sitting on a log and slicing up a piece of rotting fruit between his fingers. Ajay observed the rips in his black T-shirt, a few sizes too big, and his trousers were practically brown with the amount of Fo Doktrin dust having made its mark. Ajay caught his initial reaction on his appearance; that the man was Unworthy. He still couldn't help himself, judging whether people were or weren't, even though it meant nothing.

The man coughed, sounding unhealthy, before leaning forward and muting the Light, its voice abruptly stopping and being replaced by the night's noise. It was a nicer sound. Ajay didn't move but wondered if the man was a mirror into his future. *Is this how I'll end up? Lonely, old and dirty?* Closing his eyes and slowly sliding down a nearby tree, he didn't let himself think about it as he fell into his exhaustion.

'You're coming tonight,' Haro barked as he thumped Ajay awake.

Ajay registered how he was slumped against the tree trunk, and he instantly looked back to where the old man had been sitting to see only a vacant log. He pulled himself up, stunned that the day had been and gone.

'What?' he mumbled.

'Climbing.' Haro casually pulled a tin from his pocket, tore its lid upwards and slurped its contents down his throat.

'No, Haro. I can't climb yet.' Ajay stared at the open tin, hunger pranging in his belly. He couldn't do it; his legs were working, marginally, but his muscles were wound up like a tight coil.

'You can clearly walk,' Haro said, licking the juice around his lips.

'Well, yes, but . . .'

'I'm not leaving you here again.' Haro pulled him up, ordering him back to camp. 'Remember, I said I'd be your babysitter.'

Ajay glanced down at the tin in Haro's hands; a few peaches bobbing around, moist and slippery in a cocktail of juice and his saliva.

As they got back, Ajay apathetically clambered into his suit, stained with his dried blood, thinking about how, in some ways, he'd enjoyed being left alone for a day. These people who were so self-absorbed with their little Command hatred party that they couldn't even muster some compassion for a kid who got a few things wrong. *OK, a lot wrong.* Ajay knew it was unhealthy to keep making excuses for himself, but he couldn't help it. *I've worked so hard, and this is what life is giving me?* With both legs now into his suit, he paused from his internal rant.

It was Charlene who distracted him. She was walking, her hair tied back and wagging behind her like a camel's tail. Ajay felt sad, instantly. It felt good to have had a friend, if only for a short time. Charlene had given him faith in the group. She had made him wonder if maybe some of them were normal people. It occurred to him that most people he'd met here, minus a few, were not too dissimilar to people he would have respected in the City. Yeah, they were all angry, but fundamentally, could he blame them? Thinking about it, his friends in the City could have easily wound up here. Mila, who he hadn't thought about in months, had never been happy with her job, despite being well-merited for it. Blake, with his leg situation, could have decided to turn on Command. And Genni, with her overdose and the lack of acceptance for her painting – she could have been here too. Maybe they all felt as if something had been stolen from them. Yet the difference was, Ajay reminded himself, those people *weren't* here. *We powered through and got our reward. Instead, this lot are so conceited that it means Long Legs can't even cut me a little slack.* He knew he shouldn't be calling Charlene that as she hated it, but luckily for everyone, including himself, no one could hear inside his head.

Grabbing his balaclava with a hot-tempered sigh, he dragged himself through the forest behind Haro and the rest of the detestable group. Yet a small part of him still wanted to be liked. Even by them. *What in Tulo is wrong with me?*

The deep perplexity of his mind troubled Ajay until the gunmen shouted, 'All clear!'

What was he supposed to do? Stay with them and facilitate another massacre? One Charlene had expressed her contempt for, and yet she was angry at him for trying to escape it? Callum and Ki argued civilians wouldn't get hurt, but that still didn't make it right. Consumed by his thoughts, Ajay barely noticed as Haro started to trace his fingers around his waist, pulling a rope close to Ajay's skin. It pinched.

Ajay hissed. 'What are you doing?'

'Can't have you running off.' Haro led Ajay with the rope, like a fox on a lead, to the base of the nearest tree.

Haro proceeded to tie the rope securely around the trunk and then another smaller one around Ajay's hands. Deep down, Ajay knew it made sense. Without another word, Haro stared at Ajay with regret in his eyes and readied himself, disappearing up the tree.

Ajay understood why he was being treated like a prisoner. It didn't mean it wasn't infuriating. Everything was building up inside him, festering like a crushing tumour and adding to the weight of his regrets.

Slumping and cursing, Ajay flopped to the ground, bracing out his legs, looking lifelessly at the bushes around him. There was nothing there. Just impenetrable darkness; not even the yellow moon could manage to peep through the cloud cover.

Ajay froze.

He stared at something else, wide-eyed. It seemed to stare back at him, the two of them suspended in a moment of mutual understanding; allowing each other to exist and share the solitude.

No one had ever mentioned they were *this* beautiful. Ajay felt like they'd been misrepresented.

Seriously, you're sympathising with a lizard now? Ace would have thought him pathetic for thinking it, but these lizards had been denied the credit they deserved for their beauty. He'd only heard about their vicious bite and their toxic insides, but never about the shimmering spectacle that was staring back at him. Its green scales covered its entire body, with small delicate specks of blue and a lighter green running sporadically down its tail to meet small, spindly legs and fingers. So precious. Elegant. He almost felt like talking to it. *Don't worry, I've been cheated too.* After all, the fruit was theirs in the first place. He watched the repeated notion of its forked tongue slipping in and out of its mouth. Until the laser ricocheted up its back and tore apart its body, squishing it over the ground.

'What are you doing?' A lad with big arms stared urgently, hypothetical smoke still coming from his laser gun. Ajay said nothing, staring blankly at the lizard's remains, feeling the shock of its loss. His insides started to boil with rage. *How could you?*

'Lizards! Move.' Black silhouettes dropped down from the trees immediately and Ajay listened to the scuttling of fast feet and aghast shouts of breath.

'Ajay, move.' Haro had fallen from the sky, loosening Ajay's bondage quickly and forcing him to move with the dispersing crowd. Ajay resisted for a moment, looking back at the lizard, dead and splattered with its poison leaking into the leaves.

'You said it was clear!' Ajay watched the gunman's spittle fly into the face of his fellow. Ajay stared at the gun; the weapon that took the lizard away. Seeing its small, delicate body exploding again layered even more of his angered fog over the moment. *It wasn't doing anything wrong.* He couldn't control his anger, he just watched the murderer cradling his weapon, as if what it was used for was righteous. Ajay had the monster in his sights and as soon as Haro took off his ties, he would break his nose.

'It was!' she snapped back at him. 'They must have arrived after us.'

'Toxes don't do that,' barked the gunman. Sten? Was that his name? *It didn't matter.* Ajay didn't take his glare off him as Haro came and fed his rough hands around

311

the ties on Ajay's wrists. Ajay felt them slacken, he was free. He bounded towards the gunman, fists clenched, ready to avenge the innocent.

'You . . .' Ajay launched himself at him, spit escaping from his mouth. The man lifted his gun, like an instinct. *Figures. You would just shoot anything, given the chance.*

'Eh, eh, Ajay!' Haro grabbed him round the waist before Ajay could lay a solid fist on the man. He couldn't get loose; Haro's grip was too strong.

'Get off me!' Ajay struggled, the man only staring at him like he was crazy. *I am not crazy.*

'He killed it. He's a psychopath.'

'I'm the psychopath?' The man raised his eyebrow, pointing to himself. 'It would have killed you if I hadn't dealt with it. Maybe I shouldn't have bothered.'

Ajay went to go again, he and Haro falling forwards in a wrestle.

'Ajay, mate, stop this.' Haro pushed him away, Ajay only looking at the gunman.

'He's a lunatic!' the man shouted as they edged away.

'Oh yeah, what does that make you? Or do you just destroy whatever you want?' Ajay roared, unable to get the angered fog to clear. The gathering of people around them wasn't even a concern.

'Swen, put the gun down,' Haro said calmly, before addressing Ajay in a whisper; almost like a parent would when discipling a child, keeping their voice low, away from any listening ears. 'You're embarrassing yourself. What are you doing?'

Ajay looked straight into Haro's eyes, flustered and breathing deeply. 'He . . . it wasn't doing anything. It was tiny and . . . he just . . . it wasn't . . .'

'It was a baby, Ajay. They never stray far from the pack. It meant there could have been up to fifty of them there. Swen only did what he's trained to do.'

Ajay breathed more deeply, the fog clearing slightly. He glanced beyond Haro to see Charlene staring at him, along with everyone else. He didn't say anything, only nodded with gritted teeth, trying to ignore the disbelieving and judgemental eyes. *They all think I'm crazy?*

Haro turned back to the rest of them, leaving Ajay on the edge of the circle, still reeling from the loss.

'He's delusional, Haro. I don't think we should have him here,' Swen said, loud enough for everyone to hear, swinging his gun around his back. 'It was only a lizard.'

'Well, it shouldn't have been there,' Haro snapped back at him, opening his pit. *Was that in my defence?*

'Exactly. *She* said it was clear.' Swen nodded at the woman from before, who rolled her eyes.

'It was clear!' she snarled.

'How could it have been clear?' someone else piped up from across the circle, anger pulsating through every word. Ajay wanted to throw his hands over his ears, the unpleasant air infecting him again. All the frustration within him just wanted to pounce at someone, anyone.

'Let's calm down.' Haro looked drained.

'Calm down?' Swen towered over Haro's small stature. 'You mad? Someone could have been killed.' He flicked a glare back at Ajay, as if to say, 'because of him'. *You want to try it, mate?*

'Alright.' Haro took a deep breath. 'Let's be rational about this.'

'Rational?' Swen's voice bulleted through the trees, forcing more people to mirror his irritation.

'We need food, we'll starve,' someone else cut in.

'There's another drop-off in a few weeks. The leaves should see us through.' Haro was clearly trying to hold it together. Ajay was still staring at Swen.

'Yeah, and then what?' Another vexed voice.

'Then,' Haro sighed, 'we reassess. The Hunters will be out during that time. Hopefully they'll make a big enough impact on the population for us to go out again.'

'And what if they can't?' Charlene stepped forwards, her figure emphasised by the way she'd pulled the torso of her suit down to sit on her hips. 'What if the lizards come into the camp? They're clearly changing. What if they aren't scared of us any more?'

'That's ridiculous,' another woman said, who Ajay recognised as the one Charlene had ordered him to stay away from.

'Oh yeah? And who made you an ecological expert?' Charlene snapped.

'Erm, the Education Centre. You know, that place where we learnt stuff. Oh wait, you were too lazy for that, right?' the woman responded sardonically. *You camel. Don't you dare talk to her like that.* Ajay could feel himself clenching his fists again before a sense of reason fell over him. Almost like a sudden realisation of his own anger, only fuelled by discontentment. *She doesn't want you to fight for her, and it was only a lizard.*

'Hey, now,' Haro said. 'Let's stop this. Don't make enemies of each other.'

Ajay knew it was a little late for that, but Charlene nodded discreetly before her glance threw daggers across the circle. Ajay then caught her eye, smiling instinctively. She just flicked her head away. He cursed himself. Why did he keep expecting her to like him? Why did he even want her to? There was nothing, absolutely nothing, that would incite Charlene, or anyone, to praise him. He wasn't Glorified, never would be, and he certainly didn't have the right to throw his weight around. A recognition of his foolishness hit him dead on, and all he wanted was to curl up into an embarassed ball where he couldn't be seen or even found.

CHAPTER
THIRTY-THREE

The house had that smell. *The same as in all these boxes they call homes.* Dry, dusty, unpleasant. Like the stench of the desert; rock, plant and animal matter all mushed up together, along with the odour of the City's camel pastures wafting its way downwind. Rod bounded down the hallway, feeling strong as he stretched his toned arms out beside him, strutting himself into his role. He was their guest, after all.

'Anyone home?'

Stopping at the doorframe, he scanned the kitchen to find a petite woman looking flustered by an electric stove. The lines of her hair were damp with sweat, and it was tied back ungracefully, in keeping with the apron around her waist: dirty and laboured. She was alone. *Shame, I would have liked a bigger party.*

'Upstairs.' Rod turned to the two Command guards, eyes submissive and armed with laser guns, impressive against their purple jumpsuits. 'Bring anyone down here.'

At his words, the woman flinched, bounding towards them.

'No.' She stopped moving as Rod raised his hand to impede her exit. 'My mother – she's not well.' There was defiance in her voice and a stubbornness in her eyes.

'Too ill to move?'

'Not currently.'

'Well, OK, then.' Rod smiled without showing his teeth, watching her curveless body move back into the kitchen; she was stroking her arms as if she was cold.

'Mind if I sit?' Rod pointed to one of the crooked, unsanitary-looking chairs, wondering if it would stand his weight. The table had chipped wooden legs, and before sitting, he stared at its display of crumbs, with distaste deliberately emerging in his face.

'I'll just wipe it for you.' The woman didn't hurry but grabbed a towel and wiped the crumbs into her cupped hand. *Good girl, though it's still dirty.* Rod tapped at his wrist, summoning one of his drones to sanitise the area. The mist from the solution rose into the air, freshening it up.

Rod pulled the chair out, grimacing at the shriek of it on the concrete. Sitting down, he put one leg over the other to exaggerate his relaxed façade. He loved to play this game. 'So, husband home?'

'No. He's not back from work yet.'

Rod saw her swallow. Fear, he liked that a lot.

'We can wait.' Rod glanced around casually, wiping a finger along the rim of the table. The truth was, he couldn't wait much longer. Despite not being concerned by Jona's threatening message, he didn't imagine the Hevases would be pleased if he took all day about this. At the same time, he didn't want to waste the opportunity for a little fun, as it was becoming increasingly hard to find.

'Would you like a drink?' The woman spoke without resistance, surprising Rod with her offer. He liked her style.

'I'd like an iced water,' Rod smirked. 'If you have it.'

She nodded and slowly moved across the kitchen. First, she retrieved a glass from the cupboard, its door falling on its hinges, before opening the fridge to reveal its flickering light bulb. She pulled a water jug from it, her hands shaking as she poured it into the glass, her fingers smearing the condensation.

'Tell me.' Rod nodded his head as she set the glass down in front of him. He wouldn't be drinking it. 'What's your name?'

'You already know that, don't you?' Her tone was light, sassy.

'And what does your husband do?' He would push her a little further.

'You already know that, too.' She poured herself a glass of water and took a slow sip, leaning on the counter, steadying her trembling legs against it.

'Hmm.' Rod nodded. 'I can see he's not just a railway man. The place looks . . .' Rod paused, casting his eyes down a wonky home-built cabinet in the corner of the dining room, '. . . adequate.' He looked back at her with a smile.

'Well, we've maintained it the best we can.' Her eyes darted up at the ceiling with worry as the old woman's voice resounded around the house.

'I'm coming. Get your hands off me.'

Rod grunted and raised an eyebrow. 'She doesn't sound very poorly.'

'Her mind is younger than her body,' Keli said, looking down the hallway as her mother's voice got louder.

'Keli. Keli!' Her mother was shouting, her voice strained.

'She won't let them bring her down.' Keli looked at Rod in request to leave the room.

'Well, go get her, then.' Rod widened his eyes. 'I'm not stopping you.' She scurried from sight as Rod stood and wandered over to the back door.

It was automatic, opening out into the garden. *Funny,* he thought. An automatic at the back but an old-fashioned one with a handle at the front. He examined the frame, seeing the gap between it and the electrics, its wiring visible. A scrappy replacement. He glanced over the lit-up garden with a small amount of respect. There were all manner of fruits and vegetables sprouting from the ground and hanging in vines under a protective glass roof, its sides fitted with loud, groaning air conditioners and sprinklers. The air was moist and breathable. *They can grow all this. What if all that time and effort was dedicated to Worthy occupations? A pity.*

He was tempted to explore it further, but a loud, croaky voice suddenly demanded his attention.

'Now, let's get this straight, love. This is *our* house.'

Rod took a deep breath, got back into character, and spun on his heel to greet her.

CHAPTER
THIRTY-FOUR

Genni's heart bashed against her chest as she listened to the movement of Rod's feet by the door. If he didn't move any further, he wouldn't see her behind the wall. When he'd bounded into the house, she'd managed to slide around its side to sit underneath the back kitchen window. Part of her didn't want to listen, but she was too intrigued. Who was her brother, really? She breathed deeply to quieten her heavy heartbeat so she could hear the familiar, dry voice.

'Now, let's get this straight, love. This is *our* house.' Ajay's Grandma had arrived.

'I apologise. Karlane, is it?' Rod's voice travelled through the window. 'I did not mean to intrude.'

Man, he's twisted. Why is he taunting them like this? Of course he meant to intrude. If he was going to arrest them, why not just do it? Fear was sitting like a weight on Genni's body, as she listened to it all unfold.

'Sorry to hear you're not well.' His voice sounded different, still carrying its usual haughtiness but with a light playfulness that made her skin crawl.

'I'm as well as I've ever been, thank you very much.' Genni smirked at Ajay's grandma's fighting spirit. She wondered what game Rod was playing here. Was this his usual approach? Toying with the people he'd come to arrest – did he just enjoy it, or was he trying to intimidate them into some sort of confession? She considered his likely distaste at the house and its less than sanitary conditions. She'd already seen the sanitising mist from a drone come through the window once. *How long until he orders it again?*

Simultaneous squeaks on concrete. They were sitting at the table, and she imagined Rod's calculating eyes standing firm against Ajay's grandma's soft yet challenging glare.

'Your Keli here has given us a nice welcome.' Genni had never heard him sound so gracious.

'I can see you've enjoyed your drink.' His grandma's tone worried Genni. She needed to be careful. Genni didn't know much about Rod as a detective, but if he treated his subjects anything like he treated her as a kid when they played 'Work', they were in trouble. He never let her play a Command Worker or a high-merit employee; she was always the Outer-Ring resident or Unworthy.

'I'm not thirsty,' Rod muttered. 'You've been around a long time, then.'

'Yes,' Ajay's grandma coughed up from her toxic lungs.

'Not for much longer though, it seems.' Rod let out an amused grunt. Genni felt sick.

'I'll go when it's my time.' Her voice remained calm.

'We all will. Some of us have more to show for life than others.' He had a point there. 'You were a nurse, yes?' Rod continued to question.

'A midwife.'

'Very good. How many babies would you say you delivered?'

'I'm not sure.'

'Try to hazard a guess.'

'Probably around 200.'

'Two hundred babies.' Rod's voice went high. 'Wow. Quite the contribution.' It went quiet.

Concentrating, Genni rose on her feet slightly to get her ears closer to the window.

'Tell me.' Rod lowered his voice, as Genni heard a chair scrape again, as if he was moving closer to Ajay's grandma. 'Do you remember which was the ugliest?'

Oh, for Tulo's sake. He's disgusting. Vile. Foul. Vermin. Everything traditionally used to describe the people he was interrogating, who had been nothing but kind to her. She couldn't quite believe where she was; listening to her brother knock Unworthies from the Side about, like he was a fox and they were his chew toy.

'Excuse me?' the old lady responded.

'It was a joke.' Rod's stabbing laughs startled Genni, catching her off-balance. She managed to stop herself from kicking a chipped pot housing soil beside her. Her ears flicked back as the front door slammed alongside rustling movement and hot, heavy breathing. 'Ahhhh, the master of the house has arrived. Welcome home, sir.'

Ajay's father had returned.

'Come in.' Rod was quieter again. 'We're just chatting.' Genni tried to imagine how the men were looking at each other. Were Ajay's father's pupils burning with anger, meeting Rod's cold, reptilian gaze? Or was he quivering, fearful as Rod held him in his arrogant, superior position?

'Are you both OK?' His father's voice was soft but restrained.

'We've all been fine.' Rod's voice boomed over him. 'I've been admiring the garden. It's exquisite work.'

Genni didn't hear any sort of response, just bodies shuffling.

'It's a compliment. You're supposed to say thank you.' Rod's voice had levelled off, no longer playful, but stern.

'Thank you,' Ajay's father stuttered.

'Actually, I'm sure my men here wouldn't mind taking a few potatoes back for their families. What do you reckon, lads?' Rod was high-spirited again.

Genni closed her eyes, wanting to keel over. She couldn't take it any more; she didn't want to listen, just to wait for the inevitable. How was she related to such a taunting animal?

CHAPTER
THIRTY-FIVE

Rod gave internal praise to the guards, as they stood patiently by the door while he played, and they agreed that some potatoes would go down well with their little ones. Rod felt giddy, the provoking going swimmingly. Just a little longer until the strike. He'd have to make it dramatic. A show to remember. This would go in his book of fame; the list he held in his head of all the best arrests he'd made. These guys might even make the top ten. Especially with the lip he was getting from the women. The father, though? Poor effort. The compassion in asking if his ladies were OK, the pathetic look of terror on his face. *He's not up for playing . . . Let's give him a bit more to bat against.*

Rod deliberately watched the flat backside of his wife as she walked too slowly out into the garden, carrying a cotton mesh bag for the potatoes. *How will he react if I check out his stash?* Rod looked back, smiling at the man whose face didn't change expression, but his hands were clenched by his sides. Were they like that before? Didn't matter. Seeing the feeble little man get enraged would be fun. Rod decided to stay silent, flashing alternate beams of joy at the father and the grandmother, awaiting his lovely fresh potatoes. They were slung on the table in front of him soon enough, making a thud as they dropped.

'Ah.' Rod grabbed a potato from the bag, cupping it with his large hand. 'They're big ones.' He raised his eyebrows at Keli, who moved backwards, shielded by her husband.

'How can we help you?' the father asked.

Rod continued to examine the potato, without really looking at it, considering his next move. 'How do you make sure they don't die?'

'Sorry?' the father asked.

'The potatoes.' Rod looked at the couple, who were now holding hands. A sweet but useless act of comfort. He stood quickly, startling Karlane, the grandmother, with the chair's shriek. Circling the kitchen island, he tossed the potato from hand to hand, its soil irritatingly dirtying his fingers. 'And all of the other stuff out there. How do you protect them?'

'With the glass roof and pesticides,' the father said, following Rod intensely.

'Pesticides?' Rod nodded. 'Why use them?'

'As you said.' Karlane, coughed again, a disgusting sound from a disgusting woman. 'To stop them from dying.'

'But who would kill them?' Rod put out his hands questionably, potato still in hand. 'It's the bugs, yes?' He looked out the window, towards the flourishing garden. 'Those little critters come in and nibble away at *all* your hard work and excellence.' He displayed the potato and admired it as if it were a trophy. 'You come to collect your crop and they have all but destroyed what was there. So, you use the chemicals to stop or . . .' Rod paused, '*kill* that which stops its growth. An ingenious strategy, I agree.'

The kitchen was silent as Rod smiled at the entire company, even at his drones floating ominously above his victim's heads. He then glanced at the garden and back at the potato, feeling its firmness on his palms and noticing its bumps and imperfections. The potatoes back home were faultlessly smooth. *OK, time to finish this up. Time for the final punch.*

Rod sighed and placed the potato down on the worktop and tilted his head, opening his mouth to speak.

'So, I'm sure you'll understand—' Then he saw it. A picture on the shelf by the mother's head. Of that young woman. Number four in his book of fame.

'Who's that?' he asked, staring intensely at the digital picture. The woman was sitting at the table, displaying some sort of vile celebratory cake, her smile sickly sweet.

'That's . . .' Keli hesitated. 'Tara. Our daughter.'

'Ajay's sister?' Rod moved closer to her, causing her to step further behind her husband, nodding. Rod couldn't help himself. He felt the unattractive smile move itself across his face until it emerged in full glory. The laugh that came out was almost uncontrollable.

Of course. That young girl, wearing the rainbow tights and hair up in pigtails, beaming from that photo Ajay had, was the same girl he'd once arrested. His sister. Fantastic. It had all fallen perfectly into place. *I am the master of this squirmy clan of worms.*

'What are you laughing at?' The father had let go of his wife's hand, his fists now rising to his torso. *Uh-oh, someone wants to fight.*

'Oh, nothing,' Rod sighed and let his lip sit in a smirk. 'Do you know where she is?'

It was fun. Oh, so much fun.

'No,' Karlane piped up from the table. 'She disappeared a few years ago.'

'Oh, yes, she did, didn't she?' Rod grunted, rubbing his jaw, reminiscing. 'I remember the way she kicked me across the chin before I took her in.'

CHAPTER
THIRTY-SIX

'Where is she?' Ajay's father spaced out his words, sounding enraged. Genni couldn't breathe, hoping the truth wasn't what she thought.

'She's been dealt with.' Rod was still laughing under his breath. 'And she won't be coming back.'

There was silence. Genni instinctively threw her hands to her ears. It had to be a sick joke. *No, no, no.* Her brain turned to brick, heavy and weighted in her head, scraping the sides of her skull with its disbelief. Rod arrested Ajay's sister and that led to her death? Really? *What is going on?*

With every moment that passed, it was as if she had been transported to some other reality. None of it could be real. Ace being dead. Ajay being Karle. All of it. It must be a nightmare. Yet as hard as Genni squeezed her eyes closed and pressed her clammy hands to her ears, the terror didn't fade. The weight of The Guiding Light Ajay's grandma gave her was digging into her lap as she curled inwards, reminding her that *this* was what she was living through.

She opened her eyes, latching them onto the tomato vine in front of her, its fruit plump and red. Her heart was thumping again, her Watch vibrating. Its beat was like a camel galloping across the desert, never stopping its run. It had gone to reckless speed when his mother had come out for the potatoes. Bending down, yanking them from the soil and lumping them in the bag, her eyes darted to Genni, wild and bewildered. 'What are you doing?' she had mouthed, fear engulfing her face. Genni hadn't responded, merely giving her an expression to tell her she couldn't leave. Not when they were in danger, and she needed to know more. Her motives were confused. Everything was.

Genni was paralysed, staring out at the garden. She wasn't surprised Rod had focused on it; the abundance of its life would have made his blood boil. What good is a garden when society needs you? He'd be racking his brain over their hard graft, like she still did. Everyone had always called them lazy and slow. Yet they'd created something so beautiful. Not quite the garden she'd dreamed about, but aspects of it were mirrored; the colours of nature in greens and browns, and the vibrancy of fruit in reds, yellows and oranges. Genni didn't notice the tears that streamed until she opened her mouth to gasp, covering it with her hand, knowing she couldn't make a sound.

Was Rod's job to do with the Side and getting rid of them? That's why he was always heading that way, always outside the Quarters? That was wicked. *Despite their anti-constitutional lifestyle, they don't deserve that. Do they?* She supposed that's why Command would keep it so quiet. To avoid questions from the public. If what she was thinking was even the truth. It couldn't be. Could it? She held on as she heard his voice again.

'Hey, in my defence, she was making a nuisance of herself.' Genni could hear Rod's sickening feet moving around on the concrete.

Just, someone please – knock. him. out.

'She was a bit far from home, wasn't she? Her and her little friends bringing that unauthorised material into the City. Hmm?'

Silence again. A terrifying, deafening silence.

Genni longed to see them. Were Ajay's father's arms tensed and ready to fight? She could only imagine what his grandma felt inside; her frail body holding back her sprightly mind. Or was it something else? Did they know it was no use? Was the pain of the revelation, or the confirmation of Tara's death, too much to bear? It was agony trying to evaluate the situation from behind a wall. Yet she got through by focusing on one plump tomato on the vine in front of her. It gave her something she couldn't describe. A feeling. Not negative but something quite different.

'OK, are we done with talking, then?' Rod had stopped playing. This was it.

CHAPTER
THIRTY-SEVEN

Rod was bored. *Time's up.* He understood that the man was angry, but not responding to his questions was just rude. And if that was how it was going to be, he would waste no more time on them. The game had been won. It was a triumph. They'd been patted and thrown between his paws in every direction, leaving behind three silently crying people, pressed hard under his will.

The Sparkle Eyes thing was a bonus point. Sparkle Eyes, or Rara or Tara or Lala, whatever her name was. Rod didn't remember names. Not even the ones in his book of fame.

She was number four, and he remembered her for her gutsy moves and her eyes, so sparkly in the City nightlight. It was quite a chase through the alleyways. She was fast, but not fast enough. He'd been tracking her movements for months, her and her accomplices. Finally, he had the evidence to bring her in and caught her red-handed delivering a device to an Inner-Ring resident. *Naughty, naughty.* The resident was severely punished too – a sharp drop in merit, of course, and a strict re-Purification course. He was back to contributing soon enough. She, on the other hand, was straight in the hover van and swooped off to Command. He remembered her sparkling, wide eyes as they led her towards her execution; they were sad, fearful but carried an irritating defiance.

Rod turned from his thoughts as he approached her quivering family, telling himself that business needed to be done.

'It's a real shame. What you've done. I can see why the boy felt like a desert mouse trapped in a very . . .' Rod looked around, moving his face into a sharp expression, '. . . unpleasant cage.'

He stepped forward, close enough to the father's face for their noses to be almost touching. He could smell his fear. Yet it wasn't like fear he wanted to smell. It had a defiant air to it. *Like father, like daughter. That won't do.*

'You gave Ajay that computer?' Rod deliberately kept his voice snappy.

'Yes.' The father hesitated at first, his tearful eyes flickering behind his slanted glasses.

'You knew what he was doing?'

'Yes.'

'You knew his plan?'

'Yes.'

'And all this time, as he's been playing dress-up, you never reported a word.'

A pause.

'No.' His father's shoulders moved slowly up and down in a strong, heavy breath.

Rod let out a tight smile and shook his head, tutting. He snapped his gaze to the guards, who lifted their wrists to prepare the drones.

'Take them.'

As he gave the command, Rod closed his eyes briefly to listen to the sweet symphony of the drones taking flight, their tasers electrifying their bodies; their grunts and wails, the shouts of the guards, and the dragging of feet across the rough concrete floor. Until finally, there was the drop to silence. Rod sighed in victory, lolling his head back towards the garden. Valiant work but wasted. He lifted his wrist, chuckling inside, congratulating himself for his brilliance and his new idea. Stroking the air, he expanded his screen, the garden becoming a haze behind him, and he hurried to input his next command.

Rod tapped the 'commit' button, picking up the dirty potato from the worktop, bouncing it between his hands. He walked away enjoying the drones as they flew in convoy into the garden. Closing his eyes, walking down the mouldy hallway, he heard a new orchestra as the tomatoes, potatoes, apricots and every other product of their hands was blown apart; glass smashing, air-conditioning vents crashing, all of it left to the desert air. Reaching the front door, he pulled it open eagerly and stepped out into the hot night. He headed towards the hover van and ignored the looks of the neighbours, but relished their cries of concern. To his delight, their startled moans intensified when he spun around and hurtled the potato at the closed front door, its starchy flesh splattering over the woodwork.

Victory was bliss.

CHAPTER
THIRTY-EIGHT

Ace's eyes sprang open.

Ajay couldn't breathe.

Ace was alive but not the same.

His eyes were like frosted glass, and while the blood on his arms slithered back into his body, his skin stayed cold.

Until he was gone, and Grandma was there. Standing in front of him, back in the Side, then in his office, and his manager Mr Hollday was holding a gun to her neck.

'Only the Worthy deserve to live.' His lips moved, but it wasn't his voice. It was the voice of technology from every drone, wardrobe, dressing table, door and checkout service. Too perfect to be a person.

Mr Hollday smiled. Then there was a bang, then darkness, then a light.

'Karle,' it whispered.

Ajay yelped as he woke, his legs in a spasm, shoes denting the damp dirt. Without a moment to process the dream, he jumped at Callum sitting on a log beside him, just staring at him.

'What . . .' Ajay paused, catching his breath. 'What are you doing?'

'Bad dream?' Callum looked down at the ground, unfazed.

'Why do you care?' Ajay wiped his forehead, bathing in a sweat shower.

'I don't.' Callum paused. 'Heard about your escape.' He smirked.

Ajay stared at him, vexed. He didn't have the energy for this. Part of him wanted to pull his red, dirty headband off Callum's head and whack it around his scar-ridden cheeks. The other part was desperate. He searched for the timid, kind boy he'd once known, lost within this abrupt, unyielding character. Ajay wondered how he could find his old friend again. If he couldn't make things right with Genni, or Grandma, or Ace – *I can never make it right with Ace* – maybe he could with Callum?

The silence between them lingered as any hope of reconciliation faded and Ajay lay back down, closing his eyes and pretending Callum wasn't there.

'You know, I didn't join the Rogue to get back at Command,' Callum mumbled, stretching his legs out in front of him, staring up at the trees. 'I joined to get back at you.'

Ajay's eyes flicked open, but he didn't move.

'Or people like you. So obsessed by the City and a Glorified status that other people were just like . . . I don't know . . . collateral.'

Ajay didn't want to hear it. *He doesn't understand.*

He turned his back, his brain having no space for what he'd done wrong, or what he should have done. It was a war; a battle between what he wanted and what was right. Except he didn't know what was right. Or he didn't want to know. Round and round his thoughts spun, like he was running on a wheel. He needed to turn the symphony of distraction up louder.

'So anyway. I got some information on your gran.'

'You did?' Ajay sat up, whispering, only half-believing him.

'Yeah. Command has searched them a few times; that's on the news, actually.' He ran his tongue over his teeth before picking food out of them. 'I ran an errand in the Side so I sneaked round the back.' Ajay observed Callum, who didn't break eye contact. *That doesn't mean he isn't lying. How can I know? I can't – I have nothing left but to trust him.*

'So?' Ajay got closer to Callum, practically on his lap.

'They looked fine. Your mam and gran . . .' He hesitated. 'And dad.'

'What were they doing? Grandma was ill. If she was in the kitchen, that must mean she's . . .'

'Don't tell anyone I helped you. Ki and Maze would have me for it.' Callum stood, walking away as Ajay noticed a deep sadness in his stare.

Ajay, disappointed, stared at his feet before quickly shouting back.

'Hey, thank you.'

Callum nodded, and put out a hand, not looking back.

Why did he look so distraught? Perhaps because he'd just helped the guy who ruined his life. Did he ruin his life? Did Callum believe that? If so, Ajay could imagine helping him wasn't easy. So there was something left of the Callum he knew? Or was it visiting home that had hurt him? Or had he seen something different from what he'd said? Ajay knew he shouldn't be negative or think the worst, as that wouldn't help him. He was still in despair, but believing Grandma was safe did make life more bearable.

Grandma's safety had lifted a gram off Ajay's heaviness. His head didn't feel quite so foggy, his anxieties had subsided, and he'd even managed to sleep without a nightmare disturbing him. Things *could* be better. Though the pain of what he'd done would never leave, maybe it wouldn't always taste so strong. And perhaps he'd be able to shake away the embarrassment he felt over his behaviour from the last few days. *Why was I so upset over a lizard?* Ajay sat up and rubbed his dry eyes, glancing at the empty spot where Charlene used to sleep. As the thought passed, he heard her voice and watched as she and others joined Haro at the entrance to his pit.

'Everyone come round.' Haro stayed quiet enough so the main camp wouldn't be disturbed as they prepared for sundown.

Ajay shuffled across the ground, moving closer and noticing the breeze; clammy and moist against his skin, sending stray twigs and leaves scuttling across the dirt. Bending back his neck, he observed the increasing size of the clouds and the disturbing sway of the trees as the sun began to set. The air felt unsettled and tentative, the way it always did before a storm.

'We need to suit up.' Haro rushed to his next sentence over the disgusted looks. 'This is an opportunity. We know the lizards shelter from storms. If we set out as the rain starts, we should be able to finish our pick before the height of the thing.' Haro pulled his suit out from his pit. 'You've all done enough climbing now to deal with the impaired visibility.'

'I'm not sure about this, Haro.' Charlene stepped forwards, arms folded. 'It's dangerous.'

'So is running out of food,' someone said. 'I agree it's the right plan.'

'If it gets too hazardous, which according to the weather predictions in the City, it won't,' Haro flicked out his suit and squeezed his small legs into it, 'we'll come straight back.'

'If we don't get struck by lightning, that is,' said a man with red hair.

'Or set on fire. It's been so dry, the trees could go up if they were hit,' someone else commented.

'Oh, seriously? Fine.' Haro huffed into his pit, his suit hanging on his waist, before returning with a Watch. 'For your reassurance.'

A weather alert cried out into the musty air. It took Ajay back.

The coming storm is expected to be mild, only reaching twenty rings per hour with minimal electrical activity. Citizens shouldn't be affected.

Report anything suspicious. Make Tulo safe again.

Those last words were new. Were they tagged onto everything now? Something about them cut deep into Ajay. An ominous reminder of the threat to their society; the very people who surrounded him now. The City didn't know them like it thought it did. Yes, they're dangerous, and downright delusional at times, but not the mindless murderers they'd been branded to be. It was Command these guys wanted. Not Tulo itself.

'OK?' Haro traced his dried bottom lip with his small tongue. 'We go once it starts.'

Ajay looked around at the group; some were instantly willing, nodding their heads enthusiastically. It was like they were drugged up, getting ready for a war. Others, including Charlene and the twins, appeared less excited, which was fair enough. These storms had destroyed homes before; it was never just a light rainfall, no matter what the weather alert said. Ajay took himself through it as people dispersed; if they set off on the first crack of thunder, the peak of the storm shouldn't arrive until at least an hour afterwards, depending on which way the clouds were moving. That should give them time to pick something at least, which would be an improvement on the last couple of days, as more lizard sightings had banned climbing altogether. So, to be fair, it didn't seem an insane suggestion. Not to him, anyway. Ajay remembered his opinion didn't matter to them, but agreeing internally gave him a small sense of inclusion.

He decided, as he pulled on his suit for the hundredth time, that if that tiny speck of involvement was all he had now, he could cope with that. A feeling of acceptance came and mingled with all the pain and the loss. *Maybe this had to be home.*

CHAPTER

THIRTY-NINE

The climb was not easy, not when he was recovering from a beating. He'd forgotten that his legs were about as useful as a smashed Watch screen and as he stared at them through the increasing darkness, pressed up against the trunk, Ajay hissed with the ache. He hadn't missed the harsh, tight pressure of the rope around his waist, holding his weight. The rain had started, and thunder was rumbling above, sending a tingle of fear up his spine. Visibility was only partially affected, but Ajay still wondered if anyone would notice if he took the coward's ticket. He could jump back down and wander back to camp, awaiting their arrival and his unsatisfying, flavourless dinner.

No. He dismissed the plan, knowing he needed to earn his keep. It was confusing; wanting to be accepted somewhere he hated, but it was all he had. Maybe, if they trusted him again, he could continue trying to convince them not to go through with it. Killing people from Command wasn't the answer to overthrowing the merit system. It wouldn't solve anything, but only create more chaos, and stifle more hope.

Ajay stopped himself. A loud roar from the sky reminding him it wasn't the time for this. He needed to focus; the tree was his mountain and he would overcome it. He had to be strong enough.

What do you want more than anything? Charlene spoke in his head, her lost friendship painful but spurring Ajay on. Imagining not only his grandma now, but all of them, everyone he'd ever loved. That's what he wanted more than anything; to be loved and accepted by them.

Come on, Jay. Ace's voice came. *You wouldn't want me winning again, would you?* Ajay could feel tears moving in his eyes, the reality that he could only ever imagine that voice still hard to take.

How could you have done this to me? I'm broken. Genni's voice. He didn't want to lose her, but he knew he already had.

Let your heart lead with love. Grandma.

Out of all the voices, he knew which was going to get him there. He needed Ace's motivation, the brotherly competition and victory. It always felt good to win; every Watch game, every round of dodgems, every wrestle. But should he let Ace have this one? Because of what he'd done to him? *No,* Ajay thought. Ace only loved winning when the competition had given everything. Ajay should give everything for him, so he imagined himself racing Ace up the tree.

No. Ajay inhaled. The pain was too real. Their last fight ended in the most horrific way possible. It was too raw, and Ajay tried to steady his breathing through his intermittent sobs and groans, thinking about Ace and how they'd never race again.

All he ever wanted was to be Ajay Ambers; successful and praised. But really, he was Karle Blythefen: a rejected boy, an Unworthy murderer, alone and unwanted, even *by* the unwanted. In thinking all this, he found himself at the top of the tree, and he flung his legs up around the branch and grasped for the fruit, its green skin barely distinguishable in the dark and the rain. Panting, Ajay smiled beneath his mask. His legs were on fire, but he felt alive, ready to cry out in the triumph and the suffering.

But his moment was stolen.

The speed of the rainfall increased and began to batter his body. The thunder was getting louder, and Ajay watched the forks stab themselves across the sky. *Beautiful. And refreshing.* It had been so dry recently, there was something pleasant about the water on his skin. His appreciation was flattened as the wind took his body and threw him off-balance on the branch. Forcing his body down, he managed to avoid tipping over and falling. *Twenty rings per hour? Are you kidding me?*

Ajay was concerned. This didn't feel like the breaking of a mild storm. Then again, it wasn't the start of a ferocious one, either.

They'd be OK. It would be OK.

Ajay's sack was almost full. Getting up the second tree had been less taxing, but he could see that people had been dropping from the trees much sooner than usual; not that he blamed them, he was just determined to achieve, battling through the increasing gale and threatening thunder. *Just a few more picks and then we'll be going.* Ajay wouldn't admit it, even to himself, but he was getting unnerved. He'd soldier on, like he always did, and his thoughts then turned to Charlene. How was she coping? Could he offer her any help? Not that she'd accept it. Surely, she would forgive him soon if she saw he was sticking around.

He forgot all about her as the lightning struck and the scream rippled through the rain. Ajay immediately hung onto his tree, instinctively assuming he needed protection.

His heart sank. In his fright, his sack had come loose. Watching it drop to the ground felt like all his life's achievements had fallen from his grasp; falling, falling, falling. What was he without it? The sack on the ground, presumably with mashed-up fruit inside, was a sombre sight. Anger pulsated through his veins, knowing how it would all go rotten quicker now it had been exposed to the air. Ajay then realised something more alarming; flames engulfing a tree a few trunks down. He could hear the crackling of the smaller branches and the cries of other climbers, calling for a retreat. Trying to brace himself against the trunk, fighting the wind smacking his back, Ajay squinted under his goggles.

He could just decipher the silhouette of someone hanging beneath the flaming tree, arms and legs flayed outwards and head bent back.

No.

His heart collapsed, everything feeling hollow as he stared at the hanging body. *Who is it? No time for that, get down.*

At once, he bent his legs and propelled himself down the tree. He'd been here before. The thunder roared, the lightning continued to lash the trees and Ajay was taken back to the attack. The lightning was the laser guns, the thunder was the bombs, the cries of hurrying climbers were the terrified shrieks of injured civilians in their glamorous attire. Back on the ground, Ajay shrivelled into a ball, trying to find comfort from the trigger. Until the screams became Ace's, clinging to his arm as the *SkipSleep* needle cut through it.

No, no, NO. GET OUT.

Ajay needed these memories to leave him; he needed to fight through the trauma to survive the current one. The fear was paralytic, his body felt frozen, giving in to the power of nature as the rain battered his entire being. Then, another voice came. A small, quiet whisper.

Karle, move.

Grandma? What was happening to him?

What's happening is you're pratting about. Get a grip, lover-boy. MOVE.

Ace? Ajay arose from his fetal position, observing the flaming tree again, detaching himself from the hanging silhouette. Who had died at the hands of the storm?

You can't help them now.

He couldn't recognise any of the moving, black figures as they ran through the chaos, heading back towards camp. Ajay couldn't even see Haro's stumpy stature, nor could he find Charlene's long physique. It was all blurred, like being in a hover vehicle, wipers fiercely sliding to give you vision in the rain.

Just run. That's all he could think. The thunder was deafening, the storm swirling right above them.

He kept running, not sure if there was anyone in front of him. His legs were burning, but it didn't faze him, he was only focusing on staying on his feet. He couldn't succumb to the storm; it would leave him for dead. Every cell in his body felt terrorised as a crack of lightning grounded beside him. Startled, Ajay leapt to the side, rolling across the ground, it's hard surface painful. Straight back up, disorientated, he ran again. He wasn't going to make it back. The storm wasn't relenting. He wouldn't win.

Ajay knew he needed to find shelter. Where? There was nothing but trees towards camp, and he didn't want to veer off towards the perimeter. Lightning hit again, the thunder clouding his thinking. It was at least a forty-five minutes' walk back to camp. So, he could do that in, what? Twenty minutes at a sprint? He was terrified, alone, and vulnerable. All the foggy silhouettes of the other climbers had become nothing but a stormy mist. He'd have to keep running. There was nowhere to hide from the angered sky.

His vision clouded; he never saw it, only felt it, when he pelted hard into a tree, and everything went black.

CHAPTER
FORTY

It was perplexing to open his eyes to rain; the water tapping at his eyeballs intermittently as he blinked. At first, he told himself he was lying on the floor of his shower room, back in his apartment on the Inner-Ring, letting the hot water fall over him in a quick moment of relaxation. It was only for a minute, until reality returned. A few trees swayed above him, their green disguised by the night; he noticed how the leaves were settling in a breeze, not a gale. The rain was lighter too, starting to only tickle against his suit. Coming around, he became aware of the dead ache in his forehead, throbbing, like he was carrying a small piece of lead behind his skin.

Struggling, he mindlessly turned back to see the offending tree, unscarred by the collision.

Well, that went well, Haro, didn't it?

Ajay laughed cynically as he made it onto his knees, but the laughing stopped when he threw up.

Breathing, and puking again, he was unsure what caused it. It may have been getting knocked out by a tree, or the nauseous recognition of everything that had happened to him in the last few weeks. Making the biggest mistake of his life, being criminalised for it, then kidnapped; beaten, starved; beaten again, and to top it all off – being caught out in a Country storm. He'd ticked them all off the experience list and no merit had even been earnt. *So,* he thought, looking down at his green, leaf-filled vomit – *what's next?* Standing up, his legs burning, he wished he hadn't asked that question.

Scanning around, able to see clearer as the darkness began to lift with a new morning, he noticed there were fewer trees. They were thinning out, becoming more bush-like, and the dirt was more orange too. Ajay knew instantly. He'd run in the wrong direction.

He was lost.

A rhythm of expletives unravelled from his mouth.

He wanted to throw, kick and destroy something, anything. He battered his fists into the ground. Ripping some leaves and flowers from their roots and crying into the late-night air, he disturbed the Wingsparks in their glitter. Exhausted, he fell onto his back.

I have no energy to find them. I will never get back.

As he caught his breath, and the rain fully gave up, he saw the fading stars. Ajay looked up at them and he cried; his life ran through his head, fluttering like the Wingsparks above him. His life in the Side, loved by people he didn't want to love. Thriving in the City, respected by the people he was desperate to impress. Existing in the Rogue, hated by people who only knew how to hate. Until finally, he was dying beneath the same, constant stars, or a part of him was.

Numb, done, he closed his eyes, letting everything disappear.

The burnt skin around his eyes ripped as he woke and sat up, touching his face. Dry, cracked and sore. The lump on his forehead was now even bigger and the desert sun was beating down, the only remembrance of the storm being in Ajay's head. His suit was completely dry, sticking to his dehydrated skin. His first thought was to rip it off, not caring if a drone wandered into his path as it didn't protect him in the daylight anyway.

Ajay stopped thinking when he heard it.

He followed the noise and there it was – a forest mouse tucking into a leaf, nibbling sweetly. The thought of food alerted him to his hunger. He hadn't eaten anything as substantial as a mouse in weeks. How would he cook it? *Does that matter right now? Grab it.*

Ajay jumped at it, grasping its tiny body in his hands, squeezing out its air.

It was good.

Having managed to make a fire using the glass from smashing his goggles and directing the sun to a pile of leaves, Ajay had cooked the mouse to perfection. That's what it felt like when it hit his tastebuds. Absolute perfection. Finishing up his little meal, he scrambled over to one of the remaining trees and took shelter from the furnace in the sky.

Feeling pleased, he considered how he might be able to survive in the wild. Until he realised that the mouse was a piece of luck. He would die here. Unless . . . *What if Charlene and Haro come to find me?* Ajay dismissed the thought instantly. Not only was he a 'traitor', but the Rogue didn't seem to risk their own lives for others. Anyway, Ajay suspected the camp would be moving. It wouldn't have surprised him in the chaos of last night, that a drone had managed to fly past the perimeter undetected. The Alert Bands would have been activated, the pits filled, and once the drone had been and gone, the camp would move on to wherever another had been prepared.

Despite his distaste for them, he had some respect for the Rogue and their operation. They'd achieved a lot to survive. Maybe to see that ingenuity and determination before he died was good. It was different from that of the City; more raw, more emotional and driven by the pain others had caused. *But that wasn't the good life, was it? That was in the City. Wasn't it?* Ajay had no idea. Life was an ungraspable concept to him now, sat on the edge of death.

In fact, it was the first time his brain didn't feel so fogged up. Ace, Grandma and Genni were still there, but without all the baggage. Only the good stuff. Those moments in their relationships were real and he should have harboured more of those memories. *I never did make it to the Glorified Quarters.* His disappointment wasn't quite as poignant as City Ajay would ever have expected. Sitting against a tree, alone in a barren land, he decided the life he'd lived so far would have to do. Even if all he'd done was to deserve *this.* He closed his eyes again, not even hoping for a second chance.

'Karle.'

A light whisper.

'Karle.'

Ajay opened his eyes, letting in the evening darkness.

'Karle.'

He thought of the movie he'd watched for merit about the stages of dehydration. There was value in knowing how to ensure the proper regulation of water intake; the extreme thirst, the dry mouth; the headache, swollen tongue, and fatigue. He couldn't remember hallucinations or voices being on the list. His condition must be severe.

'Karle.'

Although the voice felt very real.

He closed his eyes again, letting his head flop on his neck.

'Karle.'

It was louder. *Shut up.*

'Ajay. Karle Blythefen. Wake up.'

I don't want to wake up. I'm dying, remember? Even in death, Ajay couldn't believe his ability to argue with himself. Until his mind went silent. Peace at last.

A small trickle of light sneaked itself underneath his eyelids. Squinting them open, he looked out to see a small glow beneath the sandy dirt, about 100 metres in front of him, a little light flickering underground. Intriguing, but all in his head.

The light got even brighter.

Not able to suppress his curiosity, Ajay struggled to his feet. Even though he was losing it, he figured, why not investigate what his mind had conjured up for him to enjoy in his last moments? If he was even dying – Ajay wasn't sure now. He felt like he might be, but then logically, it wouldn't be that quick, that simple. Limping his way towards the glow, he fumbled over branches and plants, into Wingsparks and other bugs, letting them camp on his shoulders and face.

'Karle.' The whisper was back.

Kneeling by the light, Ajay lifelessly swiped his hands over the dirt to uncover its make-believe source –

although the coolness of its hardware was tangible. Ajay widened his drooping eyes to bring himself round. More determinedly, he hurried to wipe away the sand. He saw its hard, steel exterior, so familiar and regrettably unforgettable. He leant back, shaking his head, before reaching forward and flipping over the oblong-shaped device.

The dancing figure of light sprang from its top, illuminating the few trees around them and setting Ajay into a cynical, uncontrollable laugh.

Letting the light into his disbelieving eyes, Ajay rasped through his hysteria.

'You've got to be kidding me.'

CHAPTER
FORTY-ONE

The sound of something being destroyed was harsh and unrelenting. All-consuming and overwhelming. It was all Genni could hear, even when the dust settled, and the garden could only ever be the remains of what it once was. Barren. Lifeless. Empty.

Until there it was.

She could just make it out, but it was there; impossibly still hanging on the vine, alive.

Having sat, frozen, in the garden for at least twenty minutes, covered in its ashes, her ears were still ringing from the blasts of shattering glass; soil, rocks and produce were thrown skyward as the lights cut out. The force of the lasers had done enough to obliterate most of the garden, and Genni was thankful for her hiding spot under the kitchen window. The dust coat over the air was beginning to settle in her throat, heaving itself up as she coughed. It was time to move.

As she stood, she unintentionally cradled The Guiding Light from Ajay's grandma in her hands, the only constant thing about the last half an hour. She tried to see the wreckage around her in the night, feeling it to her core. A moment before, something whole, alive and innocent had been there; now it lay in fragments. She held onto the steady weight of the unbroken device given to her; herself, that and the tomato on the vine, sole survivors of the destruction. Her thigh muscles were tight. Body, numb. Slowly, she tiptoed over to the vine, clocking her head sideways to check she was alone. Wiping the dry tears from her cheeks, she felt the scratch of soil on her skin. Using the light from inside the house, she managed to pick the tomato from the vine, it coming off with a satisfying pop. Her hands still shaking, she closed the tomato beneath her brown, encrusted fingernails. It felt better to save something.

Moving steadily, Genni stepped over shards of glass and chunks of vegetables, her feet rustling over singed leaves. Reaching the door, she bit back a yelp as she pressed her hand onto a jagged edge of the automatic door, also shattered. Genni stamped her foot in pain and frustration. Unthinkingly, she dropped the tomato and The Guiding Light, pressing her hand onto the other's cut palm, stopping the blood from dripping between her fingers. The tomato rolled under the table, almost bouncing. The device crashed onto the concrete, causing Genni to grimace, not only from the pain. *Don't make any more noise. No one can know you were here.*

She'd always known it had been reckless. She could never have imagined how much. Stumbling over the broken doorframe and the device, lying surprisingly undamaged, she silently made it to the tap. She bit her lip as the water splattered down onto her hand, screaming through its sting. *OK. That's OK. Now, get that towel there. Not the blue one. The green one. It looks cleaner.* Genni grabbed the green towel and pressed it into her palm forcefully. *Now, have a look at it.* Genni peered down into her hand. *It doesn't look too bad. Superficial, but needs to be kept clean.* Relieved, Genni rustled through the cupboards, quietly, to find some silicone plasters. She didn't think she'd ever worn one. The skin sealants back home were always much more effective and more sanitary. Genni wondered if she could be allergic to the blue, sticky-back material she was now laying across her skin. It was a risk she'd have to take. Instinctively, she went to return the green towel but she stopped. Was she crazy? Was leaving a blood-covered tea towel, smothered in her DNA, in the house of recent convicts really a good idea? Genni took a breath. She needed to clear her head and think straight.

She thought over the facts: she needed to go back to the City, and she was covered head to toe in dust. So, point one was to make herself presentable, to not arouse any suspicion as a girl coated in dirt and blood. Point two was her prints were all over the house, never mind a tea towel. So next would be to wipe down where she'd been, as a precaution. Then she'd deal with the inevitable question of what she was going back to do.

After sneaking up the stairs, trying to silence the creeks of the floorboards, and following a deep scrub down in the bathroom, Genni hesitantly raided Keli's wardrobe. She was still momentarily surprised to open it and not hear its voice banging on about today's trends. It was a random assortment of clothes; varying faded colours and thin, worn-down materials. That wasn't the fundamental problem, though: everything was too small. Too petite to fit over Genni's pear-shaped physique. She reminded herself she'd have to look at least a little bit Worthy until she made it home. All in all, Keli's wardrobe was not going to grant her that. Perhaps she could wash her outfit. And what? Wait for it to dry? She couldn't stay here any longer than she needed to.

Creeping out onto the landing, skimming over the ripped wallpaper and childhood graffiti, her eyes moved towards another room. *No, no. I can't. It's disrespectful.*

The door was proudly ordained with Tara's name in stickers. In a similar way to Karle's, there were other stickers littered around it, but hers were more colourful. Trees, animals and insects; one bug had a glitter effect on its legs. Genni had never seen a fly like that before, she thought briefly, before cursing out loud at what she was going to do. With a strong clog in her throat, she reached forward and pushed the door, its creek startling her. *Calm down. There's no one here.*

As she stood in the open doorway and swiped on the light, an emotional shockwave hit her hard. Was it simply because it was a dead girl's bedroom? Or the shock at how many photos were proudly displayed along its walls? Printed graphics hanging delicately along string on little wooden hooks. She'd never seen so many in one place. Her grandma's gallery had nothing on it. So many faces, with Tara's dotted throughout. Genni's tears got thicker as she scanned from one to the next. Was this sudden emotion because this person, who she never knew, was dead too soon? Or was it because she knew she would never have so many faces hanging along her wall?

Stop it, Genni. Get out.

Wiping away her tears, Genni moved quickly to the wardrobe, pulling out the first dress she saw. A floral navy-blue number, tight at the waist with a flowy skirt. Genni smiled sweetly. Tara must have been a pear too. As she threw off her clothes and stepped into the borrowed garment, she still expected the mirror to judge her choices. She appreciated its silence as she glanced around the rest of the room. It was ordinary, so simple; the dusty window looked out over the Country, the forest far in the distance. A small bed and touch lamp were tucked underneath it, with an old, *quiet* dressing table opposite; a red hairbrush lay on it, hair stuck in there giving the false pretence it was still being used. Beside it was another picture, this one in a frame.

Dressed, the fabric soft against her, Genni went to inspect it, curiosity trapping her yet again. It was *Karle* with Tara. Four youthful brown eyes beaming at the camera, Tara's tiny arms wrapped around Karle's shoulders, him holding her legs as she hung off his back. The shot was slightly obscured with the glow of The Guiding Light on the kitchen worktop beside them. Genni thought about what she saw downstairs the other night. It was brighter than she imagined. A little like the dancing ball of light in her dreams, yet more like a person and not as big. Dismissing it, Genni stared into Karle's eyes and she, for a moment, saw Ajay. The smile, the lightness, the joy. It was the Ajay only *she* seemed to see. Those times when the City was shut outside one of their apartments and they were still working, but were fully themselves with each other. They complained, yelled, slept, wasted time and sometimes, very occasionally, talked honestly about life. Those were the early days. Genni now knew he hadn't been in the City for that long. He'd come from somewhere different, and as time went on, he'd hardened, and those talks became even rarer than sleep.

Would Ajay even know Tara was gone? Probably not. *Good*, Genni thought. *He deserves to be in the dark.* She longed to hate him. Closing her eyes, gripping on to the picture, she told herself to hate him. There shouldn't be even a scratch of love in her bones for this man. Yet, she realised as she sighed, she couldn't not love him. *You're in so much trouble, Genni.* Shaking her head, she put the picture back and darted out the room.

After dashing to find some cleaning products in the bathroom, she did her best to wipe down every surface and room she had so much as breathed in. The blood-covered tea towel would have to come with her, she thought, as she stood in the kitchen, slightly breathless. Ready to go, she looked briefly at The Guiding Light lying by the broken back door. *Have you wiped that?* She picked it up, rubbing a disinfectant wipe over every angle of its robust metal casing. Genni half-hoped the figure would appear. Maybe it could inspire her with what she was supposed to do now? But really, she was deliberately light in her work, not wanting to wake it up.

Right, done. Go.

She put it down and spun around, feeling the flow of Tara's dress creating a breeze on her legs. Before setting out, she remembered that Ajay's mother had given her somebody's details. *What was the lady's name?* Reha, Genni confirmed as she flicked her fingers on her wrist. *So maybe she could help me?* As she moved to depart, her eyes fixated on it again: that bright red, plump tomato, slightly dusty in its new home under the table. She felt sad to have dropped it, looking at the plaster on her hand. Her prints were on the tomato too. *Time to eat, then.*

Bending down, making sure her knees didn't touch the concrete and being careful that her arms didn't scrape the clean table legs, she gathered the tomato into her right hand. Moving quietly to the sink, she drowned the fruit with water before re-cleaning the tap. The tomato shone with the reflection of the intensive ceiling lights. It was almost warming, and Genni immediately knew it would make a good painting. It stood firm through it all. She closed her eyes, imagining getting lost with her paintbrush in its lines, shapes, tones and textures. It felt . . . that was it. The same feeling she'd had when she was gazing at the tomato earlier. Even as Rod was manipulating and torturing others, it had given her an unexplainable positivity, its beauty uplifting her into something outside of her own existence. She had no idea what it meant, but one thing was certain: she couldn't just run away. There were people she needed to protect. Taking the first bite, she almost choked on the tomato. *How am I going to protect anyone? But I have to do something.*

If Command really were killing people in the Side, didn't that make them the same as the Rogue, if not worse? At least the Rogue weren't hiding their corruption.

She didn't know what she was supposed to do.

She didn't know if she could ever forgive Ajay.

She didn't know if she could ever move on.

She looked around the dirty, Unworthy kitchen before stepping into the dark garden. She continued to cry, not knowing where to go from here. She tentatively moved through the wreckage, struggling to step over the black shapes of produce, totally engulfed by the night. She glanced upwards and gasped, stopping still, her body shaking as she saw it. The stars were dotted across the sky like diamonds, with one so much brighter, bolder and more orange than the rest. *Curtan*. Had she ever stopped long enough to see it? That planet they could see during one week of the year, when it passed the line of the sun in the right way. It was staggering. Mesmerised by it through her tears, she almost forgot her circumstance. A circumstance riddled with misery, pain, hatred and fear. As she got immersed in the purity of the landscape she existed in, she questioned it all.

How have we destroyed this? Surely, we should be happy, living in a place so breathtakingly beautiful.

Wiping her face, she took a last glance at the empty house, promising them she'd make a difference. Whatever that might be. She didn't care that they were Unworthies, not any more. She wouldn't ever care again.

END OF BOOK TWO

Around 250 years earlier, a man wearing no shoes looked up and watched storm clouds gather over the planet in the sky. He breathed deeply, closed his eyes, and remembered who sent him. The grains seeped between his toes as he embarked on his future, the sky roaring with his determination. In his steady stride, his face glowed in the reflection of his fire; he was a light skimming across the otherwise black desert. Though miles ahead, nature was burdened with his destination: the twinkling windows of a small city on the edge of revolution.

The Merit-Hunters Series will return.

**The story continues in *Quiet Echoes at Night*:
Book Three of the Merit-Hunters Series**

Turn over to read the first chapter . . .

CHAPTER
ONE

She felt uneasy as she saw him checking his Watch. She was sad, disappointed.

The feelings grew stronger, like a dark fog moving in, peppered with the temptation to check her own wrist. Even then, in a moment where nothing else should matter, they still couldn't pull themselves away from the constant desire for merit.

Genni Mansald could feel a tight web of guilt spinning in her thoughts as she sat on the soft-backed chair. *Progress is strength. Missing merit opportunities is weakness.* She could see the irritation move across the room in hot ripples as every funeral guest started to fidget. Disgruntled faces turned towards the back of the large open space, all of them expecting the funeral coordinator to appear and huffing when he didn't. She could see it clearer than ever before; when it came down to it, life was about selfish productivity and there was no space for anything else, no empathy or sacrifice or decency or respect.

Despite it all, Genni managed to fabricate a smile for Blake as he looked up from his wrist, addressing her with alert eyes and a subtle wave across the rows of funeral attendants. Pearl, Jaxson and Mila were beside him. They now saw her too. It was only for a moment, before they were all pulled back in, working from their devices or posting something on *Personi,* or both.

Is Ace, your friend who hasn't even been dead a week, not worth your full attention?

And don't I deserve more than a wave? I haven't seen you since Ajay, the love of my life, murdered Ace because he found out Ajay was a fraud and had been lying to us as long as we've known him, and my life has fallen apart and you can't even stop working for a second to come and give me a hug? Some friends.

What she hated more than anything, though, was how much she wanted to join them. The woman's words on yesterday's *All That Motivation* broadcast echoed in her head: 'Progress is strength and we all have a part to play in building a greater Tulo.'

That's what I should be doing, but it all feels so dirty.

She wanted to shake off the desire to gain points, but the culture had its ropes wrapped so tightly around her neck, she could only choke rather than breathe. What she'd seen in the Side over the last few days with Ajay's family had helped her see things more clearly. The people in the Side, Unworthies, weren't everything Command claimed they were. They weren't lazy or selfish or worthless. Memories of Ajay's mother running around after her own mother and ladling endless scoops of soup into boxes for others confirmed the contrary. A shiver tingled down Genni's back as she wondered whether her thoughts were a crime. She hated that now she was back, breathing in the toxic City air, the clarity she felt in the Side was lost in a fresh cloud of merit lust.

I don't need merit. Of course I do. It's everything I know. Stop thinking. These ten minutes are about Ace. Does he not deserve my time and attention to say goodbye?

She glanced down at her legs, wiping the trousers of her silver pantsuit, as if to wipe away her accessory of persistent sadness. So much about the City felt twisted. Even the tradition of wearing silver to the funeral of someone with a M-400 plus score and only donning gold for the Glorified was perverted. *Is their memory not worth as much?* They weren't worth as much as they'd achieved less. That's what Genni had always known, but she couldn't forget what she'd seen.

She could still hear her brother's voice, coarse and evil as he toyed with the Blythefens, as if they were nothing. It was hard to believe he was an undercover command detective, not an events executive. But he was disgusting; he, Rod, just casually told that family he arrested Tara, Ajay's sister, years ago.

And then Command *dealt* with her. He treated her execution, or whatever it was, as simply as a pass in a football match.

She had tried to imagine Ajay's parents' faces but she couldn't. It was funny how she didn't really know them, but she still cared deeply, which also made her feel unhinged.

This is Ajay's family. Ajay, the narcissistic liar who destroyed your life, broke your heart and ran away from it. Not to mention the fact that he killed, killed, the friend you're supposed to be honouring right now.

Genni could feel her arm hairs standing on end as she held back the tears.

Is this why Command is taking so long to find Ajay or the Rogue? Because they're too busy with corrupt vendettas against the Side? How can I stop it? I can't. I'm just a woman, with no power, trapped in a system.

She picked at her nail cuticles and swallowed the lump in her throat as she looked considerately at the head of Ace's mother a few rows in front. Her dyed, brown hair shone under the tasteful, fluorescent lights, curling under at the back with the smooth curvature of a bowl. Genni wondered whether her eyes were welling with tears or just held their usual sharp and intimidating glare. It was hard for Genni to believe Ace came from such a ruthless woman, though she could see some of her stubbornness and vanity in him. She knew from her own mother, whose mouth wouldn't ever stay shut, about the drama when Ace was a baby. His father cheating and leaving, the merit deduction for his bad behaviour not enough to warrant any real punishment. Perhaps all that resentment had formed a solid mass within his mother and so she carried it around like a heavy burden, forcing her to treat Ace as a project rather than a son.

All parents seem to carry that burden.

At that moment, Genni's eyes gravitated towards the second row to meet her own mother's persistent stare, two large pearl earrings sitting gracefully either side of her plump face. Instantly and predictably, her mother fussed and tapped the broad shoulder of Genni's father beside her. He twitched his head in her direction, his silver hair combed back. He stared at Genni, irritated, with a disciplinary look. Genni watched his lips mouth over the rows of heads: 'Where have you been?'

She wasn't going to respond, merely moving her gaze to the front of the conference room where the Prosper logo spun on a hovering screen. Turning her thoughts to the room, she admired the quality of the painting on the cool, eye-catching feature wall; the three shades of the Prosper purple complemented each other in an asymmetric pattern. The ceiling was high and the room airy and bright with a view of the City through the windows on her left.

If she died, she wasn't sure if the room in the Beauty Dome would have a view, often hearing that they used the basement rooms for funerals. Though she'd never thought much about it, she wouldn't have imagined anyone she knew would die young enough for their funerals to be at their workplace rather than in the Glorified Quarters. Suppose it was only right, though; if there was any building worthy enough outside the Quarters, Prosper was it. Genni had never been in before, despite always asking for a tour. Ajay, who worked there for half of their three-year relationship, had promised her one once. Genni breathed through the circle of her mouth, feeling the anger brewing with the recognition of another way he'd let her down. Her suspicions were correct about the building, though; it was just as impressive inside as out.

Genni didn't even hear the swooshing of the double doors as the funeral coordinator bounded into the room, filling it with a silent relief. As he stood before his agitated audience between two hovering drones, he adjusted his silver tie knot, his voice coming out dry through the drones' microphones. Genni watched him, the sweat visible in his black locks and his blotching skin.

Genni reckoned he was mid-forties, and no higher than M-300 with his worn-out suit and general tardiness. She was surprised; she assumed helping citizens move on from grief would be a Worthy contribution. Perhaps he was well-merited and was just having a bad day. Genni closed her eyes, damning herself for the jerk reaction of merit judgement.

None of this even matters. Ace matters. Use this time for him. Don't think about anything else. Not Ajay, his family, Rod, Command or my questions. And not about the coordinator's merit score. It doesn't matter. But it has to. Doesn't it? Somehow.

'To begin the celebration of Ace's contribution, here is a short reel of his highest merit achievements.' The coordinator shuffled away as the drones swirled around to project the film.

The video flickered through Ace's jobs, his community efforts and overall statistics, but it still failed to change Genni's thought pattern. Her trip to the Side and everything after it was absorbing her; in the four days since her return, everything took her back there. She felt guilt press into her like a relentless boss; Ace deserved her full attention and she couldn't give it to him. Even as a picture of him volunteering with kids at an Education Centre stole the room, Genni saw the playground in the Side; a young girl celebrating with her father as he lifted her body across the climbing frame. *Are the Blythefens still alive? Would they have killed them already?*

She could still hear the struggle of Ajay's mother as they pulled them from their own home.

Genni tried to clear her mind, not letting the images of Rod, the drones, the arrest and their destroyed garden steal her focus. She looked back to the screen where Ace's work statistics were appearing and they managed to distract her, finally. *He was a power station.* Genni had never noticed but his work-hour tally was monumental, making her feel inadequate. *Is this why Command promoted funerals?* The service wasn't about Ace at all, but about throwing someone else's achievements around to make others compare, and work harder as a result. It felt like a Command thing to do. The Command she now knew.

She closed her eyes again, trying to erase the memories, and fill them with ones of Ace. She couldn't. As more images of Ace appeared, she was reminded of what she did when she returned from the Side and what it could mean for her future.

Pre-order *Quiet Echoes at Night* now

www.malcolmdown.co.uk

ACKNOWLEDGEMENTS

Firstly, thank you to you, the reader, for picking up the second book in the Merit-Hunters Series. It means so much that you are invested in Ajay and Genni's stories, even though at times they can be infuriating in equal measure!

Thank you again to Anika and Ben for your guidance in the draft stages of the novel. Massive thanks also to my talented sister-in-law, Sarah, for the amazing map at the start of the book. You've made the world of Tulo come alive! Thank you to Malcolm Down and Sarah Grace Publishing for believing in these novels and for assisting me in getting them out there. Thank you to Sheila Jacobs for her assistance in the editing process.

I won't do another soppy tribute to my parents or my husband, Stephen. For that, you'll have to go back to the acknowledgements in *Sun of Endless Days*, but I echo everything I said then.

While I was writing *Storm at Dusk*, I felt more of God's love than I've ever experienced before. These books are not my own; their themes reflect His guidance and intercession in my life as a young professional trying to navigate a working life today. I give Him all the praise for what these books are and what they might become.

When things let you down, there is always a more excellent way – it's a path of forgiveness, grace and love: things we can try to press towards every day.

Search me, God, and know my heart;
test me and know my anxious thoughts.
See if there is any offensive way in me,
and lead me in the way everlasting.
Psalm 139:23-24, NIV

All of you, clothe yourselves with humility towards one another, because, 'God opposes the proud but shows favour to the humble.'
1 Peter 5:5, NIV

STAY UP TO DATE WITH ALL THINGS MERIT-HUNTERS

Be 'in the know' about Merit-Hunters releases and writing updates by joining my mailing list.

In addition, you'll get access to my newsletter – 'For the Love of Dystopian Fiction' – to enjoy dystopian book recommendations, giveaways, exclusive author interviews and more. If you love dystopian worlds and stories – it's not to be missed.

Join by visiting lgjenkins.com or scan the code.

**Find me on TikTok and Instagram too –
@lgjenkinsauthor**

And remember, have a happy merit-making day!

ABOUT THE AUTHOR

Lydia Jenkins is an author, booklover and coffee drinker. When she isn't immersed in writing dystopian worlds, you'll either find her reading in a coffee shop, playing netball or spending time with friends in 'sunny' England.

Sun of Endless Days was her debut novel and she hopes to encourage others in their purpose, worth and faith through writing for years to come. Follow Lydia on Instagram and TikTok to keep up with all her antics – @lgjenkinsauthor